THE DANCE
OF DEATH

Also by Oliver Bottini in English translation

Zen and the Art of Murder (2018)
A Summer of Murder (2018)

OLIVER BOTTINI

THE DANCE
OF DEATH

A Black Forest Investigation: III

Translated from the German by
Jamie Bulloch

MACLEHOSE PRESS
QUERCUS · LONDON

First published in the German language as *Im Auftrag der Väter*
by S. Fischer Verlag, Frankfurt, in 2007, and reissued by
DuMont Buchverlag, Cologne, in 2016
First published in Great Britain in 2019

This paperback published in 2020 by

MacLehose Press
An imprint of Quercus Publishing Ltd
Carmelite House
50 Victoria Embankment
London EC4Y 0DZ

An Hachette UK company

A CIP catalogue record for this book is available from the British Library.

ISBN (MMP) 978 0 85705 743 3
ISBN (Ebook) 978 0 85705 741 9

10 9 8 7 6 5 4 3 2 1

Designed and typeset in Minion by Libanus Press, Marlborough
Printed and bound in Great Britain by Clays Ltd, Elcograf S.p.A.

For all those who had to leave

Where are we going?
Ever homewards.

NOVALIS, *HEINRICH VON OFTERDINGEN*

Prologue

He was awoken by Brahms, "A German Requiem": a swell of dark, distant voices washing into the living room from upstairs. With a yawn, Paul Niemann felt for his glasses and put them on. Three o'clock in the afternoon, it was still raining and the garden lay half hidden in a misty grey. No matter where you looked these past weeks, life ended after thirty metres in a wall of rain and fog. Brahms weather, he thought as he got to his feet – yes, but not if you're only fifteen, surely . . .

At the bottom of the stairs he stopped and listened. *For here we have no continuing city, but we seek one to come . . .* Why would a completely unmusical fifteen-year-old listen to a requiem?

He went into the kitchen, took the coffee pot from the warming plate and poured himself a cup.

Coffee in hand, he stood by the living-room door, humming along to the baritone solo and gazing out at the garden. The conifer hedge along the fence vanished into the fog, and the hawthorn and lime were invisible in a distant world.

Golden October, saturated in rain and the grey . . .

Rainy days had been more bearable in Munich. Not quite so relentless.

Noises from behind jolted him from his thoughts. A cloud of cool perfume, then Carola's voice from the front door: "Don't wait for me for dinner, Papa."

He turned his head but said nothing; the door was already closed.

Occasionally, when she was within reach, he would have loved to hold Carola tight. If anybody could put into words what was happening to him and the family, it was she.

Tell me Caro, what do you think? About the four of us. I mean . . .

He didn't know what he meant.

He sat at the low table by the broad window, sipping his coffee and thinking of Munich, of the evenings with Henriette and the Lutheran church choir, of bright, friendly rainy days.

Another world, another life.

And now? A son isolated from humanity with a requiem; a daughter ever more spectral, fugitive; the mother away, without giving an indication of where or until when; and the father . . .

The father.

He bent to switch on the standing lamp. Light helped against the heavy grey of the Breisgau.

Tell me, Caro, what do you think about me? I mean . . .

He shook his head, picked up his cup and paused. Outside, in the garden, something had changed. The fog seemed to be drifting, and for a moment he fancied he could make out the dark trunk of the lime tree. Then the fog thickened again and the trunk disappeared.

He took a sip and listened to the music. Perhaps he meant the anger that sometimes raged inside him, unable to escape because he couldn't find the words or gestures to express it. Or the boredom that occasionally overcame him, no matter what he was doing.

Boredom, tiredness, reluctance.

When he put the cup down on the table, the dark voices broke off and there was silence. The oppressive, timeless silence of weekends in Merzhausen, when the two women were not there and the two men didn't know what . . .

He removed his spectacles and rubbed his eyes. Maybe he should stop thinking about Munich so often.

"Papa?"

He put his glasses back on and turned around. Philip was standing in the doorway, his fingers on the handle, pale, pimply and thin. Tell me, Caro, what do you think about Philip. He's so . . . I feel he's so . . .

"There's someone in the garden."

"Hm?"

"I think I saw someone in the garden."

"In our garden?"

The two of them peered out into the grey. But there was only the rain, the fog, a section of conifer hedge. And somewhere, far away and invisible, the lime tree and the hawthorn he had brought from Munich.

"I can't see anyone, Philip." He turned back to the door, thinking of Brahms, of the chorus' penetrating voices, and wondering what these voices might trigger in the mind of a fifteen-year-old.

Philip shrugged. His shoulders clenched, his mouth tense, as if he didn't know how to stand there and look, how to . . . "I thought there was somebody there."

"Mama, perhaps?"

"But she's not back till this evening."

He nodded and gestured: Of course, I forgot, she's not coming back till this evening. But he had the impression Philip wasn't taken in by his charade. "I don't know either, then. You must have been mistaken, I mean, it's not surprising with all that fog."

"Yes," Philip said, but he stayed where he was and looked outside again, as if gazing into the fog was enough to be doing at that moment.

"By the way, that music you were just listening to . . ."

Philip nodded without looking at him.

"We used to sing that, your mother and I. Did you know that?"

"Uh-huh."

"When we were in Munich."

"Uh-huh."

"Every year at All Souls, you must have been with us in the church at some point." He paused to ponder what he was aiming his words at. The silence? The distance between them?

At what had gone wrong.

"You know what's peculiar about that requiem? . . . It's not meant to be a prayer for the dead, but comfort for those who've . . ."

"That's him," Philip said softly.

Paul Niemann turned to the window. As before, the fog seemed to clear, revealing a dark shape. It wasn't the trunk of the lime tree, but a man.

A man standing in their garden, peering in at them.

"You're right . . ."

"Who is it?"

"I've no idea, Philip."

The man didn't move; he just stood there in the rain and stared at them.

"One of the new people opposite?"

"Maybe, yes. Could be."

Philip came up beside him. "But he looks like a tramp."

Paul Niemann nodded. Yes, a tramp, with torn anorak and trousers, both filthy and wet. All he was missing was the bottle of schnapps in one hand and a supermarket bag in the other. A tramp who'd been driven by the rain from the bushes of some garden or other on the estate.

"Or has Mama taken on a gardener?"

Niemann was just about to respond when Philip laughed quietly, a joke. Grateful, he laughed too. "I think we'd better ask him, don't you?" He got up and went to the door to the terrace. For several seconds he stared at his reflection in the glass: a short, scrawny man with glasses, suit trousers, a shirt – dressed far too smartly for a Saturday afternoon. All he was missing was the tie . . .

He even disliked his reflection here.

As Niemann opened the door the cold made him shudder. The cold and a sudden feeling of uncertainty. What was this man doing in their garden? Why didn't he go away?

"Can I help you?"

The man said nothing and did nothing; he merely stared at Niemann. They could see him more clearly now: unshaven cheeks, shaggy, ice-grey hair, an aged, weatherbeaten face with Slavic features, Russian features . . .

Niemann stepped outside. "Hello?" His uncertainty grew. The way the man was staring at him . . . He said nothing and did nothing, just stood there in the rain, twenty, thirty metres away, a squat, unkempt shadow in the grey, *out* of the grey. A bizarre thought flashed through Niemann's mind: the man had always been in their garden, had always been a part of this garden, and before that part of this patch of earth; and he'd been waiting for years, decades for a day like this, when he could step into the light, into the consciousness of the people here, into the nightmare of every single one of them . . .

Saturday afternoon daydreams.

"Do you need help? Is anything wrong?"

No response. Just the gaze fixed on him.

Philip stepped up to the window. "Tell him it's *our* garden. Tell him to get out of our garden."

"I don't know, Philip. Maybe he *does* need help."

"Go away!" Philip shouted, sticking his arm out and flapping his fingers up and down.

They waited. The man didn't react.

"That stare of his," Philip said.

Niemann nodded. That stare, the way he just stood there. As if angling for an argument. As if he were here to . . . He rubbed his eyes beneath his spectacles. To what?

"Tell him to go, Papa."

"Shh, Philip, everything's O.K. I'll go over to him and . . ."

"Wait, Papa, there's something strange about him."

"No, no, everything's O.K.," he repeated, even though he was no longer sure this was true.

At that moment the man began to move, approaching the house slowly, approaching *him*. He felt a tinge of fear in his chest and he thought that there *was* something peculiar about this guy. "Everything's

O.K., Philip," he said again, but was struck by the certainty that this wasn't right, that something *wasn't* O.K. "Hello?" he called out. "Can I help you?"

The man continued walking towards them in silence.

"Shut the door, Papa."

"Philip . . ."

"Please!"

Niemann stepped back into the living room and closed the door. Now the man was barely ten metres from the terrace and Niemann wished he would stop there, but he didn't. He had just reached the rose bed, surely he would stop now, but the man didn't stop, he just kept walking, walked straight through the rose bed, came onto the terrace, without taking his eyes off Niemann for a second. Do something! a voice whispered in his head, but at a loss as to what to do, he did nothing, while the man wandered across the terrace towards the door as if he intended to keep going, straight through the glass, into the house . . .

Niemann stepped back in horror.

At the last moment the man stopped right in front of the garden door and placed his palms flat against the glass – huge, dark, grazed hands. Now the voice in Niemann's head said, Do something, for God's sake do something, then he became aware that the voice was Philip's and he heard Philip shouting, then he nodded and took a step towards the dark figure, in whom he suddenly saw his reflection, far more clearly than before, and he took another step towards the dark figure and his reflection, and one more, then the man stepped back, felt in his pocket, raised his right arm, pointed a black object at him from the other side of the glass, and Paul Niemann stared at the object and heard Philip shouting and felt the fear pounding in his chest . . .

Everything's O.K., Philip, he thought.

And closed his eyes.

*

An eternity passed, nothing happened. He felt tears running down his cheeks, he sensed he was breathing too quickly and he was cold again, like earlier. Images and thoughts raged inside his head, he saw a man running across a field and thought it must be his father, his father as a young man, then his father was a child and the child was running across the field, there was nobody else to be seen, and the child who must be his father ran and ran. Then Philip said, "He's gone, Papa." Niemann opened his eyes, blinked and saw the man walking off, back the way he had come, returning into the fog.

He sat in the armchair by the window, looking out onto the garden. It was still raining, still foggy, and a wall of grey ran right across the garden. And yet everything was different now.

"No, Mama, not yet," Philip said into the telephone behind him.

A cold shudder ran down his neck and shoulders. A man with a pistol.

"No, you don't have to . . . He's gone . . . No, really, you don't have to. She doesn't have to come back earlier, does she, Papa?"

He shook his head.

"I don't know, ten minutes ago . . . Oh, *Mama*, they'll be here in a minute . . . I don't know, just some tramp!"

A tramp on his way through the gardens of the estate . . .

But something, he thought, didn't match the picture in his memory.

Then he realised. Not a tramp. The man wasn't a tramp. He looked scruffy, filthy even, but he wasn't a tramp. Tramps looked different. Walked differently, behaved differently. They were different in an indefinable way.

"No, Mama, really don't . . . Yes, yes, everything's under control and the . . . for God's sake, *no*."

His eyes alighted on the footprints in the flowerbed by the terrace. After days of rain the earth was sodden and water was collecting in the hollows left by the man's shoes. He had trampled on rose stems, trodden earth onto the terrace, he had *soiled* the terrace.

Everything under control? No, they didn't have anything under control, he certainly didn't, nothing, not this situation, not his life, not the family.

Not his fear. Nothing.

His heart thumping, Niemann went into the hallway, put on some wellington boots, took an umbrella and returned to the living room. He opened the garden door and stepped into the pouring rain.

Faint traces across the entire garden, trampled grass, the half-open gate leading to the path that ran alongside the fields and meadows at the foot of the Schönberg. He closed the gate, then went back to the middle of the garden, where the footprints were more distinct. In the fog before him he saw the dull yellow of the standard lamp in the living room. Behind this he thought he could see movement – Philip, wandering around, fetching his shoes, perhaps? He saw the armchair where he'd drunk his coffee and even the cup on the table. How long had the guy been standing here, watching him? His heart was racing. He stared into the fog, spun around and at a stroke the fear returned. What if he were still here? Lurking somewhere in the fog, watching him. Go away, he thought, go away from here, then shouted the words out loud: "Go away!" No reply from the fog, not a sound, though there was sudden movement, on the path from the carport, on the terrace, where he glimpsed silhouettes. Then an unfamiliar woman's voice called his name.

"But what if he's still there? Waiting outside till . . ."

"He's gone, Herr Niemann."

He pursed his lips.

"Believe me, he's gone."

He nodded.

"O.K., so you say he wasn't a homeless person?"

He shook his head.

"Even though he looked like one?"

"Yes, but there was something . . ." He stopped.

"I understand," the policewoman said. He sensed that she didn't know what to make of him, but he also got the impression that she was trying her best to take him seriously.

The name badge on her chest read HESSE. She was no longer young, around forty-five. She seemed tired, tired from too many years in this profession.

She was sitting in the armchair by the coffee table, where his empty cup still stood, while he sat on the sofa. A second policewoman had gone into the kitchen with Philip. Niemann could hear only her voice, not Philip's; if he was saying anything, it was too quiet to hear. He felt he ought to go and check on Philip, but he lacked the strength to get up.

His strength, he thought, had stayed in the garden.

He drew air up through his nose. A strange thought.

"Are you not feeling well, Herr Niemann?"

"I don't know. I . . ." he said, turning to the window and looking out into the grey.

"He's gone, Herr Niemann."

"I'm not so sure."

Five or six police officers were on the terrace and in the garden, securing evidence, in the rose bed, on the garden door. The officer by the garden door knocked on the glass and pointed with his hand. Niemann nodded. Yes, about there.

They were on the streets of Merzhausen too. Looking for the man, for witnesses.

Yes, they were trying their best to take him seriously.

"If you don't know him, if you've never seen him before, why do you think he's going to come back?"

He shrugged. That look, he thought. He knew where he was. He wanted to come in to us. To *me*.

His pulse started racing again. Suddenly there was too much air in his lungs. He fiddled with his shirt collar, opened the second button. Now the policewoman was beside him. "Go and lie down, Herr Niemann. We'll call a doctor, O.K.?"

She caught hold of him as he slumped to the side, took his shoes off and lifted his legs onto the sofa.

"You're breathing too quickly. Breathe slowly . . ."

"What if he wanted to get inside?"

"But if you don't know the man."

He shrugged.

"Breathe slowly, Herr Niemann."

He tried. He breathed slowly. Gradually it got better.

"That's it . . . Everything's O.K., Herr Niemann."

He nodded.

"Everything's O.K. Now, try to have a rest."

"I left my strength in the garden," he said with a flat smile.

A doctor arrived, diagnosed a minor shock, administered an injection and left. Then Henriette was standing in the living room and the individual elements of the scene came together. After a few minutes she was up to speed on everything, knew all the names, all the jobs they were doing, all the provisional findings. She checked Philip was O.K., made coffee and organised a thermos and cups for the police officers. He followed her with his eyes, admiring her ability to get on with life. He vaguely wondered whether mentally she'd already built herself a new life, while he was still asking himself what had gone wrong with the old one.

Eventually she sat with him and the policewoman, on the rug by the sofa, frantically stroking his shoulder and cheek. Her small face looked troubled yet determined. "What a nasty shock that must have been," she said.

He nodded. No criticism, no questions – that was Henriette.

Anybody who felt shame nonetheless had themselves to blame. But she understood that as well.

"I'd have got an almighty fright too."

He forced a smile. No, Henriette would have had everything under control. She would have sent the man packing.

"Your husband thinks he might come back," the policewoman said.

"Let him. I'd like a word with that man. Giving you a fright like that. And look at my rose bed."

He saw the policewoman smirk. The tiredness in her face had vanished. This was the effect Henriette had on people – animating, refreshing, encouraging.

The policewoman explained what her colleagues had found. There were some fingerprints, but these were indistinct or patchy. The man's fingertips must be badly scratched or cut. Then the footprints in the rose bed, and on the path they'd picked up a half-smoked cigarette but this could have been dropped by a passer-by.

"Or Carola," Henriette said.

"Or me." He gave a restrained yawn.

Henriette's hand stopped. "Are you smoking again?"

"Sometimes. At the weekends."

"Since when?"

"I don't know. Since we arrived here?"

"That's four years! Have you been smoking for four years?"

The policewoman smiled at him. He smiled back. Four years already? Only four years?

"Occasionally. At weekends."

Henriette stared at her husband. Her hand was stroking him again, more slowly, more tenderly than before. Her eyes were full of affection, but the affection was mitigated by a distinct aloofness.

"An Italian brand," the policewoman said. "M.S."

He shook his head sleepily. "Camel."

Henriette nodded. Camel and port from the Algarve. The beginning of the old life.

For a moment the aloofness seemed to vanish.

"What about your daughter?"

"It changes. Depends what boy she's with," Henriette said. "I'll ask her."

The tiredness became so overwhelming that he closed his eyes and listened to the two women. Henriette asked whether anybody in the neighbourhood or on the footpaths had seen the man; the policewoman replied, no, nothing so far, but her colleagues were still out. Then the women fell silent and he sensed them looking at him, watching him fall asleep. He wished they'd kept talking, for the moment they stopped a heavy, menacing shadow perched on the edge of his consciousness. It was as if he could feel it physically, somewhere deep inside his head. You see? he thought, trying to open his mouth, but his lips had become numb and motionless and so he said to himself what he'd been desperate to tell the two women before nodding off:

He's back.

When he woke up the room was in darkness. He was still lying on the sofa beneath a mountain of bedclothes. The shadow in his mind had started to ache. He sat up and found the button for the standard lamp with his foot. Niemann hesitated before turning it on. But he was alone in the room and the blinds were down.

He glanced at the clock on the kitchen wall. Half past two.

Only now did he realise that he was in pyjamas. He remembered softly whispered instructions, now your left arm, now lift your bum, well done, and Henriette's small, soft hand.

Henriette, who was far away and only sometimes returned from her aloofness.

He went back into the living room and found his slippers by the sofa. He sat down and tried to work out what had woken him.

Pressure in his bladder? The pain inside his head? A sound?

He felt himself shivering. With cold, with fear. He knew that the man was inside the house. He just *knew*.

Niemann got up.

In the hallway he stopped and listened. Apart from the humming of the fridge there was silence. Silence and darkness.

He tiptoed over to check the front door. Locked, but for once Henriette's key wasn't in the lock. Had she gone off again?

He opened the lavatory door, closed it behind him and peed in the darkness. For a while he was undecided whether or not to flush. In the end he left it: too loud.

Then he crept up the stairs to the first floor. Where are you? he thought. Or was he deluding himself? Was fear deluding him? He was certain that the man was inside the house ...

Upstairs it was a little lighter; a soft glow spilled through the window from the street. He held his breath and listened. Nothing.

Philip was asleep in his bed. The display of his C.D. player was illuminated, diodes were moving. There they were again, the voices from the afternoon, so quiet that he could barely hear them. Brahms' "A German Requiem", all night long. He switched off the C.D. player.

Henriette was sleeping fitfully, making the occasional soft sound. Without his duvet she looked small in their bed. Defenceless and helpless.

A noise made him spin around. Philip's door opened.

Philip in T-shirt and underpants, blinking with small eyes.

Niemann put his index finger to his lips and closed his bedroom door. When he pointed at Carola's door and raised his eyebrows, Philip shrugged.

Carola wasn't in her bed. Her duvet and pillows were heaped up in one corner. As Carola was too slovenly to make the bed he couldn't tell whether she'd been in that night. Whether she'd been home at all.

He gestured to Philip to follow him downstairs.

In the dark hallway he said, "Do you know where she is?"

Philip shook his head.

He hurried to the telephone in the living room. He had begun sweating, he could smell the sweat, smell the fear. Not Carola, he thought, dialling her mobile. Please, God, let Carola be alright . . .

She answered straightaway. She was in Kaiser-Joseph-Strasse in Freiburg and was about to come home. Sixteen years old, half past two in the morning, he thought – but that wasn't important now.

He asked her to stay over at a friend's place.

"Why? Has something happened?"

"No, no, don't worry."

"Have you had an argument?"

"No, Caro . . ."

"Has Mama gone away?"

"What? No, she hasn't gone away, she's here, Caro. Everything's O.K., it's just . . ." He explained quickly: a tramp in their garden, and he might still be hanging around. So sleep at a friend's tonight. O.K.?

"Yes. Sure."

He hung up.

Has Mama gone away?

Philip's eyes were on him, eyes in the semi-darkness. They looked at each other in silence.

"I just think, in case he's still wandering around somewhere outside."

Philip nodded.

They went into the kitchen and sat at the dining table. Philip's face looked sickly pale in the harsh kitchen light. His red pimples seemed to glow.

Has Mama gone away?

He got up. The cellar door, he had to check the cellar door. Philip nodded.

The cellar door was locked, the key in the lock. Had he deluded himself? Had fear deluded him?

He returned to the kitchen. "Maybe we should go back to bed."

"Uh-huh."

"I mean, you to bed and me on the sofa."

Philip gave the hint of a smile as he got up. "Night, Papa."

"Goodnight, Philip."

He sat and listened to Philip's footsteps in the hallway, on the staircase. Painful phrases overlapping inside his head – has Mama gone away, four years already, only four years . . .

He went over to the front door and put his key in the lock, then returned to the living room, which seemed cold and silent. As he lay on the sofa and pulled the covers over him he thought he wouldn't be able to sleep again, not with these painful phrases in his head, and another lurking behind them: He's here, he's back.

But he must have dozed off, for at some point later he woke up with his head full of other phrases, phrases or words whose meaning he could not fathom. Phrases and words from a dream, perhaps, but he could still hear them after his consciousness had slowly and painfully struggled its way from sleep into wakefulness – phrases and words in a foreign tongue, whispered by a foreign voice from the darkness.

He sat up. "Lord God . . ."

"Shhh," the voice said softly, then continued speaking. Again Niemann couldn't understand anything, an eastern European language, Slavic, Russian perhaps, it sounded soft, bordering on tender, almost like a prayer for the dead, as if he had to die with these foreign words from the darkness.

"Lord God, please . . ."

"Shhh . . ."

He wanted to scream, but again there was too much air in his lungs, and so he did nothing, just breathed, and his breathing grew ever faster.

"Lord . . . God . . ." the man said with long, dark vowels. "Lord God, *there*." He sensed the man moving, coming very close. Then the dark vowels rang out again: "The Lord will also be refuge of the oppressed, refuge in time of trouble."

He nodded as his breathing got quicker and quicker, his lungs filling with more air and fear.

"The Lord will also be refuge of the oppressed, refuge in time of trouble," the man whispered.

"Yes."

"*Da.*"

"Please . . ."

"Go away," the man whispered right by his ear. "Go away with family."

"I . . ."

"Go away, is *my* house."

"Your house?"

"Is *my* house."

"I don't . . . understand . . ."

"Go away with family, is *my* house."

He nodded without understanding. "Yes, we'll go away."

"My house now."

"Yes," he said with another nod.

"Seven days," the man whispered. "Go away seven days."

"In seven days, yes."

"I come seven days."

"I understand."

"*Da,*" the man said right beside his ear.

A movement, barely a sound, then the man was by the door, a silent silhouette in the darkness. The familiar sound of the front door being unlocked, light and shadows dancing in the living room, then the shadows were gone, only the light remained, the light from outside, and the silence outside, and the soft, hoarse voice inside his head:

Is my house, my house now.

I come seven days.

I

Seven Days

1

Upper Silesians, not Poles – for them this was an important distinction, even though they only talked to each other in Polish. Short, dark-blond men whose voices had been droning through the walls and ceilings of the apartment block since September, and since October through the windows from outside too. Their names were Christian, Andreas, Matthias, and Louise Bonì liked them, even though she couldn't say why. Perhaps because they brought life to the building as they were dismantling it so that later, in spring, it would be beautiful, as good as new and unaffordable. On her days off, with bread and honey in one hand and a cup of coffee in the other, she enjoyed watching them dismantle through the sitting-room window. If it was raining she would sometimes pass a mobile phone, Allen key or message from one window to another to spare them the slippery walk on the scaffolding around her apartment.

The only problem was the noise. Noise from seven in the morning until seven in the evening, six days a week.

"Sorry about the noise," Andreas said.

"There's nothing you can do about it," Louise replied, stuffing the ear plugs back in.

Most tenants had moved out some time ago; the rest were sticking it out. Gambling on compensation or a better future, and suffering the consequences. Moving out was not an option for Louise – she would never let herself be driven from somewhere against her will.

"Do it *in accordance* with your will, then," Marcel said one misty Monday morning towards the end of October. Wearing colourful ear plugs they were standing in pyjamas at the breakfast bar, drinking coffee and eating biscuits because Louise had forgotten to go shopping on Saturday. The radio was tuned to S.W.R.3, in the stairwell a drill was grumbling a deep bass, which made them fear the worst.

Louise shook her head. "No way."

"When these industrious, cheerful chaps from our lost eastern lands really get going . . . taking the roof off, ripping out the stairwell . . ."

"I always thought the stairwell was ugly."

". . . making a hole in your sitting-room wall so that you can actually get into your apartment."

"It might be practical too."

Marcel raised his eyebrows.

"I never planned to move out, so I'm not going to."

"You'll end up unwell, darling."

Marcel the concerned friend. The caring friend. For the odd night his caring was O.K., she thought. But when the Upper Silesians started saying hello through the window in the morning and Marcel muttered, "Jesus, you've really got to get *out* of here," she found him slightly redundant.

"Where's the hole going anyway?" He pointed at the shelf with the hi-fi and C.D.s. "There?"

"No idea. Weren't you about to leave?"

Marcel smiled. "I'd quite like to get dressed first, my sweet."

The nice thing about Marcel was that he possessed an endless reserve of calm and friendliness. Whatever he did or said, he did it or said it with the satisfaction of a happily married man, even though he hadn't been married for a long time. Sometimes when Louise spent the evening with him – watching him read, listening to music, washing up – she had the feeling, for a whole night, of being a wife again. A feeling she needed from time to time at the age of forty-four.

But one night of marriage every fortnight was enough.

In the morning Marcel was quite happy to be thrown out.

Marcel, forty-five, an affectionate bookseller, putting on weight around the middle and with a wild shock of grey hair. She particularly liked his softness. To be able to fall and land softly sometimes, physically as well as emotionally.

The drinking was difficult. Marcel loved a glass of red wine in the evenings. As alcohol was taboo in her apartment, at first she sent him over to his own place to drink. Ever since his move to Vauban she'd been sending him out onto the scaffolding. He would stand there looking perfectly happy, despite the cold and his vertigo.

Now he picked up his coffee cup and, looking puzzled, moved it in a semicircle from the breakfast bar across the sitting room, bathroom and hallway as if to say: Is all this really so special? Is it *really* worth putting up with this nightmare for?

But he just cleared his throat.

Louise drank and waited. She sensed that something else was coming, something important, perhaps. A clearing of the throat to herald something important.

Marcel put down the coffee cup and pulled the Niemann papers towards him, carefully lining up the edges with the palms of his hands.

Pushed them to the left, then to the right.

Looked up.

"Vauban's pretty."

She shrugged.

"Very pretty. A nice place to live."

She raised her eyebrows and thought, Too many children, too many friendly people, too few cars.

Louise waited.

"Really very pretty."

"Hmm."

Marcel pushed the papers around again, and again cleared his throat. "I'm not going to put it more blatantly, darling."

She smiled. Move in with Marcel? She gently stroked his arm and shook her head.

Then came a knock at the kitchen window and Marcel disappeared with a sigh into the bathroom, while Louise pulled back the curtain for a new day in her life on the building site.

After Marcel left she got dressed then opened the front door. Moments later the Upper Silesians were in her sitting room in their long socks, visibly embarrassed. Together they cleared the shelf units on the wall facing the courtyard, through which Louise would from now on enter her apartment. They put the shelves where they found space on other walls; one was dismantled and given away. Behind the shelf units they found plenty of dust, dead woodlice and an unopened bottle of Jägermeister. The Jägermeister was given away too.

Then she watched Christian measure the wall and mark the outline of the provisional door with a red pen. "Roughly here," he said. She nodded.

A grey, burglar-proof metal door in the living room. A platform on a metal stair tower. A winter on the building site.

Eh bien?

She noted with surprise how calm she'd become. Evidently abstaining from drinking didn't just make you healthy, but calm too.

"Not nice to live," Andreas said in a sympathetic tone.

"It's only for a few months."

"Then comes balcony and living is nice again."

She showed the builders to the door and watched them pull on their worn builders' shoes. Had she ever found living nice? Here or anywhere else? Had she ever enjoyed living anywhere? Did she need a balcony?

"Thank you for shelves and schnapps," Christian said.

"You're welcome," Louise said, and shut the door.

While she pondered whether to sweep up the dust and woodlice immediately or wait until the evening, she thought about the Jägermeister.

What if it had been the Jägermeister she'd found last July, rather than the Mon Chéri?

One thing was certain: she wouldn't be standing here this morning. Nor would she still be a policewoman.

She felt a cold shudder as she put on her shoes, picked up the Niemann papers and postponed the dust and woodlice until the evening.

One final wander down the old stairwell to the ground floor, past dozens of dusty, discoloured, dirty builders, electricians, carpenters, plumbers and architects standing by walls taken down to reveal red brickwork like bloody wounds, ravaged apartments without doors, makeshift steel supports, temporarily laid cables and barriers above wooden planks, rubble, fallen plaster. So this was her home, stormed, occupied and destroyed by a friendly hostile army.

With her finger she wiped the dust from the name plate on her mailbox.

No, there was no question of her moving out.

On the way to the Schlossberg she thought about the Niemann case. She'd read the reports and interrogation protocols drafted by her colleagues and had seen the photographs, but she hadn't yet been to the house herself, nor spoken with the family. She knew a lot about the case, had formed images in her mind, but the key thing was missing: her personal impression. The images in her mind were leading her astray.

The old problem when you were called in to a case late.

Trespass and breaking and entering – her colleagues from Freiburg South police station would have dealt with this themselves. But because of the firearm the case had been passed to D11. Louise had been on call at the weekend, so Operations had briefed her. It was unclear why this hadn't happened until Sunday evening, after Operations themselves had undertaken the initial steps of the investigation, such as the questioning. Cases like this almost always involved some sort of turf war.

But Bonì had virtually no interest in this. She had become a calm individual.

Time would tell whether this was a good thing or not.

A small, red-brick church in the shadow of the Schlossberg, creepers on the walls, grass in the gaps between the cobblestones. She had been here once before, years ago, when she was still married and living a normal private life with friends, evenings at the cinema and daily humiliations. A child of some friends had been baptised here and her heart pounded when she heard the child cry. In a corner of her policewoman's heart she had still felt herself to be a woman called late to motherhood.

"Pretty pastor," Mick had muttered.

Louise had paid attention to the pastor only years later, when she saw her again at a clinic in the forest. She was still pretty, but in despair too, and lacking any will to go on living.

She opened the narrow, dark-brown portal. Traces of incense hung in the air. Candles were burning on the altar and on either side of it stood a few vases with fading flowers. The walls and pillars of the nave were bare and scarcely any daylight found its way in through the tall, slender windows. There was nobody in the church apart from her.

Not the sort of place you'd want to linger at eight in the morning.

She sat on a pew at the very back. Thoughts of the christening, of Mick, of being an older mother flowed through her mind – another life that was over, thank goodness. Then she thought of Marcel, her former neighbour, who she'd only got to know because in summer 2003 a different, a false Marcel had broken into her apartment and settled in her head for several long months. One night, when she'd had enough of the false Marcel, she'd rung on the bell of the real Marcel – who unfortunately wasn't the *right* Marcel – and got him out of bed.

I just wanted to know what you look like, she'd said. At half two in the morning? Like this, came his reply. Much better at eight in the evening at the Italian on the corner.

Another intruder came to mind, an elderly man with a pistol who spoke broken German and had issued a strange ultimatum. Who may have come originally to kill, but perhaps not.

The Lord will also be a refuge for the oppressed, a refuge in times of trouble.

An intruder who had recited a verse from Psalms. Not with absolute accuracy, but he must have learned the verse in German by heart. At least that's what Paul Niemann said.

"Louise?"

A female figure emerged from the shadow of a pillar up by the altar.

"How nice of you to come, Louise."

"Hello, Jenny."

Jenny Böhm stopped three pews away from her. Her hand on the backrest. A white hand in the dimness, a white face, as beautiful as ever, but almost as tired and forlorn as it had been in those first few days and weeks at the clinic in the forest.

"I can see you're doing well."

Louise nodded.

"And it's not hard to see how I'm doing."

"Yes."

"I mean, *you* can see it. The others can't."

"The others can see it too, Jenny."

"Yes, but they think it's because of the work. They think I'm working too hard." Jenny Böhm sat sideways on the pew. She was wearing jeans and a jumper, both black, and her blonde hair was tied into a plait. Beneath her large, inert eyes, the skin was dark.

How beautiful she used to be, Louise thought. How ill.

Neither spoke for a time.

I wanted to change something, Jenny had said in Oberberg. But *they* didn't want it. "They" were the parish council, the volunteers. The elderly people who had been there for decades, watching pastors come and go. Her husband, who found change threatening.

At the time Louise had thought that it couldn't be that simplistic. Jenny Böhm could have asserted herself or struck compromises, change parish, leave her husband. She had stayed.

"Are you still going to the meetings?"

"No, haven't been in a long time."

"Go again, Jenny."

"No," Jenny Böhm whispered.

Louise sympathised with her. She couldn't imagine anything worse than being surrounded at an A.A. meeting by people who've managed to stay on the wagon when you've failed to do it yourself. Who tell everyone their tally of dry days, whereas you haven't managed more than a few hours.

"What are you going to do to stop it, then?"

Jenny shrugged. "You are so strong and virtuous, Louise. So strict, both with yourself and others. So proud." Jenny stood up and came to sit on the pew in front of Louise. "Can you smell it from there?"

"Yes."

"Does it bother you?"

"Yes."

Jenny laughed in surprise. "I normally keep my distance, Louise. I stand to the side of people, I go behind them. I turn my back to them. I turn my back to my own children, Louise."

"The game of hide-and-seek has begun again."

"Yes."

"It's what I hated most, the hiding."

"I remember."

"It helps to be virtuous and strict, Jenny."

"Yes, you're probably right."

"I'm definitely right."

"But I'm not like that. I'm different. I can't be strict, Louise. I can't put myself at the centre of the world like you. How would that square with my job?"

"You don't *want* to."

"Yes, I do. No. Oh, I don't know."

Louise grasped Jenny's white hand and stroked it softly.

"I'm so glad you came, Louise."

"Shall we go for a little walk?"

They left the church and entered the large cemetery beside it, which was criss-crossed by a tangle of paths and tracks. Hundreds of gravestones stood between bare trees in the fog, most of them old and weathered, some sunken crookedly, covered in moss, blackened over time. Jenny said that this was her refuge when she'd been drinking or was in despair – she fled to the dead, the mute dead whose silence harboured no reproach, only peace and mercy.

Peace and mercy, Louise thought.

She saw only pain and suffering in cemeteries, greed and hatred. She saw lies, violence, fear.

Jenny Böhm saw the dead, she the living.

"Did our friends send you?"

"No."

"Because I've stopped going?"

"Absolutely not."

"Why did you come, then?"

"Because I need your help."

"Theological help?"

"Yes."

They stopped. Louise had forgotten how short Jenny was. She barely came up to her nose. So short, so in need of protection. And she really did keep her distance.

"'The Lord will also be a refuge for the oppressed, a refuge in times of trouble.' Do you know it?"

"A psalm?" Jenny said, raising her eyebrows.

"Yes. Psalm 9, verse 9."

"Sometimes they say 'stronghold' or 'fortress.'"

"Is this verse used on specific occasions? By specific people?"

Jenny Böhm turned her head to the side. Her cheeks were slightly flushed, from the cold, perhaps, or maybe out of shame. "I don't know. No, I don't think so. Other verses and other psalms, yes, but this one?"

They continued walking.

"Psalm 9 is a sort of thanksgiving hymn for salvation from hardship. The Lord who saves the poor and the oppressed from their enemies, offers them protection, you know? Who passes judgment and metes out justice by destroying the wicked and their cities. A rather Old Testament-type psalm if you take it literally. Very brutal and . . . *masculine*. But maybe you should talk to an expert on Bible exegesis and psalm commentaries. I could call a colleague of mine if you like."

"Could you do that today? It's fairly urgent."

"Have you got a murderer who's a religious fanatic?"

"Just an intruder for the time being."

"For the time being?"

"He might come back."

"And do . . . something worse?"

Louise shrugged.

"You've got so much responsibility," Jenny muttered.

For several moments they said nothing, following the damp paths and tracks, now one behind the other, now side by side, past tombs, crosses, stone angels, statues missing limbs or heads, all the dead people Jenny Böhm sought consolation from.

It began to drizzle, but they ignored this.

"I can check whether the verse is used as part of an introit. That might be why he knows it."

"What's an introit?"

"A song sung during the entrance procession for a service or Mass. Verses of psalms are recited too. If he's very religious or belongs to an order, he'll know the verse from the liturgy of the hours. Monks and clerics recite all one hundred and fifty psalms in prayer within a certain period of time. It used to be a single day, now they have four weeks."

"My God, that doesn't leave much time for anything else."

Jenny didn't laugh. "Indeed, neither for sinful thoughts nor sinful desires."

"Talking of which," Louise said, "did I tell you I was in a monastery."

Jenny Böhm stopped and swept a damp strand of hair from her brow. "In a monastery?"

"After Oberberg I went to a Zen monastery in Alsace. For a kind of withdrawal." Louise talked about the months she spent at the Kanzan-an in spring 2003, the long walks in the forest with the roshi, the grey cat, the German nun, Chiyono, who no longer had an ego but was happy nonetheless, or perhaps because of this. She talked about the tea ceremonies that in retrospect seemed so unbelievably long-winded, my God, it takes an age before you finally get a cup of tea, you're sitting there waiting, cross-legged, really thirsty and with a pain in your lower back, wondering whether there might be a drop of sake – or whatever it is the Japanese drink – somewhere to pour in the tea, and then at last the tea is ready, but the cup is so small that you've finished it in one sip . . .

She looked at Jenny Böhm. Come on, Jenny, laugh.

But Jenny didn't laugh.

They went back through the cemetery gate and out onto the road. The drizzle stopped. Jenny promised to give her a call about the psalm before lunchtime. When she saw the red Renault Mégane with its blue bonnet and blue driver's door, an uneasy smile crept across her face. In Oberberg they had raced through the countryside in it on Sunday afternoons, listening to cassettes from their late teenage years, belting out Kate Bush songs at the tops of their voices and howling duets when Udo Lindenberg came on.

A twin pack of "Lady Whisky".

Jenny stood there, transfixed, her fingertips in the pockets of her jeans. "Well," she said. "That only applies to me now."

"You did it once, you'll do it again."

A vague nod.

"Get your arse into gear, will you, Jenny?"

Taken aback, Jenny smiled.

"I want to see you at the next meeting."

A vague nod.

"Jenny?"

"Hmm?"

"You'll come?"

"I . . ." This was followed by the hint of a "Yes".

"Good."

They embraced.

When she was back in the car, Louise wondered whether she had now committed to attending the next meeting too. With a disgruntled grin she put on her Santana cassette.

It would be her very first.

"Not another *monk*," Rolf Bermann said.

"Oh, for God's sake," Bonì said.

"I never want another *monk* again, do you hear?"

She crossed her legs, yawned and waited. Bermann's Monday morning tantrums were more intense than other colleagues', but they also were substantially shorter.

"Just never bring me another *monk*, ever."

Cup in hand, Bermann rolled his desk chair to the coffee machine, filled his cup, rolled back and rubbed his tired eyes.

It was just before nine and they were sitting in his office on the third floor, the domain of the serious crime squad. Rolf Bermann was still head of this section, which had its advantages and disadvantages. A year ago he'd applied to be head of Divisions One and Three, and thus head of sections 11, 12, 13, 31 and 32. As expected, however, he had been beaten to the job by Anselm Löbinger of D23. Which was good news for Kripo; Bermann was a born section head, but would have made a poor head of division. And bad news for Bermann himself, because head of division would have been the next step in the career that Rita Bermann had mapped out for her husband. The upper echelons of the force, salary grade A14 or even A15, eventually the Ministry of the Interior and fame throughout Baden-Württemberg – those were her long-term goals for him and for herself, and the price Rolf Bermann had to pay for all those other slim, pretty blondes who populated Rita Bermann's life like a fragrant shadow army.

The consequences she had drawn from his defeat were only too clear. No colleague had seen her face since. No matter whether it was a Christmas party, a ball, a birthday party, barbecue, welcome do or leaving do, Rolf Bermann always turned up alone.

Which he absolutely loathed.

Only when it became apparent that he'd finish the evening in the company of another woman did his mood improve.

But the stigma remained. The section head who came on his own.

The *man* who came on his own.

"Right, then," Bermann said, resting his elbows on the desk. "What's the significance of the psalm?"

"We don't know yet."

"Keep me informed."

Louise nodded, raised a hand and listed on her fingers: "I'd like Alfons, Peter, Klaus, Anne . . ."

"What?" Bermann interrupted her. "You'll get Mats and he'll have to do."

"Have you read the transcripts of the interviews?"

"Stupid question."

"He's going to come back, Rolf."

"Yes, in seven days' time. Then he'll get a royal reception. But until then two people will suffice. I mean, nothing has actually happened, has it?"

"Rolf, I want Alfons, Peter, Klaus, Anne and, if you like, Mats too."

"You're going to get Mats and that's it."

"I'll go and see Bob, then,"

"You'd do that? You'd go to Bob? Go behind my back again?"

She sighed. In summer 2003 Bermann was the only one who'd been against deferring to the false Marcel. Christian Almenbroich, Kripo boss at the time, had come to the opposite decision. Louise had backed Almenbroich.

A fatal decision.

Almenbroich had been obliged to go. Bob had come.

"You wouldn't," Bermann said.

"Of course I wouldn't."

Bermann grinned. "You can have Alfons, Anne and Mats. We'll review it at the end of the week, O.K.?"

"I hate compromises."

"This isn't a compromise, Louise. It's a decision taken by your superior."

She smiled. "I hate superiors."

During her four months of detox and withdrawal in spring 2003, Louise had lost her office and desk. When she returned Almenbroich had wrested her a small meeting room from the drugs squad on the second floor. After the Marcel case they'd wanted to get her back on the third floor. Bonì had resisted and stayed on the second.

On the margins of everything and yet a part of it.

She sat on the window ledge, looking contentedly at the members of her investigation team buried in the Niemann documents. Many things had indeed changed. Louise Bonì, who because of her history of alcoholism would never receive another promotion, was heading up investigation teams. In her colleagues' minds she would always remain a pisshead. But now she was a respected pisshead.

A *dry* pisshead.

"A madman?" Alfons Hoffmann muttered.

"A Russian?" Anne Wallmer muttered.

"Funny," Mats Benedikt muttered.

"What's funny?" Louise asked.

Mats Benedikt leafed through the papers. "Did he say, 'This is my house' or 'This is my house *now*'?" He passed her the transcript drafted by the constabulary, who were the first to turn up at the Niemanns' early on Sunday morning, as well as the one from Operations.

Skimming the passages, she nodded. Paul Niemann's statements varied slightly. She made a mental note to ask him about this. "Let me sum up," she said, giving Benedikt the copies back.

They were looking for an elderly man who looked like a homeless person, but possibly wasn't. Who had wandered through gardens on a Saturday afternoon but hadn't been seen by anybody. Who possessed a weapon, probably an automatic pistol. Who had broken into a house at four in the morning without leaving any traces and given the owner of the house a bizarre ultimatum. A man who seemed prepared to do anything and had quoted a verse from a psalm. Who spoke broken German and who may originally have come to kill – but maybe not.

"We still don't know how he got in, do we?" Benedikt asked. He'd pushed his glasses up onto his forehead and was stroking his dark moustache with two fingers. Louise was looking forward to working with him. Bob had fetched Benedikt from Karlsruhe a few months earlier. An inspector with a flawless reputation and immaculate behaviour. Soft brown eyes, focused, medium height, slim. A specialist in state security, parked in D11 because there was no vacancy for him in D13.

Bob's man? So what?

"No."

Benedikt nodded thoughtfully. "He could have gone for the woman or Philip."

"But he didn't. Was he just planning to steal something and stumbled across the father? Or did he want to see the father?"

"The father says he doesn't know him."

"It would be enough if the man knew the father."

"Yes," Benedikt said.

"How could that be?"

"An unhappy customer, perhaps," Anne Wallmer said.

Alfons Hoffmann snorted quietly. "I like 'customer'." Paul Niemann worked in the council office for services and information. The office's areas of responsibility were: registration, passports, taxation, vehicles, driving licence applications and advice on waste-collection charges. Over the years he'd worked in all these areas and for the past twelve months he'd been head of the taxation section.

"Why not?" Wallmer asked caustically. All of them looked at her. She was paler than usual, more stooped than usual, more cantankerous than usual. Anne Wallmer, an over-developed muscle from head to toe. Today it seemed as if there were too much acid in the muscle. "Don't gawk like that!"

Louise grinned. Someone else with Monday morning tantrums.

"An unhappy citizen, why not?" Benedikt said.

They mulled this over in silence. Louise was grateful that nobody made a joke about rubbish or driving licences. Clearly this was an investigation team without the usual profiling rituals – male rituals, generally.

"We shouldn't focus solely on the father," Hoffmann said. "Let's not forget the mother and the children."

"And we ought to drive out and visit the Russians," Wallmer said.

Louise nodded. Maybe one of the Russians, Niemann had said on the record.

She turned around and tilted the window open. The view extended for a few hundred metres before coming to an end. No green, no blue, no *light*. Another day when the grey would refuse to break up.

A tough day. A strange case.

"The Russians?" Benedikt said.

"Russian-Germans. Resettlers," Hoffmann explained. "We've got a few in Freiburg, especially in Weingarten and out in Landwasser. Our colleagues call them 'Russians.'"

"Everyone calls them that."

"I don't."

"O.K., then, everyone bar one exception."

"I'm two exceptions," Hoffmann said, patting his belly. They laughed. Alfons Hoffmann's belly stretched from one end of the room to the other.

"In the council Niemann dealt with resettlers," Benedikt said. "Perhaps they do know each other after all."

"We'll deal with the Russians," Louise said. "But first we need to focus on the family, the homeless and our colleagues."

Wallmer said there were too few of them. They needed more people to cover everything. Louise replied that she wouldn't be getting anyone else for the time being. She shrugged. The administrative reforms in Baden-Württemberg were not supposed to disadvantage Kripo departments in any way. In reality, of course, things looked different. Less money = fewer people. Quite apart from the fact that there would be fewer promotions, and salaries would be increased less often.

They shared out the tasks. Hoffmann was given the Niemann

documents. As chief case officer he was responsible for the file and processing the material that other members of the investigation team brought him, as well as making telephone calls. "Land registry, former owners of the property, you know the routine."

Hoffmann nodded. He was a born chief case officer and it was a long time since he'd undertaken an investigation himself. He wasn't interested in looking for clues, but was passionate about assembling them, ordering them, retaining them in his memory and making connections between them. Especially if this meant he could move as little as possible. He'd bought himself a special office chair that moved for him – bobbing up and down, swinging, rolling, depending on which direction the heavy body of Alfons Hoffmann was leaning. Movement was for the evenings, he said – medically prescribed walks, fitness programmes, swimming, saunas. During the daytime his circulation demanded a bit of peace and quiet.

And food.

He reached for a paper bag on the desk and took out a chocolate croissant.

Wallmer and Benedikt would pay the homeless people a visit – Stühlinger Kirchplatz, the Colombischlössle, the airport hostel and so on. Ask about strangers, eastern Europeans, ask about a man with a pistol. A man reciting psalms.

On Wednesday they would discuss who was going to visit the Russians.

"The resettlers," Hoffmann corrected, before taking a bite of his croissant.

"Would they rather be called that?"

"In actual fact," Hoffmann said, chewing, "we could also just call them 'Germans.'"

"That would be confusing," Wallmer said.

"Could I have a bite?" Louise said.

Hoffmann froze. "A bite?"

"'We'll go and see the Germans in Landwasser'? How's anybody supposed to know who that means?" Wallmer grumbled.

"Pass it over."

"Pass it over?"

Louise slid off the window ledge, grabbed the croissant from Hoffmann and hungrily bit into it.

"A bite!" Hoffmann said in horror.

"What about you?" Benedikt said.

"I'm going to see the Niemanns," Louise said, licking chocolate from her lips.

"On your own?"

She shrugged. "Nothing has actually happened yet, has it?"

2

A Bermann phrase, she thought as she got into the car – how ghastly. No sooner had she started heading up investigation teams than Bermann phrases were slipping into her language. Did team leaders always resort to the same vocabulary? Did assuming a leadership role automatically activate a switch in the brain that opened up a reservoir of team-leader words which hitherto had been closed off?

She laughed.

How easy it was to become Rolf Bermann.

U2 helped, *The Joshua Tree*, which alongside a variety of others was one of the best L.P.s of the previous century. The cassette player hissed, the cassette droned, but nothing could really spoil "Where the Streets Have no Name".

As she drove south down Merzhauser Strasse, the Bermann phrase grumbled in her bowels.

Nothing has actually happened. Nothing has actually happened.

There was something about this sentence.

Then she remembered. These were the words with which Bermann had dispatched her to Liebau in January 2003, to Taro, the monk. She had returned with one policeman dead and one seriously injured.

That, she thought, was now definitively a Louise Bonì phrase.

She passed Vauban, the former military base in the south of Freiburg, where a colourful, sustainable district was built after the French withdrew their troops in the 1990s, with squares and paths, energy-saving houses, passive houses and all that sort of stuff. She thought of Marcel, who wanted to give it a go with her here, even though he saw her barely more than twice a month, was forced out onto the scaffolding in the evening and unceremoniously chucked out in the mornings.

She smiled. A man who wanted to live with her.

Even if it was here, in twee little Vauban.

A world away from Vauban was Merzhausen, adjacent to it but lying outside the boundaries of the city. Merzhausen was a modest place at the foot of the Kreuzkopf on one side and the Schönberg on the other, bisected by the congested Hexentalstrasse. It was substantially older than Freiburg and yet gave the impression of having been tacked on to it, as if Merzhausen ought or wanted to be part of a big city too. She pulled over in a quiet street on the western edge of the town and contemplated the white, modern, terraced houses with carports, lots of green, lots of wood, lots of glass and lots of balconies. These were bright, airy houses which didn't try to fit in with their surroundings – the rest of Merzhausen looked rather cramped and slightly chaotic.

Boní got out and went up to the corner house. She was preoccupied by the fact that they still didn't know how the man had entered the Niemanns' house on Saturday night. According to what they knew of him he didn't go to any trouble to cover his tracks – fingerprints on the garden door, footprints in the rose bed, a cigarette in the garden, assuming it was his. And yet there was still no clue as to how and where the man had got inside.

And when.

She took out her mobile, called operations and asked for a couple of colleagues from forensics.

Perhaps they just needed to search more thoroughly.

She'd arranged to meet Paul Niemann, but he wasn't there. "He's at the doctor's," Henriette Niemann said, taking her denim jacket and bag. She showed Louise into the living room, offered her an armchair and asked whether she would like coffee, juice or milk. "Or do you like coke? We've got coke too . . ."

"Tap water's fine, thanks."

While Henriette was in the kitchen Louise took a snoop around. Lots of glass and green here too, both inside and out, a light-brown leather sofa and three armchairs around a glass coffee table, glass shelves, a few books, a few C.D.s, plants of all sizes, colours, shapes. On the wall a poster-sized calendar with an Alpine landscape, photographs of two teenagers, and on the coffee table a copy of the *Badische Zeitung* and *Brigitte*. This room, indeed the house as a whole, was elegant, delicate, too tidy for her liking.

She sat down and peered out at the garden. The rose bed by the terrace, to the left a hedge, at the back trees and shrubs, then a fence. Beyond these lay fields that rose up in the grey to the Schönberg. She tried to imagine what it would be like glancing up from your coffee on a Saturday afternoon and seeing a stranger in the garden. Opening your eyes and hearing the voice of a stranger in the darkness of your living room.

Memories surfaced – one afternoon in summer, two strangers in her apartment, the American and the false Marcel, who had broken in while she was asleep. For months afterwards she hadn't felt secure at home, she had felt vulnerable and kept thinking she could sense the two men in her apartment, invisible shadows who had taken root inside her.

Henriette returned with a carafe of water, two crystal glasses and some biscuits.

"When's your husband coming back?"

"Well, that depends." Henriette smiled and offered Louise the biscuits. "Here, have one."

Louise took a biscuit. "On what?"

Henriette sat down. She had a small, elegant face, and small, alert eyes. Her brown hair was cut fashionably short, her green suit was slightly conventional. They must be around the same age, but Henriette Niemann's life was substantially different from hers. Husband, children, a home free of dust and woodlice, a regular daily routine, crystal glasses, green suit. If there had been edges in her life, then they had been smoothed down or well hidden behind functionality. Her eyes and hands remained still, and in her elegant face there was a hint of exhaustion.

Louise waited, chewing.

Henriette shrugged. "He went to see the Russians in Landwasser."

Louise nodded, took a sip of water.

He didn't want to rely entirely on the police, Henriette said. The police are on the case, he said, but they can't do enough. They can't watch over us all day and all night, they just can't, unfortunately. He thought that if he went often enough, eventually he'd find the man amongst the Russians. "So I said, what will you do then, Paul? Leave it, the police have got everything under control, I won't step outside the house all week and then we'll see what happens. But he said he had to go to Landwasser. He had to try."

Louise nodded again. "Has he got a mobile on him?"

"Yes."

"Please tell him to come home, then."

"Yes," Henriette said. She sounded relieved.

They had moved here four years ago, Henriette Niemann said, from Munich village to Freiburg village, on her insistence, admittedly, but they had all settled down well in the meantime, even Paul, who'd never moved before in his life, forty-two years in the house where he was born in Giesing in Munich, which obviously meant he had some difficulty acclimatising to his new home. But in the end he was happy, especially as being a council employee there was no problem switching to Freiburg. They hadn't moved until there was a concrete job for him at Freiburg council.

As Louise listened she thought of what her colleague, Hesse, had said. Four years already? Only four years? A sad, apathetic man, Hesse had written.

Not someone who had acclimatised.

"We didn't have a choice," Henriette said.

Louise nodded. Nodding seemed to be an effective way of getting Henriette Niemann to talk.

Someone, Henriette said, had to take over her brother's stationery shop in Freiburg after his heart attack. Who else could step in but the family? No, unfortunately they couldn't have done anything else. The wife had looked after the patient and the sister had taken care of the shop.

"How's your brother now?"

"He died three years ago."

Louise nodded.

"And my sister-in-law . . ." Henriette smiled affectionately. "She's a lovely person, but the business is too much for her. She works part-time in the shop . . . It still belongs to her and I'm an employee there. But she turns up less and less. Sometimes she won't come for weeks on end. She's not yet recovered her bearings in life."

Louise took the plate of biscuits onto her lap and leaned back. "My brother died too. He overturned his car on an icy country road in France. He was twenty-four."

"How dreadful . . ."

"You never forget it."

"You do. If you want to forget it, you do."

"Not me. I can't forget something like that."

Henriette grinned. Because you don't want to? her grin seemed to imply. Louise shrugged. Perhaps clinging to the past was one of her problems. But seeing how extraordinarily relaxed she was now, at some point she would get her clinginess under control.

"A year and a half ago I got a new brother," she said. "He's got the same name as the old one, the same hair, the same eyes, but he's only eight. Oh well, such is life." She smiled, but Henriette did not return the smile. They looked at each other in silence. The exhaustion on Henriette's face had made her eyes even smaller, and drawn lines that hadn't been there before. She'd sunk into her armchair, her hands motionless in her lap.

Louise nodded.

"Help us," Henriette said.

Then Louise's colleagues from forensics arrived: Steinle, young and sullen; Lubowitz, older and gangly. Both men stank of strong cigarettes and strong coffee, both were chewing gum and dressed as if they were colour-blind and their wardrobes were put together in dustbins. From their van they'd taken the tools they thought they might need – there weren't many of them. "The Queen of Sheba along with her entire retinue has traipsed through here since Saturday, Bonì," Steinle said in his smoker's growl.

"There was no avoiding that, I'm afraid."

"If you say so."

She waited at the door while Steinle and Lubowitz put on their white Tyvek suits and overshoes. Despite the Queen of Sheba, no technician would ever enter a crime scene without protective clothing. Forensic technicians were peculiar people, and for the most part this was a good thing.

She took them into the hallway.

"Don't go any further, Bonì." Steinle pointed at Henriette Niemann, who was just coming out of the kitchen. "The same goes for you."

Henriette opened her mouth, then closed it again.

"Any colleagues of yours here, Bonì?"

"No, I'm on my own."

Steinle put down his aluminium case. "Right then, what do you want us to do?"

She wanted them to take a look at the first floor and the television room on the second. They had seen his fingerprints, his cut or scratched fingers, and they would find similar prints upstairs. Check the door handles, the banisters, the walls, objects you might touch if you're standing in front of them, pictures, photos, the usual. The floors – traces of fibres, soil, grass, dirt. Window catches, balcony doors, both inside and out . . .

"Yes, yes, yes," Steinle growled.

She ignored him. Over the years she had learned not to listen when Steinle growled. "Look for signs of fingers, tools . . ."

"Locks?" Lubowitz asked.

"Yes, the lock on the cellar door. And the old front-door lock."

Steinle narrowed his eyes. "The *old* front-door lock?"

"We had it changed," Henriette said.

"You had it *changed*?"

"He took a front-door key with him, Steinle," Louise said.

"Did you put it in the washing machine too?"

"Your sense of humour —" Henriette began.

"I don't have a sense of humour," Steinle growled.

With the back of his hand Lubowitz swept his longish, grey hair from his face and nodded. "O.K., let's get to it."

"Straight into the kitchen," Steinle growled.

Louise forced a smile. In spite of everything, she admired her technicians, especially the growling, pug-nosed, ugly Steinle, who found everything there was to find, and often things that were no longer there too. Forensic technicians were the heroes of day-to-day police work, even though occasionally they had their problems dealing with people. They were eccentric creatures from two worlds, shuttling between the silent microcosm and the noisy macrocosm, between matter and life, always searching for the decisive nano-sized particle. They had a right to be eccentric.

"Sort us out a coffee, would you, Bonì?" Steinle said.

She found cups in a wall cupboard, a half-full thermos on the warming plate and a silver tray. Serving Steinle and Lubowitz was all part of the old game between technicians and investigators. But if a young chief inspector was kneeling in the dirt where a body had been found, throwing her guts up, the technicians were beside her. Steinle was beside her, sounding very different.

She put the tray on a chair in the hallway and returned to the kitchen.

"So you think he was upstairs?" Henriette was standing at the kitchen window, staring out. "Why?"

Louise went over to her. Raindrops ran down the glass, the road and pavement were dark with rain, while the sky looked cold and alien.

Henriette turned to her. "Come on, out with it. I want to know what you think."

So Louise told her what she thought.

That the man was strange, had behaved strangely, said strange things. That they couldn't understand why he'd come. Was it his intention to burgle the place? Kill someone? Did he want Paul Niemann? Did he know him? If so, how? How had he broken in and when? What did the ultimatum mean?

Normal burglars behaved differently. They didn't issue ultimatums. They didn't take possession of houses. But if he wasn't a normal burglar, then what was he?

Louise could tell from Henriette's expression that she was beginning to understand. Whether the man was mad or not, from now on he was connected to her life, to the life of her family.

And perhaps not only since Saturday afternoon.

They drank coffee and talked as outside the rain subsided and the sky became a touch brighter. Henriette had no explanation for what had happened, the ultimatum, the threat. For the past four years her life had consisted solely of the stationery shop, the household, the children, yoga once a week and occasionally socialising with friends. Paul had work, one or two acquaintances, but apart from that he liked being at home, watching television and occupying himself with his thoughts. Neither of them had any abysses out of which an unkempt man could have crawled, a man who claimed that their house belonged to him, a man who had a *pistol* . . . She rubbed her temples. And the children, no, that was even more inconceivable, what would their children have to do with someone like him? Louise agreed. She didn't want to exclude anything at this early stage, but if there were a connection, then it was likely to be between the man and Henriette or Paul Niemann.

"But what *sort* of connection?" Henriette asked. "We don't have much time. Seven days isn't . . ."

Louise stroked her arm. "We've got enough time."

Henriette nodded mechanically. "There's absolutely no question about the house," she said.

"No." The house was new; the Niemanns had bought it from a developer four years ago. The house, the neighbouring houses, half the estate were new.

"What about the land? Did that use to belong to him perhaps?"

"My colleagues are checking that right now."

"Maybe that's it," Henriette said. "The land." She told Louise what her husband couldn't help thinking when he noticed the stranger in the garden: that he'd always been part of this patch of earth, that he'd waited years for a day like this, to step into the light, into the consciousness of the people who lived here. "An uncanny idea, don't you think?"

"But no more than an idea. A fantasy."

Henriette nodded.

They could hear footsteps above their heads as well as other sounds – Steinle and Lubowitz pushing furniture around, laughing at one point. Henriette didn't appear to be taking any notice.

"Let's talk woman to woman . . ." Louise said.

"Woman to woman?" Henriette smiled. She paused for a moment, then said, "Of course I have dreams. Not just at night. Do you understand?"

Louise nodded.

"When I'm alone in the shop, well . . . You understand."

"But?"

"But I'm not like that. I wasn't brought up like that. I was brought up differently. I'm married to Paul and there's no question of anyone else. So you can forget it. No lover out for revenge."

Louise nodded. "But?"

"There's no but."

"From woman to woman."

"No but."

Louise nodded.

"But . . . How does that dreadful man say it? Bonì?"

Louise smiled.

"But this is just between us, Bonì."

"Of course."

"As soon as the children leave home then I'm off." Henriette screwed up her eyes and looked horrified. Once you've come out with it, Louise thought, it's practically happened. It couldn't be undone now.

"I left too. Four dozen rivals in five years – it's one hell of a wake-up call."

"That's not it."

Louise said nothing.

"To be honest, I don't know what it is." Henriette looked out of the window. A blue Audi had turned into the carport. A man got out, opened an umbrella and trudged across the paving to the front door – a slow, slim man in a beige jacket beneath a chequered umbrella. "Actually, maybe I do know," Henriette said. "It's quite simple really. But on the other hand it's really, really bad."

"When the love has gone."

"Yes, when the love has simply gone."

3

She sat at the kitchen table with Paul Niemann while Henriette made some fresh coffee. Outside the front door Lubowitz and Steinle smoked, growled and laughed, and Mats Benedikt and Anne Wallmer were on their way from Stühlinger Kirchplatz to the airport hostel for the homeless, as Alfons Hoffmann had just told her on the telephone. Niemann had not taken off his coat or shoes, as if he were about to leave again. He looked pensive, mistrustful, edgy, a stranger in his own house. Bonì sensed that his mind was far away, maybe in Landwasser, maybe recalling Saturday night – Saturday night wouldn't leave him alone.

"He could be anywhere, Herr Niemann."

"Of course, I know."

"You won't find him. Not like that."

"No, maybe not."

"And even if you did. What then?"

"Well, I'd . . ." He rather awkwardly took a digital camera from his coat pocket and awkwardly put it back again. "I'd inform the police. I mean, I've, er . . . been given telephone numbers."

She nodded. Niemann removed his spectacles and took out a handkerchief. "The rain," he muttered, and began wiping away dried water marks. He spoke in Bavarian dialect – Munich dialect, perhaps, if such a thing existed – without making much of an effort to be comprehensible, as if it would never cross his mind that she might be unfamiliar with his idiom. Bavarian arrogance, she thought, but then remembered what her colleague, Hesse, had noted: someone who hadn't acclimatised.

"I need to start from the beginning. Ask questions that you've already answered."

"Yes, I understand."

"Why do you think he's one of the Russians?"

"Because of the way he spoke."

"Like one of the Germans from Russia."

"Yes."

"How do they speak? Can you do the guy's voice for me?"

He shook his head, he wasn't good at those sorts of things, acting and impersonating, but he described the voice. Long, dark vowels and the "R" rolled at the front of the mouth, I mean with the tip of the tongue. You know, like real Russians when they speak German, the "R" and the vowels and then this particular intonation. And he said *da*. The Russian *da*.

Louise nodded. *Da* as in "yes"?

Da as in Da-Da-Davidoff.

Jenny Böhm had smuggled a bottle of Davidoff Classic into Oberberg. On their first Sunday jaunt into the country it was suddenly in her hand, while they were singing, howling. Louise had stopped, first chucked the bottle out of the car, then Jenny Böhm.

Henriette put fresh cups on the table and poured coffee from the thermos jug. Not more coffee, Louise thought, and asked for a glass of water. Henriette brought the water, sat down and looked at her for a little too long. Louise smiled. That thing you said about love? Not a word will cross my lips.

Promise?

Promise.

"You told my colleagues that he spoke like one of those Russians who learned German a long time ago, but hasn't spoken it in a very long time."

Niemann held his spectacles up to his eyes and squinted through them – it was more of a pensive than searching look. "Well, that was just the feeling I got."

"A very precise feeling."

"I used to work with resettled people for the council. I heard the way they spoke." As he wiped his glasses again Bonì wondered what he was trying to clear from the lenses.

She took a sip of water. Broken glass and an amber-coloured glinting in the rear-view mirror, Jenny sitting on the road, her face in her hands, but Louise's memory might be playing tricks on her.

Two bends, then she had turned around. Jenny was considered a suicide risk.

She hadn't thought about Jenny in months, and now she couldn't get her out of her head.

"Let's move on to the psalm."

Niemann put on his glasses. "The . . . it's a psalm?"

"Psalm 9, verse 9. 'The Lord will also be a refuge for the oppressed, a refuge in times of trouble.'"

"What a lovely saying," Henriette said.

"Are you religious?"

"No, not at all. If this is all about religion then he came to the wrong people. We don't go to church and we haven't a clue about psalms or Bible sayings."

Louise repeated what Jenny had said. A thanksgiving hymn, a hymn of protection. God had saved the poor and oppressed from their enemies and destroyed the wicked and their cities. He guaranteed protection.

"From their enemies." Niemann put his fingers on the saucer and looked at them. "What sort of enemies?"

"No idea."

"Are we the enemies?"

"Could you be?"

Looking at her, he raised his fingers, eyebrows and shoulders – a picture of cluelessness. She believed his cluelessness.

But that meant nothing. She knew she'd been ensnared by the

atmosphere of this tidy, fragile household. A family on the verge of falling apart, a love that was over, a sad, apathetic man, who she found both likeable and unlikeable.

She felt pity and this was a problem. She shouldn't have come alone.

"Why should we be his *enemies*?" Henriette asked. "We don't know him! How could we be his enemies?"

Louise didn't answer. Upstairs a door closed. She heard Steinle say, "Shit!" She heard Lubowitz laugh.

"A psalm," Niemann muttered. A psalm, she thought, quoted in German by someone who spoke broken German. The psalm was important to him, Niemann had told her colleagues from Operations. But not just the psalm, the German too. At least that's the impression he'd got. The psalm and the German played a role.

"What if he's just a nutter?" Henriette asked. "A psychopath who mumbles Bible sayings and *imagines* in his sick brain that we are his enemies? We and his neighbours and the entire world? Because he imagines that at some point somebody took something away from him?"

"It's a possibility," Louise said. "Talking about —"

"A psychopath . . . Jesus," Henriette said.

"Talking about the house." Bonì asked Niemann whether the man had said "This is my house" or "This is my house *now*". Both, he replied once one way, once the other.

She sighed. What was that supposed to mean now?

"Sounds just like a psycho to me," Henriette said.

Louise kept quiet. Her gaze met Niemann's. His eyes were watery, red and still restless. She knew that he was desperate to get away, to go back to Landwasser, this time to look in the churches, ask in the parish offices. A Russian-German who speaks broken German and quotes a psalm . . .

Keep out of this, she thought. You've got to keep *out*. But she said nothing.

"The enemies of a psychopath, well, thanks very much," Henriette said, abruptly getting to her feet. Louise heard her doing something in a cupboard. Glasses were clinking.

She knew what was going to happen now.

A shiver crept up her neck. The everyday life of a pisshead.

"I need a drink," Henriette said. "Will you have one too?"

"No thanks," Louise said. "Not right now."

Then the riddles began. A man who spoke like the Russian-Germans; Paul Niemann who four years ago had spent a few months working for the council with Russian-Germans. Had they by any chance come across one another?

Niemann said that was impossible. He would remember, he said, even after such a long time. He remembered other resettlers he'd dealt with. Sometimes whole families had come and sometimes friends who had translated and helped out. Stories you don't forget easily. Situations you don't forget. He had seen them sad, angry and speechless because education, diplomas, entire professional lives were disregarded. He'd laughed with them because their driving licences weren't recognised. Because lorry drivers who for years had freighted back and forth across Siberia had to take driving lessons in Germany. He had argued with them because he couldn't change any of this.

No, he would remember.

"What if it's further back in the past? If he's someone you met in Munich?"

"I didn't have any dealings with resettlers in Munich."

"Only in Freiburg?"

"Yes."

"Four years, Herr Niemann. You can easily forget someone in that time."

"No, I think that's . . . impossible."

"Maybe someone whose case was relatively simple? Who didn't have a difficult life and didn't come with his family?"

He shook his head. The point was, there hadn't been thousands of them, he said in his quiet voice, there may have been about eighty or a hundred. Then he had changed jobs in the council. He remembered many of these eighty or hundred, he could still picture them – old men with flat caps and wrinkled faces, old women with colourful headscarves and crocheted coats, young people wearing that dark, shiny sportswear, you know, Adidas rip-offs with three white stripes. He could still picture them as if it were yesterday. He'd felt sorry for them, for they believed they'd returned to some sort of ancient homeland, but most native Germans regarded them as foreigners, and they weren't even E.U. foreigners, no, they were "Russians", the German Russians, the remnants of a German past that no longer chimed with contemporary Germany ...

Niemann took off his glasses and rubbed his eyes with thumbs and forefingers, as if all this talking had tired him out. He put his spectacles back on. No, he said, if that man had come to see him at the council, he would remember him.

Louise nodded. Paul Niemann and the Russians. Was Henriette aware of whose story he had just told?

Shortly afterwards, Steinle and Lubowitz came noisily down the stairs, hammered on the door and called out "Bonì!" in smoky unison. She followed them outside into the clammy dampness. Niemann and the Russians, such different lives, then they meet in an office in Freiburg and for a few minutes have something in common: a new place to live where they don't feel at home.

She went over to the forensics van, watched Steinle and Lubowitz pack up, get changed, and froze as she waited for the blessing of some clue. How important a homeland was for some people. What they felt to be their homeland. The place they came from, the dialect they spoke, what they saw when they went outside in the morning, the routes they could have taken blindfolded. Smells, noises, a taste. What happened inside these people, when for some reason or other they were obliged to move away? Was it possible to live without a homeland?

In her mind elderly women with colourful headscarves paraded past, old men wearing flat caps, angry young men . . . A non-German spouse taking revenge because Paul Niemann had told him that his pension claim wasn't valid? A resettler whose driving licence hadn't been recognised?

, Nonsense.

She thought it was too soon for a conversation with Niemann. She was speaking to the right man, but they were discussing the wrong things. She needed more clues.

She needed Steinle and Lubowitz.

"Boys . . ." she begged.

"Yes, yes, yes . . ." Steinle growled, slamming the tailgate shut. He wiped his hands on his diarrhoea-brown woollen jumper, which stretched down to his knees. Beneath it he wore green cords, while on his feet he had holey socks and Adilettes. Crime-scene clothes; technicians spent enough time squatting in filth.

"Will you get the report done by tomorrow?"

"She wants a *report*." Steinle acted amused; Lubowitz grinned. They got in and Steinle started the engine.

"It would be a pretty short report."

Louise moved between him and the door. "You're not saying you didn't find anything, are you?"

He shot her a brief glance. "I'm not saying anything."

"You didn't find anything? Nothing at all?"

"Nothing that would justify a report. Would you step away?"

"Shit."

Steinle grinned. "I see we understand each other now."

"Total shit."

"Move away, Bonì."

She didn't budge.

"She's a stubborn woman," Lubowitz said. He leaned towards her. "You're a stubborn woman."

Steinle nodded. "You certainly are."

Louise looked from one to the other. For a moment she hadn't been sure, but now she knew that Steinle and Lubowitz were playing one of their games.

Sometimes it paid to wait.

"Really stubborn."

"Are you going to stand there until it gets dark?" Steinle said.

"Let's tell her before we run out of petrol."

"He was everywhere," Steinle said.

Louise bent towards him. "Everywhere?"

He nodded. He became a little uneasy; suddenly the two of them were in close proximity. His pug nose looked enormous in the middle of the white smoker's skin with large pores, above it his eyes twitched in shock. He smelled of cigarettes, sweat and mould.

Lubowitz leaned forwards again and outlined their findings, now soberly and professionally, without any of the shenanigans that technicians loved, these two in particular. Her man had been in the parents' bedroom, the children's rooms, the bathroom, the attic room, had sat on the sofa opposite the T.V. and touched objects. He had been everywhere. They didn't have much, but what they had was better than nothing and scattered across half the house – fingerprints, fibres, soil residues, footprints.

"Shit, I was right, then."

"Slightly," Lubowitz said.

Steinle still hadn't said anything, was still looking at her, unmoved.

"So how did he get in?"

Lubowitz shrugged. "Well, how do you get into a house? Through the front door." They'd examined the old lock and found faint scratches and notches – a wire, a picklock, a tool, something he was able to rapidly and expertly pick the lock with.

She took a step back. He had come through the front door and had been everywhere.

This is my house, this is my house now . . .

Who *was* this man? What was going through his head?

"You've got a right weirdo there," Lubowitz said.

Weird, unpredictable. She nodded.

Before she could say thank you, Steinle pulled the door shut and simultaneously put his foot on the accelerator. She watched the van drive off, still thinking of the man, unable to banish him from her mind, a man who lumbered through a strange house at night, making no effort to cover his traces. Not a tramp, Niemann had said to her colleagues in Operations and to Hesse from Freiburg South, not a dropout, not an alcoholic, not someone who was resigned to poverty and homelessness. Too confident for a tramp. A man who felt invulnerable.

What had he called him?

The van had turned around and now shot past her. Two dark silhouettes, two glowing dots at mouth height. She raised her hand in a fleeting wave; it wasn't returned.

A warrior, Niemann had said. There was something of the old warrior about the man.

Bonì heard the tones of Erik Satie tinkling from the house, but she wasn't quick enough. She took her mobile from her shoulder bag – Alfons Hoffmann. As she called back she stepped outside again.

"Louise," Hoffmann said, "we've got something."

A trail – but it was no longer new. Their colleagues from the station in Lahr had called, internal surveillance. At the beginning of October, a patrol in Lahr were checking up on two homeless men. One ran away, disappeared just like that, as if he'd been swallowed up by the ground. The other was a homeless man well known in the city, a German who lived in the pedestrian zone. The two of them had sat together for about an hour, sharing a drink and smoking. The Lahr man claimed he didn't know the other guy, he'd met him for the first time that day. At any rate, he matched the vague description from Freiburg – clothes, height, appearance.

"Tell them to scoop up their local beggar."

"Will you drive up there?"

"This afternoon."

"Alone?"

"Our colleagues in Lahr will look after me, don't you think?"

"Our lone wolf," Hoffmann said tenderly.

"Don't talk rubbish."

"Always on your own, Louise, even now that everything's better."

"Cut the crap."

"Think about it."

"In seven days."

Hoffmann giggled.

She slipped her mobile into her trouser pocket, went back inside the house and thought, slightly irritated, lone wolf – utter crap! She turned her mind to her colleagues in Lahr. An old trail, a vague trail.

But one fact made this trail highly interesting: more than 20 per cent of Lahr's population were Russian-Germans.

Henriette stood in the kitchen, desperate to clean, hoover, sweep – she wanted to sweep this man out of their house. May I do it now? She smiled feistily. Of course she could, Steinle and Lubowitz had what they needed, there wouldn't be any more to find. Louise lifted her hand and stroked Henriette's arm. "Hang on in there, O.K.?"

"Oh, I'll cope, don't you worry."

Louise took her hand back. Yes, Henriette would cope. The problem was Paul.

Lahr, Niemann said at a loss, no, no connections with Lahr, apart from the annual family excursion to the Chrysanthema in late autumn. They'd planned on going again next Saturday, but that wasn't going to happen now . . . A colleague of his came from Lahr, he commuted every day, but Niemann only rarely sat next to him in the canteen. "What's Lahr got to do with it anyway?"

"We don't know yet," Louise said and told them about the old, vague lead, partly to discourage him from returning to Landwasser or Weinberg, to emphasise how pointless it was to go anywhere, even Lahr.

She suspected this wouldn't work.

"Lahr . . ." Confused, he shook his head.

She bent forwards and leaned her elbows on the table. "You've got to keep out of this, Herr Niemann. Keep *out* of it."

He turned pale, even paler than he'd been before. All of a sudden his eyes were misty – now she had him, now there was a closeness between them.

"Try to forget the guy for a few days, Herr Niemann. Look after your family. Go to work. Resume your normal life. Go to Chrysanthema. O.K.?"

He nodded.

"Good."

"But . . ."

"But what?"

"Lahr, I don't understand. What's he got to do with *Lahr*?"

She sighed and leaned back. Upstairs a vacuum cleaner roared into life, then a door closed and the noise was quieter. She would send Anne Wallmer and Mats Benedikt over here, let them chat to Paul and Henriette Niemann again, without sympathy, without compassion and without impatience. She wasn't particularly good at questioning witnesses and victims anymore; over the past few months, perhaps years, she'd lost her distance. She liked these people, or she didn't like them – this was becoming an ever more frequent problem. She liked the man in this house and didn't like him at the same time, but she had to think logically, coolly and keep track of it all.

"Lahr," Niemann muttered. "I really couldn't say what . . ."

Calmly, Louise explained that at the beginning of an investigation there were always long roads, diversions, plenty of false leads. But avenues *always* opened up, now they had one linking the case to Lahr, and if this didn't get them any further then another would. Each avenue needed answers and all answers were important, even the negative ones, for they closed off one lead and maybe switched the focus to others.

"I understand," Niemann said, looking down at his hands.

Their moment of closeness was past.

"What about your colleagues? The technicians? What did they say?"

"They need to compile a report first and that might take time."

He looked up. "Didn't they find anything?"

"Let's wait for the report, shall we, Herr Niemann?"

"But if it drags on . . ."

She rolled her eyes. "It won't be *that* long." She got up and repeated what she'd said to his wife earlier: they had time, until the weekend at least. When she put her hand on his shoulder she felt him flinch, which made her flinch too. Her hand hung in the air for a moment. "Would you mind if I took a look at your garden?"

He shook his head.

She was already in the hallway when she heard him speak.

"How do you count the seven days?"

She turned around. He looked at her, leaning on his elbows, his back hunched, his head half sunken into the collar of his coat.

"I mean, when did the seven days begin? If he includes Saturday, then Friday is the seventh day. But if he starts counting from Sunday, that makes Saturday the seventh day. But 'in seven days', does that mean that he . . . that he comes on the seventh day following a particular day? Or does he let the seven days pass and . . . I mean, does he only come on the eighth day?"

"I don't know, Herr Niemann."

"I can't stop asking myself this."

She nodded.

"How he counts. When he's coming."

4

In the garden, beneath the heavy, grey October sky that choked the air and made her eyes ache, she had no desire to think of Paul Niemann and the old warrior, to speculate how he counted or when he would come. Have a break, she thought, then tried to unpick the feelings she'd had for Steinle earlier.

Steinle and romantic urges?

She walked along the conifer hedge, letting her hand run across the damp twigs. Another garden came to mind, a garden in Günterstal on a summer's night before the rain, during the rain. Richard Landen and her on the terrace, later in the living room, before Thomas Ilic rang and the hunt for the false Marcel began.

Being in love, she thought – this was what was missing from her life. The last man she'd pestered was Richard Landen, who shuttled between three countries and hundreds of cities, and sometimes rang, and if she went to his or he came to hers, that feeling returned for a few hours, both at his place and hers, and they spoke about how, in different circumstances, in another life, at a different time . . .

Wonderful conversations because that other life and other time would never exist.

It hadn't been easy to wave goodbye to the aspiration of having a family, which Mick had represented until four years ago, as had, rather surprisingly, Landen until eighteen months ago, but coming up with an idea of what should replace this seemed even more difficult. Sex twice a month with different partners?

Oh well, she thought, why not?

But Louise suspected that this was not enough. Other emotions wanted to be expressed too.

She turned and saw Niemann standing in his unlit living room, looking in her direction, more an inkling than a body, saw him traipsing through the streets, digital camera in hand, searching for an old warrior who would be practically impossible to find.

She walked on, along the fence, beyond which lay steep fields and meadows, paths, woodland all the way up to the Schönberg. After the Niemanns' overheated house the cool dampness of the air was refreshing. She took a deep breath and felt in good spirits on the edge of the fields, in the damp air. To one side a house, a place where she could talk to people; to the other an indeterminable expanse, a place where she could be alone. It was how she had organised this phase of her life and it was perfect. To be sometimes here, sometimes there, for as long as she wanted, then to return to the centre, a narrow ridge that constituted the boundary between the two, neither the one nor the other, but a place of possibilities. Here, on this narrow ridge, you could feel lost too, and occasionally long for something that you would seek to abandon a few hours later, so as to return to the ridge where you felt at home . . .

Louise opened the garden gate, near to where the cigarette butts had been found that weren't Niemann's nor his daughter's. She stepped onto the gravel track that ran alongside the gardens. Niemann, who was still standing in his living room and still hadn't switched on any lights, seemed to be gradually dissolving into the grey. By contrast, the first floor was brightly lit, windows and balcony doors were open, and somewhere Henriette Niemann was on her knees cleaning, in an attempt to banish the intruder from her house and her life, which she wouldn't manage today. Even if he never returned he would remain for a few weeks, a few months.

Her gaze wandered along the neighbouring houses. Like the Niemanns' there was lots of glass, lots of wood, lots of green, gardens, everything so pretty and homely and peaceful, and yet just a whisker away from a nightmare. How easy it was for that feeling of being at home in a particular place to be shattered. All it needed was for a man to break into a house one October night or two strangers to be standing in your apartment one summer's afternoon and something fundamental was destroyed. As if home were something inside you as well as a physical place. As if the home inside you were destroyed when the boundaries of the physical one were violated.

She looked out across the fields and meadows up to the Schönberg. To the right in the distance two dogs were frolicking and a little girl was riding on a huge brown horse, while to the left walkers were heading into the forest and a man was standing on his own. She wondered whether Niemann's warrior had come from there, out of the forest and across the steep fields. A warrior from the forest, she thought, from the fields, an aged, muddy warrior who'd lived in those fields for centuries, had risen from the fields one Saturday afternoon, a myth and archetype, the shadow of humanity.

She giggled.

In the distance the little girl made the huge horse turn in a tight circle, twice, three times, four times, as if it were a lapdog. A light-sport aircraft descended from the grey of the clouds and she heard barking, even though the two dogs had disappeared from view.

And the man stood there, as still as a statue, facing Boni.

He was a good fifty metres away, staring at her. He could have been anyone – a walker waiting for his dog, a farmer checking on his field, whoever. But suddenly she knew that this was the man they were looking for, and she knew why she felt so certain: the man did indeed give the impression that he'd always belonged in this place, as if he'd been standing there for years, waiting . . .

Her heart began to race, her mind was in a spin. But she acted slowly and with focus. Turning away as discreetly as possible, she returned to the Niemanns' garden and closed the gate. Only when she found cover behind the patchy conifer hedge did she take out her mobile.

Hoffmann answered at once.

"What? Are you sure?"

"Pretty much."

"What sort of . . . Just keep away from him, do you hear me?"

She walked over to the house, not daring to turn around. Niemann was still standing where she'd last seen him, looking at her. Two motionless men, she thought, just standing there – one inside, one outside – barely one hundred metres apart, and one was going to drive off to Landwasser or Lahr to hunt for the other.

"Do you hear me, Louise?"

"Yes, yes."

"O.K., what do you need?"

Niemann unfroze and moved to the garden door. Not that, she thought. She stopped by the rose bed and gave him as relaxed a smile as she could muster.

"Louise?"

"Yes . . ." She needed all the patrols in the vicinity, as many officers from Freiburg South as possible, plus Wallmer and Benedikt. If one of the Stuttgart choppers happened to be in the Breisgau area then she needed that too. And the dog unit, of course.

Hoffmann panted. That cost money.

"Stay on the line," he said. She heard him roll on his chair, pick up the other phone and mumble to himself, "What sort of bloke is this?"

One who returned to the scene of the crime, she thought. Who perhaps had never gone away.

Turn around, her instinct told her. He's not stupid, he's understood.

"I'm going to hang up now, Alfons," she said, even though she knew he couldn't hear her.

Niemann stepped out onto the terrace with a furrowed brow.

This one's not stupid either, she thought. He's understood too. She smiled again.

"Don't hang up, O.K.?" Hoffmann said.

She cut him off. Niemann said something, but she made no effort to understand him. She went back to the garden gate.

The man was running and already a fair distance away.

Cursing, she set off herself, running parallel to the man and below him, on the gravel path alongside the gardens. Although she made quicker progress, two to three hundred metres ahead of him were houses, streets, the south-western fringes of Merzhausen, where he would disappear from view. As she ran she pressed last number recall. Hoffmann took his time, he had Benedikt on the other line, send the patrol cars at once, she screamed, he's getting away, south-west Merzhausen, near Hexentalstrasse, and he said, they're on their way, promise me you'll keep your distance, do you promise me that? "Yes, yes," she said, still running, not taking her eyes off the man, who briefly turned his head, but only once. She thought she could see him slowing, an elderly man struggling through the wet, deep earth of the field, and she thought she might in fact catch up with him before he got to the houses. Behind her in the distance came the wailing of police sirens and on Hexentalstrasse to the south-west she saw flashing blue lights. From the corner of her eye she glimpsed the man stumble, but he rapidly regained his balance and ran on, again a little more slowly, but nimbly and with determination, as if he were used to fleeing. Suddenly there were walkers in front of her, two old ladies who'd stopped, she held up her service badge, shouted, "Police!", waved the women to the side, but instead of moving aside they just stared at her in shock. Leaping into the field to avoid them, she sank into the deep, heavy earth, before scrambling back up to the path. Now she'd reached the crossroads almost simultaneously with the man, but when she changed direction and headed southwards, he was already running into town and she lost sight of him. Police sirens were now wailing from all directions and up ahead a patrol car was coming towards her. She counted the seconds as she was running: five, six, seven . . . When she got to ten she reached the junction and turned.

A narrow, quiet street, cars parked on both sides, the man nowhere to be seen. At first she thought he was hiding behind one of the cars, but then she saw the footprints in the middle of the road, clear prints of two deep sole profiles, sticky with earth.

Twenty metres further on the footprints ended abruptly.

She stopped.

He'd taken off his shoes.

And vanished.

They didn't find him. Ten patrol cars drove around the neighbourhood, another thirty officers searched gardens, cellars and yards, while a helicopter from Stuttgart circled above Merzhausen, the Schönberg and the Hexental. Bonì, Wallmer, Benedikt and six Kripo officers questioned the local residents: nobody had seen anything – no man on the run, no car starting. They tried using the dogs, got them to sniff the footprints, the cobbles where he may have been in socks, but this yielded no results either. They checked almost one hundred and thirty parked cars – every one could be accounted for and there was no reason to run a check on any of the owners. The fact remained: they couldn't find him. He'd needed barely fifty metres head start to vanish without trace within a few seconds.

Carrying his shoes.

When darkness fell Louise brought the operation to an end. Apart from Wallmer, Benedikt and a few constables from Freiburg South, she sent all the officers back to their stations. She organised coffee and sandwiches, then sat with Wallmer and Benedikt in one of the patrol cars. She'd borrowed a policewoman's green jumper because her coat was still hanging up in the Niemanns' house. She stank of cold sweat and was freezing. Time and again she saw an exhausted, elderly man before her, standing in the middle of a road, shoes in hand, before he took a step to the side and disappeared.

"Shit!" she said.

Wallmer and Benedikt said nothing. They were exhausted and frustrated. Benedikt had called home, Wallmer had cancelled her plans for the evening. Overtime had begun.

A handful of residents were still in the street, but most had gone back inside. For a few hours there had been commotion in Merzhausen; with the darkness peace had returned. He could have made use of the commotion, Louise thought, and now he could make use of the darkness. He wasn't just used to running away, but going underground too.

"Shit!" she said again.

Rolf Bermann turned up at 7 p.m. One of his many children was lying asleep in the back of the black Daimler, a child's birthday party in Ehrenkirchen. Now father and son were on their way home. I thought I'd just pop by, the father said.

"Nothing," Louise said. "Absolutely nothing."

Bermann nodded. Hoffmann had kept him up to date. "You'll get back-up. Bob's got contacts in Schwenningen, there are a few trainee inspectors with time on their hands."

"Trainee inspectors from Schwenningen."

"Yes," Bermann said gleefully. "Swabians."

She nodded. The inelastic world of Rolf Bermann couldn't get along without enmity. Badeners v. Swabians – that was tradition.

"Get them to sharpen your pencils, do some photocopying, that sort of thing."

"Go home, Rolf."

"Yes," Bermann said gleefully.

As they watched the black 4×4 drive off, she tried to remember a phrase she'd heard over the course of the evening in Merzhausen. A phrase that hadn't been thought through to its conclusion.

But she couldn't put her finger on it.

"Luck," Wallmer said. "It was just luck."

"These things do happen," Benedikt said with a yawn.

"Luck pure and simple."

They were standing at the spot where the trail ended. Where the man had vanished. Where time and again he stopped, took his shoes off and just disappeared.

Luck, Louise thought.

The air was cold and damp, and a mist had gathered. Dogs barked in the darkness and in the distance traffic roared along Hexentalstrasse. The fog turned the light of the streetlamps milky.

Luck pure and simple.

On either side of the street stood detached houses with front gardens and alleyways through to gardens at the back. The old part of Merzhausen. Wooden sheds, dog kennels, shrubs, cellar steps, basement utility rooms with unlocked doors. Yes, with a bit of luck you could bide your time here unnoticed, even if dozens of police officers were creeping through the front gardens, alleyways and back gardens.

But she didn't really believe this. No warrior relied on luck in what presumably was a foreign country.

On what then?

No answer came to mind. She was tired, fixated, her head was blocked. She wanted to be alone, sit here alone, in the darkness, to understand how this man kept vanishing. She wanted to spend all night with him alone, to understand what sort of person he was.

What sort of warrior he was.

Benedikt yawned. Wallmer yawned with him. A man stood in the mist, took off his shoes and vanished.

"Let's call it a day," Louise said.

Benedikt shook his head. "I didn't mean it like that."

"Yes, you did," Wallmer said.

They laughed softly. The laughter relieved the blockage. If someone didn't want to rely on luck, they made a plan. A plan in case something went wrong and they only had another fifty metres to escape.

An escape plan pure and simple.

"That's what she's like," Wallmer said, shaking her head.

"That's what I'm like," Louise said.

"No evening off, no private life, and just when you think she's going to collapse with exhaustion she starts all over again."

It seemed a little harsh, a little curt. "Sounds awful," Louise said.

Benedikt nodded. "Sounds like an illness."

"I just hope it isn't contagious," Wallmer said.

Again, a little harsh, a little curt. Louise smiled warily.

Wallmer opened the back door of one of the patrol cars from Freiburg South. "I'm sticking with the line that he was lucky. I mean, a tramp with an escape plan? Per-lease."

"Go home, Anne," Louise said. "Get yourself some private life."

Wallmer nodded, got in and shut the door. For a moment her face behind the window was expressionless. Then she gave a brief smile and waved.

The car drove off.

"Is there something wrong with her?"

"Like what?" Benedikt said.

Louise shrugged. "Forget it."

She thought about the meeting that morning, Wallmer's Monday morning tantrum. Or had she expected Bermann to give *her* the leadership of the investigation team. But Wallmer wasn't the type for professional envy. She wasn't ambitious enough. She'd fitted perfectly into the hierarchical structure and endeavoured to be a good policewoman, apart from the fact that she tried to be as hard and steely as Bermann. A few years earlier Bermann had issued threats to banish from the corridors of police H.Q. the rumour that she was a lesbian. In return she'd worshipped him ever since.

A rumour, a hobby, unconditional dedication to her job and her boss – they knew very little else about Wallmer.

"An escape plan," Benedikt said thoughtfully.

"It can wait till tomorrow, Mats."

"It's plausible, anyhow. It would explain a lot, not just how he was able to escape this afternoon. But his behaviour at the Niemanns' too. That he wasn't worried about being caught. That he didn't worry about whether or not he left any trace. He knew that all he needed was a few metres' head start to vanish."

"Yes."

They went to his car.

"If you don't mind I'll come back here tomorrow," Benedikt said, as if he were sure he'd find answers. If someone had devised an escape plan, other people could figure it out. That was how he said it.

She nodded. She was glad he thought like this. With all the chatter in her head about old warriors, homelands old and new, Germans from another time and another country, somehow her sense of what was obvious, logical and simple had gone astray.

If someone had a plan, the plan could be deduced. She liked this. It was so wonderfully sober.

Benedikt offered to drive her to the Niemanns'. She declined. She wanted to walk, be alone, finally identify the word that might be important and which was hidden in her tired brain between the many words that might be unimportant.

Walk back alone in the fog and darkness along the narrow ridge where she felt at home.

And perhaps not only she, she thought.

5

She followed the road towards the Schönberg, the fog growing thicker with every step. From a nearby house she could hear the clattering of pots and pans, a child laughed, an engine hummed. Otherwise peace reigned again in Merzhausen. The strangers who, with their cars, helicopters, dogs and questions, had brought spectacle and menace to Merzhausen, had gone. Sometimes when questioning people on operations like this she saw in their eyes the fear of a malevolent visitation, of the unfamiliar intruding into what was familiar. They wanted to close the door and say nothing, for along with the police officer the criminal had entered their houses, and their heads too. Spectacle and menace, desire and fear – only when the police officer left did peace return. The police officer embodied the criminal. When the one had gone, the other no longer existed.

Irrespective of whether he was still waiting somewhere in the darkness.

For a few minutes she wondered whether she shouldn't chance it. Whether she shouldn't sit and wait herself. Maybe the escape plan specified that he'd wait until it was peaceful again in Merzhausen.

She knew now that she had to rethink. They were waging an asymmetrical war using the techniques of symmetrical warfare. They had come with dozens of people, dogs and helicopters, with their technology, their questions, their theories. They did what they always did because they assumed the man they were looking for did what the men they usually looked for always did. Now they knew, however, that this man was different.

So she wondered whether she should sit and wait in the darkness. But she was too tired for an asymmetrical war.

She stopped at the end of the road, at the edge of the fields and meadows where she'd lost sight of the man. In the light of the street-lamps all she could see was a strip of earth and white fog and a few headlights slowly approaching from the east. She had a hunch and her hunch was confirmed. A blue Audi from a carport by a house with lots of glass and lots of wood, now the Audi stopped, behind the windscreen a slim, pallid face with glasses, searching for a nightmare and finding an inspector. She went over to the passenger door, opened it and let herself sink into the warmth and tranquillity of the car interior. Classical music, the smell of fear, of questions, how does he count, when is he coming, what sort of enemies . . . She briefly stroked Niemann's arm and said nothing.

Landwasser, Lahr, Merzhausen, a lonely search without any point – where could it take him? But she kept quiet. She allowed herself to be driven through fog, accompanied by Mozart or Bach or Beethoven or whatever the choir was singing. Music for being carried away, music for solitude, she thought, dangerous music for people who lived in semi-abandoned buildings without stairs, entered their apartments at the wrong end and were beginning to understand that perhaps they would have been better off moving. That surely they couldn't be indifferent to where they lived.

She ran her finger across the C.D. player.

"Turn it down?" Niemann said.

"Off," Louise said.

"Of course."

The music fell silent.

"Don't you like Brahms, then?"

"Not when I'm hungry."

She grinned, but Niemann just nodded thoughtfully, as if this were an answer worth thinking about. But then he said, "We sang that, my wife and I, when we lived in Munich." He glanced at her. "Not this recording, obviously . . . I mean, the Requiem."

"You were in a choir?"

"A church choir." Not a special choir, a small, dedicated choir, the choir of the Lutheran church in Giesing, that's where they lived, in the Giesing area of Munich, beneath the Giesinger Berg where the apartments were simple and sometimes shabby, and the people like-wise simple and sometimes shabby, Yes, but they were good people, just simple people like you and me, and above them on the hill the mighty Church of the Holy Cross, and in its shadow the small, rust-brown Lutheran church on a busy road, sometimes we were told to sing against the traffic and that's what we did, sing against the traffic and everyday life and the anonymity of the big city . . .

They turned into the Niemanns' road. The fog in front of them became a sunny yellow; the glass house was brightly lit.

Music against everyday life, light against the fear.

"What about now?"

"Now we don't have any time for singing."

"It's got nothing to do with time, Herr Niemann."

He didn't respond.

"Sorry, I just get like this sometimes when I'm hungry."

"You must be hungry fairly often then."

When she saw him smile she smiled too. The victim and the inspector were joking with each other like the therapist and the patient used to at the hospital bed in January 2003.

She knew now that Wallmer's curt remarks had been right. Why did she always start all over again when the others had clocked off work to enjoy their private life?

Because for her, job and private life had long been one and the same.

*

Niemann switched off the engine in the carport, but made no move to get out. Louise already had her hand on the door handle. She didn't fancy listening to any more stories from Giesing in Munich, but she sensed again that closeness to Niemann, around whom everything in this story revolved. So she would listen a while longer.

But Niemann said nothing.

A movement made her turn her head. Now the front door opened and a girl with short, red hair stood on the threshold, looking in their direction. The small face and assured poise were reminiscent of Henriette Niemann. At first glance nothing reminded Louise of Paul Niemann.

The girl waved and Niemann waved back and smiled. "My daughter, Carola."

"Yes."

"You should talk to her. She is . . . I mean, she sees a lot and she thinks a lot. Maybe . . ." Niemann broke off.

"Tomorrow," Louise said. "I've got to go back to the office now, and then to bed."

He nodded.

"I'm getting out now, Herr Niemann."

"I . . . I took a picture of him."

"The man?"

"This afternoon, when you . . ."

"Show me."

Niemann took the digital camera from his coat pocket, switched it on and gave it to her. "Press this one to scroll through." Yes, that was him, the warrior, running in the distance, taken diagonally from behind and barely visible against the dark field, the dark forest, more a shadow than a person. In the next photograph he was closer, it was zoomed in slightly, although not focused, a blurry figure, the only discernible feature of the head being his ice-grey hair. The third picture showed him a little closer still, now his head was turned and the left-hand side of his face was visible. Niemann must have taken it at the very moment the man had turned to her.

"That's all of them, I'm afraid I couldn't take any more."

"Where's the zoom?"

"Top right."

She zoomed into the man's face until it became completely pixelated. She knew the technicians would be able to get something, even from this blur.

"I don't believe it . . . You photographed the guy."

"Well." Niemann gave an uncertain laugh.

"I don't believe it."

"I . . . I'm afraid the pictures aren't good, I mean, I was so far away and I couldn't run or . . ."

"It'll be fine for a first mug shot."

"Do you think so?"

"I do."

They got out and went over to the girl who looked at them with dark, serene, watchful eyes. A peculiar strength emanated from her, a natural dignity. Henriette might be the protective brace around this family, Louise thought, but the girl was its core.

Tomorrow, she thought, not now. I'm not going to start over again, just as it's coming to an end.

"I'll have to keep hold of the camera for the time being."

"Yes, of course."

"We won't be able to do it by tomorrow morning. Just in case you're . . ."

Going to Landwasser or Lahr or Merzhausen – she didn't have to say it out loud.

"Oh, it doesn't matter," Niemann said, pulling a second digital camera from the other pocket of his coat.

*

Then Bonì was introduced to the girl, who still came across as digni-fied, but also slightly cold, and afterwards to the boy, who reminded her more of the father and was equally pale and uncertain. Henriette came and asked whether she would like a tea or coffee, or a glass of something stronger, perhaps now? She felt quite seriously tempted, a tea, she thought, followed by something to eat, then a bath, which she pictured as large, white and elegant, and then to relax on the sofa on the second floor beneath a mountain of blankets, watching a bit of telly, and being woken in the morning by Henriette with a mug of coffee, and then they would talk more, woman to woman ...

She shook her head: another time.

On the way back to the office it occurred to her that Jenny Böhm hadn't called. At a traffic light she dialled her mobile number, but it was no longer working. As she drove on she called directory enquiries and was connected to Jenny's landline, but neither she nor her hus-band picked up, nor did they have an answerphone. She had herself put through to the parish office and listened to the recorded message as she waved to the cameras operated by her colleagues in the traffic police. They never sent a penalty notice, just the occasional photo. "Frau Böhm," she said softly. "It's Frau Bonì here. Please call me back."

At ten o'clock she was in the office and by eleven she had read and countersigned the documents that Wallmer, Benedikt and Hoffmann had placed on her desk, recorded a verbal report of the day's events on her dictaphone, and filled out the form for the D.N.A. analysis of the cigarette, which required judicial authorisation. She went to Hoffmann's office, where a light was still on, but he wasn't there. When she put the documents and Niemann's digital camera on his desk she noticed that his hi-tech chair wasn't there either. Then, from a corner of the room, from amongst yuccas, ferns and other fronds, she heard a grunting and a snoring: Hoffmann slumped in his chair, as if he'd rolled in his sleep across the room and into the plants. Super-Chair Abducts Police Inspector . . . She laughed quietly and Hoffmann woke up. He stared at her from the green undergrowth. "Enough of the jokes, I'm an old man."

"An old man in a wheelchair."

He got up with a yawn and freed himself and the chair from the foliage. Back at his desk he sat down again. "I could have fallen over, Louise."

"It wasn't me, I've only just come from my office."

"Then it was Rolf."

"Rolf left ages ago."

"Who was it, then?"

"The chair."

"The chair?"

"Doesn't the thing have a wheel lock? Like on a pram, you know, the mummy clicks it with her foot when they're on the tram, the mummy and her little darling."

She grinned. Hoffmann grumbled.

"It doesn't say anywhere in the manual that the thing can move of its own accord."

"You've got a manual for your chair?"

"Health is a complex subject and needs explaining, Louise."

"What if you had fallen off it?"

"Then," Hoffmann said with a smile, "the chair would have caught me."

They went downstairs together, from the third to the ground floor, which took some time with Hoffmann in tow, but there was no taking the lift in the evenings, the evenings were for exercise. The evenings were his "other life". Hoffmann had married a dragon uprooted from her native Lower Bavaria, and the dragon went to bed at nine thirty on the dot. And so Hoffmann stayed at the office long into the evening, took lengthy walks along the banks of the Dreisam, sat on the fitness machines in the academy, living his "other life", his life without the dragon and fantasising that he'd never got married, or at least not to a creature who only ever smiled at Christmas.

"Lahr called," Hoffmann said on the second floor. "They wanted to know what to do with the homeless guy. I said they should keep him in and we'd go up tomorrow, we couldn't do it today."

"Tomorrow morning, right after the meeting."

"The land registry office called back," Hoffmann said on the first floor. "The land used to belong to a farmer from Au who sold it to the developer eight years ago. An old codger who's never done anything wrong, but you never know . . ."

"Get Schwenningen to look him up."

"Bob was here," Hoffmann said on the ground floor. "He wanted to know how things were looking. I told him it doesn't look great at the moment."

"It looks a bit better now," she said and told him about Niemann's photographs.

"Well, if we don't get him now . . ." Hoffmann said. "I mean, how's the guy going to hide if we've got a photo?"

They entered the courtyard.

"Unless he's gone to ground somewhere different entirely," Hoffmann said.

Louise didn't respond. Suddenly the phrase she'd been looking for was there – going underground. It hadn't been spoken out loud, she had merely thought it. He wasn't just used to running away, but going underground too, she'd thought.

"Get a plan of the Merzhausen sewer system for Mats tomorrow," she said.

"Good God . . ."

She nodded. Maybe the old warrior had been lurking beneath them for half a day.

Waiting for peace and quiet to return to Merzhausen.

*

At midnight she was standing on the ground floor of her building, staring up at the stars. No more stairs, no lift, just a shaft up to the sky.

As arranged, the new key was in her mailbox.

She climbed a metal tower in the courtyard, stepped onto a metal platform and stood in front of a metal door. At her feet was the door-mat. She thought it looked slightly crooked, so she set it straight, then made it crooked again – come on, getting all neurotic because of a metal door? You're a *calm* person now. She slipped out of her shoes and put the key in the lock. The door didn't creak; well, that was something at least.

She felt for the light switch and pressed play on her answerphone. A call from Richard Landen from Japan, a call from little Germain from Kehl, no call from Jenny Böhm. Landen said he'd be back on Wednesday. Her brother said he wanted to visit her at the weekend. Louise said, I've no time, guys.

On the coffee table stood a rose in a beer bottle. So this was how Upper Silesians, who for inexplicable reasons had a bad conscience, said "Welcome".

It was only when she noticed the fine layer of red dust covering every surface in her sitting room that she understood the bad conscience.

This spelled the end of the new, relaxed Louise.

6

The meeting began at eight a.m. and ended at eight, at least as far as Louise was concerned. Anybody over forty who had spent half the night cleaning up fine dust had a right to be unconscious at eight in the morning, she thought. She wiggled her hand and Hoffmann took over. With half-closed eyes and her skull humming, she heard incomprehensible words resound in her head, and now and again stood up to spit dust into the sink. When she heard an enticing rustle from Hoffmann's direction she muttered, "Could I have a bite?" and was given a scrunched-up ball of newspaper. She turned it over in her hands before realising that it was never going to turn into a chocolate croissant. "The taxi's waiting," Hoffmann said cordially at some point, and accompanied her to the lift.

Soon afterwards she was in the back of a Golf being driven to Lahr; a female officer was heading there coincidentally. She fell asleep before they turned out of Heinrich-von-Stephan-Strasse. Boni dreamed of the narrow ridge where she felt at home and this ridge was a blue motorway between the Vosges to the left and the Black Forest to the right. In the dream her French family was waving on the left and her German family on the right. Is Germain with Auntie Natalie again? a voice asked, and another voice said, Yes, *ma chère*, he's with Auntie Natalie in Upper Silesia. "Nonsense," Louise said, opening her eyes. They were at a service station, her colleague was filling up and the sun was shining for the first time in a long, grey week. She got out. The shop's air conditioning was freezing and beside the till were the descendants of that Mon Chéri which had led her into temptation eighteen months earlier. This time she only wanted chewing gum, two chocolate croissants and two takeaway coffees. Her colleague blushed, evidently delighted that Chief Inspector Bonì had thought of her too. During the last few kilometres to Lahr, Louise wondered with satisfaction whether within a year and a half she might have turned from the problem child of D11 into the legend of Freiburg Kripo.

Lahr police station was a "terminus"; officers who came here generally stayed until they retired. Arndt Schneider, chief of the station, late thirties, had arrived eight years earlier, but his office gave the impression that he was leaving the following day. It was a bare, cold room, as empty as only a police office could be. A desk, a P.C., two chairs and a lockable metal cupboard.

"A minimalist," Louise said.

Arndt Schneider smiled.

She liked his smile. It was very friendly, very open and, as it subsided, fleetingly very sad. She liked his eyes too, warm, light-grey eyes that looked at her steadily rather than darting about her face like those of so many other people.

"We've met," he said.

She nodded. The face and eyes did seem vaguely familiar. "Some operation?"

"No, I don't think so. From before."

"From before? Hopefully nothing comp . . ."

"Compromising? Complicated?"

She wiggled her hand – take your pick.

He smiled again, then said with a shrug, "To be honest, I can't really remember."

"Must be a long time ago, then."

"It feels like S.S.U. times."

"Ah, the special support unit, those legendary parties . . ." She grinned. "After my time, I'm afraid."

"You joined before '87?"

She nodded. Eighty-two, after the obligatory trip around Asia and the obligatory where-am-I-going semesters of Romance studies, before the S.S.U. was open to women. She could remember it clearly: as Emma Bovary was dying an agonising death, she suddenly hit on the idea of trying her luck as a policewoman, perhaps because at the time no other profession had such a strong whiff of the nineteenth century about it . . . Then Germain had died and she had been saved by her training. "Baby course", constabulary course and Kripo course, followed by her first postings as a detective sergeant in Stuttgart and Freiburg, study at Villingen-Schwenningen at the beginning of the nineties, then back to Freiburg. Schneider shook his head, different places, different times; he'd done all his police courses in Freiburg. In her head Louise ran through the "mid-course parties" during the training she'd taken in '86 and '87. At the time she was twenty and definitely used to notch up young bucks.

Had Arndt Schneider been one of these young bucks?

"We'll get there in the end," he said.

"I don't know if that's a good thing."

He laughed as he stood up. "Shall we go?"

Schneider held the door open. He was tall with long legs, slightly ungainly, not a powerful, virile street cop in the Rolf Bermann or Mats Benedikt mould, more like James Stewart in "The Man Who Shot Liberty Valance".

She didn't remember a James Stewart at any of those "mid-course parties".

"Tell me something about your homeless guy," she said.

"Tell me something about your case," Schneider said.

Bonì nodded. She'd noticed that those warm, light-grey eyes had become alert. The homeless man and the Russians in Lahr – Arndt Schneider's business.

Quite apart from the fact that he was a chief superintendent and thus three grades above her.

She briefed him on the case, but only the essentials; he was a minimalist, after all. By the time they'd got down to the ground floor she was finished, and now had the opportunity to consider that when he reached her age he would be five or six grades above her and still five or six years younger.

She resolved *not* to think about this.

Although she possessed the best qualification a woman could have for a career in the police – no children – she had the worst too: she was an alcoholic.

So why should she doubt the system when this time she herself might be to blame?

Schneider opened the security door.

"Where are we going?"

"For a little stroll around town."

"So you didn't keep him in?"

"Of course not. How can I detain someone who's not committed a crime?"

Louise sighed inwardly. Something she was able to do now and then.

"He'd turn my detention cell into firewood if he wasn't supplied with a litre of booze every half hour."

Yes, she understood that better.

"But we're keeping an eye on him."

She nodded. A warrior with a pistol, a bizarre ultimatum, and a homeless man who might know something.

Arndt Schneider's business and he was dealing with it.

Lahr at the end of October was one big sea of flowers – chrysanthemums wherever you looked, in shades of yellow, red, violet and white, hanging in the bright sunshine from window sills, canopies and balconies, growing in pots, beds, boxes, crafted into arches, animals and landscapes. There was barely a metre of the pedestrian zone without chrysanthemums and they were lovely to look at, even if, like Louise, you knew next to nothing about flowers. Mick had loved flowers. The Chrysanthema had been an obligatory fixture in their marriage ever since its inception in 1998. For three years Louise had come home from Lahr laden with colourful blooms.

They bought coffee and continued on their way.

"Listen, then," Schneider said. Nobody knew what the homeless man was called, how old he was, where he came from or how long he'd been living in Lahr. He just appeared one day, and one day he'd be gone again; they knew little else. The Lahr police called him "Friedrich" because he'd first been apprehended on Friedrichstrasse, several years ago now. Because he was always there, always watching, always saying what he had seen, over the years he'd become something akin to a chronicler. A chronicler of banalities in a world that extended no further than a crossroads in the pedestrian zone. He was probably in his mid-thirties, surprisingly educated and usually entertaining as he chatted about harmless, everyday stuff – Lilly from the flower stall has a new admirer, he's as fat as old Helmut Kohl. You know Lukas from the takeaway? His toupee went flying into a puddle . . .

"When isn't he entertaining?"

"Don't mention the resettlers."

"How's that going to work if I'm looking for a resettler?"

"Just oblige me, would you?"

"What's he got against resettlers?"

"Everything and anything."

"He seems to talk to them, though."

"Your resettler had booze on him. Alcohol lets alcoholics overlook their reservations, I suppose."

Did it? She mulled this over for a while as they wandered along

Marktstrasse with its half-timbered houses. The street still had an early morning feel to it – clean, fresh and unworn – even though many people were already out and about. As Schneider was in uniform, heads turned – the tall, friendly, serene policeman, whose high rank was easy to surmise even if you didn't know what the two gold stars on his epaulettes and the gold band on his cap signified; beside him the medium-height, dark-haired woman with sunglasses, the legend of Freiburg Kripo in a classically understated look: denim jacket, white blouse, jeans, shoulder bag, Geox shoes.

"Strange," Schneider said. "Ever since I knew you were coming to Lahr I've had a certain type of music in my head, seventies' rock or pop, you know, bombastic, guitars, keyboards . . ."

She began to laugh and linked arms with the chief superintendent, who probably *had* been one of her young bucks. The pieces of the puzzle were gradually fitting together. A 1987 course on sex cases at Freiburg police academy, a "mid-course party" after seven out of fourteen days, Barclay James Harvest at high volume on the morning of the eighth, sleepy, warm, light-grey eyes, two naked people with mugs of coffee in one hand and their partner's genitalia in the other.

"Now you mention it . . ." Schneider stopped.

"Don't think for a moment that it gives you any rights now."

"Any *rights*?" He looked at her, slightly bemused.

Louise laughed again. She had yet to meet a chief superintendent she couldn't faze.

Schneider had called the officers who were keeping an eye on Friedrich. As usual he was sitting by the Stork Tower, and that's where they found him, cross-legged in front of a low wall, surrounded by colourful, decorative chrysanthemums. He was a stooped, lifeless figure with thin, longish hair that fell into his face. When Louise made out his eyes behind the hair she realised that he'd been staring at them for a while.

"Hey, Arndt!" Friedrich raised a hand. A broad, gold wedding ring circled his fourth finger.

"Morning, Friedrich," Schneider said.

Friedrich's eyes were red, his lips dry, his face dark and leathery. Sweeping his hair behind his ears, he said, "The lady from Freiburg?"

Schneider nodded. "Yes."

"Hi, Louise! One answer for ten euros, two for eighteen." Friedrich gave a flat laugh, revealing grey teeth. "Just a joke. I'm a good man. Aren't I?"

"Yes, you are," Arndt said.

"I just stink, unfortunately."

Louise smiled. "Stink" was right. Any time even the smallest part of Friedrich moved a stench floated up to her nose.

Friedrich took out a dark-blue tobacco pouch and began rolling himself a cigarette. "DRUM" – another memory from the early days, her first few wild years as a policewoman . . .

"What has the guy done, Louise?"

"He broke into someone's house and threatened them with a pistol."

"No good person would do that, would they, Arndt?"

Schneider shook his head.

"Come on, sit down you two," Friedrich said.

"Like a coffee?" Schneider asked.

"Yes, coffee would be great, Arndt, but put a little something in it, would you?"

"You'll have to do that yourself."

Friedrich lit the cigarette. "A man with principles, Louise. A good soul. Despite everything that's happened. Can I tell her, Arndt, while you get my coffee?"

"If she wants to hear, then you can tell her."

They watched Schneider walk away.

"Would you like to hear, Louise?" Friedrich said.

She sat on the wall. "What?"

"How Arndt's little boy died."

"How . . ."

She looked into those red, torpid eyes. No, she thought, she didn't want to hear. Not this way. Not from Friedrich.

But when Friedrich began to tell the story she didn't say anything.

One summer's day five years ago, a reversing lorry, a boy on a yellow bicycle. The boy wasn't watching and the lorry's reversing alarm wasn't working. The bike slid under the lorry, the boy lay on the cobbles with a broken neck. Friedrich pointed to the spot, over there, on the corner, and he saw it, he was sitting here and saw it. A yellow bicycle beneath a lorry, a boy on the cobbles. Louise looked to see where Schneider was, but couldn't find him. Her eyes returned to the spot on the corner. A yellow bike, a boy on the cobbles. She asked Friedrich what the boy's name was, but he didn't know. She thought of the bare, cold office with just the essentials. For a split second she fancied she understood why it had to be that way.

Then Schneider came back holding a cup of coffee and a paper bag. Friedrich took both with a gesture that almost hinted at an intimacy between the men. Thanking Schneider, he opened a dark glass bottle and added to the coffee what needed to be added. Arndt Schneider, the policeman; Friedrich, the homeless man – she now knew what linked them. What had Schneider called Friedrich? A chronicler of banalities. Lilly from the flower stall has got a new admirer, Lukas' toupee went flying into a puddle, Arndt's little boy died today . . . Once again she felt for a brief moment that she understood Schneider. That she understood what he was doing when he let Friedrich talk.

"She knows, Arndt," Friedrich said.

Schneider nodded.

Louise said she was terribly sorry and Schneider nodded again. "It was five years ago," he said, sitting down beside her. "It's O.K. now."

"Is it?"

"Yes."

How could it be O.K.? Louise thought. But she said nothing.

Schneider asked Friedrich for the tobacco pouch and rolled himself a cigarette. He said it was O.K. for his wife now too. They'd accepted what had happened, accepted it by and large. But they hadn't wanted more children. He looked up. They'd had one and lost him, such was their life.

He lit the cigarette and Louise breathed in the smell, the smell of that wild first time. She thought of the morning she probably hadn't thought about for seventeen years. A morning like many at a time which had been marked by the memory of her dead brother, her daily struggle in a man's world, desire, depression, loneliness and the wherefore and whither. She recollected all of this vividly, but barely remembered Arndt Schneider, which strangely pained her. Barclay James Harvest, warm, light-grey eyes, the hint of a man and a voice – there wasn't much else.

Years later a little boy died.

She looked at Schneider. "Would you roll me one too?"

They smoked in silence amidst the chrysanthemum splendour, the passers-by, the memories. Louise felt a strange lethargy well up inside her; it may have been tiredness, perhaps something else. A lover from the past, a dead boy – all a bit much for half a morning.

Hoffmann jolted her from her lethargy.

"You're not going to believe this," he said as she moved away from Schneider and Friedrich, the mobile to her ear.

They thought they'd worked out how the old warrior had disappeared in Merzhausen. He had indeed sat and waited in the sewers. He'd lifted a manhole cover, climbed down into the shaft, closed the cover and waited. Less than fifty metres from where the trail had ended.

"You were right," Hoffmann said.

She nodded. The phrase she'd been looking for and had then found. The phrase and the idea that maybe she should sit in the dark and wait . . . With her hunches she was closer to him than she'd considered possible.

She must have been thinking in asymmetric parameters. But wasn't she fundamentally asymmetric anyway?

She couldn't help smiling. Maybe that would be useful now.

Bonì dropped the half-smoked cigarette. She'd had it with smoking, with smoking and drinking. Schneider and Friedrich were watching her; she gave a small wave. Neither waved back. She turned her face to the sun, closed her eyes and leaned back against the wall of a building. "Did Mats find the manhole?"

"Yes."

Mats Benedikt had traced all the possible routes. Routes where you became invisible after just a few metres, routes that ran between houses, into gardens or simply behind front-garden hedges. He'd counted the steps, timed the seconds, marked potential areas. Then he had searched these areas. "A manhole in a parallel street," Hoffmann said. "A designated play zone with no parking, so he could assume that there wouldn't be a car above the manhole."

Louise nodded again. An escape plan that wasn't 100 per cent certain. There was room for a bit of luck and risk after all.

There were marks on the manhole cover, Hoffmann said. He'd lifted it with an iron bar or similar. Forensics were now searching the shaft for fingerprints, fibres and other clues.

"Steinle and Lubowitz?"

"Yes."

Louise laughed gently. She pictured Steinle in a sewer shaft, heard him curse, growl, grunt. No Queen of Sheba along with all her entourage had shuffled down the sewer shaft. But Steinle was hanging in the bowels of Merzhausen.

She heard a woman's voice, answered by a child's, and opened her eyes slightly. Yellow chrysanthemums shone in the sunlight, more and more people, more and more activity. "What did we do wrong yesterday, Alfons?"

"Nothing. First it was foggy and then it was dark."

"We should have thought of it. I mean, a sewer – it's not *that* original."

"I don't know. We've got to get to know him first."

"Yes," Louise said. Slowly they *were* getting to know him. They knew he was different and acted differently from how they expected. That he didn't run away when it looked as if he did. That he didn't care about leaving traces when breaking into someone's house. That he had a pistol but didn't use it, not even when in danger.

And they knew that a single investigator achieved more than a dozen officers with dogs, a helicopter and all the technology. An investigator who was on the right track. But the usual questions didn't seem to put them on this track – how does he think, how does he operate, how does he react in such and such a situation?

So what were the key questions about this man who was so different and who acted so differently?

Why did he think the way he did? How had he become the man who thought in this way?

"Louise?"

"I've got a bad feeling . . ."

"I've always got a bad feeling."

She remembered Niemann's questions. How should he count? When would he come? What if the old warrior behaved differently from how they were expecting, here too?

"How many patrol cars have we got in Merzhausen?"

"Driving past the Niemanns'? Two."

"We need more. We need at least four. They have to be going past at short, irregular intervals."

"I'll sort that out."

"And we need a task force."

"We won't get one, Louise."

"Tell Rolf."

Hoffmann sighed, but said yes.

They had to be quick. They needed all the information they could muster and as fast as humanly possible. Possible fingerprint matches, information on the shoes, fibres, the results of the D.N.A. analysis. Task forces worked more rapidly and efficiently than investigation teams. Got what they wanted more quickly.

The D.N.A. analysis was a problem. As soon as they had judicial authorisation Hoffmann would send the sample to the Baden-Württemberg Criminal Investigation Bureau in Stuttgart, because no murder had been committed. Which meant four weeks if they were lucky, six months if unlucky. "Send the sample to the forensics lab in Freiburg. We need the result in twenty-four hours. Tell them that. If we want to prevent something dreadful from happening we need the result in twenty-four hours."

"And what if there's no match?"

"Maybe we'll get lucky and he's in some database."

"Luck," Hoffmann said gloomily.

"Anything else, Alfons?"

"No. What about you?"

"Later. Bye."

Louise kept her eyes closed, her face to the sun. The lethargy and tiredness had returned. The questions.

What was important about this man?

Why he thought as he did. Why he'd become like that.

She turned around. Schneider and Friedrich were still looking over as if waiting for her to come back. The friendly chief superintendent, the homeless chronicler. A yellow bicycle beneath a lorry, a boy with a broken neck.

Over there, on the corner, Friedrich had said.

The corner she was standing on.

Then they spoke about the Russian, "our man", as Louise called him, to avoid having to say "Russian". She showed Friedrich her copy of the photograph Niemann had taken, and Friedrich nodded. "Your man" had been sitting here one morning before Friedrich arrived, in Friedrich's place, so he'd said, you can't sit here, no, maybe you don't know, but this is *my* place, no, no, you can't sit here. He had shuffled to the side and Friedrich had sat down, all very civilised, That's how we settle problems over people's places, Louise, us civilised individuals. Friedrich laughed, smoke rose from his mouth, masking for a moment the stench of his clothes, hair and skin.

"Did he say anything?"

"Not a word, Louise, he didn't say a word. He just listened and nodded and smoked and shared his slivovitz with me."

"Then the patrol car came."

"Then the patrol car came." Friedrich opened the dark bottle and drank whatever was in it. She thought how she'd done the same for a few years – opened bottles and drunk whatever was in them. But secretly, hidden, in lavatories, shielded by cupboards, in dark shadows. As if she'd been trying to conceal it from herself. But maybe the hiding had been important. Maybe it had been a clue that at some point she'd be ready to stop.

Perhaps those who didn't hide it didn't have to stop.

She thought of Jenny Böhm who'd started hiding again. Who hadn't called back.

"The officers didn't come because of the two men," Schneider said. "They were just getting a coffee."

"They park their car there," Friedrich said, nodding to the left, "and head for Tschibo" – he nodded his head to the right – "but being such polite gents, they want to say hello to me, so they come up to us. Your man leaps up and clears off at a pelt, they go after him, but how he *runs*, Louise . . . Blink and you've no idea where he's gone." Friedrich flicked away his cigarette butt, laughing softly and with admiration.

"Did he have anything on him? A bag, a rucksack?"

"A rucksack."

"What type?"

"Smallish, Louise. Like your bag."

"Colour?"

"Dark. Maybe blue. Black."

"What was he wearing?"

"Well, he wasn't wearing black tie, Louise."

"What then?"

"Definitely not black tie . . ."

Schneider touched her arm and she followed his gaze. At the crossroads stood three elderly men in dark-blue tracksuit bottoms and anoraks, one with a flat cap and another with a walking stick. They were smoking, talking, gesticulating.

"Look at them," Friedrich said. "Do you see them, Louise? Our Russians."

"What was he wearing, Friedrich?"

"Oh, I dunno, trousers, a coat and surely something underneath too . . . Can you see them, Louise?"

"Yes, I can. But I'm not here because of them, Friedrich."

"How old are they? Fifty-five, sixty? Do they work? Study? Do they do anything useful? No, they do *nothing*. They get benefits or an early pension, so they don't have to work or study or do anything useful."

"Describe him to me, Friedrich. Face, hands, voice . . ."

"He had all of those, Louise, face, hands, voice." Friedrich laughed and now the tone of his laughter was different – menacing and aggressive. "And what language do they speak, Louise? Do they speak German? No, they speak Russian or Kazakhstani or Siberian or whatever. And why? Because they're not Germans, Louise."

"I think that's that," Schneider said, getting to his feet.

Friedrich nodded. "Yes, he doesn't like to hear this, our Arndt. Doesn't like hearing the truth sometimes."

"The truth, Friedrich?"

"Yes, the truth. What I see, what I hear. The truth, Arndt."

"Let's go," Schneider said.

Louise looked at Friedrich. So many questions remained. But Schneider was right. That was that. She stood up.

"Don't you like hearing the truth either, Louise?" Friedrich muttered, without taking his eyes off the three men at the crossroads. Then he continued with his litany: they were lazy, uneducated, filthy, they'd swamped Lahr like an epidemic, their daughters were whores, their sons drug dealers, the old ones just held out their hands, they were Russians after all, and suddenly there was violence in Lahr, violence, Louise, just wander along Kanadaring at night and you'll see what I mean . . .

Louise bent down to him. "Bye bye, Friedrich."

He looked up at her with his red, torpid eyes.

"And thanks."

Friedrich nodded.

Schneider was already a few metres away. Louise wondered what was going through his mind. Friedrich, who had seen what happened to his little boy. Friedrich, the Russian-hater.

"Louise," Friedrich whispered behind her.

She stopped and turned her head.

"I've got a word for you."

"I'm not sure I want to hear it."

He grinned. "A word from your man, Louise."

She stepped closer. "What sort of word?"

"He had a cigarette case and there was a word on it, engraved on the inside. A word and a date."

She nodded and waited.

"'Wapolwo,' it said, Louise, and a date. The year was 1945, I don't remember the rest."

She asked him to spell the word, which he did.

Wapolwo 1945. A name, a place, an expression – and a year. "Do you know what Wapolwo is?"

Friedrich shrugged. "Never heard of it."

"Describe the cigarette case."

"Silver-coloured, some metal, possibly aluminium. It was light, you know? Tatty, tarnished, dirty. And inside, on the lid, there was this word: Wapolwo. A nice word, don't you think? Now you should go, Louise, if you don't want to hear my truths."

She nodded, raised a hand, thanks in spite of everything. Wapolwo, she thought, her excitement mounting. Perhaps now they had a start, the start of a story, a life. Someone would know what Wapolwo was – a name, a place, an expression.

A past.

Wapolwo 1945.

Schneider had no idea, nor did Hoffmann.

They would find out.

Rather than returning to the station they went in the opposite direction, passing a big wheel decorated with chrysanthemums, then the town hall, before leaving the pedestrian zone. Schneider had told her that if she wanted to know anything about resettlers she had to speak to some. He had arranged an appointment for her in K2, the counselling service for resettlers, Kanadaring 2. A patrol car would take her there.

"Kanadaring," Louise said. "I hear quite a lot about that, and not just from Friedrich."

Schneider shrugged. "You mustn't believe everything you hear."

"What should I believe, Arndt?"

Another shrug. "If only it were so simple."

But she wasn't having that. Tell me something about the Russians, Arndt, about little Lahr and its thousands of Russians, I hear quite a lot. Schneider smiled his friendly, sad smile and said, "Lahr doesn't have any Russians, Louise. Lahr has Germans from Russia."

"Whatever. I wasn't being mean. It's just a word."

"Words are part of the problem."

Was that really true? She didn't know. Words were words. Words were neutral. It was people who imbued them with meaning through what they did or thought. "Is that so, Arndt?"

"Yes," Schneider said. "Always." And particularly with regard to the resettlers. In the east they had been "Germans" and thus foreigners. In Germany they were "Russians" and thus foreigners again. Whether you meant to or not, if you called them "Russians" you were stigmatising them. You were saying: You don't belong with us. You're not Germans. You're foreigners.

Yes, words were part of the problem.

"The problem of integration?"

Schneider nodded. A home-made problem. A small town in the nineties, around 35,000 inhabitants including thousands of Canadian N.A.T.O. troops, who tended to be affluent and well liked. Then, in 1993, after the end of the Cold War, the Canadians moved out and hundreds of apartments stood empty. The town bought up the apartments and made them available to Germans from the successor states to the Soviet Union. Nowadays Lahr had roughly 44,000 inhabitants, around 22 per cent of which were resettlers who made up 25 per cent of the town's youth. Most of the resettlers lived in three residential areas. Unlike the Canadians they were neither affluent nor well liked. They were foreigners.

Russians.

If you move thousands of "foreigners" into a small town, Schneider said, it should not surprise you that integration proves tricky. If the locals call certain neighbourhoods "Little Kazakhstan" or "Little Moscow".

A home-made problem.

"What about Kanadaring?"

"A bit dismal, a bit ghetto-like, the odd punch-up. A few locals, a few immigrants and three quarters resettlers. And lots of prejudice on both sides."

"Doesn't sound *that* bad."

"I don't want to make it sound better than it is, Louise. But I don't want to overdramatise either." The old problem, Schneider said – objective data, subjective experience. Fear of the foreign, the other, amplified in the case of the resettlers because here what subjectively was foreign was claiming to be of the same ilk. The foreigners were claiming to be Germans, even though they didn't look like – Schneider made inverted commas with his fingers – "Germans", didn't speak like "Germans", didn't think like "Germans", didn't eat and drink like "Germans", didn't shop like "Germans" and didn't raise their children like "Germans".

He pursed his lips and shrugged. A touch of resignation, a touch of incomprehension, a touch of impatience, in short: a shrug.

A patrol car stopped next to them. Schneider opened the back door for her. Louise closed it. "And the objective data?"

"Statistics," Schneider said. More criminal resettlers than criminal locals? No. More jobless resettlers than jobless locals? No. "The only serious problems we have are with the young men. Drug users. Drug deaths, alcohol-related diseases, violent crime, theft – here the Russian-Germans are disproportionately represented in comparison to the locals." Schneider outstretched his arms. Not a surprise, is it? Uprooted, loss of self-esteem, homeland. Torn from their social milieu at the age of ten or twelve, shipped over to a foreign country where they don't speak the language, or not well enough, labelled as Russians, second-class citizens. "The politicians shouldn't be surprised, nor the parents who do that to their children," Schneider said. "I've got to get back, Louise. Meeting."

Louise opened the rear door. She thought of the yellow bicycle and the little boy. The bare, cold office to which Arndt Schneider would now return.

Where everything was O.K., by and large.

"Right, then."

"Pop by again sometime."

She nodded.

"To toast old times."

They shook hands and kissed left, then right.

"Thanks for your help."

"My pleasure."

She got in. "When it comes back to you . . ."

". . . I'll call you."

"Or I'll call you." She smiled. "By the way, the bombastic music in your head is called Barclay James Harvest."

"Barclay James Harvest . . . Wasn't 'Hymn' one of theirs?"

"It was."

Schneider smiled, nodded and pointed at his head. Something was happening in there, finally something was happening, and she nodded as well – in her head too.

"Wasn't there a balcony, Louise? A balcony and a naked woman in police boots?"

She grinned. "And a naked man in the stairwell, Arndt Schneider," she retorted, and closed the door.

7

They drove along a dead-straight road towards the railway station. Louise found Lahr a bit haphazard outside of the centre, a bit unorganised. Here and there stood tall apartment blocks, then period houses again, industrial areas, car dealers. A mixture of town and periphery, without boundaries, without a master plan. The road remained straight, stretching endlessly ahead. It could have been two kilometres before the officer behind the wheel pointed outside – Kanadaring.

Lahr changed its face yet again. Perpendicular to the road stood simple terraced houses, three storeys high, all in a row, all identical and painted an identical beige colour, then trees and grass, eight-sided tower blocks, wide, balcony-access apartment blocks from old films, old times.

And net curtains at all the windows.

The police officer stopped the car and indicated where the K2 was – in one of the uniform terraced houses. As Louise made her way to the entrance it struck her that something wasn't right. The man she was looking for didn't fit in with terraced houses, balcony-access blocks or net curtains. Nor with language courses and integration programmes, or men with walking sticks and flat caps who spent their mornings hanging around in Lahr, chatting about Russia, Kazakhstan and Siberia.

She crossed the threshold of an open door, went up to the first floor and pressed a bell. An old warrior in Freiburg, a harmless old man on Kanadaring?

No, the man she was looking for didn't fit in with Kanadaring.

Which didn't mean, however, that he hadn't fitted in once upon a time, before becoming the man he was now.

A man who perhaps fitted in nowhere.

Shortly afterwards Bonì was sitting at a cluttered desk in a cluttered room, stirring black tea and balancing on her lap a small plate with two slices of marble cake. Her tiredness had returned and along with it a feeling that something wasn't right.

Kanadaring and the old warrior, something not right.

On the other side of the desk sat Sophie Iwanowa, a golden-blonde, energetic Kazakh – no, a German from Kazakhstan in a light-blue woollen suit. Sophie Iwanowa, late thirties, a physics teacher in Kazakhstan, in Germany a cleaning lady, carer for the aged and for the last two years a council employee at the bilingual advice centre for resettlers, known in short as K2. Her mother was a Volga German, her father a Russian, Sophie Iwanowa said in rather routine fashion, as if she trotted out this explanation every time she talked to native Germans. Sophie's mother had always wanted to move to Germany, but the father had not. When the father died, Sophie and her mother left.

Sophie smiled, nodded, shrugged, that's how it was, you understand? That's why I'm here. She spoke quickly, intently and virtually accent-free. Her hands, arms, shoulders and head were in perpetual motion, her hair flew around, a cheerful whirl amongst all those inanimate shelves, books, folders, files, card-index boxes and papers. Here, Louise felt, the mysterious, foreign world of Kanadaring was concentrated into a few square metres. Thousands of people, data, lives. Decades, centuries between East and West.

"Your German is fantastic," she said.

"So's yours," Sophie said.

"Mine too?"

Sophie beamed and gesticulated. "Louise Bonì is a French name, isn't it?"

Louise nodded. Mine too? Deep inside her an ugly feeling stirred. Anger?

Deep inside her anger stirred.

A joke, Bonì, it was just a joke.

A joke that called into question something fundamental. That took something *away* from her. A joke that had perturbed some unspoken classification. I belong. You don't. You lot don't.

What crap! she thought. A joke is a joke, nothing more.

But the anger wouldn't go.

Sophie poured more tea, pushed the sliced cake towards Louise and asked chattily, "French parents?"

"French father, German mother. My father has always wanted to be German and lives in Kehl. My mother has always wanted to be French and lives in Provence." Louise shrugged, that's how it is, you see? She took a sip of tea and a mouthful of cake. Just a joke, Bonì.

"Just like my family, but the other way around," Sophie said. "My mother wanted to be German, my father wanted to stay Russian." She smiled. "What about you? What do you want to be?"

There it was, the question behind the joke. A joke with a whole string of questions. What do you want to be? Do you know that you don't really belong? "I've never thought about it and I'm not going to start now."

"Good. I like that. Just keep going down the road."

"Yes."

"My husband can't do that. He gets onto a roundabout and can't get off." Sophie smiled. "He's Russian. Like my father he didn't want to come to Germany. He's still going round and round in Kazakhstan. More tea, Louise? Cake?"

"No, thanks."

"Russian men can be difficult sometimes. They can be terribly anxious. Like my father and my husband. Are they O.K.? No! But they don't want to change anything. They're frightened of changing anything. They'd rather stay on the roundabout. Going the wrong way round." There was a triumphant spark in Sophie's large dark eyes, while her hands, now holding a cigarette as if by magic, danced in the air. "That's how it is, Louise."

Her anger had dissipated. It had persisted a moment longer before subsiding, withdrawing to the swamps and morasses of the unexplained.

Waiting for the next joke.

"Are you divorced?"

"Oh, no! I love my husband. Don't we women always love men who go the wrong way round, Louise? Three times a year he jumps on a plane and comes to my home country, and three times a year I jump on a plane and go to his. We're a modern German–Russian–Kazakh couple with a long-distance relationship. That's that."

Louise had to laugh and Sophie joined in.

"And the language, Louise! Kazakh!" With a groan, Sophie slapped her forehead. "Russia used to be the official language of Kazakhstan. But since the dissolution of the U.S.S.R. it's been Kazakh. I don't speak it, it's very hard, a Turkic language rather than a Slavic one. The school I taught at wanted me to speak to the pupils in Kazakh. I said it was irrelevant whether Newton's apple falls in Russian or Kazakh, just so long as it falls! The headmaster said, Sooner or later you're going to have to learn our language or you'll have to leave. So I left." Sophie stubbed out her half-smoked cigarette. "Do you speak both? German and French?"

Louise sighed, put the plate on the desk and nodded. Born in Germany – her father had won that battle. Brought up bilingually – her mother had won that one . . .

"Let's get on to why I'm here, Frau Iwanowa."

"Sophie."

"Sophie."

"But we're on that subject already!" Sophie had raised her hands and splayed her fingers in all directions, as if trying to point to the index-card boxes, documents, people and lives that were gathered in this room. "Home," she said. "There's no other subject for us."

Louise nodded. Of course. Expelled, deported, emigrated, losing one homeland and finding another. In cases like that, nothing but home could be of importance. "I understand."

She hadn't understood.

"For us *all*, Louise," Sophie said. "You, me, native Germans, my compatriots. Some know, the others don't. For us all."

"O.K., I don't have much time, Sophie. Do you know why I'm here?"

Sophie nodded. Schneider had mentioned it. Have you got some time for a Kripo colleague from Freiburg? She's looking for a man. Perhaps you know him.

"A man who might be a resettler," Louise said.

"You see, it *is* about home." Sophie smiled, but her lips quivered. She leaned forwards. "You're looking for a man, Louise, and we've lost one."

An oldish passport photograph, a few words, numbers, information on an index card, a name, a vague feeling: Yes, possibly.

The hair was right, the shape of the head was right. The nose, perhaps. A narrow, bony face, narrower than that of the man they were looking for. In the eyes lurked something dark, tired, cold.

Johannes Miller, born 1940 in Friedental, Russia. Family deported to Siberia in 1941. Childhood in Krasnoyarsk, Siberia. Employed at the Krasnyy Profintern locomotive factory. Married 1965, widowed 1966. No children. Moved to Karaganda, Kazakhstan, with sister's family in 1970. Moved to Germany with sister's family in 1996. Friedland, other reception camps, finally Kanadaring, Lahr.

"Friedental, Friedland," Sophie said.

Louise nodded.

"Not a very good . . . what do you say?"

"Omen."

"Yes."

Louise scanned the index card again. "Wapolwo" wasn't on it. She looked at the face and again thought, yes, possibly. The short, grey hair, perhaps the angular forehead, the nose. The face was narrower, but he could have put on weight since. Sophie had said that the photograph was six or seven years old.

"'Friedental, Friedland, Johannes,' I always told him. 'You're in the right place in Germany.'"

"Did he want to go back?"

"To Krasnoyarsk. To the past." Sophie frowned, shook her head, her hands and hair flew about: to the *past*! "He didn't have any work here, he never found any. He was quiet, but in a way that made people afraid of him. Made them think he might be violent. Nobody wanted to give him work. Three years ago he started drinking and I became afraid too."

"What about his sister?"

"She moved with her family to Hamburg in 2000. Johannes Miller didn't want to move. I don't know why not, perhaps he didn't want to move *again*. He'd rather stay here, without family, without work. But things got worse. He came to see me a lot. Sat there, silent, listening to me. Kept coming back, but did he talk? No. He barely uttered a word. Whenever I said, Johannes Miller, you've got to stop drinking, he nodded and closed his eyes, and I knew he'd try. He was ashamed of drinking, of having no job. Once, in the street, he was walking towards me. When he saw me he crossed to the other side. That's what he's like."

Twice Johannes Miller had vanished for several weeks. Then he'd reappeared, sat opposite Sophie again and said nothing. Now he had been missing for two months. Sophie had put her hands together on the desk and was quite still. "What has he done?"

"That's assuming it's him." Louise took out the copy of Niemann's photograph.

Sophie rocked her head from side to side. "I don't know."

"Is that more of a yes or more of a no?"

"I'm not sure."

"But what do you think?"

"I don't know. Maybe. It's very blurred and far away." Sophie paused for a moment and blinked. Her eyes were moist. "What do I think? Yes, it's him, Louise. I sense it. Friedental, Friedland, it wasn't a good omen for Johannes Miller. It's him." Nodding, she handed back the picture. "What has he done?"

Louise told her and Sophie listened without moving a muscle. The psalm seemed to be what finally convinced her. Johannes was religious, a "Lutheran". Service on Sunday, assembly on Wednesday, Bible study on Thursday, assembly on Saturday. Then at some point he only came to church on Sundays. And then, when he started drinking, he even stayed away from the Sunday service. Not a zealot, but devout, at least "before", before the drinking, the shame, the despair. Like many of the older people in the neighbourhood he never owned a television set, television only showed what ought not to be shown, what ought not to be, it showed sin. It didn't teach you compassion, Johannes said, and it didn't teach you honesty.

But all that was in the past, when his sister still lived here, before he'd started drinking.

That was Johannes Miller.

Louise nodded. What people did when they drank.

And what they stopped doing.

She called Hoffmann, passed on the information relating to Johannes as well as the address of his sister in Hamburg. See if you can find anything, it's possible that it's him. Possible? Yes, possible, but not certain. Bonì stared at Sophie, who returned her gaze. Her teeth were nibbling at her lower lip, her fingers stroking each other, yes, Sophie, now it's official. Up until a few minutes ago, Johannes Miller had been under Sophie Iwanowa's protection. But no longer. Now he was a suspect and the police were searching for him. Sophie had handed him over to the state. To the natives.

Is this what was going through Sophie's head?

"Listen, this Wapolwo," Hoffmann said. "There's something not right about it." He'd started by searching the internet. Not a single result. He'd swapped some letters around. Nothing. So he'd abandoned the search. Not a single result? It wasn't worth pursuing, something wasn't right.

"Wait." Louise asked Sophie, who just shook her head. "Keep trying, Alfons. Call a historian. Call the university. Do I really need to tell you this?"

"But if the internet doesn't know . . ."

"The internet can't make associations, can it, Alfons? It can't pull up something similar."

"I thought it could."

Hoffmann and the internet. Up until two years ago he didn't even know what it was. Then he'd worked with Elly, the red-haired queen of digital research from the organised crime squad. The inevitable happened: he fell in love with Elly paternally, and probably in other ways too. Because he couldn't have her paternally, let alone in any other way, as a substitute he fell in love even more ardently with the internet, Elly's medium, Elly's passion.

The internet says. The internet thinks. The internet knows.

"Alfons?"

"Yes, yes."

She hung up.

"That's Johannes Miller for you," Sophie said.

"But then again, maybe not. Maybe we're after someone completely different."

Sophie shrugged.

"Something's not right, Sophie."

"I've got a hunch it *is* him. The man you're looking for."

"Let's wait and see."

Sophie just nodded.

Silence descended on the small room bursting with so many lives. Louise thought of her conversations with Friedrich and Hoffmann. A cigarette case. An engraving. Wapolwo 1945, something wasn't right with that word. Just as something wasn't right with the old warrior and Kanadaring.

She would ask Friedrich again. She had to show him the photograph of Johannes anyway.

Friedrich, the chronicler and Russian-hater who drank slivovitz with a Russian.

Something wasn't right about this either.

8

They left Sophie Iwanowa's office and stepped out into the sun. They walked across a patch of grass to one of the apartment blocks. Johannes Miller had lived with his sister and her family, but ever since they'd left he'd been subletting at "Waldemar and Emma's". He got his food, his streusel cake, company, familiar customs and a bit of warmth. But none of it helped. He couldn't get any work.

Sophie told the story of Waldemar and Emma Kaufmann; Louise listened with one ear only. Volga Germans, deported in August 1941, this much she took in before switching off. Too many stories for just a few hours, she thought. First the "mid-course party" and the young buck, then the little boy with the yellow bicycle, Sophie Iwanowa and the roundabout. And finally Johannes Miller, who might be the man they were looking for. But then again, maybe not.

Enough stories for a few hours.

Sophie waved up at a window. Behind a net curtain a hand waved back.

"Do you know what Johannes drank?"

"What he drank? No, I never asked him."

"Did he drink slivovitz?"

"I don't know. I don't know what those people drink."

"Those people? People from Friedental?"

Sophie's hands, shoulders and hair became animated. No, not *those* people.

No, Sophie?

"People who drink."

I see, Sophie. Those people. Louise gave a tired nod. They start with wine and beer, Sophie. Then they get to the point where that's not enough. And so they drink Jägermeister, vodka or bourbon. Or Davidoff or ţuică. Or slivovitz. Or all of the above. Then it's enough.

She said nothing.

"We'll ask Waldemar and Emma."

"Good." Louise nodded and thought: those people.

A little understanding, Sophie, instead of fear – how about that? Friedental, Friedland, that can turn you into an alkie. A failed marriage, a dead body in the snow, a brother in a car crash. Hmm?

She grimaced. That's enough, Bonì.

She asked how good Johannes' German was. Not good, Sophie said. In Friedental the family had spoken German. In Krasnoyarsk it was better to speak Russian. In Kanadaring Johannes had attended the language courses, but learned hardly anything.

Louise thought of Niemann's statement. Someone who'd learned German as a child, but then hadn't spoken it in a long time.

Finally something else that matched.

They entered the apartment block. Sophie pointed up, down, right and left. It needs renovating, Louise, don't look. Louise looked. Everything was faded, outdated, neglected. Renovations were expensive, Sophie said, the town didn't have any money for renovations. She threw up her hands. Language courses were more important. Lahr did a lot – the council, churches, police, schools, volunteers. But it wasn't enough. To achieve integration more had to be done. Offer more advice services, recruit more Russian-Germans, have more Russian-German council employees. Most importantly, they urgently needed a Russian-German police officer.

"My compatriots need to do more too, Louise. They need to learn German. They need to be open towards Germany. Integrate. They need to move away from Kanadaring, Langenwinkel and Kippenheimweiler, and into mixed areas. They need to regain their confidence. They've got so much to offer, Louise! So much experience of Russia, of the East! They're familiar with two cultures, two languages, two political systems. They can help Germany in its dealings with the East! And they come with children, Louise! Sophie opened out her arms. "New children for the old homeland. Do you have children?"

"No. Do you?"

"No. While my husband keeps going round the wrong way . . ." Sophie shrugged.

On the first floor she opened a plywood door to one of the balconies. Louise touched her arm. "Wait."

They stopped.

"Go on alone, Sophie. If Johannes is there, stay and have a bit of a chat. If he's not there, come back and get me."

Sophie's large eyes grew even larger. "Because of the gun?" she whispered.

Louise nodded.

"Have you got a gun too?"

"Go now, Sophie."

"I can't," Sophie whispered.

"Yes, you can. He won't do anything to you."

"Will *you* do anything to *him*?"

Louise shook her head. "If he's there I'll just wait."

"Wait," Sophie whispered.

"Just wait."

Sophie nodded.

"Go now."

Louise shut the plywood door and listened to Sophie's footsteps. She heard a knocking, a door opened and a delighted woman's voice said, "Well, well, look who's here! It's Sophie!"

The door closed, the door opened. Johannes had not come back.

*

Waldemar and Emma Kaufmann, both over eighty, small and wizened with white, sagging faces and soft, cool hands, were shy, polite individuals. They stood in their overheated sitting room as if they'd been caught in the act, casting uncertain glances at the policewoman from Freiburg, while Sophie spoke and the lunch on the table went cold: potatoes with dumplings, steamed cabbage, one glass of beer and one of water. "Well, then," Waldemar said affably, before falling silent.

Now Louise wished she had listened earlier, Waldemar and Emma Kaufmann from the Volga Republic, deported to Siberia sixty years ago, a long road from Lahr. It seemed to Louise that the sitting room told some of the story of this long road, which for them was so foreign. A handful of icons and Jesus statues, a dark-brown shelving unit from the 1950s. Plenty of plastic, plenty of oilcloth, an ancient foxtail on the sofa, above it a huge painting of a winter landscape. On the shelves were family photographs and small houseplants. A lamp in the form of a candle, a ceramic vase in the form of a fish, vodka glasses in the form of fish, standing on their tailfins with mouths pointing upwards. And on the wall beside the corridor to the kitchen, a baby-sized plastic doll with long, blonde hair.

"Listen," Emma said, beaming, and pulled something on the doll's back.

The doll sang an American folk song.

It hung on the wall, squawking "Oh My Darling, Clementine".

Then things got difficult. Neither Louise nor Sophie wanted to eat anything, and so neither Waldemar nor Emma would finish their lunch. In front of guests? Impossible! That's what they're like, Sophie said with an impatient smile and Louise wondered who she meant. Waldemar and Emma? The Germans from Russia? Those people? They stood there, looking at each other, at a loss as to what to do now. What should we do now? Waldemar's eyes said. Do something, Sophie, Emma's eyes said. Why, Louise thought, do people invent customs that merely make living together more complicated? People who were hungry should eat. People who weren't hungry should be able to say no. It could be so simple.

She sat and said softly, "O.K., pass the cabbage, then."

The sun shone into the room, the old-fashioned, colourful, plastic room, making the doll's hair shimmer and warming Louise's cheeks and hands as she ate. Waldemar didn't say a word, eating coyly and rather noisily. In a whisper, Emma and Sophie discussed friends and relatives, people with Russian names, German names, wonderful, unusual names such as Rotärmel, Beifuss, Buchsbaum. One was simply called Weber and had been a farmer in Neu-Hoffnung, Ukraine, but then "they said he was a Kulak", Emma whispered. Weber was deported and died in the mines of Chelyabinsk, and his wife was shot in Neu-Hoffnung, because she had run through the village as if out of her mind, screaming, "Uncle won't let us down, Uncle will help us!" And the story was that Erika from Kippenheimweiler had married the Webers' grandson, and Erika knew both Emma and Sophie, as did the Webers' grandson.

Neu-Hoffnung and Chelyabinsk, thought Louise, and Kippen-heimweiler in Lahr. Everyone she'd spoken to these past few days seemed to tell of unbelievably long roads.

"Do you know who the uncle was?" Sophie asked.

"The uncle who was supposed to help?" Emma said. "That was Hitler."

"I see."

Louise returned Sophie's searching gaze. Well, Louise, the gaze said, what do you think of us now? If they weren't communists they were Nazis? Is that what you think.

No, no, Sophie.

Just a bit, Sophie, perhaps.

What *did* she think about the Germans from Russia? She didn't know. Here they were, three million distant relations from the East, packaged in a few neat categories: Russians, expellees, resettlers, Friedland, Kanadaring – those categories.

The terms helped in the difficult process of familiarisation. As a person lacking the time or opportunity you put up with the fact that they might be telling other stories than the true ones. Until you found the time and opportunity – and maybe even the inclination – to unpack these people from the neat categories.

To eat potatoes and steamed cabbage with them.

That was roughly what she thought.

Emma Kaufmann stood up and drew some heavy curtains in front of one of the windows. In the dim blue light she cleared the table. Sophie was allowed to help, but not Louise. Louise had learned and fell into line. Things didn't need to be complicated; they could be simple.

She sat in the dark, yawning discreetly, growing ever more tired. Johannes Miller, Wapolwo 1945, Friedrich and the slivovitz, the old warrior. Those were the important stories, everything else was too much.

The long roads of the Germans from the East.

But perhaps, it occurred to her, she too would have to travel a long road to find the man with the pistol, before he returned, in three days, in four days, depending on how he counted.

Maybe even earlier or later or never.

"Well, then," Waldemar said, scratching his unshaven cheek. Emma had started washing up, Sophie was drying. From the kitchen Louise could hear Emma's voice, the ancient, unfamiliar German which had survived in the East, *It were indeed shown to me, but understand it I did not . . . And the examination, when is this to take place? . . . Them that could write it, they . . .*

"Well," Waldemar said.

"I'd like to talk to you about Johannes Miller."

He nodded. "Right. Johannes Miller."

He'd been living with them for four years, a good man, but life hadn't been kind to him. A man with a firm faith. That was him, Waldemar said, just like Emmi, she had a firm faith too. She wouldn't go to church without a headscarf on, because that's what the Bible told her. And because you couldn't know what Paul's letter to the Corinthians actually meant, she also wouldn't go shopping without her headscarf, nor anywhere else for that matter. Johannes Miller was the same, a man of firm faith. He would say grace before they ate, while in the mornings and evenings he prayed and sang together with Emma, the old songs from the East: "Jesus, Still Lead On", "The Home Over There". He used to go to church three or four times a week. A good man, but life hadn't been kind to him, that was Johannes, and now he was gone and a policewoman was here.

The policewoman placed a hand on his arm. Perhaps Johannes wasn't the man they were after at all; to be honest a few things didn't add up.

Waldemar turned his lined, white face to her and said nothing. She fancied she could tell what was going through his mind: If you don't look for him then someone else will. Life hasn't been kind to him and now it's dealt him something awful.

She stroked his arm then took back her hand.

Asked about slivovitz.

Slivovitz? Waldemar shrugged. Here in the apartment it was just beer – one glass at lunch, one in the evenings – and one or two little glasses of vodka. When Johannes was out? He didn't know. But why should Johannes drink something that didn't come from Germany or Russia.

She smiled in surprise. Things didn't need to be complicated; they could be simple.

She asked about Wapolwo? Waldemar shrugged. Was it called that? Wasn't it called Valpovo?

"Valpovo?"

Waldemar nodded. Valpovo, a place somewhere in Yugoslavia, but that didn't exist anymore either, Yugoslavia.

"In Yugoslavia?"

"Aye."

"Do you know where, Herr Kaufmann?"

"Hmm. Well. No, I don't." Not on the coast, at any rate. His daughters had gone on holiday to Istria, it wasn't there. Maybe it didn't exist anymore. "Them that talked of Valpovo were Germans from Yugoslavia. They said there were a camp for Germans from Yugoslavia and many of them that went to said camp died of hunger, exhaustion and the cold, they did. Like our lot in Siberia, eh?"

"A camp for Germans from Yugoslavia?"

"Aye."

"Help me, Herr Kaufmann – who were these Germans?"

"Them Germans that went there two centuries or so ago."

"To Yugoslavia?"

"Aye, and a good many of them there were, hundreds of thousands, it's said. Back in the day we went to every corner of the East, not enough farmland here there weren't and taxes were high, and there were always a war going on, and so the emperor and empress said, Come to the East, every man will have his patch of land, get work and have a good life. And we went, we did."

"Which emperor? Which empress?"

"The Habsburgs, of course, them that owned half of Europe at the time, and in Russia, Empress Katharina II – a German herself too."

"Princess Sophie," Sophie said from the kitchen.

"Aye," Waldemar said with a nod.

Hundreds of thousands of Germans who migrated to the East centuries ago, to Russia, to Yugoslavia, everywhere, invited by the Habsburgs. Bonì had known about those in Russia, of course, but not about the Germans in Yugoslavia. Or had she? Words came into her head that she'd read or heard over the years, without being able to place them accurately. Sathmar Swabians, Banat Swabians, Swabian Turkey. Was that Yugoslavia? Transylvania, but that was Romania. She took her notepad and pen from her bag and wrote these words down. All those long roads – it was easy to get confused.

"Back to Valpovo."

"Aye."

"Who built the camp?"

"The communists."

"What communists, Herr Kaufmann?"

Waldemar frowned. In his eyes there was polite surprise. It was silent in the kitchen; Emma and Sophie were staring at them. She raised her eyebrows. Nobody can know everything, can they?

"What communists?"

"Tito's partisans," Waldemar said.

She nodded. Tito – she knew him. Died in 1980 – she knew that. Thomas Ilic had mentioned it on the way to Offenburg. Thomas Ilic, half-Croat, her favourite colleague, on sick leave for the past eighteen months because in a clearing near Heuweiler he'd failed to close his eyes. To have to watch someone be murdered changed everything. It didn't matter whether or not you were a police officer. He ought to have known this.

That night he shouldn't have worked a moment longer. *She* ought to have known this.

But she'd taken him to the Rappeneck, where the false Marcel had concluded his hunt. Now Ilic was on sick leave and being treated by trauma specialists. Not even they could say whether he would ever come back to work.

She tapped the pen against her brow. Don't think of Illi now.

"Do you know when the camp was built? The Valpovo camp?"

"No, them that talked of it didn't say."

"Did it exist in 1945?"

"Yes, I'm sure, in '45 it must have been there – that Tito had been driving the Germans out since '44."

"The Germans from Yugoslavia?"

Again, surprise in Waldemar's eyes, again silence in the kitchen. She grinned. Don't make such a fuss.

She got up and pulled back the curtain. Her head was reeling in the blue gloom. She needed sunlight to be able to think. An engraving in a cigarette case: "Valpovo 1945". Valpovo, a Yugoslav communist internment camp for ethnic Germans from Yugoslavia.

Yet another history, another long, foreign road.

She sat down. "Who did Tito expel, Herr Kaufmann?"

"Right, well. Expelled them all, he did, the Ustaša Croats, the German soldiers, the Yugoslav Germans, all of them together. He expropriated and expelled the Germans, just like Stalin expropriated and expelled us Germans in the Soviet Union."

She wrote: *Ustaša Croats? Yugoslav Germans? War in Yugoslavia? Expropriation/expulsion?*

"Can you remember who told you about Valpovo?"

"Not exactly, no, I can't." Waldemar was a member of the Russian-German fraternity. Sometimes they met with other Germans from the East, and these included Germans from Yugoslavia. They must have mentioned Valpovo at some point.

Louise nodded.

Valpovo 1945. Paul Niemann had reckoned the old warrior was about sixty. Which meant that in 1945 he would have been two or three.

It struck her that the cigarette case didn't necessarily mean anything. He might have found, stolen or bought it somewhere. "Valpovo 1945" didn't necessarily have anything to do with him.

But equally he could have been in Valpovo in 1945. A small boy of German descent in the post-war chaos, somewhere in a camp in Yugoslavia. Someone crafts a cigarette case and gives it to him.

If so, she thought, they would have the beginnings of the story.

*

A bed, a cupboard, a chair, a small desk, its edges battered, the wood dried out, having passed through numerous hands and rooms. Now they were in Johannes Miller's bedroom. The bed was made and photographs were affixed to the cupboard door. On the desk a vase with white chrysanthemums. Lace curtains in front of the window, dust, the smell of loneliness, anonymity, stasis. The sort of room she'd seen many of during her years as a policewoman – in hostels for the homeless, hostels for single men. As a rule, she thought, this was how the bedrooms of stranded men looked. Women were stranded differently.

Only the bed was unusual. Three enormous pillows with lace pillowcases and tassels. It took her a moment to think of the name: "throw pillows".

"Right, well," said Waldemar, who'd taken her to the room. "I'll leave you alone, then."

She nodded.

Johannes Miller, she thought, born in Friedental, Russia, deported to Siberia – that other story again. The other Germans from the East.

Widowed after a year. No children. Moved to Germany in 1996 with his sister and her family. Alone since 2000.

Friedental, Friedland, not a good omen.

Somehow all of this was written in the bedroom.

She put on a pair of disposable gloves and went to the cupboard. At eye level were four black-and-white photographs and two in colour. The parents, a young couple, simple, proud, pale, he with moustache and bow tie, she in a frill dress. The parents a few years later, the father holding hands with a young boy, the mother with a young girl. Johannes Miller as a teenager in a sort of sailor's suit. Johannes Miller and a beaming, plump woman. The colour photographs were portraits of a young, blonde woman and a brunette girl about eight years of age. The niece, the daughter of the niece.

In the cupboard were underpants, socks, trousers, shirts. The clothes you would expect an impoverished man to possess and not a scrap more. A toothbrush mug with toothbrush, a disposable razor. She put the mug, toothbrush and razor into separate clear-plastic bags.

The only drawer in the desk contained dozens of letters in a neat pile. As far as she could make out, all of them had a Hamburg postmark and were ordered by date. She opened the top one, but it was written in Russian. She opened the next one, a child's handwriting, this time in German: *Dear Grandad, Bergedorf in Hamburg is so beautiful.* At the bottom a name, *Hanni.*

The oldest letter was four years old, the most recent three months. Louise put the letters back.

A few clothes, a few bathroom items – there was nothing else here. At the door she turned. The bedroom of an impoverished, lonely man who no longer knew where he belonged. Who'd thought he would come back to this room.

She would show the photograph Sophie had given her to Friedrich and Niemann, pass the toothbrush mug, toothbrush and razor to forensics and have them compare the fingerprints with those recovered from the Niemanns' house. Then they'd have proof for what she thought she already knew.

Johannes Miller was not the man they were looking for.

Waldemar Kaufmann was silent, Emma Kaufmann wore a broad smile. She handed Louise some streusel cake in aluminium foil, a recipe from Engels on the Volga, "So you don't forget us, my child." The curtain was drawn again, the light blue, Waldemar and Emma's faces pale, exhausted and incredibly old. Sophie escorted her downstairs and into the street, to the edge of the neighbourhood. It felt to Louise as if she were nearing the invisible border to another country.

They kissed on both cheeks.

"You promised me," Sophie said.

"What?"

"If you find him, wait."

Louise nodded.

"Just wait. Please."

"It's not him, Sophie."

"It is. I know."

Louise smiled. "Because of the omen?"

Yes.

Then Sophie walked away, a short, round woman in a light-blue suit, her blonde hair flying in the air. What remained was the memory of a few strange moments of anger and confusion. Louise was surprised to realise that she had learned something from Sophie Iwanowa.

How it was possible not to belong.

She walked the two kilometres back without really knowing why. Perhaps she thought that on foot the certainty of belonging might return. A dead-straight road that led from Kanadaring to the centre, from confusion to certainty.

What rubbish, Bonì.

But walking felt good.

Somewhere in the no-man's-land between Kanadaring and the town centre was a supermarket. In the car park she saw the other Germans from Russia, the young ones, for whom resettlement had perhaps been most difficult. They had formed a kind of wagon fort with their cars. They squatted on the bonnets, on their heels, music was playing, bottles were passed around, none of them was without a cigarette. A few girls in their late teens were there, dressed up to the nines, the boys wearing baseball caps, bursting with testosterone and aggression. She wanted to approach them, sit on a bonnet and listen to *these* stories too, but without Sophie Iwanowa she didn't have a chance, she knew that. Neither with the older ones nor the younger ones.

Bonì still had Kanadaring in her head when she came into the centre. The crossroads where Schneider's boy had died, the fragrance of the chrysanthemums, all the colours, Friedrich lying asleep on his side. Ignoring the stench, she squatted and nudged him.

"Friedrich?"

He opened his eyes. "Hey, Louise." His eyes were sleepy, dull and lifeless. "More questions?" he said softly.

"The engraving. Might it have said 'Valpovo'?"

He nodded. "Got the letters mixed up, didn't I, Louise? And you noticed." He yawned, she waited. "Anything else?"

"A photo." She held out the index card.

"Shit, a Russian."

"Is that him, Friedrich? The man with the cigarette case?"

"That's one of the Russians, Louise."

"I need an answer."

"That *is* your answer."

She nodded. Now everything fitted. This was quite simple too. Friedrich would never smoke, drink or chat with a German from Russia.

"Are you hungry?"

"I'm thirsty, Louise."

She grinned and thought, I was thirsty for a few years too, you know? Friedrich's gaze followed her hand as she put it in her pocket, took out Emma Kaufmann's streusel cake, placed it before him and unwrapped the silver foil. Four slices. A recipe from Engels by the Volga, Friedrich, but hatred doesn't stretch so far that you can see, taste or sense it.

"All we're missing is the candle and a cup of tea, Louise."

"A tea with a drop of something, I assume?"

He laughed silently. "A drop of something with tea."

"I was thirsty for a few years too, you know. Not a good time."

"I thought you were a special woman." He sat up. "Eat with me, Louise. It's been a long time since I shared cake with a special woman." She shook her head. "I've just had lunch."

"Oh, come on, Louise. A piece of streusel cake. Catching criminals is a tiring business. Especially one that runs like your man."

"On one condition."

He nodded. "Special women have conditions."

"Not a word about the Germans from Russia."

"Agreed. Not a word about the fucking Russians."

Already one word too many, she thought. But she stayed where she was.

In silence and crouched on the cobbles, they ate Emma Kaufmann's streusel cake, the cake from Engels somewhere in the East, at the end of the world, one slice for her, three for Friedrich. Then he carefully folded the aluminium foil, put it in his coat pocket and brought out his tobacco. Louise got up and left, all those stories in her head, half a day's worth of stories from Lahr, stories of the dead, home-lands, long roads and an encounter seventeen years earlier. But when the taxi arrived to take her to the station, only one story remained: Valpovo 1945, which might be the beginning.

9

Sunshine in Lahr, rain in Freiburg; the weather divide had been about halfway between the two. But the fog had dissipated and the view from her office window extended far beyond the city. In the west it was bright and blue. For a moment Provence came to mind; it was bright and blue there too. And yellow, of course. Blue were the lupins and lavender, yellow the light and her mother's house.

Inside her mother's house it was dark.

She had called the Niemanns' but got only the answerphone. She had called Jenny Böhm but got only the parish office secretary.

Jenny was ill.

Ill?

A bad cold.

She'd wanted to drive over, first to Jenny, then to the Niemanns'; you never knew. But at the Niemanns', at least, everything was fine. The patrol cars were keeping Hoffmann updated. And she didn't have time for Jenny – the investigation team meeting was scheduled for 5 p.m.

So instead of driving anywhere she had sat on the window sill, recording her reports about Lahr on her dictaphone, gazing out at the rain and the light-blue western sky, and somehow at Provence too and the long roads travelled by the Germans from the East. Now she was waiting to go upstairs to the meeting, to return from the periphery to the centre. Again she felt the urge to get into her car and drive away, this time to her mother's in Provence . . . perhaps turn the light on, Mama, in your dark house and my comical life.

*

"Croatia," Hoffmann said.

"Again," Wallmer said.

Illi, Louise thought.

"Illi," Bermann said.

It was half past five and they were sitting in the small meeting room. Wallmer and Benedikt had talked about Merzhausen and their conversation with Henriette, Philip and Carola Niemann – nothing in particular to report, except that Paul Niemann had indeed gone to Lahr. Louise had talked about Lahr – Friedrich, who had seen their man, the Germans from Russia, Johannes Miller, who was missing but probably had nothing to do with the Niemanns, and Valpovo 1945. Hoffmann had compiled information on Valpovo and the Yugoslav Germans, and photocopied it – impressive piles of paper, but these were long roads too.

"Do we need him? Illi?" Bermann said.

"He's on sick leave," Louise said.

With a sigh, Bermann rubbed his eyes. "You could pay him a visit. A patient visit?"

"We're going to leave him in peace."

"He'd be thrilled. A visit from colleagues. A little chat about home. What could be nicer?"

Louise smiled. "Being left in peace by your colleagues."

A moment's silence. Bermann grinned menacingly. Louise had heard that he'd been to see Bob that morning and had to spend two hours justifying himself. Bob didn't like the way in which Bermann was running his section, or so the rumour went in the corridors of D11.

Bermann had been on the warpath since.

Bermann and Bob – from day one there had been no love lost between the two men, nor would there ever be.

She wondered if, like her, Bermann had a fundamental problem with superiors. He didn't even like Hubert Vormweg, the Freiburg police commissioner. Too many differences that could be summed up in two types: the old '68er and the old macho. The only one Bermann had respected and rated was Almenbroich, Bob's predecessor as Kripo head. Almenbroich, the father figure.

"I don't think we need Illi, Rolf," Hoffmann said. "It's probably more about Germans than Croats."

"Germans in Croatia?"

"Probably."

"Because of Valpovo?" Wallmer said.

"Yes," Louise said.

Hoffmann slid around in his seat and grimaced in discomfort. A chair for medium-sized people. "Valpovo has a German name too, by the way: Walpach. If you search for 'Valpovo', 'Walpach' comes up as well."

Benedikt nodded. Spectacles on his forehead, two fingers stroking his moustache – a sight Louise could get used to. "A camp with a German name."

"Valpovo is a place. A small town."

"Where?"

"Eastern Croatia, by the Hungarian border." Hoffmann put his hand in the air and pointed: Hungary, Serbia, Croatia. Slavonia in Croatia. Valpovo in Slavonia.

"And during the war or after it there was a camp there," Benedikt said. "The Second World War, that is."

"Yes."

"What does this camp have to do with Paul Niemann?" Wallmer asked.

"We don't know yet, Anne." Louise pointed at the pile. "Homework for this evening." She smiled. No evenings off, no private life – it was a contagious illness, after all. Forced infection, so to speak.

Wallmer just frowned.

"Let me get the chronology straight," Benedikt said.

Beginning of October, Lahr. Friedrich, the homeless man, found a stranger in his regular spot in the pedestrian zone. They drank and smoked together. The stranger had a cigarette case engraved with "Valpovo 1945" and a bottle of slivovitz. When some police officers turned up he scarpered. End of October, Merzhausen. Presumably the same man broke into the Niemanns' house and issued an ultimatum: Leave within seven days, otherwise . . ."

Well, what *would* happen?

Everyone looked at Louise, no-one came up with an answer. Then Bermann said, "And what if nothing happens?"

She nodded. What if nothing happens?

"Good for the Niemanns," Hoffmann said. "Good for us."

She stood up and went to the window. The brightness and the blue had gone; far away on the horizon lay a last vague streak of light. It seemed as if a deep darkness were creeping from the clouds.

She briefly considered this possibility. A lunatic who had broken into the Niemanns' and let off steam, merely intent on sowing fear and terror. Who had come by again on the Monday afternoon to see whether it had worked. Who would never show up again.

"In that case the bosses of Kripo and D11 would have a few questions for the leader of the investigation team," Bermann said. "Questions about the relationship between the offence and the police effort that has gone into investigating it. Those kinds of questions, you know."

She turned to look at Bermann. Those questions.

But she didn't believe it. An old warrior who was just a loony? No. He had a plan and was going to try to execute it. He had come a long way; he wouldn't just vanish again like that.

She stiffened and felt a sudden chill on the back of her neck. She thought she could sense the darkness moving behind her.

"He's coming back."

"Yes," Benedikt said.

Bermann stretched out his arms. He looked serious. "If he comes back and we don't catch him, you'll get your task force."

"Not before?"

"Not before."

She nodded and sat down. The "otherwise" question remained. *Leave within seven days, otherwise . . .* That was the problem: they didn't have the slightest clue of what he was planning. Or if he was planning anything at all.

They spoke about the next day. They would look for the farmer from Au, the former owner of the land on which the Niemanns' house now stood. They would consult historians for information about Valpovo and the Germans from Yugoslavia – Hoffmann was already arranging appointments. They also needed to find out whether there were Yugoslav-Germans in Lahr too. Their man had been seen in Lahr, after all. And for obvious reasons they had to talk to Niemann again. He had put them on the Russian-German track with the accent and his contact with Russian-Germans in council services. All that had somehow fitted together nicely. Now, with Valpovo and Yugoslavia, nothing fitted together. They needed to confront him with this. And as a formality they had to show him the photograph of Johannes Miller.

They stood up and grabbed their sheafs of photocopies. In the corridor Hoffmann said, "Tell me, what day are we now?"

It took Louise a moment to comprehend. "Depends. The third if he's counting from Sunday. The fourth if from Saturday."

They stood in a tight circle, Bermann too. Unspoken questions hung in the air. Questions such as what would he do if the Niemanns didn't leave. What would happen on the seventh day?

"Because I wondered how I would react after what happened yesterday," Hoffmann said. "I mean, would I really wait until the seventh day? Or would I react straightaway?"

"Well?" Louise said.

"Well, I *would* react straightaway."

"Me too," Wallmer said.

"I wouldn't," Bermann said. "I have a plan. I'm going to see it through. On the seventh day I'm coming back. The Biblical seventh day, do you get it? I cite psalms, I come on the seventh day."

Louise stared at him. For one bizarre moment she felt like laughing. I have a plan, I cite psalms, I come on the seventh day. She'd never heard Bermann talk like this before. It wasn't his style to slip inside the mind of the criminal. Surrender his distance. Bermann always put the greatest possible distance between himself and the criminal. He needed the certainty that they shared nothing in common.

Were the skirmishes with Bob wearing him down?

He raised his eyebrows. What's wrong? his expression said.

She turned to Benedikt. "What would you do?"

Benedikt shrugged. "Dunno. You?"

"Hmm. No idea."

"I think I'd react tonight," Hoffmann said.

Louise looked at him. "On the other hand, he always does what we're least expecting."

Hoffmann nodded.

"Which means we're expecting him *not* to react immediately."

"Also correct."

"So it would be logical if he reacted tonight. And it would be just as logical if he waited until the seventh day."

Nobody spoke. Louise checked the time: just after six.

"Are you going back out?" Wallmer said.

"Yes."

Wallmer chuckled.

Absolutely right, Anne, that's the woman I am. No evenings off, no private life. No beginning and no end.

In a flash the anger had returned. The anger which Sophie had unleashed that morning. And with the anger all the questions, what do you want to be, where do you want to belong, why do you have no private life, no evenings off, no children, no husband, where do you actually belong, all those stupid, stupid questions. Hadn't she answered these already?

Which wall is the door going in?

Dust in the apartment . . .

She gesticulated. "For God's sake, my apartment's covered in dust."

"You mentioned that this morning," Hoffmann said kindly.

"I don't fancy sitting around all evening in *fine dust particles*."

"Sure," Wallmer said, and Louise sensed that it wasn't meant sarcastically. In her own way she was trying to be nice; it was a peace offering. Wallmer was still in a foul mood, but she was making peace offerings.

"You really shouldn't spend the night there anymore either," Hoffmann said. "I bet it's not healthy."

Bermann suggested she stay at the police academy; they had small, simple rooms. He'd used them on occasion, he said, grinning. She couldn't help smiling too, but not because of Bermann and the blondes who had now cost him so dearly, but because she was thinking of Arndt Schneider. The police academy, formerly the regional police college, was where she had met Schneider. What significance did it have, she wondered, on the day she'd met one of her "mid-course" young bucks again, her seeking asylum from fine dust particles at the academy?

Chiefly it meant one thing: she had nobody she could hole up with for a few nights. Richard Landen was in Japan, and Marcel would have rushed off to buy rings the following day. Apart from them there was nobody.

"You can stay at mine," Wallmer said. "I've got a guest room." Hoffmann said they had a guest room too. Benedikt said they'd converted their loft. Bermann said Alex was away on a school trip so she could have his bed. Louise thanked them all and warned them not to complain if she took them up on their offers. "The important thing," Bermann said, "is that you don't pee standing up."

They laughed.

Then they went their separate ways. Wallmer accompanied Louise to the staircase. "It would be nice, Louise. We could . . . chat."

Louise nodded. Sensing Wallmer's eyes on her as she went down the stairs, she looked back. A peculiarly naked expression, she thought. I need to talk, Louise, the expression said.

"You know what I'd bring with me?" She smiled.

Wallmer shook her head.

"Work."

The parents were out, so Carola, the daughter, showed her into the house. In the living room sat three boys, schoolfriends, who tried to look cool as they shook hands with Bonì. "We're keeping watch," a tall, fidgety beanpole said, nodding towards the darkness beyond the window.

Carola rolled her eyes.

There were more of them outside. In the garden, by the fence. Keeping watch in case he came back.

"Heavens," Louise said. She saw tall, fidgety beanpoles lying under bushes, in the grass, in the field, waiting for the old warrior. "Watch out for yourselves, for goodness' sake."

She went upstairs with Carola.

"They wouldn't have gone out otherwise," Carola said. "They didn't want to leave us alone."

"Where did they go?"

"To the doctor's."

"What's happened?"

Carola shrugged. They were standing beside a closed door. Carola just stood there, staring at the door.

Louise put a hand on her shoulder. "Carola?"

"Everything's going wrong, you know."

"Did they have an argument?"

"Not an argument. They just talked. Cried. Papa cried."

Carola knocked on the door and Philip answered. They went in. A large, virtually dark room, a few candles. Choral music similar to what she'd heard in Niemann's car, perhaps even the same piece. A computer monitor with a screen saver of white birds flying through darkness. Philip was sitting on the floor, a book in his lap, which he could barely have been able to read. Now he stood up and looked at his sister for help. A fifteen-year-old and this music . . . The darkness.

What was going on with these people?

"She wants to show you a photo."

"A photo?"

Louise shook his hand. He reminded her so much of his father, even the hand. Cold, small, feeble, a hand that stirred impatience within her, but also the need to protect this scrawny, insecure, rudderless boy. Somehow she wanted to give him the strength that nature had denied him.

"Brahms, right?" she said. "The Requiem?"

A shake of the head. "Mozart."

"Did he compose a requiem too, then?"

A nod. "Uh-huh."

"Let's turn it off for a bit, shall we? Otherwise I'll start howling." Carola smiled, Philip stared, and then switched it off. Louise asked what sort of doctor their parents had gone to visit. Carola shook her head and jutted her chin in Philip's direction. Not here, please. Louise nodded.

She showed Philip the photograph of Johannes Miller.

"No," he said very softly.

"Are you sure?"

"Uh-huh."

Nobody spoke for a few seconds. Philip was still staring at her, but she couldn't make out his eyes in the darkness. She believed she could sense his fear, fear of what the man would do, fear of what his parents would do. She wanted to offer some words of encouragement, but what could you say to a fifteen-year-old who had to watch his family fall apart?

She took a business card from her trouser pocket and gave it to him. "In case you need anything. Doesn't matter what."

He nodded.

They went to the door. "Turn the light on if you're going to read," Carola said.

On the landing she pointed upwards and they went up the stairs to the television room. The man had been here too, wandered around, sat on the sofa, had thought and planned who knows what.

My house, this is my house. And they still didn't know why.

"They're with a friend. A therapist," Carola said.

Louise nodded. "Perhaps things will get better again. If they get help. Therapy is bound to help."

"Yes," Carola said.

"And when all this is over. When we've got him."

"Yes."

The phrases echoed in her head. Perhaps things will get better again, therapy is bound to help. Louise realised that these phrases sounded familiar. Someone had said similar things to her. Senseless things. So obvious, so empty. Even back in the 1970s, when those new but at the same time ancient doctrines of salvation reached the middle classes, infecting half of the population. Gurus from the East, therapists from the West, then everything would be fine. She had leaned against the kitchen table while her mother had wrung her hands and implored, if you come with us, if we all do family therapy together, then . . .

If we go to France, to Paris, then . . .

Then. Then everything will be fine. Then: the magic word.

She stepped over to the panorama window. The garden, the fields, the Schönberg all lay in darkness. Somewhere down below a few boys were hanging around, imagining they could stop a man who was waging an asymmetric war. On the other hand, tall, fidgety, teenage beanpoles on an October evening, beneath bushes and in the muddy field – what could be more asymmetric?

Was he outside right now? Observing the lit-up house from the darkness? Observing *her*?

She felt the case was slipping away from her. Paul Niemann driving to Landwasser and Lahr. Young boys taking on the work of the police. A man who did what no-one expected and was always one step ahead.

A family that was falling apart. But she had no control over this.

Bonì turned around and asked Carola to send her friends home when her parents got back. All of them, including those outside in the field and under the bushes. Carola laughed bleakly. Oh them, they're just playing a game. But she promised all the same.

"Listen, this man . . ."

"He's of no interest to me," Carola blurted out.

"Well, he ought to be."

"I mean, I know you're going to catch him. So I don't have to be worried about him."

"You're worried about your parents."

Carola had slipped her hands into the back pockets of her trousers and stood there, legs apart. Her wild red hair was an armour of spikes, her eyes dark and clever, and her mouth seemed to be asking angrily: How can I stop what might happen?

Things were slipping away from her too.

A sixteen-year-old who felt responsible.

"Mama wants to leave. Leave us."

"Has she said that?"

Carola sat on the sofa, one hand on the armrest, the other in her lap. Narrow, colourful rings adorned each of her fingers. "No, but it's obvious."

Louise said nothing, but thought: When the love has gone. The silent dialogue with Henriette Niemann, that thing you said about love? Not a word will cross my lips. Does that apply to this conversation with Carola too? "I can't imagine her going away while the two of you are still at school. While you're still living here."

"Yes. Sure. But now . . ."

"Now?"

Carola nodded towards the window. "Now everything's moving faster. This man, he's . . . I don't know."

"He's what?"

"Philip says he's a sort of symbol. He represents what's broken on the inside and now he's coming from the outside. Inside our family, I mean. Do you understand?"

Louise nodded, confused.

"Our inner disintegration transposed to the outside world. That's what Philip says. He's a modern-day mystic, that's how he thinks."

"A modern-day mystic?"

Carola smiled. "So he says."

"What's a modern-day mystic?"

"No idea."

"Your brother needs help."

"I know."

"Psychological help."

"I know."

"He sits there in the darkness, listening to depressing music and losing touch with reality."

"Well, reality's a pile of crap."

"You might be right."

Carola shrugged.

"Do you think the same? That the man is a symbol for your family falling apart?"

"No, but I do think that everything's moving much quicker now. My parents are scared, and because they're scared they're losing control of themselves. It's all coming out. Everything that's broken on the inside."

They heard voices from below, the hallway. The beanpoles were calling for Carola. Laughing, shouting, "Caro!"

"Oh, well." Carola stood up.

Louise asked if there was anything she could do. Whether she could help. Carola shook her head.

They went downstairs in silence and shook hands in the hallway.

"Can I have a card too?"

"Of course." Louise took out a business card and wrote her private number on it.

"You keep them in your trouser pocket?"

"Sure. I'm a modern-day practitioner."

Carola smiled and briefly her dark, clever eyes smiled too.

No new desert of fine dust particles, but there were endless hairline cracks in the wall of the corridor to the stairs, a strange pattern of vertical and oblique zig-zag lines, as if the wall, or even the whole building, had started to shift.

It couldn't go on like this. She had to move. She didn't need a balcony; she needed a home. And until then a room at the academy. Or at Wallmer's?

Jenny hadn't called.

But little Germain had. He wanted to know if it was going to work out at the weekend. "Shit!" Louise said. She had forgotten little Germain.

She dialled the number in Kehl. Her father picked up.

"Shame, he was really looking forward to it."

"Shit."

"Are you sure you couldn't arrange something, chérie?"

"Not this weekend."

"That's a real shame."

She said nothing. Her odd, grey, French father and his accent-free, deliberate, stiff German. At least he knew where he belonged. Which country was his home.

But I know too, she thought.

They hung up.

Over supper she looked through the documentation on Valpovo. But she was too tired for those long roads out to the East, from the East. She stared at the black, jagged lines in the wall and the metal door opposite. What had happened to her life? Everything was coming apart. For months now she'd been living with a temporary solution because she refused to be driven out. Refused to accept that what was happening was happening.

Refused to accept the reality.

This is the reality, she thought. There is nothing else.

She liked this thought and pondered it for a while.

Then she went to bed.

10

In the middle of the night she was woken from her sleep. She had been dreaming that the house was still moving. That the walls were collapsing. But it wasn't the dream that had woken her.

Both her phones were ringing.

She rushed into the sitting room and grabbed her mobile.

Carola, crying. Then gone, abruptly.

Bonì wrenched the cordless phone from its dock. Another female voice, Hesse, her colleague from the constabulary. In the background: shouting, screaming and noises she couldn't place.

Hesse said something, but it was drowned out by the noise.

"What?"

"You've got to come!"

"Shit, where?" she shouted.

As if she hadn't known straightaway.

From Vauban she could see the glare of the blaze and blue lights coming from all directions. In Merzhausen police had stopped the traffic so that emergency services vehicles could pass unhindered. The officers waved her on, the colourful Mégane which was by now familiar.

But she couldn't get as far as the house because dozens of fire engines, police cars and ambulances were blocking the road, not to mention more and more people. She leaped out of the car. The sky was in flames. The air was thick with the smell of burnt petrol.

My house, this is my house, a voice said inside her head as she ran.

He had set his house on fire.

*

The wall of people grew ever denser. She shoved and shunted and swore until she reached the lane that uniformed officers were keeping free. She showed her I.D., then started running again. Up ahead she saw a black, smoking carcass illuminated by spotlights, a few steel joists, the ceilings, the stairs, everything else burnt, exploded, collapsed, the neighbouring house in flames, and the one next to that. Houses of wood and glass, through which flames and water from the hoses were shooting, now the nightmare she'd pictured a couple of days ago had become reality, everything so pretty and homely and peaceful and destroyed. She dragged a constable with her, but he didn't know what had happened to the Niemanns. A fireman pointed at an ambulance, in the back of which sat Paul Niemann, a slouched, limp body wrapped in a light-blue blanket. With him a uniformed officer who must be Hesse. A few metres away stood Henriette Niemann in her dressing gown, gesturing to two constables. Then, out of the corner of her eye, Louise glimpsed a shock of red hair, Carola, who sped towards her in tears and fell into her arms. Louise held her, infinitely relieved and infinitely surprised because she was so relieved.

"Philip," Carola whispered into her shoulder.

Philip had disappeared.

He had got out of the house in time, had stood outside with them as it burned to the ground, then the numbers of emergency service personnel and neighbours around them swelled and they lost sight of Philip. Later Carola had seen a figure wandering up the road in the direction of the Schönberg, but she couldn't tell if it was Philip. Louise thought of the boy in the dark room with the dark music, of the fear she believed she could sense. She looked up, but the Schönberg lay in darkness beyond the flames. It struck her that if she'd lost her home, she might wander off into the darkness too. She would walk up a hill to be above what had happened rather than remain in the midst of it.

She looked at the houses at the foot of the Schönberg. The third house was no longer alight, the second was still in flames, the first no longer existed.

My house, this is my house. He had destroyed his house.

"They say they haven't got enough people to look for him."

"I'll sort that out in a minute."

They had taken a few steps to the side, holding hands. Having turned her back on the destroyed house, Carola was now staring at Louise, clutching onto her with her hands and eyes, while Louise tried to work out what had happened here, what all this meant.

He had destroyed his house.

"You've got to look for him, I mean, he's on his own!"

"In a minute, Carola, just let me think for a moment."

Niemann was still in the back of the ambulance, but lying down now. With him were a doctor and the policewoman. Henriette was talking to another officer, a mobile in her left hand, her right on the seam of her dressing gown. Louise recognised the officer, Helm Brager, a gaunt chief inspector from Freiburg South. She'd heard sad stories about him, all of them to do with illnesses.

"He woke us," Carola said. "He was in the house."

Louise nodded. "We'll find him. Wait here, I'll be back in a sec."

"You don't understand . . ."

"Give me a minute, Carola."

She hurried over to Henriette Niemann and Helm Brager. The closer she moved to the scene of the fire the stronger the stench of petrol became. He had doused his house in petrol and set fire to it.

He'd returned on the third or fourth day and destroyed his house.

She shook her head. She didn't understand anything anymore.

With relief she saw Henriette move away from Brager to make a telephone call. She wouldn't have known what to say. Something along the lines of what she'd come out with two days ago?

We've got enough time. Hang on in there, O.K.?

Something along those lines?

"Brager?"

"Bonì." Brager turned his grey, sunken face towards her. When she was beside him she could see that it was completely hairless. No eyebrows, no lashes, no beard growth. She had never seen him like this. Beads of sweat had collected on his brow and cheeks. But his eyes glowed with implacability. "Your case?"

She nodded. "I'm looking for a boy. Fifteen years old."

"The Niemanns' boy. The daughter says he went up the Schönberg."

"Are you sure he got out in time?"

Brager looked at her but didn't respond. His eyes were small and pinched in the corners, as if anticipating that a pain would shoot through his body any moment. Seeing him like this, you could imagine it happening often.

"Brager, say something, for God's sake."

"He woke them before it started."

"The boy?"

Brager shook his head. "The arsonist."

He woke us, he was in the house . . . Now she understood what Carola had meant. "He was in the house."

"Yes," Brager said.

He was in the house and poured petrol everywhere: the cellar, ground floor, first floor and second floor. Then he'd opened the doors to the parents' and children's bedrooms. The parents woke up immediately, smelled the petrol, heard the footsteps on the stairs and understood. They rushed to the children's rooms and raced downstairs with them.

By that stage the cellar was already on fire.

"He meant for them to get out," Louise said. "He wanted to burn the house down, but didn't want anything to happen to them."

Brager said nothing, just stared at her. His eyes now looked larger and brighter than before. Louise wondered whether the pain had come.

She touched his arm. "Is everything O.K.?"

His eyes didn't move.

"Brager?"

"Yes, yes," Brager growled. "Take a few officers and look for the boy, alright?"

As Bonì hurried back to Carola she pictured his eyes in her mind – large, bright eyes that expressed a pain whose origins she didn't know, and perhaps, she thought, the deeds of the old warrior were the expression of a pain whose origins she did not know either. Sometimes the answers to all questions lay in human pain.

Now Henriette was beside her and, like Carola, she threw her arms around Louise and began to talk while still in an embrace. They were going to stay with her sister-in-law, she still had a house in Au and was on her way to pick them up, they would stay in Au till they found a new house, it was only a tiny bit further from the children's school, and would make no difference to Paul or to her. "It's virtually the same distance into town," she said, pulling away from Louise and bursting into tears.

Bonì set off with six colleagues from Freiburg South and Carola, who was determined to come along. They walked up the road to where Carola had seen the figure, and plunged into the darkness at the foot of the Schönberg. The road narrowed and curved. To the left lay steep gardens, between which steps led down into the village; to the right was a vineyard. They snaked their way up to the Jesuitenschloss, which stood somewhere in the blackness above them. They switched on their torches. Louise kept Carola close beside her, while the other officers had their hands on their holsters – you never knew. Many arsonists liked to watch what they had set alight burn to the ground; maybe this one did too, maybe he was standing somewhere up here in the dark, gazing down at the flames and the house that no longer existed. Feeling the chill, Louise buttoned up her denim jacket. It was a cold, black night. A small section at the foot of the hill was brightly lit, a suppurating wound at the edge of Merzhausen – flames, flood-lights, blue lights. The firemen now appeared to have the blaze under control; the flames were noticeably lower than a few minutes earlier. Beside it, where the Niemanns' house had stood, was a rectangular patch of black and embers that occasionally glowed in the wind.

"I can't see it," Carola whispered.

"I know."

"Has it completely gone? Is it all gone?"

Louise nodded.

"All gone," Carola said.

Louise put an arm around her shoulder. She felt she ought to say something but nothing came to mind apart from: I'm so sorry, I should have known, I should have looked after you, I mean, I knew something was going to happen.

She would say it tomorrow. Now was not the right time.

Louise sensed that Carola was weeping silently, but she also sensed a peculiar strength in this slim body, which nothing could unsettle, and although she knew it wasn't right she pulled Carola tightly to her, so as to be closer to this strength.

It was more by chance that they found Philip, when the beam of a torch swept a field below the road. He was lying curled into a ball, facing downhill. Carola called his name and began to cry when he didn't respond. She wanted to run to him, but Louise held on to her and sent three officers instead, watching tensely as they approached Philip. A shiver ran down her spine. All of a sudden she pictured Niksch, the young policeman from Liebau in winter 2003, who she'd also looked for in the darkness and who'd also been found lying in the dirt. They'd buried him a few days later.

Now the officers were with Philip and shouted something over to her. She repeated it in her head, without immediately grasping the meaning of the words: Everything's O.K., nothing's happened, he's alive.

They stood in a circle around the two children, who sat there hugging each other in the dirt and the darkness. A wall of adults, as if trying to protect the siblings.

As if they were able to protect them.

Louise had telephoned Brager with the news. Everything's O.K., he's alive, he's just a bit bewildered, apart from anything else. She wondered what the "anything else" might be. Whether Philip had come here looking for the man too.

First the father, then the son.

"Inspector?" said one of the officers who had moved away from the group. His torch was pointing down the hill. In the circle of light she could see footprints. The officer slowly moved the circle of light towards Philip. The prints ended a couple of metres away from him.

"Show me his shoes," Louise said.

The light focused on Philip's feet. He was barefoot.

She shook her head. The old warrior had been here. Had stood here, barely two metres from Philip. The question was, when? When Philip was already lying here?

She froze. "We need to take an impression."

"I'll see to that."

Louise went back to the children and kneeled beside them. In the darkness she could only make out their faces. "Philip?"

"Uh-huh?"

"Did you see him up here? The man?"

A vague movement: a shake of the head?

"No?"

"No."

She stroked his shoulder and stood up. He had been here, had stood here. He'd doused his house in petrol, woken the Niemanns, then climbed up the hill, maybe to watch the house burn, but maybe just to escape across the fields and into the forest.

Was that it? The "otherwise"? Leave within seven days, otherwise I'll burn the house down?

Your house, my house.

Was it over now? Would he go back to where he belonged? If such a place existed. Or would he come back?

She looked up at the Schönberg. The moon was behind clouds, the hill lay hidden in darkness. She thought of Helm Brager and her reflections on pain. They might be able to answer the questions if they knew the nature of the pain expressing itself in the deeds of the old warrior.

Valpovo 1945. The Germans from Yugoslavia.

They had a handful of clues, which they would follow up. Perhaps these clues would lead them to the pain.

Taking a deep breath, Bonì stepped back to rejoin the wall of adults.

As if they were trying to protect the children.

As if they were able to protect them.

II

The Dance of the Dying Fathers

11

Another dream about a house, sometime between six and seven in the morning, once again the house moved and when the walls collapsed she saw flames instead of daylight.

Louise was woken by voices. Someone was knocking at the window, laughing. The room smelled of burnt wood. *She* smelled of burnt wood.

She took a shower, but the smell lingered.

She ate breakfast standing up and imagined that, like the smell, what had happened in Merzhausen had stuck to her skin too. As if the smell *was* what had happened to the Niemanns and would keep happening.

Jägermeister meditations without the Jägermeister.

Outside on the metal platform stood the Upper Silesians. They wanted a word. She thought of the cracks in the wall, thought how it couldn't go on like this, people were still living in the building. But then cracks in the walls weren't that important so long as the walls were still standing.

In the courtyard a tall, gaunt man suddenly appeared at her side. He wanted a word too, and talked about a replacement apartment in St Georgen and a guaranteed return in the spring at a higher rent, all uttered rather gruffly with a slight Bavarian dialect, accompanied by broad, aggressive hand movements. He had longish, wavy hair, spoke legalese and whenever they passed builders all conversations stopped.

The Bavarian, she had heard of him.

"But it's your choice, of course," he said.

"Correct," Louise said.

"It can't be any fun living like this, Frau Bonì."

"Correct."

"And now the wall on the street side needs to be stabilised with steel joists."

"Does it?"

"Very funny. How do you think we're going to do it without joists?"

Now they were out on the pavement. Louise said nothing. She was thinking of Carola's questions. Has it completely gone? Is it all gone? She knew that she would never forget these questions, nor Carola's voice as she asked them. The questions and voice of a girl whose home had been taken away from her.

"We need to find a solution, Frau Bonì," the Bavarian said. His tone was rather one of boredom than any particular urgency.

"The solution is fifty thousand euros."

The Bavarian laughed.

Louise unlocked her Mégane.

"We don't pay five-figure sums."

"You can transfer it in four-figure amounts." She got in.

The Bavarian laughed again. She'd had enough of him after a couple of minutes, this Bavarian and his high-handed manner. But she knew, of course, that he would win in the end.

How had Mick put it? The Bavarians always win.

Bob was waiting in her office. Standing at the window, he nodded "Good morning" to her. She could tell from his focused yet distant look why he wanted to talk to her. He was searching for mistakes, transgressors. Nobody aiming for the top must carry any blame around with them. He needed to lay the blame on others' shoulders so it wouldn't stick to him. Bob's favourite lines were: You ought to have done it like *that*. You ought to have put it *differently*. You ought to have done it *earlier*. His favourite colleagues were the really good cops like Mats Benedikt and – with the occasional reservation – Rolf Bermann.

He knew he needed the best to make it to the top. Knew that he had to tell them afterwards – always afterwards – what they should have done differently. His favourite suits were expensive and elegant, but off the peg. The gap between the top and bottom mustn't be too great.

Stepping away from the window, he spread his arms. "How could that have happened?"

Louise sat at her desk and deliberated whether to answer him. She didn't.

"I hear you were asking for a task force already yesterday."

"It wouldn't have made any difference."

"Your section head told you that . . ."

"I know what my head of section told me."

Bob nodded and moved over to her. "You're trying to protect him."

"Who?"

Bob smiled patiently. His smile was handsome, he was a handsome man, the type you wouldn't mind having around, were he not so devoured by ambition.

"Louise."

"Robert."

Bob smiled again. "Fine. Let's leave it." Back at the window, he glanced out at the sunlight, then turned around. "Is it over? What do you think?"

She looked at him but said nothing. How clever this man was. How cautious. She didn't like the idea, but Bob's caution, his fear of making a mistake by overlooking something, ignoring a valid warning or being a victim of his own prejudices, almost always benefited their investigations.

"No."

"Is he going to come back?"

"Yes."

Bob nodded. "What makes you think that?"

"I don't know. Just a hunch. It's not over yet."

"What's he going to do?"

She shrugged.

"Will he kill someone?"

"I don't know, for God's sake."

"What do you *think*?"

"He might try."

"Last night he protected the Niemanns."

She gave a bitter laugh. You could see it that way.

"He didn't want anything to happen to them," Bob specified.

"I know."

"And yet you still think he might try to kill someone?"

She nodded.

"Who, Louise?"

"Paul Niemann."

"Because there has to be a connection between them?"

"Yes."

Bob pursed his lips. His arms were crossed and he appeared to be in thought. A couple of minutes passed, then he went to the door, said, "I'll see you at the meeting," and was gone.

Louise snorted. Bob. Younger, smarter, more handsome and more successful than good old Almenbroich, who had made mistakes because he had been nicer, more honest and more humane.

She forced herself not to think of Bob and Almenbroich, and went back to her hunch. That the old warrior would return. There was nothing to suggest that he would try to kill Paul Niemann. On the contrary, twice he'd had the opportunity and twice he had refrained from doing so. Last night he had "protected" Niemann and his family.

And yet she couldn't shake the feeling that he would come back to kill.

The first "Merzhausen" task force meeting began at 8 a.m. Bob, the media spokeswoman, members of the investigation team and a handful of other colleagues sat in the room along with Bermann, who was heading up the task force. For the third or fourth time that morning, Louise reported what had happened the night before, and for the first time outlined what had happened since Saturday afternoon. Task forces tended to unleash adrenaline – the hunt was on, the dogs were picking up the scent. This morning Louise found the proceedings stultifying. She was desperate to get back to Merzhausen, or rather, Au, where the Niemanns were staying. So many things needed to be resolved, and one in particular: what connected Valpovo 1945, the Germans from Yugoslavia and Paul Niemann?

But then she realised that mainly she wanted to go and see Henriette and Carola. She wanted to apologise, and check that they were O.K. in the circumstances.

At around 9 a.m., Bermann allocated the various tasks. The Valpovo lead, Louise learned, was just one of several. They still had to follow up on the Russian, the homeless man, the farmer, the lover, the psychopath.

Bob's handwriting.

She said nothing. Bob was right. Someone had to think of everything. Another reason why she didn't find it too difficult to accept that, because of her history, she would never lead a task force. The price she had to pay for the intensity with which she worked was an overview. Piecing together the overall picture and plummeting into the abyss were mutually exclusive.

Benedikt accompanied her into the abyss.

They drove in Benedikt's car to the scene of the fire. Benedikt got out, Louise stayed in the vehicle. Yesterday an attractive house made of wood and glass; now all that remained was the skeleton: four joists and the staircase up to the first floor. The ceilings and the staircase up to the second floor had collapsed.

Has it completely gone? Is it all gone?

She looked away and watched Benedikt chat to one of the constables responsible for making the site safe. Then he walked around it, registered what he was seeing and made notes. It felt good to watch him, to know that there were colleagues who could be wonderfully sober, who could step into the abyss and then step out again.

The sister-in-law's house in Au was large, old and somewhat neglected. It stood in a road perpendicular to Hexentalstrasse. Thick, white walls beneath a dark, defiant roof. Henriette greeted them in an apron and rubber gloves. She had black rings around her eyes, and her face was crossed with thousands of tiny wrinkles. Her mouth was a thin line, but she managed a smile. "I bet you'd like a coffee. I made far too much, for the smell . . ." She turned and hurried ahead into the kitchen.

"For the smell?" Benedikt whispered.

Louise shrugged.

But then, when they were standing in the huge, bare kitchen, she thought she understood. The smell of coffee . . . If you closed your eyes, you might imagine you were in a house made of wood and glass.

They sat at an enormous, dark wooden table. A glass door led out to a vegetable garden that was overgrown, full of weeds, neglected – a thicket of twigs, leaves and vegetables that had burst open.

The sister-in-law who could no longer find her bearings in life.

Henriette put cups and a thermos in front of them, fetched milk from the fridge then stood beside Louise and muttered, "I can't find the sugar."

"I don't take sugar, thanks," Benedikt said.

"Me neither," Louise said.

"But you do," Henriette said.

"Not today." Louise stroked her arm. Henriette nodded. Her eyes held dozens of questions, but she said nothing. The daughter who didn't want to look. The mother who didn't want to ask.

"She's a bit . . . slovenly."

"Your sister-in-law?"

"Sometimes the sugar's here, sometimes it's there. Sometimes in the kitchen, sometimes in the living room, sometimes in the dining room. Sometimes it's in the fridge. Today . . ." Henriette took a deep breath. "Today I can't find it at all."

Benedikt cleared his throat and Louise said, "I'm like that too. Slovenly, I mean. Nothing has a fixed place. It drove my husband up the wall."

"Yes," Henriette said.

"When I threw him out he couldn't find any clean socks."

Benedikt gave a fake laugh.

"So he left without any on."

"Without socks," Benedikt said and laughed again.

"Please, sit down," Louise said.

"Only for a moment. I've got to tidy the house. She's a bit . . . slovenly." Henriette sat opposite her at the table. She stared at Louise, her mouth narrow again, her small eyes exuding disappointment. Louise nodded. Talk, Henriette. Talk to me. Say it, then it's out.

But Henriette just looked at her.

Benedikt asked about Paul Niemann and the children. Niemann was upstairs, he'd been sitting by the window ever since they'd arrived a few hours ago. Philip was in bed, hopefully asleep. Carola had gone shopping with the sister-in-law. They didn't have to worry about Caro, Henriette said. Caro was like her. Always on the go. Always on top of everything. If your old home was gone, you simply moved into a new one. She gave a strained smile. Philip was different. She didn't understand Philip. He was very distant. She didn't know what he was feeling. Whether he could take this in his stride.

Benedikt offered to call Hartmut Prader, the police conflict counsellor. He would come at once, talk to the children, to Paul, liaise with counselling centres. With psychologists if necessary. Henriette nodded, but declined. Her eyes were again fixed on Louise.

You said we had time.

She nodded. Say it.

Henriette said nothing.

"I'm so sorry," Louise said. "I thought we had time. I didn't know he'd . . ." She broke off.

Benedikt tried to come to her help. Nobody knew, he said. There was no suggestion that the man would come back so soon. That he'd burn down the house. "His" house. He did say it was *his* house.

Henriette looked at him and nodded. Her gaze returned to Louise.

"I knew something was going to happen," Louise said. "But I didn't know what."

"We *couldn't* have known," Benedikt said, turning to her.

"We doubled the number of patrol cars. One drove past your house every few minutes."

"We *couldn't* have known," Benedikt repeated.

Louise shrugged. "I had a hunch."

"Hunches, Louise," Benedikt said softly.

She looked at him and smiled. That's what it's like working with me, Mats Benedikt. The abyss. You have been warned.

"What sort of hunch?" Henriette asked.

"That something would happen. Something we weren't expecting at all."

"You didn't tell us that. You said we had time."

"I know."

"Hunches," Benedikt said. "We all have hunches, and then something completely different happens. We can't —"

"You should have told us."

"We can't make our procedures dependent on *hunches.* All we can do is try to find clues that *confirm* our hunches. Only then can we act accordingly."

"Yes," Louise said, without taking her eyes off Henriette.

Benedikt leaned forwards and rested his arms on the table. "It would have been irresponsible of us to let you know our hunches. You might have panicked, especially your husband. And what good would it have done? We wouldn't have been able to protect your house around the clock just because we had *hunches*. He would have waited until we'd gone and then set the place on fire."

"He's superior to us," Louise said.

"No!" Benedikt said fiercely. "He's one step ahead of us and he's unpredictable. But he's not superior."

"He's . . ." Louise paused. "He's strange. He's waging a war. But we don't know why, nor against whom. Nor when the war's going to end."

"Against us," Henriette interjected gruffly. "He's waging war against *us*. That's obvious, isn't it?"

Louise said nothing. Benedikt said, "Against your husband? Against you? For the house? The land? It's *not*—"

Henriette snorted. "It all boils down to the same thing. He's destroyed our house. He's taken away our home."

For a while there was silence, then Henriette asked, "What about now? Have you got any hunches now?"

Louise nodded.

"For God's sake," Benedikt muttered.

"What are they?"

"No, Louise—"

"I believe he's going to try to kill your husband."

Henriette froze. Her eyes filled with tears, which ran down her cheeks. She took a tissue from her apron, wiped away the tears and blew her nose. "I'm not going to tell him. But now I can keep an eye on him."

They went upstairs to the guest room where Henriette and Paul Niemann were staying, a small, dark room with a view of the neighbouring house's windowless wall. Heavy rustic furniture, a rug that swallowed the sound of every footstep, light years from the house made of wood and glass. Niemann was sitting in an armchair by the small window at which hung two dark-brown curtains. He didn't react when they came in, not even when Henriette went and spoke to him. He was wearing a dressing gown that was too big, beneath it pyjamas that were too big and slippers that were too big. The sister-in-law must have kept her dead husband's clothes for four years, and now it was paying off.

"Paul," Henriette said again. "Paul."

Eventually he looked at her.

"Kripo are here." Her voice was soft, but she did not touch him.

Niemann's eyes wandered to Benedikt and Louise, then returned to his wife. His hands lay in his lap, his head was inclined slightly to the side. Feelings of pity surged through Louise, followed by a wave of anger – at him, at herself. Niemann was the key, but he hadn't talked and she hadn't found a way of making him talk.

"Just a few questions," Benedikt said in a friendly tone.

Just a few questions? Louise thought. No. As many questions and as much time as was necessary to find out what linked Niemann to the old warrior.

Henriette sat on the bed. She had offered to go downstairs if the two officers wanted to talk to her husband alone, but Louise asked her to stay. She had no intention of speaking of the love that had gone, but she would use what she knew to find out what she wanted to know.

Benedikt looked at her and gave the faintest of nods: begin, let's have a go, you first then me. He was unable to disguise his scepticism, knowing full well that she would rely on her hunches again. Louise felt a touch melancholy; that's how it was with colleagues. Only with Thomas Ilic had it been different. He had been willing to work with hunches. He could allow himself this with his orderly folder, essential for dealing with Louise Bonì's abyss. Ilic's folder had contained maps, photographs, telephone numbers, names and all the blue words he jotted down to avoid them getting lost in the morass of hunches.

But Ilic was ill; he hadn't managed to climb back out of the abyss.

She nodded. Right then, dear Mats, first we'll do it my way, welcome to my realm, home to duplicity, amongst other things.

Louise began with the photograph of Johannes Miller, one of the other Germans from the East. She showed Niemann the index card, with her hand over the name. She knew he would respond in the negative, and he did, shaking his head. Louise put away the photo. Johannes Miller – there were too many things that weren't right, he was just an old man without a homeland, not an old warrior. The fingerprint comparison would give them the objective proof. Sophie Iwanowa's feeling had been wrong; Friedental/Friedland may not have been a good omen, but it hadn't turned Johannes into a criminal. He remained missing, though, and they would search for him, even if he was no longer a suspect.

She glanced at Henriette, then back to Niemann. "Does the word 'Valpovo' mean anything to you?"

He seemed to mull this over for a moment before shaking his head. "Frau Niemann?"

"No."

Louise nodded and paused. Her eyes landed on a series of square pencil drawings on the wall beneath a bookshelf. Portraits of a man, always the same man, drawn by an amateur, but there was a clear similarity between the faces, just as there was a similarity between the man and Henriette. But when she looked more closely she noticed that the man changed from drawing to drawing, and at the end looked different from how he had at the beginning. The resemblance to Henriette had vanished too, as if the man had gradually become a stranger. She wondered whether the woman who must have drawn these portraits – the woman in whose house they were – had noticed the change in the man.

And what this might have made her feel.

"What is Valpovo?" Henriette asked.

"A place in Croatia."

"In Croatia? But . . . I don't understand."

"The man we're looking for has nothing to do with the Germans from Russia," Louise said.

"But with Croatia?"

"Probably with the Germans from former Yugoslavia."

"But why Yugoslavia? Is it because of Vapol—"

"Valpovo, yes."

"O.K. So how did you come up with Valpovo?"

Louise told the story. A homeless man in Lahr, a foreigner with a cigarette case, an engraving, a place in Croatia where there had been an internment camp for the Yugoslav-Germans, and a year, 1945, when the camp still existed. Henriette was frowning, she listened in disbelief, of course, none of this was convincing. "Hmm," she said.

Niemann said nothing. His gaze flitted from the window to Louise and Benedikt, then back again. To look at his wife he would have had to turn around. He made no attempt to do so.

"Not a Russian-German," Louise said. "We have to assume that this lead is a dead end. That you don't know him from your work at the council."

"So where from, then?"

"From earlier."

"Earlier?"

Louise nodded. "From Munich."

"Impossible . . . I would remember."

"You'd remember if you'd met him in Freiburg."

Niemann turned away.

"But Munich," Louise said, "was different, wasn't it, Herr Niemann?"

She looked at Henriette, who returned her gaze. "Something like this can't have started in Munich, can it? Not in Munich."

"No," Niemann said.

"Not in Munich where everything was different and better. Where you and your wife sang in the choir. Where you had time for each other."

Niemann said nothing.

"It wouldn't fit with Munich, would it?"

"It wasn't in Munich."

"Of course not," Louise said.

"It must have been in Freiburg. In council services."

"I know."

They looked at each other. He appeared very calm, very tired, very distant and she felt as if they'd lost him at some point between yesterday and today. Henriette would cope, her husband would not.

"To begin with I wasn't sure . . ." he said.

"That he was a Russian-German?"

He nodded. "But I am now."

"The way he spoke?"

"Yes."

"Maybe the Germans from Yugoslavia speak in a similar way."

"I didn't have any contact with Germans from Yugoslavia." A barely noticeable shrug of the shoulders. Either believe me or don't.

Yes, they'd lost him.

"In Freiburg."

He nodded.

"What about Munich?"

"Not there either." A hand movement, almost impatient. Leave Munich out of it, Munich won't get you anywhere. Bonì gave a cold laugh. Her hunches were getting stronger. It couldn't have anything to do with Munich. Munich was where the answers were.

"What exactly did you do in Munich?"

"I was in social services."

"For the city council?"

"Yes."

"What were you responsible for?"

"The elderly. Provision of facilities for the elderly in the various districts." Another shrug. Look, Munich isn't going to get you anywhere, there's nothing in Munich.

"To start with you said you couldn't have met this man in council services without remembering him. On Monday."

"That's right."

"But now you think it's possible."

"It must be."

Louise caught Benedikt's pensive look. She pursed her lips. Facilities for the elderly . . . admittedly that didn't seem particularly promising. But it was obvious that Niemann was protecting his life in Munich, that he'd put up an idealising wall around Munich, which in his feeble way he would doggedly defend.

She mouthed the word "Munich". Benedikt rocked his head from side to side and behind his glasses his eyes remained thoughtful. He touched her arm and she nodded. Fine, your turn.

He asked the Niemanns whether they had any connection to former Yugoslavia. Whether they'd ever been there, had contact with people from there, either now or in the past. His calm, neutral voice dispelled the tension, created order, was full of consideration for the victims. Not a trace of pity or anger, just professionalism. No hunches in which order could become entangled. For a moment Louise wished she'd come on her own. But she knew that Benedikt wasn't just good for the Niemanns, he was good for her too.

"Take your time," Benedikt said. "Have a good think. What links you to former Yugoslavia? A holiday, a person, maybe a neighbour. A schoolfriend, a colleague, a friend of your parents. Perhaps you went on an anti-Tito march when you were younger. Or a pro-Tito one."

Louise smirked. Benedikt smiled.

"He's a Russian-German," Niemann said. "He spoke like a Russian-German."

Benedikt ignored this. "Maybe you were involved politically. Think back to the nineties, the Balkan Wars. The N.A.T.O. operations, Kosovo. There were demonstrations about these too. Maybe you simply drove through Yugoslavia once to go to Greece on holiday and met someone. Herr Niemann?"

Niemann shrugged, again at a total loss, again Louise believed him.

"Anything," Benedikt said. "Anybody. A few months ago, a few years ago, a few decades ago."

Henriette shook her head. Niemann shrugged.

"What connection is there between you and former Yugoslavia?" He said this softly and calmly, as if intending to repeat the question until he received a satisfactory answer.

"Yugoslavia or Croatia?" Henriette murmured.

"Yugoslavia. Perhaps Valpovo plays a completely different role, we don't know. The states of the former Yugoslavia. Slovenia. Croatia. Serbia. Montenegro. Bosnia and Herzegovina. Kosovo. Is that all of them? Macedonia. What's the connection, Herr Niemann?"

Niemann cleared his throat. "There isn't one. We've never been to Yugoslavia. We don't know anyone from there."

Louise kept her eyes fixed on Henriette. Her voice, her expression had changed almost imperceptibly. She had narrowed her eyes, looked slightly horrified as she had on Monday when she'd said she would leave her husband once the children had gone.

Henriette began to understand.

"There must be a connection," Benedikt said. "Think hard. Maybe a brief encounter, which might have been of no further significance for you, but for someone else it was. It doesn't have to have been our man. It can have been *anybody*. Think. Try to remember. What links you to former Yugoslavia? Herr Niemann?"

"I . . ." He cleared his throat again.

"Yes?"

"Nothing. Nothing at all."

"Frau Niemann?"

Henriette shook her head.

Benedikt looked at Louise, to be sure she was happy to let him continue. She nodded and wondered if he too had sensed that something in Henriette Niemann had changed. "O.K.," he said. "Let's try something else. What do you think of when you hear the word Yugoslavia? What's the first thing that comes to mind? Frau Niemann?"

Henriette hesitated. "The war."

"The war in the 1990s?" Benedikt said.

"The Bosnian War."

Louise looked at Benedikt. A shiver ran down her spine and arms. An old warrior, a war. And a link to the Niemanns?

"The Bosnian War," Benedikt repeated calmly. "Herr Niemann?"

Niemann didn't respond. He had turned away and was staring outside again, at the grey, windowless wall of the neighbouring house. His eyes were half closed, his hands tightly clenched in his lap.

"Herr Niemann?"

No reply. Louise's heart started beating more quickly. She knew they were on the verge of some answers. And she knew she wouldn't hear these answers from Niemann.

"Tell him, Paul," Henriette muttered. Now she was staring out of the window too.

Niemann said nothing. Louise resisted the urge to go to him, lay a hand on his shoulder and tell him he *must* speak if he didn't want to lose the respect of his wife. Don't you realise that this is all there is left?

Niemann closed his eyes.

"He's thinking of the Bosnians," Henriette said.

"The Bosnians?" Benedikt said.

"The war refugees from Bosnia."

"Did he deal with them in Munich? In social services?"

Henriette looked at her husband. "Paul?"

Niemann said nothing.

Henriette stood up. "Come with me."

"In a sec," Louise said.

Benedikt nodded and followed Henriette, who had already left the room.

Louise touched Niemann's shoulder. He looked up at her and said, "No, that's impossible."

"I know."

Niemann nodded. She could feel him trembling.

"I know," she repeated, before going to the door, past the portraits of Henriette's brother, who was a different man by the end of the series, and it occurred to her that this was what happened – the past changed the more time went on. She wondered whether this was true of the old warrior as well. Or had a moment of pain buried itself so deeply in his memory that this moment would never change? And the pain would never subside?

They went back into the kitchen. Henriette poured three cups of coffee, put milk on the table then hesitated. Louise smiled. The sugar. Henriette shrugged and sat down. She was pale, but looked composed and determined. The decision had been taken, the final link was broken. When love was gone, that was one thing. When you'd decided to leave, that was something else.

Then she spoke.

In the late 1990s Niemann had been seconded for a couple of months to the foreigners' registration office of the Munich administrative region. After the Dayton Agreement came into force the city had begun to send Croatian and Bosnian refugees back to their respective homelands. There were so many of them, however, that the office had to call in staff from other departments. Some, including Paul Niemann, had no choice in the matter. He began in May or June 1998, fell ill that summer and after his recuperation returned to social services. They had never spoken about it, but Henriette knew he'd found it really difficult to send people who wanted to stay in their new, secure home back to their old one, now in ruins.

She couldn't remember the precise details of the war refugees' repatriation or which tasks Niemann had been involved in. All she knew was that the name of his new department had been "312 B.W.R." and it wasn't located in the main building of the foreigners' registration office, but in Untersbergstrasse in Giesing. There had been more than forty administrators working in Giesing, including Niemann, having to make decisions without ever coming face to face with the people whose destinies they controlled; only the main building was open to the public. That was where the refugees had first come, where they had applied for extensions to their right to remain, where they had pleaded all the legal and not-so-legal circumstances that might give them a right of permanent residence. The administrators in Untersbergstrasse ascertained all this only by way of more forms.

Henriette got to her feet and wandered around the kitchen, opening drawers and cupboards. When she came back to the table she was holding a lit cigarette. "My sister-in-law only had one left and now I need it," she said apologetically.

Louise nodded and thought: An old warrior, a war, a possible connection to Paul Niemann if the man they were after had lived in Munich as a war refugee. A pain that might have branded itself on the old warrior's memory for good: being sent away from his new, secure home. This offered a possible motive: revenge.

This is my house, she thought. This is my house now.

You took away my house, so now I'm going to take away yours?

She wondered how many cases Niemann had processed in the two months he'd worked for the foreigners' registration office. Fifty?

Two hundred? Five hundred? They had no name, just a blurred face, an approximate age, fingerprints. They had the engraving in the cigarette case: "Valpovo 1945". The German lead.

They needed to see the relevant documents from 1998, assuming these still existed. They had to get Niemann to talk to them about Munich.

To talk about things that cannot have happened in Munich.

She took a sip of coffee – how she hated coffee without sugar.

An old warrior, a war. Sometime in the 1990s he flees to Germany, to Munich. Years later an administrator in a makeshift office of the Munich foreigners' registration office picks up a form and arranges the refugee's repatriation to Bosnia. A few more years pass, then the refugee appears in a garden in Merzhausen near Freiburg, issues an ultimatum and sets light to a house.

Was that the story?

"We need to talk to your husband," Benedikt said.

"Yes."

"Not now," Louise said. "He won't talk now."

"Let's take him with us."

Louise shook her head. "He won't talk, Mats. Not yet."

They looked at each other. Benedikt shrugged.

"We'll get the documents from Munich, then we'll talk to him."

He nodded.

Henriette accompanied them to the door.

"I'll just be a minute," Louise said. Benedikt nodded once more and left the house. In silence they watched him open the front gate and get into the car.

"I'll ask Carola to talk to her father," Henriette said at length. "He listens to her."

"Yes."

They looked at each other.

"Your children need professional help, Henriette. Even Carola."

Henriette brushed fluff from her arm. "We'll manage."

"No," Louise said.

"We just need a little time. We'll get on top of it."

"You will. Your children and your husband won't."

"Another hunch?" Henriette smiled aloofly.

Louise nodded. "Experience too."

Benedikt was on the telephone. She knew he was talking to Hoffmann, telling him about Munich, the old warrior, Paul Niemann and department 312 B.W.R. She pondered what "B.W.R." might mean and then it dawned on her. Of course, "Bosnian war refugees".

"I'll send Hartmut Prader over to you," she said.

"No. Not yet."

Louise sighed.

They shook hands. Henriette's was cold and rigid. "How are you going to protect my husband?"

"For the time being by increasing the number of patrol cars. We need to think about everything else."

"Don't think for too long."

They looked at each other. Louise knew what Henriette was thinking, and was grateful that she didn't say it out loud – for we have no time.

12

"Hunches," Benedikt said. It sounded neither sceptical nor friendly, but slightly pensive.

"And?" Louise said.

They drove through Au and Merzhausen. The colours of Vauban shone in the sudden sunlight. After a week of rain and grey, an explosion of light, of warmth.

Benedikt didn't go on. In any case Louise had no desire to justify her hunches; having to justify hunches really wasn't necessary now, Mats Benedikt, we police officers know how important hunches can be.

She felt a little sad, but not because of the hunches. To her surprise she realised it was because she hadn't seen Carola that morning. She would have taken her in her arms, to give her strength this time rather than take it from her. She would have liked to say how sorry she was. That she'd had a hunch, that she ought to have looked after them.

Then she thought of the house made of wood and glass, and tried to imagine how it might have been there on a sunny day like today. Dust hovering in the bright light and everywhere warmth, silence, tranquillity, a secure life, even though she knew the Niemanns had never led a life like that in Freiburg.

She didn't know why she thought about the house so often, and about the Niemanns, perhaps because both represented the life she didn't want to lead, a life with children, a husband, fences that prevented you from running straight into the abyss. If you were slightly asymmetric, a life like that didn't work. If you wanted to be on your own.

And then you met a woman like Henriette Niemann and a daughter like Carola and thought that you'd have loved to have a daughter like that, *only* one like that, not a different one, a daughter with wild red hair, an armour of spikes, with dark, clever, furious, sad eyes. That you might have been happy with a daughter like Carola, entirely free of abysses and hunches and stressful Louise-Bonì-style operations.

Has it completely gone? Carola's voice said inside her head. *Is it all gone?*

A daughter who couldn't look and the next morning went shopping and tried to get her own life and that of her family back on track.

"I don't want you to go thinking I've got anything against hunches," Benedikt said.

"O.K."

"I don't have anything against hunches."

"O.K."

"Hunches," Benedikt said wistfully.

Louise waited. They pulled away from a traffic light, but Benedikt said nothing more.

"O.K.," Louise said, looking away.

"I don't have them."

"Hunches?"

"Yes."

"You could call them feelings too."

He shrugged. "I don't have them."

"Feelings?"

Another shrug.

"Are you telling me you don't have feelings?"

No response.

What a bizarre conversation, she thought.

"Yup," Benedikt said.

"This is a bizarre conversation."

They looked at each other and laughed.

"I see it like this," Benedikt said. Where other people had feelings – in their head, their heart, wherever – he had . . . He hesitated.

"Well?"

"Things."

"Things?"

"Things wrapped up. Like little, dark, shapeless presents."

"And you don't want to unwrap them?"

"I wouldn't know where to start."

Louise couldn't help smiling. The sadness had returned, the vision of the destroyed house of wood and glass, Carola's voice early in the morning, but the conversation with Benedikt helped. "Start with the sticky tape."

"Yes," Benedikt said with a laugh, "with the sticky tape."

"This really is a bizarre conversation."

"It is."

"Why are we having it?"

"I just wanted to make it clear that I don't have anything against hunches," Benedikt said. The only problem was that hunches became a sort of truth the moment they were spoken out loud. Especially when uttered by police officers. The moment police officers revealed their hunches to other people, for those people they became certainties. And possibly not only for those people. Maybe for the police officers who articulated them too. You had to bear this in mind.

Louise nodded. She hadn't borne it in mind. "So what does that mean?"

"Well," Benedikt said, hesitantly.

"That he might now do something completely different?"

Benedikt nodded.

"Yes," Louise said. "Shit."

Of course Benedikt was right. It might be a case of revenge, revenge exacted by the old warrior on Paul Niemann in department 312 B.W.R., who on the basis of a smattering of information, some forms and regulations, had decided the fate of dozens, hundreds of refugees. But what significance did that have? How could they know that the old warrior's thirst for revenge would be satisfied by killing Niemann?

They *couldn't* know.

"In truth we can only be sure of one thing," Benedikt said.

"That it's not over."

"Yes."

Louise touched his arm. "And what do you call that, Mats?"

Benedikt grinned. A man with a hunch.

Late that morning a small group of them were sitting in Hoffmann's office – Bonì, Wallmer, Benedikt and Bermann, who'd been summoned to see Bob again and was following the conversation silently and with narrowed eyes, a man on the verge of revolt, on the verge of an impulsive decision. This immediately became clear to Louise.

They outlined their discussion with the Niemanns and Hoffmann told them about his conversation with their colleague Bereiter from Munich police H.Q., who would seize the 312 B.W.R. records for them, but hadn't sounded overly happy. No time, they had a spectacular murder case on their hands. A celebrity, Hoffmann (the Lower Bavarian) said, quoting Bereiter, and they all laughed. Typical Munich, typical Bavaria: even when it came to crime it had to be something exceptional.

Less amusing was the prospect that their matter might get stranded in the shadow of Bavarian exceptionality.

"Maybe we should go to Munich and sort it out ourselves," Louise said.

"Forget it," Bermann growled.

"Hmm."

"That's why Edison invented the telephone, fax machines and e-mail."

"And scanners and pdf files," Hoffmann added.

"Nobody's going anywhere," Bermann said.

Louise gave a dismissive wave. Men on the verge of revolt were immortal, unreasonable, unbearable. Of course she would drive to Munich if they didn't get any information in the next hour or two, a telephone call at the very least.

Bermann's eyes were still fixed on her and she returned his gaze calmly. It was a lengthy, grim stare that wasn't really aimed at her, but at life in general, the circumstances, Bob, the future that was forcing him to revolt – him, who had always been part of the system. But then Bermann smiled briefly and she sensed that he felt closer to her, closer than ever. Rolf Bermann had always been an integral element of Freiburg Kripo, one of the few really essential cogs. Now she suspected he felt hustled out to the margins, and margins were where Louise Bonì preferred to dwell.

She smiled back. Bermann gave a curt nod.

Then Wallmer told them about her conversation with a historian from the University of Freiburg about the Germans from Yugoslavia, which hadn't really been a conversation, more of a monologue, a confused, mumbled, largely incomprehensible monologue, but she did get some material, essays, résumés, books, and this afternoon or evening she was going to go through them in peace and tomorrow morning draft a report. There was only one thing she understood and could remember, which was that the Germans from Yugoslavia belonged to the so-called Danube Swabians, emigrants chiefly from the south of Germany who moved in their thousands to south-eastern Europe from the eighteenth century onwards, mostly on boats down the Danube, departing from Ulm. Hence these boats were called "Ulm Boxes".

Bermann grumbled that he didn't care what some eighteenth-century boats carrying whoever were called. Louise asked why the Danube Swabians went to south-east Europe back then. Bermann didn't care about this either. Wallmer said that unfortunately she hadn't understood this entirely, but she thought it was because the Austrian emperors had recruited settlers for these regions.

"Who gives a fuck?" Bermann said.

Everybody fell silent and stared at him, until Louise said, "That's quite enough of that." Bermann threw up his hands and said that even a section head was allowed to be in a bad mood from time to time, wasn't he?

"But not permanently," Louise replied gently.

For a while nobody spoke, then Hoffmann said with glee, "Dead famous, us Bavarians." Everyone laughed, even Bermann.

They all returned to their offices with another pile of photocopies and waited to hear back from Bereiter in Munich, from Lahr, where council employees were searching the database for individuals born in former Yugoslavia, for the results of the D.N.A. analyses, the forensics reports, and not least for some unlikely success in their manhunt. Louise dropped the pile of paper on her desk, then called the various numbers she had for Jenny Böhm. She discovered that Jenny's cold had got worse and spoke to two answerphones: Frau Böhm? Frau Bonì is getting properly worried now. A cold? A likely story.

Louise sat on the window sill and in the bright sunlight read everything that Hoffmann had managed to assemble the previous day. In the warmth she nodded off, dreaming of innumerable faceless figures stepping aboard wooden boats, disembarking in foreign cities, continuing their journeys on foot or in covered wagons and then, after days or weeks or years, arriving and settling down in a place called Valpovo. Valpovo, how beautiful it sounded, the first syllable short and soft, the second heavy, carrying the emphasis, Valpovo, it sounded so Italian and this was how she saw Valpovo in her dream, a bright Italian city beside a tranquil sea, lemon trees under a blue sky. She dreamed that one day she would journey to this city, board a wooden ship amongst innumerable faceless figures, set off and make her way to Valpovo, and in her dream it was a strange feeling, an inexplicable longing, but not for a place, only for its name, for the word "Valpovo", and when in her dream she stood in this place the longing turned to sadness, because she understood that you couldn't visit a word, that you could arrive in places, but never in words.

She woke up.

Valpovo 1945, the beginning perhaps.

The beginning of *one* story. Another may have begun much earlier, in the eighteenth century on a Danube boat in Ulm.

She washed her face and went to the window, her thoughts occupied by Paul Niemann and Munich, by the fact that so much information was missing and now they had to wait. In virtually every case there came a phase of waiting. Louise hated the hours or days when all you could do was wait, wait, wait, while somebody somewhere collated leads, and at some point would send over their results . . . or maybe not.

She picked up her bag, grabbed a bottle of water and thought, well, if not Valpovo, then Munich at least.

"You can't be serious," Hoffmann said, sitting in his chair with a red watering can and tending to the plants in the corner of his office.

"Between four and half past five. If it gets any later, I'll call."

"You cannot be serious."

Louise pointed to a yucca. "You're overflowing."

"For goodness' sake!" Hoffmann rolled over to the sink, rolled back with a cloth and wiped the floor using his foot. Holding the wet cloth in front of him, he returned to the sink. "What am I going to say to Rolf?"

"That I'm in Munich and I'll be back late this evening."

"You really can't be serious." Hoffmann rinsed the cloth, wrung it out and laid it carefully over the rim of the sink. Louise was struck by the considerable degree of neatness and care with which he approached this trivial task. Perhaps this was why he was such a good chief case officer. This was why all those important and unimportant details of a crime were in such good hands with him. "He said nobody was going to go to Munich."

"I heard that."

"And he's the boss."

"He's frustrated."

"And?"

"Frustrated bosses make the wrong decisions." A sombre smile appeared on Hoffmann's lips. Louise pointed at the yucca. "Still over-flowing."

"Goodness gracious!" The cleaning-up process was repeated. Now breathing heavily, Hoffmann rolled back to his desk.

"Will you call Munich now?" she said.

"Yes, yes, I'll call them."

She thanked him and left. As she wandered along the corridor of D11 she thought how strange it was that she was behind the revolt yet again.

Of course she was being serious. Instead of waiting, waiting, waiting, possibly until tomorrow or the day after, she was going to get what she needed – Bermann could scream and shout all he liked. She didn't bump into him on the way downstairs, nor did she see him in the courtyard. Maybe he was in Bob's office again, listening to his cold criticism and grumbling about a revolt and life on the margins. She thought how she'd love to tell him over a beer – beer for him, water for her – about life on the margins and how to cope there. She was an expert, after all. Louise grinned. Rolf Bermann on the margins – that wasn't right. With a wife, five children, his own house in the countryside, a 4x4 Daimler and an Audi for everyday use, he was a hopeless case as far as the margins were concerned.

As she sat in the car with U2 on the stereo Hoffmann called to confirm an appointment between 4 and 4.30 p.m. in Munich district council, department II: residency, sub-department 3: foreign citizens, room 1066 with Heidelinde Zach, and our Kripo colleague Bereiter will make it too if his celebrity murder case allows.

"Bet you anything he doesn't make it," Hoffmann said.

"Is that the impression you got?"

"Yes. Have you got a map?"

"I don't need one. I've got G.P.S."

"No, you don't."

"Oh, I thought it was integrated in the radio."

They laughed.

"I'll ask passers-by."

"In Munich? You won't understand a word they say, my dear. They speak Bavarian. That's if they answer you at all."

"Then I'll call you."

"Just what I was going to suggest. By the way, Illi's going to give you a buzz."

"Illi?"

Hoffmann sighed "Yes". Louise turned off Heinrich-von-Stepan-Strasse and onto the B31. Hoffmann kept talking. Bermann had rung Illi, your colleagues all say hi, your Croatia has cropped up again, give us a call, we need your help, that sort of thing. Louise shook her head, speechless with rage and a bad conscience. Thomas Ilic, a wonderful policeman, sometimes all he needed was someone to take decisions for him, and in one such moment back in summer 2003 he'd had the misfortune to end up with her.

"I'll kill him," she said.

"I was worried you'd say that," Hoffmann said and hung up.

13

With the autumn sun in her rear-view mirror, Bonì followed the B31, drove past the Flaunser and thought of Taro, the Japanese monk who had frozen to death up there in winter 2003. She drove past Kirchzarten and thought of the false Marcel and the marvellous village policeman Heinrich Täschle. She drove into the Höllental and thought that her memory was increasingly being filled with past cases and the people involved with them, as was her "love life". There was Richard Landen, who she had met in winter 2003 because of Taro, and now the real Marcel, who had only come into her life and her bed because the false Marcel had borrowed his name . . .

What did this mean?

Maybe just one thing, she thought, slightly depressed: that she met interesting people in her line of work.

When she got to Titisee-Neustadt she called Thomas Ilic, who in his own way was still entangled in the Marcel case too.

She tried not to cry, but without much success.

"Hey," Ilic said. "I'm better now. I'm in good shape."

"O.K."

"I'm alright. Really I am."

She sniffled. Words from that dreadful night in summer 2003. She didn't believe him back then and she didn't believe him now. Touch him or howl, she thought, and she couldn't touch him.

"Hey," Ilic said.

"It's O.K."

It had been too long since she'd last seen or spoken to Ilic, she thought. To begin with she'd visited him once a month, then less frequently. He had given the impression he wanted to be alone, didn't want any contact with his colleagues. Victims of crime and psychos went through trauma, but not police officers. Police officers helped, they were strong. Psychologically, at least, they were invulnerable. When you understood that this narrative didn't correspond with reality, it destroyed the very foundations of the profession. They didn't want to understand. Not even Thomas Ilic. Not even him, who was so different from Rolf Bermann and the other chauvinists and alpha males.

So she had visited less frequently.

One day his wife called. Don't come anymore, she said. Write him a card from time to time, from holiday and at Christmas. Call occasionally. But don't come anymore. It's not doing him any good.

So she'd stopped coming.

"What's all this about Croatia, Louise?"

"Only if you promise me."

"I promise."

"Good."

They laughed.

"Come on, then, Croatia," Ilic said.

"I want to hear it, Illi. What you're promising me."

Ilic sighed. "I'll only phone. I won't come to H.Q. and I won't meet anybody. I won't step into any clearings or climb up any mountains. Only phone."

She nodded. The clearing in Glottertal, where Ilic should have closed his eyes. The Rappeneck, which she should never have made him climb.

"Right, then," Ilic said. "Croatia."

Louise told him the story from the beginning and Ilic knew nothing, which almost brought her to tears again. Illi, who'd always known everything, even if he'd had to check his folder with all the documents and the blue writing . . .

She swallowed the tears.

A man in the Niemanns' garden on Saturday afternoon, then at the garden door, a pistol in his hand. That night he roamed the house which in some way was *his* house, threatened Paul Niemann and issued an ultimatum. Leave in seven days, otherwise . . .

"Otherwise?"

"Wait."

Two days later she caught sight of the man in a field in Merzhausen. He ran away and disappeared into the sewer system because he'd prepared for contingencies. The following night he broke into the house again, doused the floors and walls with petrol, woke the Niemanns, then vanished again and from the Schönberg watched the house, which in some way was *his* house, burn to its foundations.

That was the "otherwise".

"The fire in Merzhausen. Perhaps you saw it on the news."

"No," Ilic said. No news, no papers since summer 2003. "But not because of *that*."

"No."

"Really not. It just doesn't interest me anymore. All the political hot air."

A moment's silence.

Then Louise continued. A man who spoke broken German as if he'd learned it a long time ago, but hadn't used it in ages, Niemann had said, an ethnic German. An old warrior, he'd said, and that seemed to fit. He was quite openly waging a war, but they didn't know what sort of war it was, who he was waging it against and why. They did, however, know now that Niemann had worked for the foreigners' registration office in Munich and had sent Bosnian refugees from the civil war back to their country when the war was over. Maybe it was about *that* war. And maybe it was about the Germans from Yugoslavia.

"But what's that got to do with Croatia?"

"Oh yes, I forgot that part." She told him about Lahr, Friedrich and the cigarette case, about Valpovo 1945. Valpovo in Slavonia in Croatia.

"*Val*povo," Ilic corrected her.

She nodded, disappointed. It no longer sounded Italian, but unfamiliar, the first syllable heavy and dark, then two short, barely audible ones. No bright Italian city with lemon trees beneath a blue sky, but something different, unknown, for which there were no pictures in her head. "*Val*povo," she repeated obediently.

"Yes, we put the emphasis differently."

"On the first syllable."

"For instance."

"Have you ever been there? To Valpovo?"

"No, but nearby, in Osijek. I had an uncle in Osijek."

Osijek, she thought and remembered having read something in Hoffmann's documents about a town called Essegg. If Valpovo had a German name, then maybe Osijek did too.

"Valpovo," Louise said in the Italian way, before reluctantly correcting herself. "*Val*povo has a German name too: Walpach."

"I see."

"Where is it? Valpovo, Osijek, Slavonia?"

"Between the Sava and the Drava."

She sighed impatiently. "Illi . . ."

Ilic laughed. "Between Hungary in the north and Bosnia and Herzegovina in the south. A long way from the coast, from the tourists." Lots of arable farming, not much industry, he said. Beautiful churches and cathedrals, a comfortable small-town life where everything proceeded at a more leisurely pace than in Zagreb and on the coast – progress included – but they were almost on a par with the rest of central Europe. It was a lovely place, peaceful, rural, and Osijek, a good one hundred thousand inhabitants, lots of cafés, students and in a gorgeous position on the Drava. Ten years ago the Serbs had stood on the other side of the Drava, fired across the river and mined the forests. There it is again, Louise thought, the war that all this might be about, the war from which the old warrior had fled to Munich, maybe to the homeland of his ancestors . . . But these were just hunches; they didn't know any of this for sure.

Yes, she thought, a case that gave her many hunches, as if there were mysterious connections, as if she were involved in some way.

Which was utter nonsense, of course.

Ilic was still talking, talking about the war, the war in Vukovar, which must be somewhere down there too, in the country between the Sava and the Drava; no, it was on the Danube and on the other side of the river lay Serbia. Vukovar, he said, the Croatian city that suffered the worst devastation during the war, 90 per cent, just imagine that, and do you know what they bombarded first? The cathedral, the water tower and the hospital. She nodded, she didn't want to hear these stories, stories of Serbs and Croats, at least not from Thomas Ilic, who in summer 2003 had said something she would never forget: Sometimes you're a German, sometimes not.

She interrupted him to ask about the Germans from Yugoslavia, the Danube Swabians. Ilic said he'd heard of them, but didn't know any details. Did he know that thousands of them had settled in the Danube Basin? No, he didn't know that. But yes, he knew Croats who had German ancestors, they called them "Švabi", "Swabians", a name that was sometimes used kindly and sometimes unkindly. There was a type of beetle they also called "Švabi", "buba švaba", and that too could be intended kindly or unkindly, depending on one's point of view.

Perhaps the beetle liked it.

Ilic gave an apologetic laugh.

Then he wanted to know how things were at H.Q., with Anselm Löbinger as head of Division One, with Bermann who was still "only" section head, with Bob, plus who was new and who had left. She told him bits and pieces, all the while trying not to forget what Ilic had told her about Slavonia. Impulsively she said, "Do you know what I miss most of all. Your folder. Now I have to write down everything or remember it myself, and I'm not cut out for either." Ilic laughed again, then fell silent, and it occurred to her that she shouldn't have mentioned the folder.

"Can I come and visit you?"

"I don't know."

"You don't know if I can?" She laughed.

Ilic didn't laugh. "I don't know if it's a good idea."

"How about calling?"

"Calling, sure, yes."

"And postcards from holiday?"

"Since when do you go on holiday?"

Now both of them were laughing.

"Think about your promise."

"I am thinking about it."

She paused. "Why do I get the impression you're not being serious?"

"I don't know," Ilic said and hung up.

Only some of the Danube Swabians had actually come from Swabia, Louise thought, but somehow the name had stuck. A German story, a European story she had been unaware of, and yet it was part of German and European history, maybe even the present too – who could tell?

In the eighteenth century tens of thousands of married couples and families, predominantly from Swabia, Bavaria, Franconia, Hessen, Westphalia, Lorraine and the Palatinate, embarked in Ulm in search of a better, freer, simpler or more peaceful future in south-eastern Europe, invited by the Habsburgs Charles VI, Maria Theresia and Joseph II. For their part, these rulers had been thinking about

Austria's future. Following the Turkish Wars they were intent on reset-tling the severely depopulated Pannonian Basin on both sides of the Danube, primarily for economic reasons, but also to afford their borders better protection. In three major "Swabian treks" and many smaller ones, the emigrants journeyed on the Danube to Budapest via Vienna, then southwards, eastwards or northwards on land, settling on the plots of unfamiliar soil that had been alloted to them, especially in Swabian Turkey, the Banat, the Bačka and later Slavonia, foreigners in a patchwork of peoples, languages and traditions, comprising Hungarians, Serbs, Croats, Muslims, Romanians, Albanians, Roma, Jews and others.

Bonì wondered whether the emigrants had also gone to live in Valpovo at some point and then, in the 1940s, died there of hunger, exhaustion and the cold, as Waldemar Kaufmann had said. No, of course it wasn't a bright Italian city of lemon trees, but a city of suffer-ing and death, perhaps.

A city of pain.

Hoffmann rang when she was close to Munich. Forensics had sent in their reports, or, more accurately, partial reports. Nothing new, but they did provide objective confirmation. The footprints in the flower-bed by the Niemanns' terrace were identical to those in the field when he'd run away and those on the slope of the Schönberg. The fingerprints in the house and sewer shaft were identical. On the sofa in the television room that no longer existed, Steinle and Lubowitz had found fibres from dark-blue corduroy trousers, and from the floor they'd recovered crumbs of soil, grains of sand, bits of grass that were identical to comparable particles in the footprints. The man in the garden was the man in the sewer and the man in the Niemanns' house and the man on the Schönberg. Important for the public prosecutor and the judge. Nothing new, just objective confirmation. And obviously it told them nothing about what the old warrior was planning, about the pain that might lie behind it all or about the Germans from Yugoslavia. For that they needed as much additional information as possible.

And hunches.

As she drove through Munich in the afternoon twilight it struck her that it didn't look so different here, just bigger and the roads were longer, they never ended. One was called Verdistrasse, another Arnulfstrasse and that one really did just keep going, all the way to the main train station. She got lost, asked someone, got an answer, saw nothing but Turkish people and Turkish shops for several streets, got lost again, asked again, drove down Lindwurmstrasse – another of those long roads – and couldn't find a space so she parked illegally. At half past four she was outside the district council office.

Hans Bereiter, the celeb murder investigator, had come along after all. He was leaning against the glass porch, tall and slim with a man bun, bags under his half-closed eyes, utterly exhausted, lost in a reverie. As they shook hands he suppressed a yawn. "Pardon me," he said in High German with his deep, smoker's voice. "I've been on my feet for forty-eight hours." She nodded, well familiar with the experience. They reported to reception and went down a narrow, windowless, corridor into a labyrinth of more empty corridors and empty staff-rooms. Bereiter smelled of cigarettes, coffee, doner kebab, sweat and adrenaline – Louise was familiar with this too.

No differences, only the longer roads.

Hoffmann had done well; Bereiter was up to speed on the essentials. He seemed uninterested in details, but perhaps he was just too tired. At any rate he didn't ask. Somewhere deep inside the labyrinth he knocked at a door and a woman called out, "Come in!" At a desk sat a stout blonde woman in her mid-fifties: Heidelinde Zach, head of sub-department 31, pen in her right hand, cup of coffee in her left, her body squeezed into a yellow dress with green trees, leaves and birds.

"*Servus*, Heidi," Bereiter said.

"*Servus*, Hans."

Louise grinned. There it was, that teeny-weeny difference.

"Paul . . . He didn't get on here at all, you know?" Unlike Bereiter, Heidelinde Zach spoke dialect, a soft, confident, vernacular Bavarian, sometimes comprehensible, sometimes less so.

"You remember him."

"Of course I do."

"He was only here for a couple of months."

"It was such a difficult time, you know? You wouldn't forget anyone."

At the time Heidelinde Zach had been deputy head of the department and also responsible for Untersbergstrasse. The stress had made all the staff rally together. You remembered everyone, even if they were only there for a couple of months. More than 20,000 war refugees, more than 18,000 repatriation decisions, a separate department consisting of ten staff to begin with, then forty-five, the confrontation with a not-too-distant war and horrendous personal stories, external pressure, especially from the conference of German interior ministers who were urgently pressing for as many people to be repatriated as soon as possible, the frequent changes in legal parameters, the frequently counter-productive reporting of the press – years which nobody who was there would forget in a hurry, and you couldn't hold it against anyone for not being able to deal with it.

"Like Paul Niemann."

Heidelinde Zach nodded.

"What was wrong with him, exactly?"

"You can never say for sure with men." Heidelinde bent forwards and smiled at Bereiter. "Us women have nervous breakdowns, while men get backache or sudden hearing loss or a cough."

"Or they beat their wives," Bereiter said.

"That too."

"What about Paul Niemann?"

"Pneumonia. He was on his back for three months, you know? In high summer." Heidelinde shrugged and leaned back.

"Were you informed about the cases he processed?"

"Only if there were problems."

"Were there problems?"

"Not any unusual ones, at any rate none that I remember. But haven't you asked him yourself?"

"He's not being desperately cooperative."

"Oh yes, he's a quiet one, our Paul. I was convinced he would come back to Munich. He never wanted to leave here in the first place, you know? His wife was the one who wanted to go."

"Yes."

"And now someone burns his house down." Heidelinde Zach had been informed too, she knew the essentials. A former colleague, a former war refugee. The break-in, the threat, the fire. She nodded grimly and everything about her wobbled: cheeks, chin, breasts, tummy, while the pen in her hand clicked against the desktop. It was bound to happen, she said, even then the circumstances had been difficult, the boundaries between staff members and refugees were often crossed. Outbreaks of rage, despair, threats, tears, tales of rape, murder, war, a lost home, traumatised children – all of it was horribly personal and intimate, you couldn't forget it, you couldn't forget any of these stories. Staff were rung at home, sometimes they found refugees outside their front doors first thing in the morning . . .

But, so far as she knew, not Paul.

Yes, it was a difficult time for everybody. Each staff member had to deal with 160 cases per day, the council building heaving with people, numbered tickets exchanged hands for money in the cafeteria. Political chaos. All the litigation, the opposition proceedings, summary proceedings, legal decisions. Greedy lawyers who earned fortunes. And not least the injustices – nurses and doctors were given leave to remain because of staffing shortages in the healthcare system here. The others had to go if they weren't covered by the right to remain ruling, which was in any case introduced far too late. If they refused, usually the father was arrested, while the family was collected and deported with only hand luggage. Whatever they left behind in the way of possessions or furniture was sent to Bosnia with the next transport.

That's how it was in the years after Dayton.

Louise enquired about the procedures involving refugees of German descent. Heidelinde replied that they were dealt with by the citizenship office. Anybody already here had to leave Germany again first, because residency applications from individuals of German descent could only be submitted from abroad.

"Did you have cases like this?"

"A few. But only a few, you know? And I can't remember whether Paul ever had one." Heidelinde stood up and adjusted her dress at the shoulders. "Come with me, you've got a lot to get through."

"Dinner in the Hofbräuhaus?" Bereiter asked.

Louise smiled. "Dinner in Freiburg."

"No way," Heidelinde Zach said.

More empty corridors and empty staffrooms, perhaps the same ones, perhaps different ones; Louise had lost her sense of direction. Then they took the lift down and for some moments the only sounds apart from their descent were Heidelinde's sniffling and a metallic clicking – she had brought the pen with her and was tapping it against the wall. The longer they were inside the lift the more clearly Louise could detect a strange smell – it was actually like being in a forest, as if Heidelinde's dress were giving off the fragrance of trees, lush leaves, pine needles and moss.

In the basement they wandered down more corridors before finally arriving at the archive. Twenty-three kilometres of shelves, Heidelinde said with a mixture of pride and tedium. She showed Louise into a small room with a desk, chair and dozens of cardboard boxes containing hundreds of files. Since Bereiter called that morning two members of staff had been searching through the twenty-three kilometres. As most of the files were ordered alphabetically by name, they had used the electronic database to sort them first by country of origin, Croatia and Bosnia–Herzegovina, then by repatriation date: between May 1998, when Niemann started at Untersbergstrasse, and the end of 1999, when repatriation was concluded after all legal possibilities had been exhausted.

"Someone's taken a lot of care over this," Louise said.

Tapping the pen against her chest, Heidelinde smiled and for a moment her soft face looked beautifully maternal. "If he's in here we'll find him." She pointed at the cardboard boxes. "You can make a start on these."

"Make a start?"

"There are more to come."

"More to come?"

Heidelinde smiled again, a sunny face in whose warmth Louise wanted to bask for days, weeks, months.

"Dinner at the Hofbräuhaus," Heidelinde said, "and breakfast in the district council building. How do you like your coffee?"

"With milk and sugar."

"Anything to eat?"

"A croissant, if that's possible."

"You eat croissants? Seeing how thin you are I thought you'd only eat vegetables."

"I get shot a couple of times a year, the recuperation keeps the weight down."

Heidelinde hesitated before opening her mouth and laughing, a magnificent, heartfelt, thunderous laugh that must have filled the empty corridors and empty staffrooms right up to the roof with joy and love, and seemed to resonate in the walls long after she had gone.

Now Louise sat alone, in awe of the towering cardboard boxes, and made an approximate count of the number of files. After two hundred and thirty she continued more roughly in fifties. There must be around eight hundred here in total, and there were more to come. For ten minutes she wondered whether it might be possible to purposefully break the symmetry of the alphabetically ordered files by means of an asymmetrical search. In the end, however, luck seemed as good a solution as any, so she closed her eyes, picked one of the boxes at random, took off the lid and stared at a photograph attached to a personal information form, the dark face of an elderly lady from Tuzla. Slowly it dawned on her: photographs! She hadn't dared hope for these.

At around six o'clock a young man with walking difficulties came in pushing a trolley with more boxes. She helped him unload, went to the loo, and returned to her cubbyhole to continue with the search. At seven Heidelinde appeared with a glass of water and promised to pick her up half an hour later for the Hofbräuhaus. Louise gulped down the water and asked, why the Hofbräuhaus, do you lot really think that everyone who's not from Munich wants to go to the Hofbräuhaus?

"Don't you want to?"

"Certainly not."

"We'll try somewhere else, then."

"If I find him before . . ." Louise began, but Heidelinde raised her hand wielding the pen that she never seemed to put down, waggled her index finger and said, "It doesn't matter. People need to eat, you know? Even Freiburgers, and if they don't want to eat then they can just sit there and watch others eat."

They laughed and Louise agreed, thinking of the sunny face. A spot of sunshine in the evening was no bad thing.

Moments later she found the old warrior.

She'd already put to one side around a dozen men, possible candidates given their appearance and age, when suddenly she came across his photograph. Taken in a photo booth, lit by flash, it showed a vivid face, very different from Niemann's image, but she didn't have the slightest doubt – ice-grey hair, gnarled, weatherbeaten. The eyes were slightly lowered, the cheeks looked tense, almost as if the pain that must have troubled this man was already visible then, in the early nineties, here in Munich.

She leaned back and felt a tingling in her belly.

They had him.

Antun Lončar, born 2/11/1942 in Štrpci, nationality "Bosna i Hercegovina", resident in Štrpci, married since 18/5/1979 to – she turned over the form – Biljana. Entered Germany on 30/11/1993, living in Munich, Tegernseer Landstrasse. On the back, almost illegibly, had been scrawled "War in Bosnia" in response to the purpose of his stay.

Welfare needed? Yes. Criminal record? No.

Then followed information on Biljana, also from Štrpci, "Bosna i Hercegovina", considerably younger than her husband – born in 1959 – and their daughter, Snježana, born in 1982 in Štrpci.

Antun Lončar's signature consisted of small, neatly written letters, very different from the signatures on the other forms Louise had looked at. As if everybody reading it should be able to decipher his name at first glance.

She turned over and examined the photograph. The eyes slightly lowered, the tense cheeks. This didn't necessarily mean anything – of course you were going to feel tense in the foreigners' registration office of a foreign country.

Antun Lončar.

Another very foreign name, like Valpovo when it was pronounced correctly. A name she had no associations with.

Apart from the personal form, his file contained correspondence between the authorities and Lončar or his lawyer, an exit certification and an eleven-page stapled document, entitled "Enforcement of the Aliens Act; rejection of residence permit to the Bosnian national Antun Lončar, born 2/11/1942 in Štrpci".

Under point 2, stamped at a slight angle, stood the date by which Lončar had to leave Germany: 01 09 1998.

Right at the top, under "Administrator", was written Paul Niemann.

Yes, they had him.

She was already at the door, Antun Lončar's file under her arm, when it struck her that Biljana and Snježana must have their own files too.

She found them in the same box, of course, the very next files: Lončar, Biljana and Lončar, Snježana. Like Antun, both had photographs, taken with flash and with all the overpowering intensity of photo-booth pictures, as if the aim was to hold up these faces and people to ridicule.

Biljana, the mother, had a soft, narrow face, whereas Snježana resembled her father, with the same intense expression; eyes lowered, cheeks tense, she looked severe and aloof.

In her features, too, Louise thought, there was an invisible pain. In 1993, when the photograph was taken and the application submitted, she would have been eleven years old, which meant she must have lived through the first phase of the Bosnian War. A child in war, then in flight. A child in a foreign land, in which like so many refugee children she had sooner or later felt at home – she must have gone to school in Munich, made friends, fallen in love for the first time.

Then, in 1998, this child had been allowed to finish the school year, before being deported at the end of the summer holidays – a trip from which she'd never returned.

In Heidelinde Zach's office she faxed the documents to Hoffmann and looked up the number of the lawyer, Dr Georg Thomas Seidl. He was one of the unscrupulous ones who made a killing, Heidelinde said, his name could be found in every second refugee file. He'd specialised in wars and refugees and made a fortune, I must say. She bent over and scornfully spat air onto the floor. Louise had already taken out her mobile, but then decided against calling him, it would be too precarious, she should go via the public prosecutor, no mistakes now, Bonì, don't break any rules, certainly not when it came to an unscrupulous lawyer.

While Heidelinde was shutting down the computer and clearing her desk, Louise thought of a question that had been on her mind since she'd come across Antun Lončar's form in the basement. Niemann had looked at this form and presumably the photograph too, so how had he not even vaguely recognised the face when Lončar appeared on his terrace? When he saw the picture on his digital camera?

One face among hundreds, obviously, and a difficult time for the administrators as well, the stress, the frequent changes in the legal parameters. All the same, these were faces that represented difficult stories, and hadn't Heidelinde said that you couldn't forget any of these stories?

She recalled her first conversation with Niemann, when they talked about the Russian-Germans he'd dealt with in the council. He had said how he remembered many of the people he'd come face to face with, he could picture as if it were yesterday the old men with their flat caps and wrinkled faces, the elderly women with colourful headscarves and crocheted coats, and the young people in dark, shiny sportswear. People who thought they had returned to an ancient homeland, but once there were regarded as mere foreigners, not even E.U. foreigners, no . . . they were "Russians".

She remembered that Niemann had said he felt sorry for these people. Had he not felt sorry for Antun Lončar? Why had he forgotten his face? Had he suppressed the memory? Because of Munich? Because Munich mustn't be associated with this man who had burst into his life like the worst possible nightmare?

As Louise helped Heidelinde into a flowery wrap-like coat, she thought of Paul Niemann who hadn't been able to cope. Who had fallen sick after a couple of months, because it had been his job to send people from their new homeland back to their old one.

They stepped into the corridor and Heidelinde switched off the light. Louise stared into the dark room and then it dawned on her.

Perhaps Niemann had lacked the strength to look at the photographs on the forms.

They went out to eat without Hans Bereiter, who had cancelled because he had to question a new witness in the murder case. Heidelinde directed Louise up Lindwurmstrasse, a few minutes later they were on the endlessly long Nymphenburgerstrasse, and eventually they turned off. "Over there," Heidelinde said, pointing to an Italian restaurant, which glowed a warm yellow in the Munich night. The small terrace behind a wall and bushes was full of people and Louise thought, this is just like Freiburg, sitting outside at the end of October. But maybe three or four hours weren't enough to register the subtle differences.

"And now comes the nice part of our day, you know?" Heidelinde said as they parked a few streets up from the restaurant. "Pasta with red wine, or do you prefer white?"

They got out. Louise linked arms with the flowery coat and forest dress, holding on to a warm, padded forearm. Somehow she felt it was time to talk again. And what could be better than a balmy October evening in a city she didn't know, with a chance acquaintaince she'd only just met . . .

"Let's talk woman to woman, Heidi," she said.

Vegetable rigatoni with litres of water, followed by two espressos and lots of talking. Two short, friendly Italians scooted from table to table, a man and a woman who were clearly the owners, joking, laughing, sweating, while once again Louise attempted to dress up in words what was so difficult to explain to someone who didn't have the same problem.

Especially as she was still trying the words out a year and a half later.

To begin with she had lied – *I can't take alcohol / I don't like alcohol / I don't like red wine / I don't like beer / I want to have a clear head.*

Then she no longer wanted to hide, having spent years hiding her addiction, just as Jenny Böhm was doing again now. And so: *I drank / I drank too much / I needed alcohol to feel good, if you know what I mean?*

For those she wanted to shock: *I was a pisshead.*

Her favourite psychologist, Katrin Rein, had suggested "alcohol problem", "you had an alcohol problem", but her experience of this term wasn't positive, not as far as she was concerned, but with regard to the term itself. "Alcohol problem" was depressing, it sounded so unsolvable, even when used with the past tense, a term that had got stuck in its three "O"s and could never free itself. It didn't reflect the present, her physical and psychological status quo, which she was largely satisfied with. She had a problem that had been solved, not one that had got stuck, and she deserved kinder terms than that.

In this phase of trying out words she usually prefaced her story by saying, *I don't drink, I used to be dependent, but that's all in the past now.*

"Oh!" Heidelinde exclaimed while they were still in the street and briefly the flowers and forest froze.

They stood there for several seconds, halfway between the car and the Italian restaurant, before Louise added, "You know?"

"You know!" Heidelinde repeated, then burst out laughing, and before they were at their table she already knew half the story.

Louise set off around 10 p.m., leaving the large, dark city of Munich, which didn't appear to be so different from the smaller, distant city of Freiburg, not in the first few hours at least. On the passenger seat were copies of the Lončar family files, on top Antun Lončar's personal form with the photograph Niemann perhaps hadn't looked at, just as he perhaps hadn't looked at any of the other photos of people he'd had to send back to their destroyed homeland. She managed to keep these questions at bay as far as Augsburg and preserve the evening's sunshine, but then Heidelinde's smiling face faded along with the pleasant memory of an intimate conversation, woman to woman, and the questions burst forth, one in particular, which seemed to grow in importance with every kilometre:

Where were Biljana and Snježana Lončar?

She arrived in Freiburg at around 2 a.m. On the ground floor she stopped where the stairwell used to be and gazed up at the stars. Then, in the darkness, she climbed the metal scaffolding to the metal platform that led to her metal door. Halfway along the platform she stopped in horror. All of a sudden she knew she wasn't alone, that someone was here, staring at her from the darkness. Then she heard breathing and grabbed the pistol from her bag. Bonì noticed a figure sitting by her door, saw movement, a shimmer of blonde hair, a white hand pointing at her . . . she raised her pistol before finally realising who was sitting there, waiting for her in the Freiburg night, hiding from her own children and the whole world.

14

"You should have done it."
     "You're insane."
"If only you'd—"
"Shut up, Jenny."

Jenny Böhm laughed softly. "I thought you were going to. I was hoping you would. You almost did, didn't you?"

Louise said nothing. They were standing in her sitting room, both holding on tight to something, Louise to the kitchen counter and Jenny to the armrest of the sofa. Three metres between them and Louise could still smell the alcohol.

"Policewoman shoots pastor," Jenny said.

Louise nodded and rubbed her aching tummy. Just a few seconds, no more, a few seconds and two lives would have been destroyed.

On the scaffolding in the darkness she had been thinking of Antun Lončar. Had pictured his face in the photograph.

No hunches this time, just fear.

Then she'd seen the white hand and recalled that Monday morning in Jenny Böhm's kitchen.

"Have you got anything on you?"

"What?"

"Anything to drink."

"No."

"Don't lie to me for Christ's sake."

"No."

"You're lying, Jenny."

Jenny moaned and pointed feebly behind her. Somewhere outside on the scaffolding, where only moments ago they'd come within a whisker of disaster. She would go out and smash the bottle just as soon as her strength returned.

"Hiding and lying," she said. "Like in the past."

Jenny laughed sadly. She didn't appear drunk, probably she wasn't. But she spoke more slowly than usual, no doubt trying to articulate her words. She knew the dangers. She had got to that point again, where hiding and disguising were automatic.

Where drinking was automatic.

"Does your husband know where you are?"

"No."

"He'll be getting worried."

"Hardly."

"Of course he'll be worried."

"He keeps a diary. A diary of mistakes. *My* mistakes. Fourth of October, 8 a.m., J stinks of booze. Fourth of October, 4 p.m., J is sitting on the sofa and can't get up. That sort of diary. I've seen it, his shitty diary."

"For therapy?"

"For his lawyer."

Tears ran down Jenny's cheeks. Louise heard her gulp. The man who found change threatening was preparing for divorce.

"Show it to me," Jenny whispered suddenly.

Louise froze.

"Is it there, in your bag?"

"Get stuffed!"

"I just want to see it. Not touch."

Louise reached for her bag, felt inside, removed the magazine from the Heckler and Koch and slipped it into her trouser pocket. "One more word, Jenny, and you'll be sleeping on the street tonight."

"So strict and self-righteous, Louise—"

"Take a look at yourself first, Jenny, then you can go accusing me of being strict and self-righteous."

Jenny said nothing, just nodded mechanically. Then she lowered her eyes, splayed her trembling fingers and stared at them, as if her fingers could confirm what Louise had said.

"I'm sorry, Jenny, I . . . Look at me. Look at me, Jenny."

Jenny looked up. The tears were streaming, her mouth was open.

"I'm sorry, O.K.?"

Another mechanical nod, no words, then Jenny raised her trembling hands and pressed them to her cheeks.

"I'm in shock, for God's sake," Louise said. "A few more seconds and I'd . . ."

Jenny slid to the floor and began to laugh and cry. "If only you had, dammit!"

When Jenny no longer had the strength to laugh and cry, Louise took her into the bathroom, undressed her and manoeuvred her into the shower. Jenny cowered on the floor of the shower, a small, trembling heap of misery, resigned to her fate. Her fate came in the form of ice-cold water, as much and as powerfully as the old system allowed.

Jenny screamed.

After a couple of minutes Louise took pity and turned off the tap. "Come on," she said, grabbing a towel.

Jenny just sat there shivering, her hair stuck to her body.

"Come on, Jenny."

Jenny covered her face with her hands and said something incomprehensible. She didn't stop speaking and sobbing, speaking and sobbing simultaneously, one word as unintelligible as the next, but her hands stayed where they were, as if she were trying to efface her words immediately. Louise squeezed into the shower, laid the towel around Jenny's shoulders and pulled the pastor towards her. When the sobbing finally subsided, she said, "I didn't get any of that, Jenny."

The hands opened a fraction. "I was there."

"Where?"

"At the meeting yesterday."

Louise nodded. She'd thought about it on Monday, then forgotten it again.

"I thought you were coming. You said you were coming."

"I know."

"But you didn't."

"I forgot. I've got too much on at the moment, Jenny, I simply forgot." She didn't say that she wouldn't have gone anyway.

Jenny turned to look at Louise. Tears, snot and water on her face, hollow despair in her eyes.

Louise wiped her face with a corner of the towel. "I'm sorry, O.K.?"

"That man with the psalm?"

Louise nodded. The man with the psalm who on Monday, when she'd told Jenny about him, had merely been an intruder, but soon afterwards had become an arsonist.

Who now had a name and a face.

"Did he come back?"

"Yes."

"And do something worse?"

"He burned a house down."

"Burned a house down!"

"Come on, Jenny, stand up."

She helped Jenny to her feet and started to dry her. Mother and child in the bathroom, she thought, very close. With one hand she held the towel around the narrow shoulders, with the other she gently rubbed Jenny's back.

"I was going to find out about the psalm, but I couldn't." Jenny slumped against Louise and rested her head on her arm.

"It's fine, it doesn't matter."

"I don't want anything more to do with it."

"With the Bible?"

"The Church."

"I can understand that."

"I really was going to find out, but I couldn't."

"It's fine."

On Monday, after Louise left, Jenny had started drinking and that night hid in the cemetery, among the dead who offered peace and mercy. On Tuesday she drank again, argued with her husband and children and the parish office secretary, went that evening to the A.A. meeting and then back to the cemetery, where suddenly she realised that she was disturbing the peace and quiet of the dead, who had a right to peace and quiet, and she was ruining this peace and quiet and silence—

"Rubbish," Louise said.

Jenny laughed and leaned into Louise. She said she loved that word, the way Louise pronounced it, more closed and impatient than when others said it, when Louise said "rubbish" then you knew it really was rubbish, whatever it was.

"But it *is* rubbish."

Jenny just shrugged, leaned her head against Louise's cheek and leaned backwards into her arms to be hugged, naked and wet as she was. Mother and child in the mirror, more like two sad women now, Louise thought, her left arm between Jenny's breasts, warm skin on cold skin, and somewhere, barely discernible, the rapid beating of her heart.

"But today I drank less."

"Good."

Jenny nodded. "A good sign, don't you think?"

"Yes."

"But now I want a drink."

"I know."

"I really want one."

"You just need to go outside to your bottle."

"You wouldn't let me in again."

"Of course I wouldn't."

"Strict Louise. Strong, strict, self-righteous Louise." Jenny smiled. She closed her eyes and Louise looked at her in the mirror, Jenny Böhm, late thirties, so dainty and beautiful, long, blonde hair, sensuous eyebrows, her eyes large and gleaming when open, now there was a touch of tiredness in this fine-looking face that would forever remain young. Beside Jenny, Louise, her dark hair up in a bun but coming loose, dark landscapes beneath her eyes, crows' feet she hadn't even seen before, an exhausted, overstrained face. Which one looked ill? Which one looked like a piss artist?

She really didn't have the time or energy for this sort of thing. For crises in the night, for a confusing private life.

For people like Jenny Böhm.

She shook her head in disgust at herself.

Jenny opened her eyes. "They're too big, aren't they?"

"What are?"

"My boobs."

"No, they're not."

"A pastor ought to have smaller ones."

"Rubbish."

Jenny giggled. "They all stare at my boobs. All the men."

Louise said nothing. Even Mick, if she remembered rightly, had stared at Jenny's boobs all those years ago during a christening in the little red church. Pretty pastor, he'd muttered, what a pair of *tits* she's got!

But maybe she'd just got used to putting all those dumb things men say into Mick's mouth.

"Then I imagine them undressing me," Jenny said, "and I'm sad when they don't."

"Then you feel ashamed."

"And then I drink."

"That's too simplistic, Jenny."

"I want them to fuck me and that's why I drink."

"Way too simplistic."

"Ever since I became a pastor I've wanted them to fuck me. From the front, from behind, everywhere. Up the arse, Louise." Jenny's voice had become quiet and throaty, her cheeks were red. Louise saw herself shrug in the mirror. Her eyes met Jenny's. She'd already heard this in Oberberg, Jenny Böhm and her fantasies. Jenny Böhm who couldn't stop thinking about sex and drank because she felt ashamed, and because when she was drunk she didn't think about sex.

But as an explanation it was too simplistic.

Surely the question to ask was why Jenny had become a pastor. That was the problem. Not the sex.

Perhaps she was trying to use sex to solve the problem.

Then, from one moment to the next, Jenny fell asleep, naked and flushed in Louise's arms. Louise woke her and half-carried her into the bedroom, manoeuvred limp arms and legs into pyjamas and dropped her onto the bed. There had to be some payback for crises in the night. Jenny opened her eyes, frowned and fell asleep again. Louise put on a dry T-shirt and lay beside her. When she realised there was no way she would fall asleep now, she got up.

On the kitchen counter were the photocopies from Munich, the photograph of the face she'd pictured in her mind on the metal platform in the darkness. Antun Lončar, who might be somewhere close by – in Freiburg, Merzhausen or Au – or perhaps had gone back to Bosnia–Herzegovina.

She stared at the face.

Here they were again, her hunches. No, they said, he hadn't gone back, he was still here. To exact revenge on the man who sent him away from Germany in 1998. He had robbed this man of his security, then of his home.

In the end he would take his life.

*

On the sofa she read the Munich documents a second and third time. At some point she dozed off, at some point she woke up. It was the middle of the night; the digital display on her video recorder said 03:43. She lay on her side, her legs tucked up, in a chaos of documents. Again she had dreamed of faceless figures, sailing down a river on wooden boats. This time Valpovo was a country and this is where the figures settled, in the country called Valpovo between the Sava and the Drava. She couldn't remember if she'd featured in the dream herself, but she wanted to. For a brief moment she felt bizarrely pained by the idea that she wasn't amongst these figures, hadn't arrived in the country called Valpovo with them. She looked along the arm supporting her head and bent her fingers inwards, one for each year in Freiburg, from left to right, then again from right to left, ten years without interruption. Prior to that a few years *with* interruptions.

It was extraordinary what a word could unleash, this strange word "Valpovo". And now ten years in the same city plus a few more felt like far too long, and she wished she had left Freiburg so she could have come back at some point later, rather than still feeling the need to get away.

She smiled crookedly and sat up.

As if she *had* to get away. From the city she loved.

Her father and mother had always wanted to go away, one to here, the other to there; perhaps that was why it had never occurred to her to quit Freiburg for any length of time.

She checked on Jenny, who was lying on her stomach, sleeping silently. Crises in the night, she remembered them well. The disease and the crises, they came in a twin pack – that was the worst.

The shame, the loneliness.

The dreadful loneliness when you'd started to hide and to lie.

Then you drank to stop feeling lonely.

She felt that, in her own way, Jenny had begun to fight again. She was here with Louise, not on her own surrounded by darkness and the dead. No, she had sought protection in the strictness and self-righteousness of Louise Bonì, and surely only those who were willing to fight would come here of their own accord. It wouldn't be much fun otherwise.

She was sleeping, another good sign.

And she hadn't gone out onto the scaffolding where she'd hidden the bottle. Where she herself had been just a few seconds from . . .

As Louise went back into the sitting room she wondered what it was about the scaffolding, apart from those few seconds. Marcel serenely drank his glass of red wine outside, then it was the Upper Silesians and their beer, now it was Jenny and her bottle, and anybody coming to see her had to go via the scaffolding that clung to three sides of her block like a clamp.

She made herself comfortable on the sofa again with Hoffmann's photocopies on the history of the Danube Swabians. The first found death, the second found hardship, the third found bread, she read. It took generations before the immigrants from Germany led a halfway tolerable existence in the south-east, on either side of the Danube, before they stopped falling victim in their hundreds and thousands to new diseases, floods, wars, poverty and hunger. Some managed a modest level of prosperity, especially with hemp – the white gold – wheat, maize, cattle-breeding, a willingness to adopt new machinery and inventions, and with hard work that left virtually no time for pleasure. Conservative, God-fearing, industrious people, she read. First the Austrian emperors persuaded Catholics to move, then Protestants too. People who kept themselves to themselves, who nurtured their German culture dutifully and harmlessly in the midst of the burgeoning nationalism of the nineteenth century. Entire villages in the later nation states of Hungary, Romania and Yugoslavia were German at the time, others were partly or mostly German, Germans were here, there and everywhere, the hard-working, dutiful German farmer and the hard-working, frugal German farmer's wife cultivated German traditions and customs and never harmed anyone . . .

She put the text to one side. It was all a bit too much German and German culture and innocence for the moment, a bit too much rapture. She got up and drank some water, which always helped, sometimes even against too much German culture.

Now Jenny was lying on her back, snoring.

Louise went back to the sofa and kept reading, skipping the rapture which transformed into self-pity after the First World War, then into arrogance, ire and vindication. She no longer took in dates and events; the unbearable tone overshadowed everything. She tried another text, written more objectively, from the beginning again, the Swabian migrations and the areas of settlement. Valpovo was not amongst them, although Slavonia was, the land between the Sava and the Drava, as well as other regions she could finally locate thanks to the maps reproduced here: Swabian Turkey to the south of Lake Balaton; Baranya on either side of the Hungarian–Croatian border; Bačka and the Banat in the triangle where Hungary, Serbia and Romania meet; the Vojvodina in Serbia; Transylvania in central Romania and others such as the Bukovina, Bessarabia, Dobruja – all further east.

She couldn't find Valpovo on the maps either, but she kept seeing Essegg on the Drava, a few kilometres from where it met the Danube. She heaved her weighty world atlas from the shelf to the sofa, the only present she had ever accepted from the real Marcel, because it had "remaindered copy" stamped on the fore edge and because Marcel had said that the world was indeed large and difficult and didn't fit in a handier-sized format. She had thought that was lovely.

The index was likewise comprehensive and it took time to find what you were looking for, especially at half past four in the morning.

Now her finger was above "Slavonia" between "Valpovo" and, to the east, "Osijek", which were barely thirty kilometres apart. Osijek lay precisely where Essegg was on the old maps photocopied from books: on the Drava, near where it flowed into the Danube.

So Osijek *was* Essegg, or Essegg was Osijek. Whatever – let the ideologues and historians sort it out amongst themselves.

She read on, studied photographs of chessboard-like villages with broad main roads, houses whose ends faced the roads, pergolas, iron gates, city houses in an almost familiar, somehow Austrian architectural style, small and yet impressive churches, people at harvest, and then plenty of mostly round faces, children, women, men, smiling or severe, cheerful or shy, the women in headscarves and in various traditional costumes, the men with moustaches in suits or overalls – they too, Louise thought, had something imperial–Austrian about them, especially the well-dressed ones in their stiffness, severity and coldness. All of them looked foreign to her.

No photographs from Valpovo or Walpach, but plenty from Osijek or Essegg, where evidently in 1792 Württemberg emigrants founded the district of Neustadt/Novi grad, as well as photos from other towns and villages, some of them with German names: Kerndia, Semlin, Franztal, India, Peterwardein, Ruma, Josefsfeld and Ernestinenhof.

The character of the photographs now changed abruptly; they showed uniformed Danube Swabians with Croatian politicians, a rally of the "German *Volk* of Essegg" in June 1941 in front of a swastika banner, German soldiers, German tanks, then treks of refugees with horse-drawn covered wagons on narrow Hungarian roads through snowy winter landscapes.

At the end, a photo from Valpovo after all, simple wooden crosses in an overgrown cemetery: German graves from 1945.

She thought of the engraving on the cigarette case. "Valpovo 1945".

The beginning, perhaps.

Strictly speaking, of course, everything had begun a few years earlier, on November 2, 1942, when Antun Lončar was born in Štrpci in Bosnia.

With a yawn she let the papers slide to the floor and pushed

Marcel's remaindered atlas away too. For a while she focused on what she had just read, allowing the words to flutter around her head as she waited for sleep, words that made neutral readers like her think long and hard, words such as "the hardworking, loyal German", "the *Volk* accomplished its mission", "the old virtues", "the old homeland", "the task of the forefathers", the Danube Swabians as a "bulwark of the Christian West" – this she liked particularly – "then, as now, bulwark of the Christian West". Words like these.

The last thing to enter her mind before she fell asleep was that unpronounceable place name, Štrpci, and she thought, really, they could have given that place a second name too, a German one, I mean, who on earth can pronounce Štrpci?

Her very last thought was, of course, Valpovo.

Bonì woke up because someone was saying her name. Jenny Böhm was kneeling beside her, a white face with a panicked expression. Louise, she whispered, Louise, and Louise stroked her cheek, her ice-cold skin, it had got to that stage now, it was serious, but then Jenny said, have a drink with me, Louise, come on, join me in a drink . . .

"What?"

"Drink with me, Louise, let's drink together, come on, let's drink Davidoff, you remember, Da-Da-Davidoff."

Louise pulled back her hand, tears of fury and disappointment in her eyes, closed them, heard Jenny's conspiratorial whispers, Louise, come on, please, don't abandon me now. The voice got higher. Please, Louise, don't abandon me now, drink with me, it came ever closer, she could feel Jenny's cold cheek near hers, cold lips by her ear, please, Louise, just this once, one drink with you, then I can stop, my last sip ever, with you, come on, Louise . . .

Bonì pushed her away and sat up. "Piss off, Jenny!"

"A sip, Louise, is that asking too much?"

"Piss off!"

"Why won't you help me?"

Louise got up. Calm, she thought, keep calm. You know this, you know what's happening. And you're calm now, even in the middle of the night, in a crisis.

"You've got to help me!" Jenny whispered.

Louise looked down at her. The fury and disappointment returned, she was too tired to keep calm.

Jenny Böhm in *her* pyjamas, beside *her* sofa, in *her* night. Trying to lure her back to drinking.

Keep calm, she thought. She's ill, you're healthy. Calm.

But the disappointment, especially the disappointment, wouldn't go away.

"Go back to bed, Jenny."

Jenny bowed her head, stood up, a brief, desperate glance, then she went to the door, stepped onto the scaffolding in bare feet, closed the door, the Upper Silesians' metal door in her sitting-room wall, a bizarre moment, Louise thought, almost like in the theatre, the theatre of the absurd, what a theatre this life is, she thought, following Jenny out onto the scaffolding. There she sat, Davidoff Classic in her hand, gazing at her with large eyes, and Louise knew that it wasn't so bad anymore, for Jenny was waiting, she wouldn't drink, she was waiting for Louise to take the Davidoff from her hand and toss it away like in spring 2003 on their Sunday jaunt through the forest near Oberberg.

She heard the bottle smash in the courtyard.

Jenny began to cry as sometimes she used to cry in Oberberg, with no restraint, with no strength. Louise brought her back into the apartment, closed the metal door, laid Jenny gently on the sofa, lay down beside her and, close together, in a tight embrace, they waited for sleep to come, mother and child, or perhaps a couple of women, Louise thought, a couple of women who had a few problems with life, the comic theatre of life.

And that's all it was.

15

Outside it was once again rainy and grey. Inside, in the uncomfortable task force room, far too big for small gatherings like this one, were the Kripo head, the section head, ten investigators, the police spokeswoman and a secretary. At last there was a trace of adrenaline in the air, even if only because the alpha males were at war.

"No," Bermann said.

"The results are more important," Bob said. His eyes were on her, his attractive smile flickered for a moment. You're under my protection, the smile said. You're my protégée now.

She suppressed a burp.

"No," Bermann repeated. His eyes were on her too, although there was no smile beneath his moustache, only a more intense, honest, livid expression.

She checked the time. One hour, she reckoned, then her eyes would close from exhaustion, she would slump to the left against Hoffmann, or to the right against Wallmer. At the age of forty-four you couldn't easily get over nights of crisis like the one just gone.

They had fallen asleep at around five, the two women with their problems on the sofa in her apartment. At half past six the alarm on her mobile went off, one woman got up to go to the office, the other stayed where she was to avoid going to the office. Should I be worried? Louise had asked as she left. Probably not, came Jenny's reply.

At the beginning of the meeting Louise had talked about Munich. Bob praised her, Bermann cursed her. It was likely that Bob was the only one in the room unaware that Bermann's curses sometimes contained a touch of pride.

This was one of those moments.

My investigator, his curses also said, doesn't give a shit about my orders, jumps into a car and brings back results like *this*.

My school.

Now he said, "So long as I'm in charge of this section, excursions like that will not happen if I say they're not to happen."

"The way I see it," Bob countered affably, "this 'excursion' ought to have happened earlier. Time is pressing. Somewhere out there we've got a potential murderer running around. We can't sit on our hands and wait for somebody else to do our job. Or what?"

Bermann merely frowned.

"Go ahead, Alfons," Bob said.

Hoffmann waited, presumably for a sign from Bermann. When it came, a barely visible nod, he began. First the blurred photograph of Lončar that Paul Niemann had taken, which the computer experts had managed to work well with. He passed around a copy, which everyone glanced at briefly; they didn't need this photo anymore.

Hoffmann continued. This afternoon the public prosecutor, Marianne Andrele, would try to call Lončar's lawyer from back then, Georg Thomas Seidl. Maybe Lončar had contacted him in the summer too. Maybe Seidl could provide them with a clue as to his whereabouts.

In the meantime, a few names had come in from Lahr: Germans who'd been born in former Yugoslavia and thus could be Lončar's potential contact. They were still waiting, checking and gathering more names.

"Rolf?" Bob said in a very friendly tone.

"How many?" Bermann asked.

Hoffmann skimmed his documents. "Around fifty."

"Too many. Our colleagues should send over everything they've got. Names, dates and places of birth. Where these people lived before they came to Germany. Everything, basically. Anne and Mats, you compare the info with the info on Lončar. He was in Lahr, so let's assume that he's got a contact there. Look for connections. We can't turn up to fifty or sixty people's houses with the S.W.A.T. team, and we're going to need the S.W.A.T. team in case Lončar is there."

Louise saw Bob nod in agreement. She wondered who was supposed to be taken in by this performance.

"We strike this afternoon if possible," Bermann said.

Wallmer groaned. Benedikt gave a sceptical "Hmm".

"What?" Bermann said. "Time is pressing. We've got a potential murderer running around out there."

Everyone looked at him.

Bermann shrugged. "Well, we do."

"Yes," Bob said, nodding again, but this was a different kind of nod, Louise thought, a wary nod. A nod that said: It's time for repercussions.

She began to worry about Bermann.

"I'll talk to our colleagues in Lahr," Bob said.

"Good idea," Bermann said. "Time's pressing."

"Yes," Bob said with a smile.

"Let's get on to the Niemanns," Bermann said, smiling too.

Since the previous evening Paul Niemann had been given personal protection so far as it was possible – Kripo couldn't provide bodyguards. Two colleagues were sitting in a car outside the house in Au, following Niemann if he left the house, which presumably wasn't going to happen.

And they'd again doubled the number of patrol cars.

For a moment nobody said a word. Louise and Benedikt looked at each other. She guessed at the questions going through his head. Two colleagues in a car and a few patrols. Was that enough? Could they protect Niemann like this? After everything they now knew about Antun Lončar and his asymmetrical war?

But what else could they do?

At least they now had a concrete idea of what he was planning. They could take measures.

"How is he going to try? And when?" she asked.

Benedikt nodded thoughtfully. The key questions.

"Well, I would wait," Hoffmann said.

Wallmer nodded. "Me too."

"Not me," Bermann said. "I've got a plan and I'm going to see it through. I feel invulnerable. I quote psalms. I'm a nutter. I've got a divine mission: to kill the man who caused me and many others suffering. No, I'd try tonight."

Louise turned to those members of the task force who hadn't been part of the initial investigation team, including the prospective inspectors from Schwenningen. On Bob's instructions they had looked at the other theories, the Russian lead, the homeless man, the farmer, the lover, the psychopath. Now the Lončar lead could be officially added to these. "This is the key question. How's he going to react? Up till now he's always done what we've least expected. What are we expecting? And does that mean he'll do the opposite? Or does he know that by now we're expecting him to do the opposite and so he'll do what we actually might expect?"

Calm, focused faces looked at her. A few colleagues nodded. Nobody answered. Just as she was about to turn away, Dietrich, a veteran Freiburg chief inspector, said, "Please explain one thing to me."

She waited.

"In your opinion, how could he know where the Niemanns are living now?"

"He'll find out. If he doesn't know already."

"I see." Dietrich nodded and smiled. Both came across as slightly sarcastic. She knew he didn't like her. Didn't like her methods. Such as driving to Munich against the express instructions of the section head. "So, he doesn't speak German," he said, fixing his eyes on Bermann, "and this might be his first time in Freiburg, but he's going to find out. Really?"

The room became restless. Whispering, a clearing of throats, someone laughed softly. From Wallmer came grumpy sounds of disapproval.

"Yes," Bermann said.

Dietrich nodded. "But how?"

"I don't give a shit," Bermann said.

"From the children, for example," Benedikt said. "Maybe he knows where they go to school."

"Then don't let them go to school."

"Maybe he knows where the mother works," Louise said.

Dietrich said nothing, just shrugged. Then don't let her go to work, the shrug said.

Benedikt cleared his throat. "Or he followed them yesterday morning. After the fire."

"And if not, he'll find out some other way," Bermann said.

Dietrich raised his arms and splayed his fingers "All I'm saying is, it's a valid question."

Louise nodded. An important question, in spite of the sarcasm and dislike. The children's school, the mother's shop, the morning of the fire. What other possibilities were there?

What possibilities had they not considered?

Suddenly she was convinced that Lončar had known all along where the Niemanns were. On Monday he'd had a contingency escape plan. He'd known that he would have to find the Niemanns again if their house was no longer there.

He'd made provisions.

Was one step ahead of them again.

Bermann knocked on the table. The restlessness subsided. "Let's move on."

"He's known all along," Louise said.

"Yes," Benedikt agreed.

"Good," Bob said. "We'll turn Au into a fortress."

"Good," Bermann said. "Anything else? Louise?"

She looked at Hoffmann. "Biljana and Snježana are important. We need to find out where they are. What's happened since 1998."

Hoffmann nodded without returning her gaze. "Already being dealt with." He appeared slightly uneasy.

"Really?"

"Someone's been on it since this morning. It was the first thing we arranged. Where Biljana and Snježana are."

"I see. Who's on it?"

Hoffmann shifted in his seat.

"Do I know him?"

"No," Bermann said impatiently.

She nodded. Bermann, helping Hoffmann out of a fix. She frowned. Bermann was looking at her menacingly. Not now, those small, harsh eyes were saying. Later, just the two of us. Without Bob and the others. Or else . . . despite the pride.

She nodded again. Later, then.

Hoffmann was still shifting in his seat, still avoiding her eye. She knew he couldn't help it. Bermann had put Ilic on the case, and Hoffmann had just let it happen. And kept it from her.

Anger surged inside her. She closed her eyes and thought, Later, there's no point now.

Opening her eyes, she nodded, later.

Later was around 9 a.m. She was standing beside Bermann's desk, he was perched on the edge and they talked about rules – professional, moral, others. In fact Bermann did the talking, Louise listened. You don't stick to my rules, but you demand I stick to yours, some confused, irrational, moral rules, emotional rules because you've got a bad conscience. Illi will say if he doesn't want to help out, he doesn't need you for that, but we need him and his contacts, have you forgotten already, time is pressing, we've got a potential murderer running around out there. Now Bermann was grinning, shifting about on the edge of the desk.

On the wall behind him were three posters of surfers, female surfers to be precise. Bermann's latest passion, surfing amongst slim beach beauties in their twenties – wild, independent girls he only had the confidence to approach in his late forties. She'd seen photographs from south-west France: Bermann on a beginners' course last year near Biarritz.

Bermann on the beach holding a huge surfboard, Bermann sitting on the huge surfboard in the Atlantic, the huge surfboard without Bermann, who was drifting somewhere towards Ireland.

Louise smiled. Thinking about Bermann was still the best therapy when you were angry with him.

She left without another word and on the stairs thought there was something in what he'd said, something truthful. Not much – this was Rolf Bermann after all – but definitely something.

Yes, she didn't like sticking to Bermann's rules when she thought they were wrong. Yes, she had a bad conscience because in summer 2003 she'd made the mistake of not sending Thomas Ilic back to police H.Q., and took him up the Rappeneck with her. Yes, they could use Ilic and his contacts. Yes, Ilic himself could say what he was prepared to do and what not. The problem then and now was that he didn't. So others had to do it for him, people with a bad conscience, people who also regarded confused, irrational moral rules as legitimate, not just those set down in the police handbook.

So it was the same as it always was: Bermann was right, and Bermann *wasn't* right.

Reassured, she hurried down the steps to the ground floor. It would have been even nicer if on this gloomy October morning the basic laws in Freiburg Kripo had suddenly changed.

*

Ilic's contacts worked fast and efficiently. Hoffmann called while she was still on her way to Au. He apologised profusely, was sheepish and self-critical, and she excused him just as self-critically. Then he told her what he knew. One colleague in Zagreb and one in Banja Luka, which might be enough if you had a man in Freiburg who could bring them together swiftly and informally, and then piece together the puzzle they provided. A few telephone calls had sufficed to make at least one thing clear: neither Biljana nor Snježana Lončar had been born in Štrpci, which was in the Serb part of Bosnia–Herzegovina, but in Poreč in Croatia. It was obvious why the Lončars had given false information on the personal forms for Munich foreigners' registration office. Given the situation at the time, Bosnian citizens could count on better treatment from host countries than Croats.

"Did Illi say where Poreč is?"

"No, I don't think so."

"Have you got a map?"

"You mean a paper one?"

"What else?"

"One made up of noughts and ones."

"I don't really care, Alfons."

Louise heard the rustling of paper, Hoffmann's giggling, his shallow breathing which couldn't possibly transport enough oxygen efficiently around his huge body. He hammered away at the keyboard with two fingers, then located Poreč. It was on the Croatian coast.

"Which region?"

"Region?"

"Is it in Slavonia?"

"Slavonia?"

"Alfons, please . . ."

"Sorry, I'm just a bit . . . I didn't sleep well." More hammering. No, Poreč was in Istria. "Wait."

She waited.

As he clicked and hammered, he said that the forensics report on Johannes Miller's fingerprints had just come in. Negative, of course, they'd known that a while back.

Louise nodded. Johannes Miller, Friedental/Friedland.

Somebody had to notify Sophie Iwanowa.

She asked Hoffmann to do it; she wasn't in the mood for Sophie's jokes.

"Poreč," Hoffmann mumbled. "Hang on a sec."

She sighed impatiently. Waited.

"There are two of them."

"Two Porečs?"

"Yes. One on the coast and one . . . Aha!"

"In Slavonia," Louise said.

"Yes."

"And that's where Biljana and Snježana were born."

"What does that mean? That Lončar probably lived for a while in Poreč."

"Uh-huh." More hammering on the keyboard.

"Poreč in Slavonia."

"Uh-huh."

"Alfons."

Alfons apologised and the hammering stopped. Via a link from the search results for Poreč he had ended up on an Australian website offering cheap trips; he really wanted to go to Australia even though he knew he never would, because his wife only allowed them to holiday in her native Lower Bavaria. He'd slept badly because they were going there again in a few days' time. "Always Plattling," he said. "How can you get to see the world from there?"

She shook her head in exasperation. Bermann going through his second adolescence, Hoffmann his fourth. Men. All the same, all predictable, all ridiculous in their own way. Sweet from time to time, but not often enough, and certainly not on days like this when someone's life was in danger.

Bonì was just parking outside the sister-in-law's house in Au when Hoffmann called again. Ilic had rung with more news from Banja Luka.

Biljana and Snježana Lončar were dead. They both died in 1999 in Štrpci, a few months after returning from Germany.

Louise took the key out of the ignition and leaned back, her eyes fixed on the old, slightly run-down house beneath the dark roof. She thought she'd seen movement at one of the windows. But the rain may have deceived her.

Deported from Munich in 1998, died in Štrpci in 1999.

There it was, the moment of pain.

A moment. For she couldn't shake the feeling that all this had begun decades prior to 1999. It wasn't in 1999 that the old warrior, Antun Lončar, became what he was now, five years later. He'd been that person his whole life long.

Valpovo 1945, she thought, perhaps that was the beginning. A war, a camp. Then life as a German in Tito's Yugoslavia, maybe facing discrimination, maybe hostility, maybe in hiding in some way or another. The 1990s, another war, the flight to Germany with wife and daughter. Deportation, return to Štrpci, to the place where he was born.

Then his wife and daughter died.

Valpovo 1945, the beginning of the story; Štrpci 1999, the end; Merzhausen 2004, the epilogue.

She spoke her thoughts out loud.

"Yes," Hoffmann said, then cleared his throat.

"That's not the whole story, is it?"

"No."

Biljana and Snježana Lončar had been shot. Ilic hadn't yet been able to find out by whom and in what circumstances. Not by Antun Lončar, that much was certain.

"Call me the moment he gets in touch again."

"Yes."

"And tell Rolf and the others."

"Yes."

"You know what this might mean?"

Hoffmann cleared his throat again. "The wife and the daughter."

"Yes."

She hung up, stared at the unfriendly house in the rain, the words echoing repeatedly in her head:

The wife and the daughter.

16

The wife shook her hand, the daughter embraced her, neither said a word. She felt the spiky hair on her cheek, slim but strong arms around her torso, and for a moment she had a strange feeling, the absence of another feeling. The feeling of being alone.

The feeling of loneliness.

"How are you?" she whispered.

"Alright," Carola whispered.

When Carola let go of her, the feeling of loneliness returned. She shook her head. This was too absurd.

They went into the kitchen, which seemed even more vast and bare than the day before. A pervading smell of detergent hung in the air and the work surfaces were perfectly clean and orderly.

She sat at the table. "Where's Philip?"

"At school," Carola said.

"What about you? Why aren't you at school?"

Carola shrugged, sat down and jerked her head towards the door. Papa needs me, said her dark, clever eyes. Today they were tired eyes, but full of defiance and pugnaciousness.

Henriette still hadn't said anything, hadn't smiled, hadn't forgiven her yet. She pottered at the sink, then turned and leaned back against it. "So?" she said. "Another hunch?" She looked at Carola. "An inspector with hunches."

Carola didn't respond.

"Yes," Louise said.

"Yes?"

"Another hunch."

"Well?" When Louise didn't continue, Henriette came over to the table, sat beside Carola and whispered, "Spit it out!"

Louise told them about Antun Lončar.

Told them about the wife and the daughter.

For a while neither of them spoke, they just sat there looking at each other, pale, confused, scared, looking at Louise. They held hands, four interlocked hands on the table, the fingers moving, the hands pressed against each other, a gesture of the greatest possible closeness, mother and daughter, opposite them the inspector who for a second or two regretted having told them about Biljana and Snježana.

Just a hunch, she wanted to say, but what are hunches?

She didn't say it.

The wife and daughter. The act of revenge was not to kill Paul Niemann, but to kill his wife and daughter.

Just a hunch, for Christ's sake, she thought.

Henriette stood up and walked smartly to the window. She stood there for a while, her back to the room, staring outside. Then she said. "O.K. Right." She turned around. "When's he going to come? Tomorrow, in a few days, in a few weeks?"

"*Assuming* he comes."

"Assuming he comes."

"We don't know."

"What do you think?"

"In a few days."

Henriette nodded. "Is that a hunch? Or a supposition?"

Louise didn't reply. Henriette nodded again, smiling coldly, her eyes fixed on Louise.

"You should go away," Louise said.

"Away?"

"Take the children out of school and go away till we've got him."

"No," Carola said.

"What about the shop?"

"Your sister-in-law will have to take care of it."

"Ha ha! She's done a runner. It's all too much for her with us here, she needs her peace and quiet so now she's relaxing in her house up in Todtnau."

"Someone else, then."

"For how long?"

Louise shrugged. They were onto him, they were closing in, now they knew something about his life, they had the beginning and the end of the story, and with every day and every hour they would find out more, get closer. But would that be enough to find him soon, in the next few days? She couldn't promise it.

It was just another hunch.

"A few days, a few weeks."

"No," Carola repeated.

"And where would we go?" Henriette said.

"We'll sort you out an apartment somewhere. In another city, in another region. Where he won't find you."

"No," Henriette said too. She went to the table, sat down and the four hands clasped each other again. "I'm not running away from that psychopath. He's already taken away my peace of mind and my house. I'm not going to let him have any more, he's not going to drive me from my life. No."

Louise nodded. She hadn't been expecting any different. "What about your husband?"

Mother and daughter both looked at her, now with tears in their eyes.

"Where is he?"

"Upstairs."

"He's lying in bed, staring at the ceiling," Henriette said. "Do you want to speak to him?"

Louise nodded. "Later. There's just one more thing I wanted to say. It's only a *hunch*."

"And that is?" Henriette said.

"That he might be planning something completely different."

"Or nothing at all. Maybe he's long gone."

"That's another possibility. But I don't think so."

Henriette gave a high-pitched laugh. "Do you actually *know* anything? For days—"

"Mama." Carola pulled her hands away from her mother's.

"How are you going to protect us? Two of your colleagues are sitting outside in an unmarked vehicle and a police car drives past now and then! *That's* how you're protecting us!"

"Yes," Louise said softly. "We can't do any more. That's why I'm advising you to go away."

"And because we can't do *that* you're leaving us alone with this psychopath!"

Henriette got up and hurried back to the window, as if keeping a lookout. But her head was lowered, her brow pressed against the glass.

The crises of the night were followed by the daytime crises. Of course Louise was sympathetic. For one crisis as much as the other. "What's important is that you're vigilant. That you stay together, rather than going out alone. Lock the doors, listen out for unusual noises. Look out for anything that's different. Make sure you've always got a phone to hand. You know what I'm talking about."

"Yes," Henriette said.

"Stay with us," Carola said impulsively, grabbing for her hand, repeating her request, stay with us, my aunt's not here, her room is free, stay, for a few days at least, and Louise said, I'm afraid I can't, then thought, why not, I want to get out of my apartment anyway. For a while she said nothing more, just looked into Carola's sad, brave eyes, felt the warmth and strength of her hands, and sensed something else without knowing precisely what it was, a different look, different eyes staring at her, but from the inside, somewhere from inside her.

Then she knew – they were Antun Lončar's eyes.

She gave Carola and Henriette copies of the photograph of Lončar that had been attached to the identification form from Munich. That's what he looks like, keep it on you at all times, take a good look at his face, imagine it slightly changed, older, rougher, different hair, think about this face until it visits you in your nightmares. Then you'll recognise him if he comes. Carola wanted to see the photographs of Biljana and Snježana. She looked at them for a long while, then nodded and Louise sensed that she'd forgotten her own fear momentarily, that she'd been thinking of the two murdered women. Of the pain that Lončar had been carrying around for years.

Carola took her upstairs. She stopped on the staircase and said, "Will you stay?"

Louise nodded.

"Cool," Carola said with a smile.

"But not during the day."

"Yes, sure."

"And I want you to discuss it with your parents."

"I will."

"And please get some sugar. I need *sugar* in my coffee."

Carola was still smiling and Louise realised that she may have been earmarked for another task, not only to protect them from Antun Lončar, but to prevent the family from falling apart.

Her mobile rang as soon as they entered the guest room. "Illi" on the display, just like old times, and that was already too many similarities with summer 2003.

She went out to the landing and said, "Just the odd phone call, Illi, right?"

Ilic laughed quietly. "Yes, yes."

"I'm being serious."

"That's taxing enough."

She sat on the stairs, dark, rough wood under a dark, rough wooden ceiling. There was nothing light in this house, nothing friendly. Louise heard Carola talking to her father in the guest room, and heard Niemann reply. Below her she could see the vast table through the open kitchen door. Louise heard Henriette wandering around, opening and closing drawers, then suddenly it fell silent.

"So, what have you got?"

"Biljana and Snježana," Ilic said.

"Wait . . . *how* do you pronounce it?"

Ilic repeated the name. Snee-ye-zhana. Something to do with snow, "Snow White", you could say. "By the way, a *lončar* is a potter."

"And this place in Bosnia? How do you pronounce that?"

"Sh-trp-zi."

"Aha."

"It's quite simple."

"If you say so."

"We just pronounce the letters differently from you."

Louise said nothing, just thought: from you.

Sometimes you were German, sometimes not.

She got the impression that over the course of his illness, Thomas Ilic was becoming more and more Croatian. She remembered how he'd once said that his father, born in Croatia, had become ever more Croatian during his years in Germany.

"How?"

"Each letter does exactly what it says. For example, a 'C' is a 'C' but never a 'K'."

"I see. Nothing wrong with that."

"Thanks."

They laughed.

"Right," Ilic said. Biljana and Snježana, shot in 1999 in the village of Štrpci in the Serb part of Bosnia–Herzegovina – the Republika Srpska – presumably by former militiamen. "Presumably", because nobody knew the details or wanted to say, and in all likelihood the murders would never be solved. Particularly in Bosnia, Ilic said, people frequently knew who had killed their father or son, blown up their house, for often enough it had been former neighbours or friends or acquaintances. But people kept quiet. The knowledge was retained until it had become meaningless – or until it provoked a new war. "But how can the knowledge of who murdered your father ever become meaningless?" Ilic said.

Louise just nodded. Below her, in the kitchen, Henriette Niemann, invisible, inaudible; above her, in the guest room, Carola and Paul Niemann, who weren't talking either.

She wished the Niemanns would agree to go away. How could they stay and wait for the old warrior to find them?

"What our Bosnian counterparts know is that they went to his place several times."

"Who went where?"

"The murderers to Lončar's."

The murderers had probably come twice without actually doing anything. Perhaps, Louise thought, they'd issued an ultimatum just as Lončar did later, hundreds of kilometres away. On the third occasion they'd set the house on fire. The fourth time . . . The family had sought refuge in a small, empty barn. The men had come looking for them. They raped Lončar's wife and daughter and then shot them.

Louise rubbed her eyes. What a story.

But perhaps it was a perfectly normal story from a perfectly normal war.

After a perfectly normal war.

They couldn't say, Ilic continued, why all this had happened, why the men had left Lončar alive. Maybe this was another Bosnian incident that would never be cleared up.

So this was the story. Antun Lončar was doing unto Paul Niemann what had been done unto him. Niemann, who had sent Lončar's family from their safe new home back to their dangerous old one because the law on the repatriation of Bosnian war refugees demanded it. Years later Lončar had returned to Germany, had somehow tracked him down and entered his house. First he had robbed Niemann of his peace and security, then of his home. And now he might be intent on taking his family away too.

"But why wait five years?"

Ilic didn't reply.

"What do you think, Illi?"

"Nothing. I don't think anything."

Only now did she understand. Thomas Ilic was on sick leave. He was only supposed to contact a few acquaintances in his father's homeland, and otherwise was not involved. He hadn't been able to work for eighteen months. She shook her head. Perhaps it was because she'd seen the word "Illi" on her screen, just like old times, and because she was desperate to work with him again.

"Sorry, Illi."

"It's not my case. I'm . . . I mean, I'm not working at the moment."

"I know. Shit, sorry."

Ilic cleared his throat. "If there's anything else you need, just call."

"And if you find out anything else . . ."

"Yes."

"Only phone calls, Illi, do you hear? Nothing more."

A lame joke, but Ilic humoured her by laughing. "Of course."

They hung up.

What do you think, Illi . . . She put her face in her hands, stood up, and tried to suppress her bad conscience because she could sense the eyes again, the eyes of Antun Lončar, as if he were already here, inside her or within these dark walls, ceilings, floors. As she went into the guest room it occurred to her that one question remained unanswered, or more accurately a whole string of questions, all of which related to the same one – the question of whether Lončar was a descendant of those figures she'd dreamed of on several occasions, those people, mostly from Germany, who had resettled in south-eastern Europe in the eighteenth century. If so, they needed to know what happened in the years immediately after he was born.

What happened in Valpovo in 1945.

How the story began.

She didn't share any of her hunches with Niemann and said nothing about Biljana and Snježana, she merely told him that the man who'd burned down his house might come to Au. Niemann, who was sitting in the armchair by the window again, simply nodded. She wasn't sure whether he was listening, whether he understood what she was saying. Carola, who was perched on the armrest, wondered the same; do you understand, Papa? she asked softly, and repeated what Louise had said. Niemann nodded again, a little more impatiently this time, and Carola said, O.K., and reassuringly stroked his arm.

Louise showed him the photograph from Munich.

"Yes," Niemann said.

"Yes what?"

"That's him."

"I know." She glimpsed Carola's pleading face, don't do it, please don't do it, but she had to do it, somebody had to.

Somebody had to drag this man back into reality.

Had to talk about Munich.

Bonì spoke for about ten minutes. Niemann stared out of the small window at the grey wall of the neighbouring house, either listening or not, but keeping silent. Carola's hand was on his shoulder, she was gazing outside too, either listening or not. When Louise showed him the photocopy of the document with his name on it, he afforded the paper only a brief glance. Everything had been said and shown, and Niemann was still silent.

"Not a Russian-German, then, but a Bosnian war refugee who lived in Munich," Louise said.

No reaction.

She felt her anger returning, no pity anymore, just anger and impatience. You can't behave like this, you can't just shut yourself off from reality after everything that's happened, it's not about you, it's about your family, the safety of your wife, daughter, son . . .

She stood between him and the window and placed her hands on the armrests of his chair. At least then he returned her gaze.

"It can't go on like this, Herr Niemann."

"I . . ." He broke off.

"Papa," Carola said softly.

"Help me. Help your family. *Talk* to me."

"She's got questions, Papa. It's really important."

Niemann nodded. "Yes. I know."

"O.K." Louise straightened up and stayed where she was. You're not going to stare out of the window anymore, you're going to look at *me.* "Not a Russian-German, but a Bosnian war refugee. Are we agreed so far?"

Niemann nodded.

"You processed his case."

"I don't know . . ."

"It's got your name on it."

Only a shrug. She snorted, the anger was there in full now, you're not going to ignore me anymore, not now, as soon as I've gone you can do what you like, but not now. She repeated, tartly, "It's got your name on it, Herr Niemann."

"Then . . ."

"Exactly, then it must have been you."

No reaction.

"Herr Niemann, this man might be planning—"

"Please, no!" Carola said.

Louise turned to her. "Wait outside, would you?"

"No!" The dark eyes became large and fractious.

"Then don't interrupt me, for Christ's sake!" Her eyes returned to Niemann. "This man might be planning to murder you or your family."

"Murder?"

"Yes."

"That's why it's so important, Papa," Carola said.

"But . . . I really don't remember."

"Nothing?" Louise said. "Neither the name nor the case?"

"Nothing at all."

"Do you recall ever having personal contact with Lončar? Have you ever spoken to him on the phone? Has he ever called you? Did he ever wait for you on your way home?"

"I . . ."

Louise sighed. Too many questions for a man who didn't really want to talk. She repeated them, one by one, waited for the answers: no, four times. Then all was silent until Niemann said he'd never seen any of these people before, only their forms.

"And their photos," Louise said.

He just looked at her, a sad, conscience-stricken, helpless look.

"You weren't able to look at these photos, were you? You had to send these people away. You couldn't look at their faces."

"No, I couldn't."

Louise's anger had abated, her pity returned. For a moment she thought about what awaited this man when they finally had Lončar, perhaps sooner: his wife leaving, the family falling apart. What then? How could such a helpless, feeble man get back on his feet?

She stepped away and Niemann gazed outside again.

One final question remained. How had Lončar found Niemann in Merzhausen?

A shrug of the shoulders, a shake of the head, cluelessness.

She looked up. Carola was pale, one hand was still on her father's shoulder. She would look after him, of course, but she was only sixteen and she needed people to look after *her*. Her gaze wandered, across the pencil portraits on the wall by the bed, the portraits of the dead man whose face changed from picture to picture, to the door that she hadn't closed and through which Antun Lončar might one day enter, because he intended Paul Niemann to meet the same fate that had befallen him.

Outside in the soft, cool rain, a brief wave to her colleagues in the parked car, glances in all directions, but she couldn't imagine that Lončar was already here, and she certainly didn't think that he would attempt anything in the daytime. Lončar was the night, he was the nightmare who came when everyone was asleep.

As she headed slowly towards Hexentalstrasse she called Jenny. Everything was fine, she was still in the apartment, lying on the sofa and battling with herself, her impulses, desires and shame, but everything was fine, or almost fine.

From her voice Louise could hear just how hard Jenny was battling.

"There was something else I wanted to say, but I've forgotten what," Jenny said.

In Louise's rear-view mirror was a patrol car, and there was another on Hexentalstrasse. As she took a turning she saw one of the undercover investigators at a food stand. Newspaper, curry sausage, cola — life as an undercover investigator wasn't particularly healthy.

At the entrance to the village was a third patrol car. Au had become a fortress.

Calm down, she told herself. It didn't work.

"No," Jenny said. "I can't remember."

"Doesn't matter."

Another pause, then Louise said, "I'm not coming home tonight."

"No?"

"I've got to look after these people. The ones whose house was burned down."

"Night shift," Jenny said, sounding disappointed.

"Yes. Stay if you want. There's a spare key for the new door somewhere. In one of the kitchen drawers."

"Yes."

"You should be able to find something to eat. Biscuits. Pasta. That sort of thing."

Jenny had already eaten the biscuits. Sometimes biscuits were lifesavers when you were battling like Jenny Böhm was. Not for ever, but for the time being.

"You're coping well, Jenny," Louise said. "You'll do this, you've almost done it."

Jenny said yes and that she'd call to arrange everything that afternoon. Health insurance, therapist, Oberberg, all that. A stand-in for the parish. Louise asked if there was anything she could do, if she could help in any way, but she knew Jenny would say no, and she did, which was another good sign.

Yes, Jenny would do it again.

Not for ever, but for the time being.

Minutes later, when she was not far from Marcel's pretty Vauban, Jenny called again. She'd remembered the other thing she meant to say. The man in the photograph, you know, the photocopies that were on the floor by the sofa. She thought she might have seen him when she arrived yesterday evening. He was getting into a white car outside the house.

"Which house?"

"Yours."

"*My* house? And you're only telling me this now?"

"I'd forgotten. All I could think of was . . . was . . ."

Louise nodded. If all you could think of was a drink then your priorities did become skewed.

Outside *her* house. Tears shot into her eyes. Another mistake, Bonì, you ought to have been more careful, ought to have used your head, dammit! You know what he's like by now.

". . . was a drink," Jenny completed her sentence.

"What sort of car?"

"A white one."

"What *make*?"

"I don't know. Something old."

Outside *her* house. If Lončar knew where the Niemanns were staying, it was because she had led him there.

More tears, unending tears, tears of anxiety and anger with a little shame mixed in. Use your head, Bonì!

"You've got to get out of my apartment."

"What?"

"Get out, Jenny. He could turn up there any minute."

"Oh God," Jenny said.

They agreed that she would call back in a few minutes, a quarter of an hour at the most. That she would go to a hotel, or friends, or her parents and keep in regular contact.

Louise pulled over, notified Bermann and Hoffmann, then called Henriette. We must assume that he already knows where you are. You've got to leave, get the family together, for God's sake, and let one of my colleagues take you to a different city . . .

"No," Henriette said, "and I'm not going to change my mind. By the way, I've heard you're coming to dinner. How about kohlrabi soup and spaghetti Bolognese? I've found some kohlrabi in the garden."

"For *Christ's* sake," Louise said.

"I'll take that as a yes, then," Henriette said and hung up.

Louise closed her eyes and rested her head on the steering wheel. So he *had* been there when she came home last night and thought she could sense his presence, maybe not on the scaffolding, but in a white car outside the house, he'd waited for her, he must have followed her on the morning of the fire through the city and eventually home, or that evening when they'd almost caught him in Merzhausen, he'd then followed her to the Niemanns in Au, today or maybe yesterday, no, more likely today because yesterday they'd driven in Benedikt's work car rather than her colourful Mégane.

One of the possibilities she hadn't considered.

That *she* would lead him to the Niemanns.

17

Bob looked at her studiously and said nothing. Bermann threw his hands in the air and said, "Fucking shit!"

Bermann, Bob and Louise tried to reconstruct, to understand. They were sitting in the Kripo boss's office on the fourth floor, Almenbroich's old office where she used to enjoy paying him a visit. They would stand at the window staring at the rain, or at the old town, the minster, the Schlossberg in the sun. The ageing Kripo boss and his problem child. But this was Bob's realm now, a functional room devoid of human moments in which those present felt more intimate because they made allowances for their own and others' weaknesses, exhaustion and distress. By contrast, meetings à la Bob meant: analysis, swapping information, reporting, justification. Conversations in which hierarchy always played a role.

"This is fucking shit," Bermann said.

Early that morning, Antun Lončar had been seen outside the apartment of a chief inspector from the Merzhausen task force. Waiting for her to lead him to the Niemanns. He'd followed her to police H.Q., followed her to Au.

What to Louise had seemed so asymmetric, unpredictable, had been carefully thought through. Not just one plan, but several.

They had increased the number of patrol cars again. And now there were four officers in the car outside the sister-in-law's house.

"Where is she now?" Bermann asked.

"In a hotel."

"Get her here."

"We need her statement," Bob said.

Louise shook her head. "No. She's ill."

"Ill?"

"Ill through booze."

Bermann rolled his eyes, Bob nodded. He looked calm, but she knew that his mind was churning. Searching for mistakes, transgressors, what else might happen, what a disaster, watch out, old chap, make sure none of the dirt sticks to you. "That's going in the protocol. Witness under the influence of alcohol."

"Yes," Louise said. "But not her name."

Bob nodded again and Bermann grinned. Moral rules, the grin implied, emotional rules, all that women's crap again, eh, Louise?

But this time the grin also said: This is Bob's problem, let him deal with it.

They exchanged glances. Rain slapped against the windows, it was now dark inside the room. Bob got up and switched on the ceiling lights. On his first day in the job he had unscrewed Almenbroich's 40-watt bulbs and replaced them with 100-watts. Light brings insight, he'd said when his investigators squinted during their first meeting "upstairs".

"We have to get the Niemanns away," he said.

"They don't want to go."

"We'll see about that."

Louise shrugged.

"I'll drive over myself," Bob said.

"Yes."

"We *must* get them away. We can't protect them in Au."

"They don't want to go."

"Idiots," Bermann said.

Bob turned to him. "Could you *please* drop it? All the insults and foul language? Over the last couple of days I've heard nothing else but insults and foul language."

Bermann raised an eyebrow. There was a dangerous twinkle in his eyes, and at the corners of his mouth a dangerous smile.

"Pull yourselves together," Louise said. "Both of you."

"What?" Bob said.

"Don't forget who you're talking to," Bermann said.

"I have trouble remembering when I hear you speak like that."

"What's she on about?" Bob said.

"If only I knew," Bermann said.

The two of them laughed. Now on his feet, Bob asked Bermann, "Are you coming? To Au?"

"I'd like to, but I'm afraid I can't. If anything happens in Lahr we need to set off straightaway."

Bob nodded and smiled. He'd understood. There was nobody he could shift the blame onto if the Niemanns refused to be convinced.

As they went to the door Louise thought this might be the moment to tell them what she'd agreed with Carola. That she was going to spend the next few nights with the Niemanns. She had to get out of her apartment anyway, the fine dust particles, metal door in the sitting room and that sort of stuff – nobody could put up with that, and so she was killing two birds with one stone. It was a brilliant idea.

She said none of this. Bob would have said no to her brilliant idea. Bermann would have said, "Fucking shit."

In the corridor her mobile played Erik Satie.

"Where are you?" Hoffmann said.

"Upstairs."

"Come down. I've got something to show you."

Without saying goodbye, she left the Kripo boss alone with the section head. From their silence she sensed they were watching her, allowing their furtive eyes to wander across her body, two opponents in a moment of silent agreement – look at her arse, what a great arse she's got – two opponents before the final confrontation in a dirty match being staged at the worst possible moment: on the day she'd led Anton Lončar to the Niemanns.

*

When she saw Hoffmann her confidence returned in a flash. One hundred and fifty kilograms of eagerness and contentment. "Come over here," he said, pointing to a second chair by the computer.

Benedikt and Wallmer had filtered out names of a few Lahr inhabitants who had been born in former Yugoslavia, who for one reason or another might be Lončar's contact. Hoffmann had put all the names into an internet search and found extensive family trees of Danube Swabians, giving details of date and place of birth, spouse, children and current residence.

He'd come across a book too.

"A book?"

"Uh-huh."

"What sort of book?"

"You'll see in a sec."

He clicked on the website of an antiquarian book dealer in Frankfurt, and let Louise read out a title that went on for ever: *Germany the Foreign Homeland. After the Return of the Bosnian Germans from Schutzberg. A Supplement by Andreas Eisenstein to Ferdinand Sommer's Work "A History of the German Protestant Community of Schutzberg in Bosnia, 1895 to 1942".* Hoffmann had already ordered the book, which was coming by courier. Guaranteed delivery by 3 p.m. that afternoon.

"Aha."

"What do you think?"

"Bosnian Germans?"

He nodded. Evidently there had been Germans in Bosnia too, a few small villages, scattered settlements inhabited predominantly by ethnic Germans who had migrated from other regions in southeastern Europe, some even from Russia.

"And this has something to do with Lončar?"

"Yes."

"Explain."

"Right, then," Hoffmann said gleefully.

Andreas Eisenstein, born 1910 in Novisad/Neusatz in what now is Serbia, resident in Lahr since 1964. According to an online genealogy of Danube Swabians, Andreas Eisenstein lived in Schutzberg from 1914 to 1942, a village now in Bosnia–Herzegovina. The Ferdinand Sommer referenced in the title of the book was pastor in Schutzberg from 1922 to 1942. In 1942 almost all Bosnian Germans, including the inhabitants of Schutzberg, were resettled on the orders of the Nazi leadership.

Schutzberg, Louise thought. Something stirred in her subconscious. Schutzberg.

Hoffmann pulled a face. "You're not saying anything."

"I'm thinking." She stood up. "Schutzberg. There's something about that name."

With arms crossed Hoffmann looked at her, waiting for her to remember.

She went to the window. The sky was dark with rain, the kind of October day they were used to. For a moment she thought of Munich, of Heidelinde Zach's sunny laughter, of that warm evening outside which had faded in the turmoil of the night and that morning.

Then she remembered.

Schutzberg: "mountain of refuge".

The Lord will also be a refuge for the oppressed, a refuge in times of trouble.

Louise shook her head. It might be a complete coincidence. "You're not telling me that's all? The psalm?"

She cited the verse.

"No, not at all," Hoffmann said, grabbing the computer mouse. She went back over to him and leaned her forearm on his shoulder, ignoring the smell of sweat which was always a sign that Hoffmann had been working, thinking and deducing intensively without moving much more than his hands.

The results from a search engine, the last one more than forty pages long, and in all the listings the word "Schutzberg" was in bold. "That was the most difficult part," Hoffmann said as he scrolled down.

Barely a dozen results for "Schutzberg". Then, almost at the end of the list, a short entry, two lines. "Schutzberg" in bold, followed by "Štrpci" in brackets.

Schutzberg was Štrpci.

Štrpci, where Antun Lončar was born in 1942. Where Andreas Eisenstein from Lahr lived between 1914 and 1942.

Hoffmann and the internet. She straightened up and clapped him on the shoulder. "Sensational!"

"I had a good teacher."

"Elly."

He nodded enthusiastically. "Elly can do anything online.Even solve a case for you."

She grinned. Hoffmann blushed.

"Do we know exactly when the resettlement happened?"

"We do." He rootled around in a clutter of papers on his desk. "It was November 6, 1942."

Lončar was born on November 2, 1942. Four days before the resettlement. They still needed to work out what relationship he had, or used to have, with Andreas Eisenstein.

And what precisely a resettlement was. And, most importantly, where the inhabitants of Schutzberg were resettled *to*.

Hoffmann had no answers.

"When's the book coming?"

"By three at the latest."

"Read it. Is Eisenstein still alive?"

"Well, he was this morning."

Smiling, Louise went to the door, and as she opened it Hoffmann's mobile rang. "Illi," he said, glancing at the display.

A brief conversation, Hoffmann restricting himself to monosyllables: right, oh, hmm, yes?

Thanks.

He looked at her and spoke hesitantly. Well, they already knew that neither Biljana nor Snježana were born in Štrpci/Schutzberg. Now Ilic had just told him that Antun Lončar wasn't born there either.

Nobody by the name Lončar had been born in Štrpci/Schutzberg. Or by the name Töpfer, its German equivalent.

Hoffmann shrugged sadly, one hundred and fifty inconsolable kilos, two tiny, frustrated eyes. He really believed he'd unearthed Lončar's contact in Andreas Eisenstein, but now it seemed that no biographical links existed between the two.

Louise grinned. "We'll see." Valpovo equals Walpach, she thought, Osijek equals Essegg, Štrpci equals Schutzberg, O.K., there isn't a Töpfer in Schutzberg, but so many things down there have two names, so why not the odd person too?

On the way to Lahr, at the most inopportune moment possible – driving at 150 k.p.h. in Benedikt's car, Bermann in the passenger seat, Wallmer next to her on the back seat – Richard Landen called. "Can you speak?"

"Shit. No."

"Call me when you can."

"Shit. Wait."

Wallmer gave a sideways glance. Wallmer, who had offered for Louise to stay with her, who had wanted to talk to her. Who had something else bothering her besides a Monday morning tantrum.

Everything had been forgotten in these hours and days.

Louise gave her a smile, then turned to the window. They were almost at Offenburg. In the distance she could see the foothills of the Black Forest, half hidden in the grey that had reconquered the Breisgau for good.

In the front Bermann was on the phone to Bob.

No time right now, but so what? "Say something, Richard."

"I came back yesterday."

"I know. How was it?"

He hesitated. "Hmm. Lovely. Strange."

A pause.

"You know what I'm trying to say."

"Yes." A fifteen-month-old son you see only four times a year, an ex-wife, an ex-family, ex-dreams, an ex-life-plan involving Japan, Buddhism and living in the moment. For years you think you should efface your ego and your desires. What an achievement that would be; it is the path to wisdom and inner peace. Then it dawns on you that perhaps you were a little hasty in your thinking. That all these ideas and this way of living were somehow more tied up with your wife than you'd realised. That the ideas aren't quite so important now you've separated. All of a sudden the ego and the desires are back, and this is all good and enjoyable and you wonder how you managed to do without them all these years.

And then you fly to Japan, to your ex-family, right back into living in the moment and your past.

That is broadly what he meant by "Lovely. Strange."

Landen cleared his throat. "When can we meet up?"

"Hard to say right now."

"On another manhunt?"

She heard him laugh uneasily. This was something she still couldn't deal with, any joking about what she did day in, day out, and he knew it. The uncanny old warrior Antun Lončar and jokes – they just didn't go together. Biljana and Snježana, shot in 1999. The wife and the daughter. Carola. Has it completely gone? Is it all gone?

And jokes?

Bermann could do it, others could too. She couldn't.

"Cut the crap."

"It was just a joke."

"Exactly."

The days of inappropriate jokes. Sophie Iwanowa and her joke – "Your German's fantastic too" – then Richard Landen and the manhunt joke.

Maybe she was also to blame. The fine dust particles, the cracks in the walls, the door. The encounter with Carola. With all those people who talked so much about their homeland, and if they *weren't* talking about it you sensed they were thinking about it. That they felt foreign both here and there. It had to rub off on you. Throw up questions. Make you feel uneasy.

Valpovo, of course, the strange dreams, the inexplicable longing for a place about which she knew little more than that it had housed a camp for Danube Swabians sixty years ago.

This is all a load of rubbish, Bonì.

"I'm sorry," Landen said. His voice sounded strange. Something *was* strange. The strange manhunt joke.

Deep in her belly she had a strange feeling.

"That's O.K."

A pause.

"How about the weekend?" Landen said.

"Sure. If I'm off."

"Yes."

"It's lovely that you're back."

"Yes. Lovely and strange."

They laughed and rang off.

What was this strange feeling, which had reacted to the strange tone in his voice?

In the front Bermann was on the phone to Pauling, chief of the S.W.A.T. team.

Wallmer was staring out of the window.

Love, she thought.

Richard Landen loved her.

18

The raid had been well prepared. The S.W.A.T. team, stationed in Umkirch, was already there in the task-force room of Lahr Kripo, with Arndt Schneider and the Kripo head, Hermann Fried. Everyone had been properly briefed. Whatever happened it was their town, their issue; the Freiburg team were there as guests: Bob, who had been on his way to Au, Bermann, Bonì, Benedikt and Wallmer. Sixteen S.W.A.T. officers, around a dozen Kripo officers from Lahr and Freiburg, as well as the Special Support Unit. A big welcoming party for a ninety-four-year-old, but nobody knew if he was alone or if Lončar was with him.

Bob's handwriting. Just don't make any mistakes.

But clearly Bob hadn't learned from Merzhausen, when they'd looked for Lončar and deployed an entire Armada of symmetric warfare, but failed to find him because Lončar was waging his own war and had taken measures to ensure he was always one step ahead.

She tried not to think of Au and the Niemanns. She tried not to think of Carola.

Schneider stood beside Louise, having greeted her with a smile of intimacy. Her shoulder brushed his arm, she could smell his after-shave, feel his warmth. While the big and little beasts spoke – investigators from Lahr, Bob, Hermann Fried and finally Pauling, the grey-haired S.W.A.T. boss – memories from 1986–7, from that night with Schneider, now came flooding back, as if his smile and the closeness of his body had opened the gates to the past. Guitar music all night long, a tall beanpole, hungry for life and love, whose joy and passion had done her so much good at a time of inner struggle, sex on the balcony, in the stairwell, in bed and elsewhere, all night long, but just that one night – why, she couldn't remember.

Then, seventeen years later, they met again by chance in a minimalist police station office. In the intervening years a child had died, a marriage had failed, they'd come to terms with life. No more dreams, no real desire for novelty, they lived at the mercy of events, and if needs be in an apartment covered in dust with a metal door. Schneider presumably managed to circumvent the abyss, whereas she plunged into it time and again. Two different lives that had converged for one night, seventeen years ago.

She felt for Schneider's hand, and he took hers in his, as if he'd been waiting seventeen years for this moment. And they stood like that, close together, waiting to hear what needed to be said.

Now it was her turn, Chief Inspector Bonì with the most up-to-date information on their man. She let go of Schneider's hand and started talking.

A small blue house on the edge of town with a front garden, an old-fashioned garage and smoke rising from the chimney. An old man, a housekeeper, but otherwise nobody to be seen, Pauling had said in the task-force room. Lahr Kripo and the S.W.A.T. team had been keeping Andreas Eisenstein's house under observation for about an hour.

Nothing new now. An old man, a housekeeper.

And around three dozen heavily armed officers gathered in the drizzle in a side street who, on Pauling's order, dispersed in silence, the S.W.A.T. team dressed in black, forming a first ring of attack, masked, inscrutable figures bristling with such aggression and determination. Kripo and Special Support officers followed in the slipstream of their energy.

Standing with Bermann, Louise watched the front door being broken down and heard the shattering of glass from the rear of the blue house, then loud shouting when the officers entered, a woman's panicky scream, the thudding of footsteps as the S.W.A.T. team ran upstairs, more shouting and finally the all-clear. Then she was standing in a small hallway that smelled of old people and illness, and heard a calm, deep, beautiful man's voice say, "Which one of you can I speak to? I should like to speak to someone who's not pointing a gun at me."

Andreas Eisenstein stood in the middle of his living room, surrounded by a wall of S.W.A.T. men. He was a gaunt man with white hair and a crooked back, and his face, neck and hands were dotted with brown liver spots. In his arms he held a sobbing woman, who might have been a Croat or Bosnian, or perhaps a Serb – Louise wasn't an expert on the physiognomy of former Yugoslavia. He was stroking her arm, talking to her softly in his beautiful voice in Croatian, Bosnian or Serbian, while Hermann Fried, Bob and Pauling stood before him, conferring in a whisper.

Fried and Bob explained to Eisenstein in few words why on a rainy October day an entire host of police officers had forced their way into his house and asked after Antun Lončar. Do you know a man by this name, are you in contact with him?

Eisenstein had simply nodded, and turned back to the woman.

In the end Pauling gave his people the order to put down their weapons, after which he instructed the squad leader to assemble the men outside. Fried sent the Lahr officers back to the station, leaving only himself, Pauling and the Freiburg team. From one moment to the next, quiet returned to the living room; the only sounds to be heard were the sobbing of the small woman, Eisenstein's words of comfort and the gentle rapping of the rain against the windows. For minutes there was no other sound, nor barely a movement, and Louise sensed a peculiar peace descend on the room and the people in it, a dark, exhausted peace as after a very lengthy time of war and suffering. Gazing at Eisenstein she realised that this peace emanated from him, this tall, crooked, ninety-four-year-old who, like Emma and Waldemar Kaufmann, must have travelled a long road from the East to the West, from Novi Sad in 1910, via Schutzberg from 1914 to 1942, and the places that the 1942 resettlement had taken him, finally to Lahr in 1964. Two world wars in-between and probably more suffering than she would care to imagine.

"Any chance of a coffee?" Bermann said as they waited for Eisenstein to pacify the woman, and for the big beasts to decide on how to proceed from here. Who was going to stay and talk to Eisenstein?

Pauling's gaze swept over Bermann, then Louise. They had a mutual antipathy and blamed each other for mistakes and dead bodies without ever having discussed the matter. Niksch, the young policeman from Liebau, who had died in January 2003, was her dead body – Pauling's niece, Theres, had been engaged to Niksch. Peter Mladić, the Lahr officer who had died during a S.W.A.T. operation in July 2003, was Pauling's dead body. Both Louise and Pauling ought to have assumed responsibility and resigned, but they didn't.

She raised her eyebrows, Pauling moved away, and Bob turned around and said, "Louise and Mats are staying with me, the rest of you are going back to Freiburg."

"Antun Lončar," Eisenstein said in the purest Baden accent. "I could never get used to this name, even though I chose it myself, in 1946, after the concentration camp in Walpach was closed and we had to start life again under the communists." He smiled, a sad, tired, anxious smile. The voice was that of a fifty-year-old, the face that of an old man who had witnessed a century and been drained of all energy – sunken cheeks, wrinkled, criss-crossed by fine red blood vessels, his eyes swimming in water, eyelids trembling. Louise wondered what kept this man alive; somewhere inside him there must still be strength fuelling his full voice. "Antun Lončar. Anton Töpfer – 'the potter'. There was nobody in Schutzberg with the name Töpfer so I chose it for him. Nobody must be able to trace it back to Schutzberg. Have you ever heard of Schutzberg?"

"Yes," Louise said.

"And Walpach? The concentration camp in Walpach?"

Louise didn't answer straightaway. Here again was one of those terms that made it so difficult for her to engage impartially with the lives of these people, the Danube Swabians, the concentration camp in Valpovo, she hadn't read anything about gassings, tens of thousands of deaths, systematic genocide.

Treblinka, Auschwitz, Valpovo? Seriously?

"Yes," she said. "I've heard of Walpach. Schutzberg, Walpach, Essegg. Štrpci, Valpovo, Osijek."

Eisenstein nodded. "You surprise me."

"I'm trying to understand."

"To understand Antun?"

"Yes. And everything else."

They were sitting down now, Eisenstein in an armchair with a view of the small back garden, Louise and Mats on a sofa to his left, Bob on a sofa to his right, the room lined on three sides by tall shelving units, books behind glass. Behind Bob stood a harpsichord – funny piano, she had whispered to Benedikt while they were waiting. Normal harpsichord, he'd replied – behind Louise a small dining table with four chairs. This appeared to suffice after such a long and varied life, four chairs, as if no more than three guests ever came to visit Andreas Eisenstein at the same time.

The housekeeper had made coffee – a fruit tea for Eisenstein – and on the coffee table were delicate, twee cups, a carafe with water and a plate of biscuits. Only Louise ate the biscuits. She had to catch up on lunch, and dinner might be with the Niemanns.

"To understand Antun," Eisenstein repeated thoughtfully. "That—"

"Later," Bob interrupted him. Sliding forwards in his chair he asked, "When did you last see Lončar?"

"A few days ago."

Bob nodded impatiently. In the task-force room in Lahr Louise had already noticed changes in him. Bob was unsettled, nervous, speaking faster than normal, his eyes even more concentrated.

Bob was worried.

Au was a fortress, but maybe they were making mistakes. Maybe *he* was making mistakes.

She felt for her mobile in her shoulder bag, wanting all of a sudden to call Carola, but what would she say?

Have you seen him yet? Is he already there?

"When, exactly?" Bob said.

"Last Friday."

Louise and Benedikt exchanged glances. The day before Lončar turned up in the Niemanns' garden.

"Are you in contact with him?"

"Not in the way I expect you mean. We don't phone each other. But he's got my car and I rather hope he'll return it to me."

"What is the registration number of your car?"

Eisenstein gave it to them and described the car, a white Golf from the early 1990s, lots of rust, very noisy, he often let people borrow it, acquaintances from Croatia or Bosnia who used it to get around. Bob got to his feet before Eisenstein had finished, his mobile already in his hand. She heard him talking quietly in the hall. Now they could search with purpose – an old, rusty, white Golf.

He came back and stood diagonally behind Eisenstein. "Do you know where Lončar is?"

With difficulty Eisenstein turned around in his chair. "No."

"Where he might be?"

"No."

"No more acquaintances from Schutzberg?"

"Not in Lahr or Freiburg."

"Any other acquaintances?"

Eisenstein raised his hands and pointed at the chair. "Please sit down. You don't have to stand and I don't want to strain my neck any longer. At my age that would spell disaster." He smiled.

Bob sat down. "Any other acquaintances."

"One, in Freiburg."

"Paul Niemann," Bob said.

Eisenstein nodded. "A friend, probably from Slavonia, from Essegg if I remember rightly, an ethnic German like us. Came to Germany in the 1950s when we were allowed to buy our way out of Yugoslavia."

"Is that what Lončar told you?" Bob asked.

"Yes. Isn't it true?"

"Buy your way out?"

"Later," Bob said, agitated now. "Paul Niemann."

Eisenstein clasped his hands in his lap and hunched his shoulders slightly forwards as he concentrated. One day, sometime in summer, a letter had arrived. Antun asking him to find an address – somewhere in Baden, maybe Freiburg or the surrounding area – for the very same Paul Niemann. Eisenstein raised his hands, a gesture of bewilderment, a letter after years with no contact.

"Yes, yes, I understand," Bob muttered.

A pause.

Eisenstein's eyes wandered from one to the other, then fixed themselves on the window, a gaze into the distance that ended in the fog a few hundred metres behind the house. A Paul Niemann somewhere in Baden, Louise thought. On the documents from Munich it had just said "Herr Niemann", and how could Lončar have known about the move to Baden? "Get Alfons to call Munich," she said to Bob, who nodded, his eyes screwed up, then asked, "Why?"

"Lončar might have been there in the summer," Benedikt answered for her. "He could have asked someone about Paul Niemann."

"Someone?"

"At the registration office."

Bob rubbed his brow, as searching inside his head for the key question that still needed to be asked, one which would give them the answer to all the other questions.

"Do you remember where the letter was sent from?" Benedikt asked.

Eisenstein nodded. "From Munich."

"Do you know what Antun is planning?" Louise said.

Eisenstein looked at her and shook his head.

"But you know that he *is* planning something? That he's done something and hasn't finished yet?"

"You're worrying me." Eisenstein clasped his hands in his lap. "But if I'm being honest, he worried me too. He was so . . . I can't describe it. When I saw him my first thought was that he was bristling with . . . cruelty. And then I thought that something terrible must have happened to him."

"Yes," Louise said.

"Do you know what?"

"Yes."

"Later." Bob got up and said he had to go back to Freiburg, but first he needed Lončar's real name, his birth name, and he looked at Eisenstein full of hope and expectation, as if this German name were the answer to all their questions, as if it needed to be said out loud only once and everything would be over, the threat posed by Lončar, the fear of mistakes, the nervousness. But then it was just a perfectly normal name, Heinrich Schwarzer, a name like millions of others that meant nothing, didn't signal any ties, any connections, a name without answers that just threw up more questions. Bob had no time or patience for these questions, he said his goodbyes and left, returning moments later to get Benedikt. You go to Au, stay with the Niemanns, *that's* where we need people now, not here.

They left, the door slamming noisily.

Rubbing his watery eyes, Eisenstein said, "They've gone now, the men with the guns. Later you can tell me what happened to Antun and why you're looking for him. But not now." He picked up his teacup and took a sip. "Now we're going to talk about Schutzberg and Walpach and Josefsdorf, so you understand."

"Josefsdorf?"

"Poreč. Two or three streets, a handful of houses, one of the former German villages in Slavonia. Josefsdorf/Poreč."

Louise nodded. Poreč, where Antun Lončar lived, where Biljana and Snježana were born.

19

They were back, the figures, several dozen or a hundred, some with faces this time. Louise saw Andreas Eisenstein, Heinrich Schwarzer, Biljana and Snježana amongst them, even though this was obviously a fantasy. Eisenstein began his story in 1895, long before the four of them were born.

At the foot of the Dornenberg – Glogovac in Slav – in Bosnia–Herzegovina, which had passed from Turkish to Austro-Hungarian administration a couple of decades earlier, a German settlement was to be built on former swampland and impenetrable forest. The first village built by the ethnic-German Protestant families from south-eastern Europe, Galicia and Russia kept being flooded in the years that followed, so they decided to construct a new settlement on the Dornenberg.

In accordance with the regulations of the Bosnian authorities, the linear village of Glogovac was established in 1902 on the crest of the mountain. It was around six kilometres long with a crossroads, but no fields or pastureland. The settlers continued to farm the old land down in the valley, seven kilometres away. In the centre of the German village of Glogovac stood the centre of the Serbian village of Štrpci – a school and church with a rectory – for the scattered Serbian farms in the area. In 1903, following a request from its inhabitants, Glogovac acquired the additional German name of "Schutzberg" and from then on was known as "Glogovac–Schutzberg", but of course, Eisenstein said, the "Glogovac" soon got lost in German usage and it became simply "Schutzberg".

He stopped, quickly drank his fruit tea, which by now must have been quite cold, then drank down a glass of water as if he were dying of thirst. He was breathing heavily and smiled apologetically, gesturing for a moment of patience. His eyes moved to one of the shelves behind glass. "Would you please . . .?"

Louise got up. On one of the shelves boxes of medicines were piled up, and beside these a little plastic box, which is what Eisenstein asked for. She fleetingly glanced at the titles of the books on the shelves, literature on the Danube Swabians, a multi-volume *White Book of the Germans from Yugoslavia*, books whose titles contained words such as "genocide" and "expulsion", books on local history and culture, Croatian titles, English titles. She brought him the box, sat down and waited until he had taken a tablet and washed it down with more water.

"How about the psalm?" she said. "Psalm 9, verse 9."

"Do you know our psalm?"

"'The Lord will also be a refuge for the oppressed, a refuge in times of trouble.'"

Eisenstein nodded and began to weep silently. Then, alternating between tears and smiles, he said, this psalm, which gave Schutzberg its name and ultimately outlived it, was there for the entire duration of the village, was even carved onto the front of the church. The verse accompanied him and others in their life of suffering after 1942 until they found a new home in Josefsdorf as German Croats amongst German and "real" Croats. For years there, they recited the psalm in their heads only rather than out loud, because in the new, communist Yugoslavia it was better not to reveal yourself as a German. They recited it in their heads together, holding hands, he and Heinrich and Heinrich's uncle, Christian, the Schutzbergers in Josefsdorf, praying silently, the Lord will also be a refuge for the oppressed, a refuge in times of trouble.

Eisenstein had stopped crying and now laboured to his feet, then apologised and left the room. The housekeeper brought more biscuits, fresh coffee, fresh tea and fresh water. Louise thanked her, the housekeeper, who may have been around sixty, gave a startled smile and said something in her language, just one word, which sounded like "*Molim*".

While Louise waited for Eisenstein to return she called Hoffmann – no news; her colleagues in the car outside the Niemanns' – no news; and finally Benedikt, who'd just arrived in Au – no news from him either. The manhunt is gathering pace, Eisenstein's house is under surveillance, Au is a fortress, Bob thinks we'll have him either today or tomorrow.

"We know him better," Benedikt said.

"Yes," Louise said.

"He might not even be here anymore. In Germany, I mean."

Louise nodded. Perhaps he won't come back until Au is no longer a fortress, when we've forgotten him because we can't spend months, years thinking about an old warrior with a horrible plan.

But they knew him better.

"No," she said.

"No," Benedikt agreed. He gave a forced laugh. "Hunches."

She nodded again. "Frightening hunches."

When Eisenstein was back in his armchair she asked him about the word the housekeeper had used. *Molim*, he replied, Croatian for "please" or "you're welcome". "Thank you" is *hvala*. She silently repeated the words, *molim, hvala*, foreign words like "Valpovo". It was a language in which she would get completely lost, because neither French nor English helped at all. No possible derivations, no associations. She wondered how Heinrich Schwarzer, alias Antun Lončar, had fared when he came to Germany in the 1990s, to the country whose language was linked to his early childhood and its traumas. Whether he'd got lost in the language of his childhood.

*

Eisenstein continued his account with the first great tragedy of the Danube Swabians, the collapse of the Austro-Hungarian Monarchy in 1918 and the division of south-eastern Europe into nation states: Hungary, Romania, the Kingdom of the Serbs, Croats and Slovenes – later, the "Kingdom of Yugoslavia". At a stroke the key areas where one and a half million Danube Swabians were settled were cut through by national borders, Bačka, the Banat and Baranya were divided between two or three countries, former neighbours were now citizens of different nationality.

Eisenstein himself had come from Novi Sad to Schutzberg in 1914, then as a young man he moved to Osijek where he was trained as a chaplain. In his early twenties he moved back even though there was no position for a chaplain in Schutzberg. He came to an agreement with Pastor Sommer to undertake the duties of a chaplain and other tasks in return for a little money or supper.

"He wrote a book," Eisenstein said, getting to his feet again. "A wonderful book on the history of Schutzberg, but also about Germans and German culture in Bosnia, about war, Christian love, suffering, as well as the relationship between Croats and Serbs, who back then did what they did again in the 1990s – set upon each other with implacable hatred." He took a book from one of the shelves and turned to Boni. "A very simple, emotional, personal book, and full of errors too, but it says so much about the cooperation and antagonism between different peoples who had but one thing in common: they farmed the earth of the same region." He went over to her. "Look."

"Thank you. *Hvala.*"

Eisenstein touched her shoulder and she heard him laugh softly. "You don't have to pronounce the 'H' as if you were collecting saliva in your throat to spit it out."

She smiled and felt his hand squeeze her shoulder, a gesture of paternal affection which came as such a surprise that it unsettled her momentarily.

Yes, this was sometimes missing too in Boni's scaffolded house and heart – parental affection. An annoying relic from the dusty quarry of her childhood.

"*Hvala*. Better?"

"Much better. *Molim*."

The hand was still on her shoulder and it felt nice.

It said *F. Sommer. Schutzberg – Bosnia* on the simple paper cover. Inside there was a drawing of the Protestant church and rectory in Schutzberg, then the full title of the book that she already knew from Hoffmann's research on the internet: *Far from the Land of their Forefathers. A History of the German Protestant Community of Schutzberg in Bosnia, 1895 to 1942. The Painful Return. The Fate of the Bosnian-Germans 1942 to 1960.*

"He was a great Christian, a great man, Ferdinand Sommer," Eisenstein said from behind her. "An unknown man in a tiny village in a forgotten corner of German civilisation, but it's only in such places that you meet truly great people, who don't ask what they can get, but only what they may give." The hand moved from her shoulder and took the book. He put it back on the shelf and closed the glass, as if he didn't want to expose it to the air or her hands any longer than necessary, then sat back down.

"During his twenty-two-year ministry in Schutzberg he strove to find an accommodation between peoples, between us Germans and our immediate Serbian neighbours, between the Croats and the Serbs, and later between us Bosnian Germans and the Germans in the Reich, which became increasingly difficult because in the late 1930s the Reich began to co-opt the German expatriates. They turned us into *Volksdeutsche*, sent emissaries to politicise us and "co-ordinate" our organisations. Many of our young people, but older ones too, joined this movement, they assumed the leadership of the cultural association, formed youth and other organisations similar to those that existed in the old homeland, swastika flags and armbands appeared, Hitler's birthday was publicly celebrated. All this was intensified even further when, in 1941, the Independent State of Croatia was established – run by the Ustaša – which, as you might know, existed by the grace of Hitler and had the same political orientation, i.e. it was fascist."

Louise nodded, recalling that Waldemar Kaufmann had mentioned the Ustaša Croats, a word on her list from Lahr. She'd just forgotten the context.

"Of course this marked the beginning of the end for the Germans in the south-east," Eisenstein said. "I didn't see it coming myself, I was young then and I'm not smart, but Pastor Sommer knew early on what would happen. He knew that one day we'd have to pay dearly for having aligned ourselves more or less officially with the Reich during the war and in the years leading up to it. In his book you will find the sentence which says that this instigated the death march of German civilisation in south-eastern Europe, and he—" Eisenstein stopped abruptly when Erik Satie rang out from the depths of Bonì's bag.

"And he . . .?"

"And he was right."

She nodded, apologised and fished out her mobile. Jenny Böhm saying, everything's O.K. with me, how about you? She wanted to talk about the "man with the psalm", what kind of person is he, why's he waiting outside your house, tell me, Louise, I'm lying in a hotel bed worrying about you. Louise put off answering her until later and swiftly brought the conversation to an end.

Jenny's call had brought back the disquiet, the questions. Where was he? What was he planning?

The wife, the daughter. Would he really go so far?

Eisenstein was looking at her, both of them knew they had to talk about Lončar, that there was no time for a leisurely conversation about the history of a tiny village in a forgotten corner of German colonisation in south-east Europe.

She stood up and went to the window. A small, neat garden, chrysanthemums in all colours and woodland beyond. The fog seemed to be thinning, the rain easing up. Had Lončar been inside her apartment? Had he followed Jenny? Was that the plan, perhaps, to take a hostage who was not involved?

Or was he already in Au?

She had to get away from here, she had to go to the Niemanns.

She turned around. "I have to go."

Eisenstein nodded and waited for her to explain. She saw his exhaustion, saw that he didn't want her to notice *how* exhausted he was, a ninety-four-year-old who had been paid a visit by a S.W.A.T. team on an October afternoon, and was now being confronted with his own painful past.

She leaned against the window sill, crossed her arms and forced herself to remain calm.

Mats was in Au, other people were in Au. Au was a fortress.

"We need to talk about Antun. About Heinrich."

Eisenstein bent forwards suddenly and whispered, "What has he done? What hasn't he yet finished?"

Louise returned to the sofa. It was a dreadful prospect, to have to tell Eisenstein about Biljana and Snježana, Lončar's visit to the Niemanns', the fire, the fact that it wasn't over, that he was presumably planning to take Paul Niemann's wife and daughter.

"Later," she said.

"Is it that bad?"

"Yes. What happened to him, what he's planning."

"Then I'm happy I've still got a few minutes of ignorance."

"Tell me about the resettlement."

"The resettlement." Eisenstein splayed his fingers, as if attempting to apologise for the fresh tears in his eyes. "The day we took leave of our homeland."

"But why? Why did you have to leave Schutzberg?"

"The attacks by Serbian killers in Bosnia intensified in 1941 and 1942, and the situation became ever more precarious. We were shot at and could no longer go to the fields down the valley without fearing for our lives. The Croats were very stand-offish, because the political and military situation meant they weren't masters in their own house, but they couldn't do what they might have wanted to do. They did terrible things to the Serb civilians, however. In short, this 'war after the war', as Pastor Sommer called these months, posed more and more dangers. And so the Reich resorted to an old plan, which was to resettle the Bosnian Germans, because the Wehrmacht could no longer guarantee us protection. It would, moreover, kill two birds with one stone: bring the *Volksdeutsche* of Bosnia to safety and colonise areas of the lands conquered in the East with Germans. The new home for us Schutzbergers was to be Litzmannstadt."

"Litzmannstadt?" Louise said, reaching for the water glass.

"Łódź."

Her hand stopped in mid-air. "Poland? They sent the Bosnian Germans to *Poland*?"

"They needed Germans in the East." Eisenstein shrugged. "Politics. All the major migration flows are a result of callous politics."

Louise shook her head, took a sip of water and put the glass down. Poland, that didn't fit anymore. Were Lončar and Eisenstein in Łódź before coming back to Yugoslavia?

No, Eisenstein said softly. Heinrich's parents, uncle and aunt, as well as he and his wife didn't go to Litzmannstadt; they didn't leave their home, they stayed in Croatia, a dreadful mistake he would never be able to forgive himself for, because a few months later only he, Heinrich and Heinrich's uncle were still alive.

Schutzberg at the beginning of November 1942, life during the war continued its course, life before the resettlement, the timetable for which had not yet been made public. A child was born and could no longer be baptised in his homeland; the village church had already been cleared out. On the late afternoon of November 5, Pastor Sommer announced that the resettlement commission from Slavonski Brod, which consisted of barely two dozen men, had come to the village and told the inhabitants that they had to leave Schutzberg at six o'clock the following morning. One evening and a night to load onto carts everything that had accumulated over the years, decades, then in the morning the Schutzbergers set off, a convoy of more than one hundred and twenty wagons, escorted by members of the *Deutsche Mannschaft*, the armed protection force of the *Volksdeutsche*.

They left their horses and carts in Derventa and climbed aboard trains. In Slavonski Brod in Croatia the Schutzbergers were divided into two groups, one continuing by train, the other staying the night there. The Schwarzers and Eisensteins were in the second group and for a while had been planning to battle their own way northwards to Essegg, where Eisenstein's wife had relatives. That night Heinrich, together with another new-born from Schutzberg, was baptised by Pastor Sommer – the last Schutzbergers to be christened. Early the next morning the Schwarzers and Eisensteins were already a few kilometres outside of Slavonski Brod and a few days later they reached Essegg, Germans in the Independent State of Croatia, where Ustaša, the German Wehrmacht and S.S., communist partisans and Četnik partisans fought each other with extraordinary savagery.

Eisenstein drank some tea and cleared his throat.

"Did you ever go back?" Louise said. "To Schutzberg?"

No, he said. As far as he was concerned his homeland was lost, he'd never wanted to return for a visit, didn't want to be a stranger in his own street, outside his house, beneath his sky. No, Schutzberg didn't exist anymore and you couldn't visit a place that no longer existed.

Life went on until the fascist Ustaša state collapsed in 1945 and the war in the Balkans was decided. There was an exodus northwards, Croatian soldiers, Wehrmacht, S.S., Serb Četniks, as well as Croatian and a few ethnic German civilians, including the Schwarzers and Eisensteins. They no longer saw any future under "Tito's bands of killers", who regarded the Danube Swabians as a Nazi fifth column, irrespective of whether they had sympathised with the Reich, like many, or not, like many others. And they were right, Eisenstein said, for now the genocide began. Expropriation, expulsion, revocation of citizenship rights. More waves of migrants emerged, consisting exclusively of ethnic Germans, which were intercepted in Slovenia, forced to turn around and the Germans were taken to extermination camps . . .

A similar fate befell the Schwarzers and Eisensteins, who fled alongside the Croats. Fierce battles accompanied their flight, particularly in Slovenia. In May 1945 the stream of people crossed the Austrian border and were stopped by the British just outside Bleiburg, almost two hundred thousand people, the valley black with bodies, Eisenstein said in tears, his beautiful voice quavering.

He paused.

Negotiations began with the British, who were occupying Carinthia, he continued, while officers from the partisans demanded that the refugees be handed over. "A tug-of-war over the lives of thousands," Eisenstein said, shaking his head in supplication. "I can't tell you what happened then, please spare me that. All you need to know is that the Tito partisans won the tug-of-war, and one week after the end of the war, on May 15, 1945, the British handed us over. Heinrich's father, his aunt and my wife died of exhaustion on the *via dolorosa* back south, many hundreds of others starved to death, succumbed to illness or were shot . . . You can't imagine the levels of suffering, barbarism . . . I can't talk about it."

Eisenstein put his face in his hands, then looked up and kept talking, as if trying to get it over and done with. Once back in Slavonia they were taken to Walpach because they were *Volksdeutsche*. There, the partisans had set up one of their concentration camps for Germans.

And there the deaths continued – hunger, illness, exhaustion, suicide. Three thousand inmates over the course of a year, and half didn't survive, including Heinrich's mother, who died a few days before the camp was wound up in 1946.

"He saw his mother die as well as his father," Eisenstein said. "He wasn't yet three years old when he sat in the rain beside a dusty road somewhere in Slovenia, his dead father lying nearby, half-naked in the mud. He had simply collapsed and died minutes later ... He stared at his dead father, just one of many who collapsed by the side of the road on this death march, or who had been shot in their thousands beforehand . . ." Now agitated, Eisenstein cleared his throat. "And then, before his fourth birthday, his mother dropped dead from hunger and exhaustion in Walpach concentration camp, and he sat beside her, swatting away the flies and mosquitoes . . . the ants crawling over her face . . ." Having raised his voice, Eisenstein now lowered it again. "*That's* what you have to know if you want to understand him. If you . . . if we want to understand what he has done or intends to do."

Louise nodded. She now pictured Carola – the wild, sad expression, the red hair, the anxiety about her family falling apart. And Henriette, who refused to be driven away, who was going to leave her husband. Two women who'd done no different from millions of others: lead a quiet, complicated, innocent life.

Just as Biljana and Snježana had done.

A life for Biljana's life, and one for Snježana's.

Understand Antun? Never in the way Eisenstein perhaps meant.

But both of them had problems with words. Valpovo "concentration camp". Tito's "bands of killers". "Genocide".

The words were part of the problem, Schneider had said in Lahr. Now she believed he was right. Words weren't neutral. They told stories from a particular perspective.

Eisenstein was still quiet, and looked up at her occasionally. She knew he wouldn't talk about his wife, who'd died on the way back to Slavonia from Bleiburg. And then he began to cry. He cried silently for some minutes, his shoulders hunched forwards, hands in his lap, a lonely, very old man who had been taken back to the horrors of his past.

Who she had to tell what had happened to Lončar, and what he might be planning to do.

The unease returned. Lončar had made preparations. Plans. What plan did he have for the days following the fire? Was he in Au, observing the house, her colleagues in the car, on the roads? What would she do in his place? Where would she be *at this moment* if she were in his place?

Perhaps this was the mistake: to be agonising over what was happening *now*. An old warrior who forged plans did his thinking *in advance*. Thought about what he would do when he'd executed his plan.

Made preparations for what he would do.

She got up and went back to the window. It had stopped raining and the fog had almost vanished. The stone terrace was dark with rain, the boughs of a fruit tree swayed gently. On three sides of the garden were fences separating it from other properties. There was nobody to be seen.

Made preparations for what he would do, where he would go.

Was Antun Lončar in Lahr? Here, hidden somewhere, having waited for her to come to Andreas Eisenstein?

That's what she would have done in his place, she thought. She would have wanted to know whether the contact had been discovered. Whether the police were now also looking out for a white 1990s' Golf.

Whether it was safe to return to Eisenstein's without falling into a trap.

*

Understand Heinrich, understand Antun. The years in Josefsdorf/ Poreč were still missing. It was to there, to an abandoned Danube-Swabian house, that Eisenstein had gone with the barely four-year-old Heinrich and his uncle after the camp in Walpach was closed in 1946.

The first few years in Josefsdorf, said Eisenstein, now looking utterly shattered and speaking in a monotone, were peaceful, if not easy-going or even happy, because they'd all lost far too much and now they relinquished their Germanness too, not because they were compelled to, but for fear of being denounced as "fascists", and of visits from the state security service. Heinrich, who couldn't speak a word of Croatian, was not to speak German anymore, not at home and definitely not in the street. Christian, the uncle, ensured that from now on they would try to become Croats, like so many other ethnic Germans.

On the way to Josefsdorf they had given themselves Croatian names – now they were Davor Vejnović, and Igor and Antun Lončar. The papers and documents with their real names were buried in a box in the garden. Together they learned Croatian day and night, Heinrich as a beginner, the other two to get rid of their telltale accents. From now on they were Croats. The only thing they wanted to keep, Eisenstein said, was the German psalm, Psalm 9, verse 9, *The Lord will also be a refuge for the oppressed, a refuge in times of trouble.* These words were a refuge for *them* in their times of trouble.

At night the dreams came, for years. He and Christian never spoke about it, only Heinrich, who would wake up sobbing and always told them about the same dream – hundreds, thousands of men, his father among them, dancing in the rain in a clearing, very slowly as if they were hanging from threads, like puppets being operated in slow motion, and they appeared to laugh and be happy. But then in his dream Heinrich realised that the men and his father were "dancing" because they were being shot at, bullets peppering their bodies. They were crying, not laughing, and then he saw them die.

*

In 1960 Eisenstein, alias Davor Vejnović, left Josefsdorf/Poreč and moved to Germany, which had been possible since the mid-1950s so long as you had money to "buy your way out". Antun had joined the Yugoslav army, having become a Croat through and through, and he loathed everything German about himself, and about his uncle Christian and Eisenstein. When the two of them whispered the psalm he would leave the room. They began to argue about everything for no reason. Whenever Eisenstein or Christian used a German word, Antun threatened to denounce them. He'd been forced to deny every-thing German in him for so long that he'd begun to despise it too. One night he unearthed the box in the garden, took out his identifica-tion documents and burned them.

Eisenstein left Croatia a deeply divided man. He longed for Germany, and yet he reproached himself for abandoning Antun. But Antun had gone, days earlier, without so much as a goodbye. Only Christian accompanied him to the station in Požega.

Eisenstein hadn't seen Antun Lončar for forty-four years, nor heard anything from him. Until one day in summer 2004 a letter arrived from Munich, and then a few weeks ago Antun was standing outside the house in Lahr, now almost an old man himself, a quiet, stony, antagonistic man who refused to be touched or embraced, who didn't want to say what had happened in the intervening years, who wanted just one thing: Paul Niemann's address, and who took just one thing: Eisenstein's old white Golf.

A few minutes later she left, Eisenstein showing her silently to the door. Until the last moment her questions about those words were still on her tongue: "concentration camp", "extermination camp", "genocide", why these words, Herr Eisenstein, surely they tell of some-thing else – of what the Nazis did to the Jews. Are you comparing Valpovo to Auschwitz? Was the expulsion of ethnic Germans in any way comparable to the planned extermination of the Jews? And were Tito's partisans really "bands of killers"? I mean, they fought the Nazis and helped liberate the Balkans! Don't you understand that words like that make it hard for me to engage with the fate of the Danube Swabians? That they just make me sceptical, and perplexed?

But these were questions she did not ask. As she looked into Eisenstein's old, watery eyes, she thought that perhaps you couldn't expect total objectivity from people like him, people who had been in camps such as Valpovo, who had been pursued and shot at, and who for years had been compelled to deny their identity.

And who had dreamed of a dance of death.

Eisenstein asked no questions either, such as What happened to Heinrich? What hasn't he finished? He must have realised that he didn't want to know the answers. Perhaps, she thought, because he wanted to preserve an image of the past that had been with him for decades, and which should remain unsullied by the present.

Or because he knew that he would not be able to cope with the answers.

She did ask one further question, however.

A cigarette case with the inscription "Valpovo 1945".

Eisenstein nodded. A present for Heinrich from a German boy in Walpach camp.

He said nothing more, just looked at her as if this story should not be told, because there were some stories that must remain untold.

In Benedikt's patrol car she made the obligatory telephone calls: Benedikt, the officers outside the Niemanns', Hoffmann, who had taken delivery of Eisenstein's book from Frankfurt, and finally Jenny Böhm, who was still lying on her hotel bed watching T.V. series and talk shows, and in between making calls that would end the hide-and-seek and the lies. During their conversation Louise let her gaze wander across Eisenstein's house, the row of houses and front gardens opposite, and checked her rear-view mirror, in case he was actually here, Antun Lončar, who had once been Heinrich Schwarzer, a long, long time ago, back in 1942 in a German village in Bosnia, in Osijek/Essegg, on the flight to Bleiburg in Carinthia, on the forced return to Slavonia, in Valpovo camp 1945–46. On the way to Josefsdorf/Poreč he had become a child with a different name, a different language, a different family and different nightmares.

20

In Au she relieved Benedikt. The day shift had finished, the night shift was beginning, even though nobody knew she'd agreed to sleep at the Niemanns'.

They stood in the darkness by Benedikt's car.

"I'm staying the night here."

"What?"

"I need a bed that's not full of dust."

Benedikt smiled, but the eyes behind his glasses looked sceptical.

"That's what I'm like, Mats. I have weird hunches and I do weird things that aren't in the job description."

And, she thought, I led Lončar here.

"There are boundaries, Louise."

"No boundaries that you can't define yourself."

"There are things you shouldn't do for good reason. You, Louise, assume responsibility where you ought not to."

"In case something happens."

"Right. But the Niemanns are part of our professional life, not our private life. When it's time to clock off we should close the door and go home."

"And stand beside their dead bodies tomorrow morning?"

"Au is a fortress, Louise."

She had to smile. Bob's words, with which he tried to predetermine the course of the world so the world didn't get in his way as he rose higher. "I can't, Mats. I like these people. I *feel* responsible."

"You like the daughter."

"You've noticed?"

Benedikt shrugged. "I'm a good copper."

"And a nice one, too."

"Don't change the subject." He touched her shoulder.

"Everything is interconnected somehow, Mats."

"What do you mean?"

"An elderly man from a Bosnian-German village and a family from Merzhausen who didn't even know his name until a few days ago. A Kripo inspector with no husband or children and a sad, wild girl." With a finger she drew an arch in the air above Au. "A village near Freiburg and the ethnic Germans in former Yugoslavia. Present-day Germany and the history of south-eastern Europe. Everything is interconnected somehow."

Antun Lončar and her.

"Only objectively," Benedikt said.

She lowered her hand. "Not emotionally?"

"Correct."

"But if you allow it to be, then yes. If you let yourself get affected by it."

"I told you I don't have any feelings." He grinned.

"Only little shapeless things in your heart."

"Yes."

They laughed.

Benedikt got in, adjusted the seat, rear-view mirror, wing mirror and said, "Go and stay with Anne, Louise. Or come with me." He looked at her. "It's dangerous. If Lončar comes. If he gets into the house."

She nodded. In their line of work you had to reckon with a bit of danger from time to time, she thought.

But she didn't say it. Only in office hours, Benedikt would have said.

She stepped back, he closed the door and wound down the window.

"If only they'd go away somewhere," she said.

"Bob tried earlier, and Rolf was here too. They're refusing to budge. Try to persuade them."

"I will. Over dinner."

Benedikt stuck his left hand out of the window, she took it with her right.

"Don't forget to shut the office door, Mats."

"It's already shut."

She watched him pull away and waved as if he was driving off and never coming back, not soon at any rate.

As if this were a farewell.

Carola opened the door and showed Bonì to the sister-in-law's room which, like the guest room, was small and gloomy. At least the bed looked soft and cosy, a bed to collapse into, if you fancied collapsing. To have breakfast in, to be ill in, to be alone in.

Louise had popped by her apartment, stuffed clothes and toiletries into a travel bag along with the documents on the Danube Swabians, which she would continue reading in this soft, cosy bed from which you could rule the world, the pillow at your back.

Here's the loo, here's the bathroom, I've put out some towels for you . . .

Then they were standing in the hallway and Louise asked, "What's the mood like?"

"Crap." Carola slipped her hands into her back pockets and gave Louise a look that was both defiant and sad. "They're not talking to each other anymore."

"Hmm."

"I mean, they're adults. They can't just stop talking to one another. They've got to think of us, surely. They're our *parents*."

"I'll have a word with them, if you like."

Carola shrugged. "What about the man?"

"Yes, the man." Louise paused and thought: no lies, but she couldn't tell the truth either. The hunches.

"You'll get him, won't you?"

"I'm convinced of that. Au is . . . We've got lots of people here."

Carola smiled fleetingly, she seemed to want to say something, Louise could see the words in her eyes, in her smile: And you're with us.

As she was unpacking her travel bag, Hoffmann called. "We've got a right hodgepodge now," he said. Ilic had learned from his contact in Zagreb that Biljana Lončar had been Orthodox.

"So?"

"Illi says that means she was a Serb. A Croatian Serb."

Louise sat on the bed. Antun Lončar, born Heinrich Schwarzer in Štrpci in Bosnia, of German ancestry, becomes a Croat in Poreč in Slavonia. Biljana, born in Poreč in Croatia, an Orthodox Serb.

She groaned.

"And there's something else," Hoffmann said.

More hodgepodge.

The Lončars, Ilic had learned from his contact in Banja Luka, moved to Štrpci in 1992. Although no-one by the name of Lončar had lived there, there had been one family with Biljana's maiden name, unpronounceable, Hoffmann said, emitting various hissing sounds, at least that's roughly how it sounded when Illi said it. "Illi says they probably moved to Bosnia because it was too dangerous for a Croatian Serb to stay in Slavonia during the war. First of all, he said, the Serbs attacked Croatia, taking Vukovar in 1991, laying siege to Osijek for ten months and conquering half of Slavonia. No wonder he says life wasn't particularly comfortable for the Serbs in Slavonian villages.

Louise went to the little window and gazed at a section of the pitched roof. Below it, now invisible in the darkness, lay the overgrown vegetable garden. She closed the shutters and drew the curtains. Lončar had tried to bring his wife to safety, had fled with her and their daughter to the place where he was born and spent the first four days of his life.

The place where, years later, his wife and daughter were murdered.

She went back to the bed. "That's why they went to Štrpci rather than Poreč after being repatriated. Just one thing: why did they have themselves registered in Germany under the name Lončar again?"

"What a hodgepodge," Hoffmann muttered.

"It explains a lot."

"Yugo-hodgepodge, Illi says."

She nodded. Yugo-stories.

Later she wandered alone through the house to gain an overall picture of the place, rooms, windows, balconies, doors leading outside, how you got in, how you got out, were all the doors locked?

A cellar like a crypt, walls blackened by mould, dust and spiders' webs. An oil tank, a laundry room with a washing machine and dryer, and a way out to the vegetable garden. A half-empty wine cellar that clearly hadn't been in use for years.

She went back up to the first floor. It would be useless trying to work out how Lončar would proceed if he actually did turn up. He would have a variety of possibilities and would opt for those she would be least expecting. Still, she knew her way around the house now, maybe that was a slight advantage.

In her room she made the usual calls, beginning with Jenny Böhm, who wanted to talk again, and again was put off. Hoffmann had more information to report, having found out via unofficial contacts in the citizenship office that Antun Lončar, following his deportation in winter 1998, had declared himself to be German, given his real name and submitted an application for re-entry into Germany for him and his family. Because he had no documents such as a birth certificate, passport or school certificates in the name of Heinrich Schwarzer, the application was rejected.

The old homeland hadn't taken him and his family in.

*

Supper with the Niemanns in Au was indeed a silent affair: lowered eyes, gloomy faces over kohlrabi soup and spaghetti Bolognese at the huge kitchen table, which itself militated against any intimacy, because everyone sat more or less on their own. Only Carola made the occasional effort, saying things to her mother and father, whispering to Philip, asking Louise about her family, whether she was married, had children or siblings. Apart from Louise nobody wanted to answer. And in some way she understood these people. If the prospect of the family falling apart wasn't preying on their minds, then the fact that their lives might be in danger was. Who *would* want to say anything?

"Are you going to school tomorrow?" Louise said.

"Uh-huh," Philip said.

"No," Carola said.

Niemann looked up. "Maybe you ought to stay at home too, Philip. Until it's all . . . over."

"Home?" Philip said scornfully.

"Well, you know, here."

Philip said nothing.

"What do you think?" Niemann asked Louise.

She hesitated. The wife. The daughter. All those hunches. What if she was wrong? If Lončar was after the father and the son? "It should be O.K. A patrol car can take him there and pick him up. The school has been informed, the teachers know."

"Oh well," Niemann said. "I'm sure you know what you're doing."

She rolled her eyes. Only Carola noticed, and she grinned. Benedikt's warnings came to mind, you're crossing boundaries, you're assuming responsibility.

Carola's unspoken words from earlier: And you're with us.

Philip was the first to leave the room. Henriette cleared the table, Niemann asked Louise whether she'd like coffee or schnapps, then was silent. Outside it was a dark October night, the window and garden door reflecting what was happening inside, reflecting all the silence, the suffering, the fear, the apathy.

"And tomorrow morning there'll be muesli with fresh plums," Henriette said, smiling nervously. "I've spotted a plum tree in this dreadful garden."

"Don't go outside on your own," Louise said. "Only with me or one of my colleagues."

"He won't be sitting in the plum tree, will he?"

"You're *not* going into the garden alone."

"For goodness' sake. Three metres away. Aren't you exaggerating just a little?"

"The inspector is right: you really shouldn't," Niemann muttered.

Henriette ignored him. Her small eyes flashed at Louise, her cheeks were tense. How much she had changed over the last few days, Louise thought. Her face still cared for, made up, her hair coiffed, the clothes smart, but her entire body radiated exhaustion, fear and helplessness. Her movements were hectic, her voice higher than normal and she spoke frenetically.

"You're *not* going out alone," Louise repeated.

"Mama, please," Carola begged.

Henriette sighed and threw her hands up in resignation. "I imagine you'd like a pot of coffee for tonight?" she said.

Louise nodded. "But this time with sugar, please."

Now came the waiting, waiting, waiting. The doors were locked, windows and shutters closed. Before dinner Louise had checked every single bolt and lock. Outside were two Kripo colleagues in a car, two others somewhere amongst the houses in the darkness, while patrol cars were still driving through Au regularly. To all intents and purposes it was virtually impossible for Lončar to get into the house.

Quite apart from the fact that a nationwide manhunt was under way for him and the white Golf.

Niemann had excused himself and gone to bed. Philip was in his bedroom, doing whatever he was doing: listening to requiems in the dark, staring at a book with no lights on, or maybe neither of these. She decided she would speak to him in the morning; this evening it was Henriette and Carola's turn.

The wife, the daughter.

She sat with Carola on a peculiarly uncomfortable sofa in the living room while Henriette finished up in the kitchen. It was impossible to concentrate because one ear was listening out for noises in the house, the creaking of the stairs, the rattling of a shutter, the sounds of the individual doors being opened or closed, footsteps in the hallway and upstairs.

The rain, the wind.

"I feel so sorry for him," Carola said. "Papa."

"He'll sort himself out."

"I'm not so sure."

"He's a grown-up, Carola."

"I'm not so sure. The two of them are behaving like such idiots. Not grown up at all."

Louise shifted about in the sofa, which was uncomfortable on her back; something was hurting. "They're not in great shape. Don't expect them to cope with everything easily just because they're grown-ups. They'll sort things out, but they're not perfect."

Carola nodded.

"This is a crappy sofa," Louise said, sliding to the floor.

Carola slid down next to her. "I should have taken better care of him. I haven't really spoken to him in months. I've barely seen him. He's been so *depressing*."

"For God's sake, Carola, it's not your job to look after your father."

"I don't know. In some way it is. When I can see that he's hasn't been happy ever since we left Munich."

"Then talk to him, but don't start feeling responsible. He's not *ill*."

"Maybe he is. I mean, depression is an illness, isn't it?"

Louise sighed and decided that she'd get Hartmut Prader to come after all, however much Henriette might baulk at the idea. The loss of their house, the fear of Lončar, the family situation – they just needed somebody who was an expert in crisis and conflict management. "Come on," she said, placing an arm around Carola's shoulder and pulling her closer. Carola snuggled up to Louise.

Waiting like this, Louise thought happily, was actually rather pleasant.

"Tell me about him."

"Who?"

"The man who set fire to our house."

"What do you want to know?"

"Everything you've found out."

"I've already told you about Biljana and Snježana."

"The wife and daughter."

Louise nodded.

"Yes. But still, I'd like to know everything."

And so Louise talked, pausing to answer Carola's questions and to listen out for noises. She told the story of Heinrich Schwarzer, alias Antun Lončar, while she sat there in wait for him.

Later Carola crawled onto the sofa and fell asleep. Henriette came to say goodnight and that was all she seemed prepared to offer; she hadn't yet forgiven Louise for having failed to articulate her hunches before the fire. "Breakfast at half past seven," she said, closing the door.

Louise got up and followed her into the hall. "Henriette."

They went into the kitchen and sat at the table.

She tried again: You've got to leave, I beg you, go away, you're not safe here, even if there are virtually more police officers than residents now in Au. They can only stay a few days, no longer, and what if he waits weeks or months? Think of your children, they're so young, they ought to be able to live without fear, especially given the problems you have in the family. *Leave*, for heaven's sake.

Henriette simply looked at her, a thoughtful gaze at least, even though it felt distant. Then she said, "What if we take the children away? First thing tomorrow morning?"

Louise nodded.

"Carola won't want to go. Will you help me with her?"

"Yes."

"Good, that's that sorted, then." Henriette stood up, said goodnight again, then Louise heard her footsteps on the stairs and in the upstairs bathroom.

Take the children away – that was something, at least.

She sat alone at the vast table that seemed better suited to a conference room than a kitchen, and listened again. Upstairs doors opened and closed, water ran, the faint hum of an electric toothbrush. Other sounds joined the mix: cars driving past, rain lashing against the shutters for a few moments. She heard the wind, dogs barking, and now believed she could hear footsteps behind the house, voices, in her mind she saw dark figures prowling around the house, and at once Bonì felt edgy. A voice made her jump with fright, Carola at the door, goodnight, and thanks again, a tired wave, a weary smile. Louise stood up and wondered how long she would be able to stick this out, how many nights of waiting, nights full of fear, anxiety and these damned hunches.

After the crisis-laden night with Jenny Böhm, yet another night without sleep.

Around midnight she lay down on the bed, intending only to rest for a while, and promptly fell asleep. Ten minutes later she woke with a start. She mustn't sleep, she was here *not* to sleep.

That was her job. After all, it was *she* who'd led him here.

Ten minutes with the dark figures that were now so familiar. Andreas Eisenstein had been amongst them, as well as Lončar and Louise herself.

Figures dancing silently in the rain.

And a feeling. In her dream or sleep she'd felt Valpovo. As if the word had become a feeling.

She pushed the rug by the bed to one side, sat on the hard wooden floor, leaned back against the wooden bed with its edges and corners, but still she kept nodding off for a few seconds at a time.

Once an hour she did a patrol of the house. She'd switched all the lights on and all the internal doors were open apart from those to the bedrooms. Only now, brightly lit at night, did the house appear almost friendly. Between patrols she called her Kripo colleagues in the car outside: Gerd Breuer and Piet Schuhmacher. No suspicious persons to be seen anywhere. The patrol cars hadn't encountered anyone either.

"Aren't you going home?" Breuer said at around half past three.

"I'm on night shift."

"*We're* the night shift."

"The rota must be wrong, then."

"Go home, there's no reason for you to be here."

"Piss off."

Breuer laughed.

"Do you need anything to eat? Drink?"

"Just cigarettes."

"I haven't got any."

"And a sip of Jägermeister. I know you won't have any of that either."

"Piss off."

"I wanted to hear you say it again."

Banter between colleagues. Everybody hated the waiting, waiting, waiting.

*

Twenty past four. Another few hours until sunrise. Until this night was finally over.

The first of God knows how many.

She drank lukewarm coffee that was too sweet.

Everything ached, her back and bottom worst of all. She stood up and stretched.

Footsteps. Soft, barely audible footsteps downstairs in the hall, then in the living room.

Grabbing her pistol she crept onto the landing. Her heart was racing. For God's sake, be careful with the gun, she thought, don't forget Jenny Böhm that night.

It might be Lončar.

It might just be one of the children.

Paul or Henriette Niemann, unable to sleep. But surely she would have seen them. They would have had to walk past her door. Past her open door. She hadn't seen anybody.

The first step on the staircase, the second creaked faintly.

A loud, uncertain whisper from below: "It's only me."

She breathed a sigh of relief.

Niemann was sitting on the sofa in his pyjamas, his hair a mess, his glasses crooked. A shadow of stubble, which made him look unpleasantly dishevelled.

How could she have failed to see him upstairs? "Was I asleep?"

He nodded.

"You have to wake me up if you see me asleep."

"I'm sorry, I . . ."

She really hated these half sentences, this "I . . ." which went no further. This uncertainty in somebody in their mid-forties, a father.

She sat in an armchair. "What about you?"

He shrugged. "I couldn't sleep anymore."

"Bad dream?"

"No. Just a . . . feeling. In my head. Like on Saturday."

"What sort of feeling?"

"It's like a shadow sitting in the centre of my head. Squeezing my brain."

She didn't respond.

"He's here," Niemann whispered.

"What?"

"He's here, I can feel it in my head."

She nodded. For a moment she fancied she understood what was going on inside Niemann's head. Fear. Hunches, perhaps. Maybe the feeling of being partially responsible, too.

One long nightmare since last Saturday.

"He can't be inside the house," she said.

"Then outside somewhere."

She shook her head. Impossible. Au was a fortress, even at night.

Niemann ran a hand through his hair. His eyes were still fixed on her, screwed up behind his glasses, his lips pursed. A screwed-up individual, and things were getting worse as the challenges, the problems, became tougher.

You've got to get out, she thought, get *out* of there. Out of the isolation, the insecurity. Out of the memories of Munich, when everything was different, nicer – completely untrue, of course.

"I didn't want to send those people back," Niemann said.

She waited for him to continue, but he didn't, and she wondered whether his silence was a question, the question of an utterly insecure man who had lost his place in the world, in his family – is it O.K. if I talk?

She nodded.

"None of them," Niemann said. "They wanted to stay in Germany, or at least most of them did, especially the children . . . Many of the children had lived longer in Germany than in Bosnia. Germany was their home now. Hardly anybody wanted to go back and I renewed the deferrals as often as possible . . . At some point I couldn't anymore and then I had to authorise the repat . . ."

"I understand."

"Did you say September 1998?"

"Yes."

"Before the right to remain ruling came into effect. At the end of 1998 or the beginning of 1999, they introduced the right to remain. When did they arrive?"

"November 1993."

"Then they ought to have been allowed to stay. A few more months and they'd have been allowed to stay."

"I didn't know that."

"Yes. At the end of 1998 or early 1999 the right to remain was brought in." Niemann took off his glasses, examined them, then put them back on. "I didn't want to send any of them back, but I had no choice."

"You did what you had to do."

"Yes. What I had to do."

"Is that why you fell ill?"

"No. I had pneumonia."

"In summer," Louise said kindly.

Niemann nodded.

"You've got to get out of there, Herr Niemann, you've really got to get out of your head – your mind is churning around incessantly. Forget what you had to do. Forget Munich. Look after your family."

"Yes." Niemann stood up. "But now I have to go back to bed."

"Did you hear what I said?"

"Yes." He went to the door. "You ought to go to bed too. Maybe really nothing can happen. I . . . Au is a fortress."

Louise snorted and in the same moment felt an anger surging, an anger she already knew, the Paul-Niemann-anger. She really wanted to slap this man. "It's high time you got a grip," she said acidly.

"Got a grip, yes," Niemann said, about to close the door.

"And for God's sake leave the door open!"

"Yes, of course. Goodnight."

"And the lights stay on."

Niemann said nothing more. She heard him go up the stairs, and now she felt sorry for him again, but it couldn't go on like this. Shaking her head angrily, she stood up.

As she was on her way upstairs, she remembered something she'd heard Niemann say.

A few more months and they'd have been allowed to stay.

The waiting continued. She was on the floor again, leaning against the wooden bed, enduring the pain in her back and buttocks as she called her colleagues outside and Jenny Böhm, who'd been asleep in her hotel bed, but was pleased to hear from Louise. She began to talk like a waterfall, but Louise interrupted her and brought the conversation to a rapid conclusion – how could she concentrate on the noises in the house if she was on the phone?

She picked up Hoffmann's documents, then put them down again. They weren't going to keep her awake.

She drank lukewarm coffee that was too sweet.

Come on, she thought. Just come now.

He came at a quarter past seven.

She was standing outside in the dawn light, giving Breuer and Schuhmacher coffee and rolls, when the first shot was fired. She heard Carola scream, Philip scream. Even as she was turning to run back the second shot came.

"In the garden, behind the house!" she screamed, wrenching the pistol from her waistband.

Curses behind her, a car door swung open, Breuer's voice yelling for back-up. She saw Schuhmacher beside her, running towards the corner of the house.

Inside Carola and Philip were screaming, but they couldn't hear

Niemann or Henriette. He's going to kill everyone, she thought in a panic, he's going to wipe out the entire family!

She shoved open the front door.

The children wouldn't stop screaming . . . She prayed for them to continue, prayed that another shot wouldn't be fired and put a stop to the screaming.

She raced into the hallway. The screams were coming from the kitchen, Carola, Philip, then she saw them, Carola in the middle of the room, her hands clasped over her mouth, Philip by the closed glass door to the garden, his hand on the frame as if he'd just shut it. Both of them were looking outside, crying, screaming. Henriette, she thought, where is Henriette? Get away from the door, Philip! she yelled, then heard Schuhmacher's voice from outside: He's coming in, Bonì, watch out, he's coming in!

Two shots from another weapon, Schuhmacher's service pistol.

"Watch out, Bonì!"

She dragged Philip away from the door, grabbed Carola's hand, and was about to haul both of them into the hallway when a shadow suddenly appeared, the glass smashed, sending shards flying through the room, and then Antun Lončar was standing before them, his hands and face bleeding, a calm, other-worldly look in his eyes, a pistol in his hand. She shoved Philip away, raised the Heckler & Koch and fired, but Lončar had moved aside. Now he was right beside her, grabbed Philip by the hair and aimed the pistol at Carola, who shut up at once.

He stared at Louise.

"O.K.!" she shouted, to drown out Philip's cries, then placed her pistol on the floor. "O.K.!"

Lončar nodded and pulled Philip towards him. Philip screamed and tried to fight him off. Lončar looked past her and she turned, thinking, play for time . . . Breuer and Schuhmacher will be here any second, the officers on patrol . . .

Niemann had appeared on the stairs in his pyjamas, his hands clutching the banisters. He wasn't wearing his glasses, perhaps he couldn't really see what was happening.

But of course he knew.

She turned back to Lončar, whose eyes were still fixed on Niemann, and pleaded with him softly not to do it, it's not their fault, it's not going to bring Biljana and Snježana back, don't do it, Antun, *molim* . . .

Lončar looked at her, one arm around Philip's neck, the gun still pointing at Carola. The gaunt, weatherbeaten face she knew only from photographs was barely thirty centimetres away, now it looked different from the pictures, calm, almost relaxed, and in his eyes was an exhausted satisfaction.

From his eyes Louise could see that Lončar had long ceased to belong to this world.

"*Molim*," she whispered.

Then came the shot and she felt Carola's hand twitch jerkily, she held it tight, but didn't look, No, she thought, closing her eyes, no, then Carola's weight pulled her to the ground, she fell, not letting go of the hand, mustn't let go, she thought as her shoulder came crashing onto the floor, mustn't let go, then her head, she felt herself lose consciousness, all strength abandoning her body, felt one of Carola's legs beneath her, her hand, mustn't let go, she thought . . .

Bonì passed out.

III

Places of Pain

21

"Hey!"

"Hmm?"

"Everything O.K.?"

"Stop asking every half hour." She smiled wearily.

Her third week in Günterstal, her third week at Richard Landen's. She was sitting at the wooden table behind the house, just as she had in 2003. It was raining, just as it had back then too.

Landen stroked her shoulder and went back inside.

He had tamed his wild garden to bring order to his life after Tommo. In the house, on the other hand, that meticulous Landen sense of order no longer prevailed. It was important to inject a little disorder into his life too.

Otherwise nothing had changed in Günterstal. The willow beside the house that seemed to grab at the roof. The shed on the other side that had been used as a teahouse was still a teahouse. I mean, I still drink tea, Landen had said in all innocence.

Everything O.K.?

No, not yet.

Three weeks in Günterstal and she could still feel the twitching of Carola's hand in hers.

She slept during the day, mainly. At night, as she dozed in the darkness, the memories came. Lončar in the Niemanns' kitchen, the shot. Carola dying silently, the sudden blackness that enveloped her. Waking up in hospital with an oxygen mask. Beside her, Benedikt, glasses on his forehead, silent for minutes on end. Just tell me, she said.

Henriette in the vegetable garden. Carola in the kitchen. You know that.

Because *she* had led Lončar to Au.

Benedikt didn't say this, obviously; it was what she thought, her memories in turmoil.

Philip? With relatives in Berlin.

Niemann? In a psychiatric clinic. Shock.

From then on she began waking with a start at night. She would sit at the window, fixing her gaze on the dark willow outside.

Landen had made up Tommo's old bedroom for her. I'd really like you to sleep in my bed, he'd said. I have to get through this alone, she'd replied.

Three weeks and she wasn't through it yet.

But she was beginning to feel better. Gradually she was able to think of the future.

She would give up her apartment in Gartenstrasse and maybe tack a few weeks of holiday onto her sick leave. Finally go away somewhere again.

Then back to work.

Occasionally she rang her colleagues.

When are you coming back? Hoffmann asked her a week ago. It's not the same without you.

We're all missing you, Wallmer said.

That's what I meant, Benedikt said. You get in too deep.

You're not going to let something like that get you down, Bermann said.

Ilic asked whether he could visit.

"Not a good idea."

"But the odd phone call?"

"Phone calls are fine, yes."

"And postcards from holiday?"

"You're going on holiday?"

They laughed a little.

Two colleagues on sick leave, joking with each other.

She hadn't spoken to Bob, Bob had gone. He'd had himself transferred somewhere provincial; a deal had been cut, as ever. Go somewhere nobody else wants to go and we'll hold off from giving you the sack.

Searching for mistakes, transgressors. Bob had been obliged to take the blame. The Niemanns ought to have been taken away. Bob hadn't succeeded in persuading them.

That was one failure.

The other: an elderly man in a foreign country, a lone wolf without any support, or at least none since they'd found Andreas Eisenstein. They had his name, his D.N.A., his fingerprints and they knew his intention: to kill, probably the Niemann woman and her daughter.

Despite all this they hadn't managed to find him.

This, of course, was a much more serious failure.

The new Kripo boss would start in January. She didn't know his name yet, nor did it interest her.

Has it completely gone? Carola said inside her head. *Is it all gone?*

Three weeks, and still the memories came flooding back as if it had happened only yesterday.

At the start of the second week Landen had kissed her for the first time.

"I don't want to raise any false hopes," she'd said.

"O.K."

"Would you still like to sleep with me?"

"Yes."

"Lovely."

"Lovely and strange."

"Yes."

She thought he looked quite a bit older than he had in the summer of 2003. The divorce, the son in Japan, all the changes, both internal and external. The reorientation. The new sense of order, the new sense of disorder.

He seemed exhausted. Not entirely content. But there was a wonderful glint in his eye when he looked at her.

"You know I love you," he'd said.

"Yes. And you know I don't love you anymore."

"Yes."

"But you mean a lot to me."

"I know that too."

"In another life, in another time, Richard."

"That's enough for me."

She knew that soon it wouldn't be enough. That at some point she would have to go so it wasn't too painful for him.

But not today, not tomorrow, not in these few weeks. In these few weeks she took what she could get to forget everything else, however briefly.

Antun Lončar, who she had led to Au.

Carola, who died holding her hand.

Once again they had failed to apprehend Lončar. Once again he'd managed to escape. Taking Philip as hostage, he'd dragged him up the Katzental. The following morning uniformed officers had found Philip tied up in a hole in the ground. No trace of Lončar.

The last plan.

This one had worked too.

They had sent requests for assistance to Austria, Slovenia, Italy, Croatia and Bosnia–Herzegovina.

No trace of Lončar.

They had his fingerprints, his D.N.A., photographs, they knew his German and Croatian names and Biljana's maiden name, under which the family had lived in Štrpci.

In spite of all this, no trace of him.

Individuals like him couldn't be found. A man without a home, without a family, without fear. An old warrior who knew how to fight, flee and hide. Who waged an asymmetric war.

No, they wouldn't find him, she thought at the end of the third week. Not by conventional methods.

Their colleagues in Lahr had found the white Golf the very next day, in a street close to Eisenstein's house.

As she had suspected, Lončar had been in Lahr that day she spoke with Eisenstein. He had waited until they turned up at the old man's house, their visit proof that they knew his past, his identities, his story. That they were on his trail.

But most importantly, that they would keep Eisenstein's house under surveillance, making it impossible for him to go back there.

He had thought of everything.

Three weeks after the double murder the Merzhausen task force was disbanded. Lončar had vanished without trace; in all likelihood he'd gone underground somewhere in the Balkans, putting himself out of reach for ever, at least for the Germans. A small team around Hoffmann kept working on the case, condensing the information, sorting. Creating a clean file that could be handed over to a state prosecutor immediately, but which would only end up in the archive of unsolved cases. They could do no more, Louise was well aware of this. She'd seen it often enough. In a few days Hoffmann and his team would be working on other cases. Lončar was on the wanted list of countless police forces in countless countries, Interpol, Europol. He was at the heart of the machinery of modern symmetric warfare as waged by European police investigation authorities.

They wouldn't find him.

*

After three weeks, the dark figures returned to her dreams. Thousands of figures on boats, then on long marches across land. Andreas Eisenstein amongst them, holding the hand of a child, who must be Antun Lončar, or Heinrich Schwarzer at the time. Valpovo, Eisenstein said to the child. We're heading for Valpovo now, where people dance in the rain.

Wallmer wanted to stop by. No, please don't, Louise said. Can't you tell me over the phone?

And so Wallmer told her over the phone. She liked men, but she preferred women. Well. Now she was pregnant.

Ever since she found out, she'd stopped liking men altogether. She didn't want a child and she didn't want a man. In fact, she didn't want anybody. It was better being on your own. You didn't have to hide. You didn't get pregnant. She gave a raucous laugh. "We're getting married in June."

"*What*?"

"The child needs a father."

"You're going to have it?"

"It is what it is."

"Rubbish!"

"Yeah, well."

"So who's the father?"

"You don't know him. He's not a colleague."

"What you're doing is insane, Anne."

"What's happened has happened. And how are you?"

Louise sighed.

She was beginning to feel better. There was no let-up in the intensity or frequency of her memories. But she was learning to accept them.

And now there was this novel idea, a strange idea that was beginning to fill her with new life.

*

"Holiday?" Landen said.

"Yes."

"In December?"

"Yes."

"Well, why not? Where shall we go?"

"Not we, on my own, Richard."

"On your own."

She nodded.

They were sitting in the maize-coloured kitchen. The black china cat on the window sill, whose unrelenting stare used to annoy her so much, was gone. Tommo had taken it. An heirloom, Landen had explained. The wisdom of Tommo's ancestors had accumulated in this cat.

Now she could be slightly foolish without feeling uncomfortable.

"On your own, then," Landen said.

"Yes."

She could see he was struggling to digest this. He was frowning and his eyebrows were sunken. Only now did she notice that the tiny patch of grey hair in his right eyebrow had spread. In January 2003 she had fallen in love with this patch of grey.

Richard Landen could be the most important person in this phase of her life, she thought, even though she had known him for less than two years. The dramas of these two years were scored into his house. She'd sat in the kitchen with Niksch before he was shot. Outside at the wooden table she'd kissed Landen for the first time, a few hours before the hunt for the false Marcel had been launched.

She'd loved him, and then the love had gone. It wasn't right. Was she going to tell him about Lončar over dinner? About Carola?

Even now she'd only disclosed the bare essentials. A dreadful case. Two people I liked were murdered.

No, it wasn't right. Landen would have foundered in her abyss. Or let her descend into it alone.

She needed a man who let himself fall like her. Who needed a little longer each time to return to life. Who at some stage might not manage it anymore, and already knew this.

"So where are you going to go?"

She shrugged. He wouldn't understand. Nobody would understand. Rather, only one person would understand.

"For Christ's sake, Louise," Ilic said.

"I need a holiday, a bit of R&R."

"In Slavonia?"

"Didn't you say it's lovely down there? Peaceful, rural, cosy? Just what I need right now."

"Don't take the piss."

"I'm sorry."

End of November, the time had come for Louise to begin her new life. She had to get away from Landen, who had started to suffer, even though he was trying to hide it. Now he often wore an oddly distant expression. She thought he'd begun to hope.

Imagining a future – him and her.

But of course Landen wasn't the real reason.

She needed to go to Slavonia. To Bosnia.

Holiday in the Balkans.

"Why?" Ilic said.

Because she had led Lončar to Carola. Because she hadn't been able to let go of Carola's hand.

She didn't say this. Even Ilic wouldn't have understood.

But she was convinced he had his suspicions. He knew what had happened in Au.

"What are you going to do if you find him?"

"I don't know. But don't be worried."

"I *am* worried. I know you."

She laughed.

"What do you want from me?"

She needed a contact down there. Someone to travel around with her and translate. Obviously not someone from the Croatian police. An interpreter, a student, it didn't matter. Someone who could spare a few days, knew their way around Slavonia and would ask as few questions as possible. Who would accompany her to the Republika Srpska in Bosnia.

"O.K.," Ilic said. "I'll have a think."

She listed the places: Osijek, Valpovo and Poreč in Croatia, Štrpci in Bosnia. In any sequence.

Ilic didn't respond. She knew she was asking a lot of him. Nobody at H.Q. must get wind of anything. Kripo chief inspector travelling unofficially to a non-E.U. country on the hunt for a killer. Without any invitation from the authorities there. Without even having notified them. What she was planning to do would cost Bonì her job if it ever got out. Likewise for Thomas Ilic if it came to light that he had helped her.

"I'll get back to you soon."

"Thanks."

"By the way, I'm starting work again in February."

"Great," she said. The tears came and she let them run silently. Ilic back, after a good eighteen months . . .

Another thought that filled her with new life.

Soon after that there came a day when something felt strange. It took her a long while to realise what it was. It dawned on her after supper, while she and Landen were kissing on the floor of the living room: this was the first day in almost four weeks that she hadn't cried about Carola.

She lasted until dawn, then it all started up again.

Memories, dreams, tears.

*

Benedikt called.

Antun Lončar. A few answers, but so many questions were unresolved.

She was sitting at the wooden table behind the house, now her favourite place. No rain today and even a bit of sunshine. Landen was at the university and she was enjoying her solitude. She let her gaze wander across the pruned and clipped garden as she listened to Benedikt.

"In summer he did indeed enquire about Niemann at the foreigners' registration office in Munich. All the administrator knew was that the Niemanns had moved to Baden – maybe Freiburg or nearby." He had offered to ask Heidelinde Zach, who would surely have the details.

Lončar had shaken his head and left.

That was Fritz, Heidelinde Zach had told Alfons Hoffmann. He just happened to be one of the staff in 312 B.W.R. who'd worked with Niemann in Untersbergstrasse, and then had moved back to the main building once the repatriation phase was over.

This was where the questions began.

Biljana and Snježana were shot in 1999. In 2004 Lončar enquired about Niemann in Munich, wrote to Eisenstein and asked him to help find a "friend from Slavonia".

"Why did he wait five years?" Benedikt said.

She nodded. What had he done in those five years? Where had he been? "Maybe he was looking for his family's killers."

"Yes, maybe," Benedikt said.

Louise went into the yellow kitchen and made herself an espresso. She even felt comfortable in the kitchen now that the china cat had gone. So much peace and quiet. The ideal place for Jenny Böhm, in fact; she no longer found any peace amongst the dead in the cemetery.

Outside there were more answers, more questions.

"We now know that he didn't have a passport," Benedikt said.

"Neither a Croatian nor Bosnian one. And yet in 2004 he presumably came from Bosnia to Munich via Croatia, Slovenia or Italy, and Austria. How the hell did he manage that? Did he hide on a train? Did he go on foot?"

"He crossed the borders on foot."

"Yes, it's a possibility."

"It would be just like him, Mats."

The old warrior, crossing borders at night in places where they couldn't be monitored 24/7.

"And we know that he was in the army until 1992," Benedikt said. "First in the Yugoslav army, then in the Croatian one, after independence. In 1992 he fought against the Serbs in Slavonia until the middle of that year, when he moved with his wife and daughter to Shtr . . . to Schutzberg."

"Was he a deserter?"

"Looks like it. It seems as if he was injured, in his left arm, I think, and then one day he just vanished from the hospital and never returned."

"He wanted to bring Biljana to safety."

"The way you put it, it sounds almost romantic."

She nodded.

Sometimes she saw two Antun Lončars.

One who had endured so much suffering, all the way back to his early childhood. Who had seen his father and mother die. Who, years later, wanted to bring his wife to safety, but in the end wasn't able to protect her or his daughter. She felt pity for this Antun Lončar. She liked him.

Then there was the other Antun Lončar, the one who had murdered Carola and Henriette. She hated this man. She wished they were two different people.

She wondered which of the two she would be looking for in Slavonia. Which one she was hoping to find.

"But it *isn't* romantic," said Benedikt, who could sense the danger here. "Lončar is a killer, full stop."

"Yes," Louise said. A killer who years earlier had become a victim.

This was the uncomfortable element of the story. Which made judging people like him, dealing with them, so difficult.

People you liked *and* hated. Who you felt sympathy for, but ultimately wanted to see pay for their crimes.

Yes, this made it complicated if you let yourself get embroiled. Benedikt didn't and she admired him for that. Louise did, and that was O.K. too. Someone had to occasionally. And make an attempt to include the uncomfortable elements of the story too.

She heard the front door open and close. Noises she'd got used to these past few weeks. Landen was home.

She'd got used to that as well.

Another life, another time. Without people like Antun Lončar, without the twitching hand of a dying girl. Where you could be asked how your day was without having to talk about killers and people dying.

"And then, of course, there's the question of who killed his wife and daughter," Benedikt said with a touch of impatience, perhaps because she'd said nothing for so long.

"And why."

"Yes. Were these revenge killings too? Had Lončar given the killers any reason to do it during his time in the Yugoslav, or later the Croatian army?"

Questions about questions.

And finally, of course, the most important one of all: where was he?

Ilic rang again. He'd made a few arrangements. Zagreb and Osijek were the starting points. In Zagreb she would meet a woman on December 5 at 3 p.m. in the gallery of Café K. & K. in – he spelled it out for her – Jurišićeva, in the centre of Zagreb. The woman's name was Iva. She would book a hotel for Louise in Osijek and give her the name of the interpreter who would accompany her from there. She could stay the night with Iva too. But Iva was flying to the U.S. the following day, hence that specific date. "Can you do that?"

"Yes."

"It'll take you around ten hours by car from here."

"I'm going to pay a visit to Bleiburg first."

"Bleiburg in Carinthia? Then you're going to have to leave soon."

"Yes."

So: Zagreb and Osijek. She could sense the anticipation. Osijek on the Drava, near Valpovo.

Ilic didn't have an interpreter yet. He had someone in mind, but he needed to check first.

"Man or woman?"

"Does it matter?"

"No."

"A man."

Once again there was something in his enunciation that perplexed her, just as it had during their first call when he'd promised to do nothing apart from telephone. There was a particular tone to his voice, he was . . . off-hand.

Ilic didn't say things off-handedly.

"Not you, Illi."

"Then I wouldn't be having to check first, would I?"

"Just phone calls, Illi, you promised."

"Yes, yes, yes."

"You know damn well what I'd do if you turned up in Osijek."

Ilic laughed. Yes, he knew.

It was the first day in weeks that she'd left Landen's house and Günterstal. In a bookshop in Freiburg she bought maps. Zagreb wasn't a problem, but there weren't any for Bleiburg, Osijek, Valpovo, Poreč or Štrpci. In Augustinerplatz she had a coffee and familiarised herself with the route, looked up Jurišićeva in Zagreb. On the way back she drove down Heinrich-von-Stephan-Strasse and gave police H.Q. a wave. She'd be back there in January, Thomas Ilic in February – what prospects! Be happy, people!

And then, on December 3, came the goodbyes. A few days earlier she'd told Landen where she was going. He'd said he'd been expecting something like this.

They were standing by her car in front of the wooden fence.

From his expression she could see that he was reluctant to let her go. But he didn't try to hold her back. He knew that he couldn't persuade her to stay.

She had to do what she believed she had to do. Usually there was some good reason. Something always came of it.

He didn't know what it was, but he tried to convince himself.

"A few days," she said. "A week at most."

He nodded. Tall, calm, tired Richard Landen. He'd said nothing for several minutes, as if unable to utter another word.

"Thanks for taking me in."

She stroked his cheek.

In another life, in another time.

22

Bleiburg, a small town of four thousand inhabitants in Carinthia, between Völkermarkt and the Slovenian border, surrounded by mountains and trees, and with a castle on a hill that she could only vaguely make out in the dark.

Half past nine in the evening, the snow on the mountains shimmered dully.

She took a room in a gloomy hotel on the main road. A chubby blonde woman gave her the key without saying a word – provincial behaviour that betrayed indifference and lethargy, and yet somehow was not unfriendly.

Louise went up the stairs and down a narrow corridor. She sensed she might be the only guest in the place.

Four weeks of Günterstal with Landen always close by, lots of conversation, sex. It had done her good, offering a slight distraction from those dreadful minutes in the kitchen in Au with Lončar, from Carola's silent death. Now, alone in Bleiburg, the memories, images and emotions returned with a vengeance. Louise spent half the night sitting on a plastic chair by the balcony door, staring at the few lights in the darkness, streetlamps, traffic lights, neon signs on shops, some with Slovenian names, a few illuminated windows in the castle, which one by one went dark. She tried to gain some control over the memories, images and emotions, to avoid plummeting into the bottomless abyss on her first night alone.

In the darkness this sad place seemed well suited to a nosedive into the abyss.

Around 2 a.m. she gave up the fight and wept for Carola, and around 4 a.m. it was all over.

By the following morning it had stopped raining, but the sky remained overcast and it was eight degrees at most. Louise had been unfair on Bleiburg by night; the centre, a street that went gently uphill, with homely-looking two-storey houses in yellow, green and pink, was very pretty. The castle sat at the top of the hill beyond the houses. Up there, in May 1945, one week after the end of the war, mediators from the British army, the Croatian army and the Yugoslav partisans had decided on the fates of tens of thousands, mainly Croatian soldiers and civilians, who a few kilometres away were awaiting their destiny on the field outside the town, wedged between the British and the partisans. Amongst them was a two-and-a-half-year-old boy by the name of Heinrich Schwarzer. Up in the castle the decision was taken to hand over the refugees.

That's what Hoffmann had told her.

Fastening her anorak in the chilly December air, Bonì walked up the main street that ended outside a chemist's.

Well, I've got more time now, Hoffmann had said on the telephone. Not only had he read Eisenstein's book, he'd also found out more about the Danube Swabians. And Bleiburg.

But there wasn't much to go on.

In Germany there was nothing save for a handful of newspaper articles. In Britain a few books had appeared in the 1970s and 1980s. There was a trial. A historian had made certain claims that had displeased a former army general. The historian had lost.

The former prime minister, Harold Macmillan, had somehow been involved.

Details don't interest me, Alfons, she had said.

In one of the British books the editors had collected all the relevant telegrams, letters, directives and orders from members of the British army from May 1945. The point of the book was probably to exonerate someone from some accusations. Hoffmann hadn't understood it precisely. How was he going to get the chance to learn English if he kept having to go to Plattling?

Can you summarise it for me, Alfons?

No, he couldn't. It wasn't possible. Bleiburg remained a puzzle. According to one source things had happened this way, according to another, that way, and a third source had it different again. One claimed there were twenty thousand refugees, another, eighty thousand, a third, one hundred and fifty thousand. One said the massacre took place in the field, another that it didn't occur until they were back in Slovenia. The third said there was no massacre at all.

No summary, no facts that could be historically proven, that were beyond dispute.

Only one thing was clear: the British had handed over to the Yugoslav army thousands of Croatian soldiers who had surrendered, as well as civilians. As they had done with Slovenian soldiers in Viktring. As with the Cossacks they'd handed over to the Russians . . .

Alright, Alfons, alright.

Hoffmann had become an expert in the immediate post-war period. And still he couldn't produce the answers.

Apart from one: of course it had been about politics. They weren't willing to cheat Tito. Or Stalin. In this context, what did the lives of a few hundred thousand people mean?

She stopped outside the council building. A plaque listed the most important dates in Bleiburg's history. Beneath "1945" she read: *At the end of the war a Croatian army surrenders to the British occupying power and is forced to march back to Yugoslavia. Every year the victims of this episode are commemorated on the "Bleiburger Feld".*

I thought the Brits and the partisans were the good guys, Hoffmann had said, confused. Or was that not the case?

Maybe not always, she had said.

*

On her way back to the town centre Landen called.

"I just wanted to know if you arrived safely."

"I did."

"Good."

A pause. She was happy to hear his voice. His voice made Bleiburg softer.

And he was part of her life to an extent that nobody else was.

"I don't know if it's O.K. for me to call you."

"Of course it's O.K."

"Not every day, obviously."

"Call whenever you feel like it."

"Not every day."

"Not every day, that would be too often. I've got work to do, after all." She smiled. "It's cold here," she said.

"Here too." He cleared his throat. "I'm assuming there's a pistol somewhere here in my house."

She laughed. "You won't find it."

"I won't go looking for it."

The new Heckler & Koch P-2000, in a removal crate in the cellar, in the lap of one of the old stone Buddhas Landen had removed from the garden, to bring a new sense of order to his life.

The Buddha and the pistol.

There needed to be a little disorder in his new life.

Cappuccino in an Italian café, where the regulars sat at the bar, five or six elderly, worn-out men, maybe out-of-work men. They smoked, drank beer and spoke a dialect that wasn't in fact unintelligible. They gave her brief, harmless glances in the mirror behind the bar. The only other woman there was the waitress, who spoke the same dialect. All that was Italian was the name of the café.

A provincial backwater which history had loaded with a heavy burden. Even the name – Bleiburg, "lead castle" – was apt: a tiny town in a leaden corset.

Bonì didn't know why she'd come to Bleiburg. She was hardly likely to find Lončar here. Assuming she actually wanted to find him, and of that she wasn't entirely sure.

Perhaps it was because he *had* been here. Because he had been amongst the refugees on the Bleiburger Feld. A two-and-a-half-year-old boy in the chaos of the immediate post-war era.

Because Bleiburg had been one of the stations on his *via dolorosa*.

Schutzberg, Bleiburg, Valpovo, Poreč. Munich, but perhaps the family had a better time of it there. Then Schutzberg again, by which time it was Štrpci. The end: the murder of his wife and daughter.

When she was on her third cappuccino Hoffmann called again. "When are you back at work?"

"January."

"Not till *Jan*uary?" He groaned sorrowfully and asked where she was, it sounded like a café in the background.

The little café in Günterstal, you know, just behind the arch of the Cistercian monastery.

Yes, he knew it.

She quickly ended their conversation, paid, and asked the waitress where the Bleiburger Feld was.

"The Loibacher Feld?" The waitress pointed into the distance – just down there, it's not far.

She looked in the direction of the arm, went down the road and got into her car.

Bleiburger Feld, Loibacher Feld, which was right?

The field was in Loibach, the cemetery in Unterloibach, both of which were part of Bleiburg, explained the attendant at the petrol station on the way there. Unfortunately, "Bleiburger Feld" had become the popular name around the world and amongst historians – a catastrophe for Bleiburg, we've got great galleries, famous artists and the hiking around here is spectacular, but no, when anyone mentions Bleiburg they mean May 1945. And that'll never change, the attendant said, getting worked up, because "Bleiburg" the "Bleiburger Feld" and the "Bleiburg Massacre" had become a thingamy, a myth for the Croats, like Pearl Harbor for the Americans. Every May on Mothers' Day they came in their thousands from across the globe, even from Australia and the U.S. to commemorate May 15, 1945. Hundreds of cars, dozens of buses, food stalls, čevapčići grills. A mass was held in Loibach cemetery, then they went across to the Loibacher Feld, where a memorial had been erected, the piece of land there belonged to the Croatian state, as did the history, and who these days cared that they were fascists back then?

"How do I get to the Loibacher Feld?"

"Just down there, it's not far."

First Boni drove to the cemetery, where she found a memorial stone with the seated figure of a woman. An inscription beside it read: "Mother Croatia mourns and weeps". In what followed Louise spied too much "honour", "glory" and "fatherland" for her liking, so didn't bother to read closely.

Historical myths, political myths, she thought, crucial for every state, every nation, particularly young ones like Croatia. They created an identification, a sense of homeland.

Myths of victimhood were obviously best for this. Being the culprit didn't fit the myth.

Evidently the British didn't like being the culprit either.

And then along came someone like her, demanding to know the historical facts.

Next to Mother Croatia was the chessboard emblem, which Landen had talked about eighteen months ago, and Ilic too at some point. Which then, as now, was the official coat of arms of Croatia. Ilic had said the only difference was which colour was in the top left-hand corner: white or red. That's how you identify it. White in the flag of fascist Croatia under the Ustaša, and red in the flag of modern, democratic Croatia. It was what the Europeans insisted on in 1991 as a precondition for recognising us as an independent state.

White. Red.

Or was it the other way around?

At the top left in the emblem beside Mother Croatia was a white square.

She had to ask twice more before she found the turn-off to the Loibacher Feld, which did indeed seem to fill half the valley. On a gravelled area another memorial, again the red-and-white chessboard emblem, again white in the top left, but maybe that was the democratic emblem, she couldn't remember. Beneath it the inscription: "In Memory of the Victims of the Bleiburg Tragedy".

She walked into the adjoining field. A wide valley surrounded by low hills. An almost uncanny silence, interrupted only by the occasional car engine on the nearby road.

The valley black with bodies, Eisenstein had said.

Amongst them Heinrich Schwarzer, two and a half, from Schutzberg in Bosnia. Maybe the dying men from his dream had danced here. Here, in the rain, on the Loibacher Feld.

Louise turned 360 degrees. All of a sudden she felt certain that he had come back, later, after the murders of Biljana and Snježana. That he had stood where she was standing now, in the same uncanny silence, a man whose life consisted of nothing but pain, a man from places of pain – Schutzberg, Bleiburg, Valpovo, Poreč, Štrpci. That, like her, he had turned around and perhaps seen the dying men dance.

And perhaps here, on the Loibacher Feld, after the murders of Biljana and Snježana he had felt the urge to take revenge for all this pain. Perhaps he had thought of Paul Niemann for the first time in years. Drafted a plan to exact revenge on Niemann by taking away his feeling of security, his home and, finally, his family.

Bonì cancelled her booking for a second night in the hotel, threw her luggage into the car and drove off. She needed to get away from Bleiburg, which in its own peculiar way had got under her skin. The darkness from yesterday, which had coloured her initial impressions. The Loibacher Feld, where Lončar may have stood a few months or years earlier.

Carola, whose death sentence may have been conceived here.

The silent valley that gave no answers.

All the questions. The British and the partisans the goodies, the Croatian fascists the baddies, and then on one day in May 1945 everything somehow turned on its head, the culprits became victims and the victims culprits, and even today nobody could or wanted to explain precisely or with historical accuracy what had happened and why.

The castle once more in her rear-view mirror: a final farewell from Bleiburg.

Louise headed west for a while, Völkermarkt, Klagenfurt, Villach. There, the long, blue river on the map and to the left of the motorway finally acquired a name: the Drava. At a service station she checked. The same Drava, of course. Its source somewhere in Italy, through Villach, past Bleiburg, through Slovenia, along the Croatian–Hungarian border, past Valpovo, through Osijek, then issuing into the Danube.

Bleiburg, Valpovo and Osijek on the same river.

The Drava reconciled her with Bleiburg.

Then the Karawanks Tunnel, a sinister, almost eight-kilometre-long tube between Austria and Slovenia. The Karawanks, another word strangely burdened by history. Hoffmann had kept mentioning the

Karawanks when talking about the early summer of 1945. Apprehended in the Karawanks, fled across the Karawanks. Murders in the Karawanks.

Slovenia lay in fog.

A dozen sets of roadworks before Ljubljana, motorway, then highway and motorway again, a huge volume of traffic. The Mégane was old, it didn't like Slovenia one bit. She had to top up the oil and engine coolant at a petrol station.

Somewhere close to the Croatian border came the other Slavonic river, the Sava. She must be almost there, Louise thought, the Drava close by, the Sava in sight. Deep into the interior of Croatia they then ran in parallel, delineating the land between the Sava and Drava through which she was now driving: Slavonia.

23

Zagreb – at first glance it consisted of hundreds of students, colourful old trams, puzzling signs in a foreign language, street cafés and Andie MacDowell for L'Oréal on the side of a dilapidated house. At second glance the real faces appeared as well, lots of attractive young men, lots of attractive young women, confident people moving almost smugly through the chaos of the cramped, overcrowded city. She found a hotel in the centre and got a room on a busy road that was horrendously noisy. Noise, endless graffiti, extremely ugly buildings, Yugo-dreariness – that was Zagreb too.

And a foreign currency which was slightly odd after a few years of living with the euro: the kuna. Luckily it was easy to convert: 1 euro was worth 7.16 kunas.

For the rest of that afternoon she drifted about in the descending darkness, enjoying being a foreigner and yet was delighted whenever she heard one of the two Croatian words she knew: *molim* or *hlava*. The markets closed, the cafés filled up, more and more cars, more and more noise. Neon signs flashed on, flooding the city with an orgy of colours, beer logos on the front of every café, the Croats seemed to like beer, beer, mobile phones and cigarettes – there was hardly anyone in any of the cafés without a cigarette. A "Bonn" café, the "o" in the form of a heart, a "Bavaria" bar. And music blaring from every door and window, from the radio as far as she could tell, as loud as possible, from every restaurant, bar, café, shop and apartment block. In one street that appeared to consist of nothing but cafés and restaurants, she came across the metal sculpture of a woman with a bun and umbrella, who appeared to be walking as confidently and smugly as the people of Zagreb. A few roads, steps and squares further on a metal man was leaning against a metal advertising column, a combination of Freud and Lenin. It rained for a few minutes. The puddles reflected the colourful neon signs, the lady with the bun was now gleaming all over. At some point it struck Louise that she hadn't thought about Lončar and Carola for a good while. But soon afterwards, as she was standing outside a pizzeria, there they both were, Lončar facing her, Carola beside her, holding her hand, then Carola fell and she fell with her.

The following morning, breakfast in one of the many cafés, but not without a few hiccoughs. They had nothing to eat; it looked as if you had to buy something at the bakery and take it back to have with your coffee. The people around her sat with paper bags containing unidentifiable pastries.

"*Hvala*," she said when her cappuccino arrived.

"*Molim*," the waiter said.

The next culture shock – the cappuccino was an instant coffee.

Jurišićeva led down from the main square, whose name seemed to incorporate most of the tricks of the Croatian language: Trg bana Jelačića. Louise almost walked straight past K. & K., a narrow, dark café behind glass. This establishment offered nothing to eat either, and here too the radio was playing loudly. She went up to the gallery as agreed. A handful of tables, almost all occupied by young people. No woman on her own. Walls, tablecloths and upholstery in hues of dark red, on the walls lamps with green shades and dozens of black-and-white framed photographs with portraits of presumably famous people. She hoped these were Croats, because she didn't recognise a single face. Downstairs the door opened and a petite, dark-haired woman came in. Jeans, blue shirt, pale face, an unremarkable, quiet woman . . .

Iva, even though she'd never seen her before. The resemblance was striking.

Then Iva was smiling at her. "Louise?" She picked up her travel bag. "Follow me."

Iva, the sister. In 1991 she was in Belgrade, married to a Serb. Then Iva moved to be with her family in Stuttgart; her husband went to war in Bosnia. Later they divorced.

The drive to Kehl a year and a half ago, Ilic's monologue about the war.

"Does it really matter?" Iva shouted above the noise of the traffic.

"He could have told me."

"Relax, you're in Croatia."

"I *am* relaxed."

"Relax a little more, then. Croatia eats you up if you're not *really* relaxed."

Iva laughed.

One moment so unremarkable, the next so likeable and jolly.

Iva Ilic.

For ten minutes they hurried through the city centre. Iva was a whirl-wind when she moved, and perfectly still when she stopped. At a traffic light she explained the mystery of cappuccino, which usually was instant and only ever an Italian cappuccino if you said *iz aparata*, "from the machine", or *espresso cappuccino*.

"*Hvala*."

Iva laughed and uttered what sounded like an endless word in Croatian.

"I didn't understand a thing."

"I said I didn't know you spoke Croatian."

"I know *hvala* and *molim* – that will have to do."

"The ten most frequent swear words – *that* would do."

Ten minutes in which Iva was called three times on her mobile and made two calls herself.

"Where's your car?"

"Oh, somewhere down there."

"Somewhere? That's where I spend my time too."

They laughed.

"*Now* you're relaxed," Iva said.

Iva Ilic, the sister, unbelievable, Louise thought, looking forward hugely to February. To her brother.

In a steep, cobbled street they entered a charming, run-down building with tall, narrow windows and went up to the second floor. The family's Zagreb apartment, for whenever anyone was here. After the war the parents moved in here for a few years before returning to Stuttgart. The father had fought for Croatia. But he'd never been able to settle down in Croatia again.

The apartment itself was charmingly run-down too. A period jewel, no doubt, but one in need of thorough renovation.

A radio was on in the kitchen. Fridge, cooker, washing machine – all manufactured by Gorenja and all old. Here and there Louise could see the red-and-white chessboard pattern: on a tea towel, schnapps glasses, a pennant on the wall. On the window sill lay a red-and-white patterned handbag. If she were looking at it correctly, the pattern began with a red square in the top left.

Iva was now slightly more fidgety than on the way here.

"Take a seat."

Louise sat at the kitchen table. Iva scuttled out and came back soon afterwards wearing a jumper over her blue shirt. She filled one glass with beer and another with water. As Louise took the glass, she heard footsteps in one of the rooms.

"Relax," Iva said.

Louise put the glass down. "I'm going to kill him."

*

Ilic looked a few years older and many years wearier than before. His face was bloated, there was sweat on his brow and he'd put on a few kilos. When he saw the anger in her face he shrugged and gave a sheepish smile.

"Illi, I don't bloody believe it."

He sat down, visibly nervous, was given a beer by Iva and stood up again when Louise came to embrace him. This was how she had to do it, first an embrace and then make his life hell for a few minutes.

He felt soft and feeble. He smelled of medicines, sadness, sleeplessness.

She held him for a long time. Long and tight.

Then they sat down and she said, "I'm not taking you to Slavonia, Illi."

Ilic smiled. "I'm not going with you to Slavonia."

"Good, because I'm not taking you."

"I never intended on going, Louise. I'm staying in Zagreb."

She nodded. Suddenly she understood. Zagreb, a first step out of the trauma. It would have been too early for Slavonia, but Zagreb was alright.

Zagreb, and then back to work in February.

From the street below she heard the juddering of tyres on cobbles. The noise of an engine echoing off the walls opposite. On the radio an old U2 song.

"So, how do you like my country?"

"Cut the crap, Illi."

Ilic laughed.

"Shall we begin? Yes?" Louise said.

Ilic left the kitchen and came back with a folder, which he placed on the table. A few blue words on the cover, and at the top, "Louise", underlined.

Everything almost as it had been, just a few more kilos.

And a few more tears.

"A policeman?"

"An *ex*-policeman."

"A *policeman*, Illi."

"We were at the academy together. He's . . . trust me."

"I'm not sure."

"Trust me."

"Illi, I don't need a policeman down there."

"He dropped out of the force."

"Dropped out?"

"Burned out."

"Benno Liebermann," she read.

"Ben, if you want to stay alive."

Iva had left the kitchen to pack for the U.S. Louise and Ilic sat bent over the table, between them the folder with the blue writing. Outside it was getting dark and Ilic had switched the light on. He drank beer, she had water.

Ben Liebermann, forty-two, specialist in police operations abroad, worked for the border protection force in Sarajevo from January 1 to December 31, 2003, as part of the European police mission in Bosnia and Herzegovina, together with other colleagues responsible for setting up the State Investigation and Protection Agency, S.I.P.A.

"I know E.U.P.M., but not S.I.P.A."

"It's like the Bosnian version of the Federal Criminal Police Office."

"I see."

Plenty more blue words about Ben Liebermann, which she just skimmed; after all, she was only going to be travelling with him for a few days, she wasn't going to marry him. Place of birth: Hamburg. Career: Cologne Kripo, Berlin Kripo, lecturer at Freiburg Academy. Foreign operations: Tel Aviv, Priština, Sarajevo. Back to Germany

(Berlin) on 1 January 2004, dropped out on 31 May. Current residence: Osijek. Temporary work for a security firm.

"What happened?"

"He didn't feel happy in Germany. He wanted to come back."

She looked up. "Back to where? He's in Osijek, not in Sarajevo."

"Back to where the war was."

A strange answer. Ilic shrugged. Once Ben Liebermann had e-mailed him to say he wanted to be where the war was.

She shook her head. "Am I going to like him?"

"If anyone likes him, it's going to be you."

"Because he's complicated."

"Because he's a loner and always seems to be standing on the edge of some abyss."

An embarrassed silence. Ben Liebermann, a kindred spirit.

"I don't want an alkie, Illi."

"I don't think he's an alkie."

The blue writing again, languages spoken and written to a reasonable level: German, English, Hebrew, Croatian. She nodded, impressed. A man who filled his free time with useful activities.

"Good. Where and when do I meet him."

Ilic leafed through a few pages in his folder. A map printed off the internet: Osijek. He'd marked crosses on it – here's your hotel, here's the Drava, here's a pedestrian bridge. That's where you're going to meet him tomorrow at 4 p.m., in the middle of the bridge, facing westwards.

Louise nodded. Tomorrow she'd be returning to the Drava.

She leafed through the folder in search of Valpovo, but found nothing. So Valpovo remained what it had always been: a place without a face.

"What did you tell him?"

"What he needs to know."

"Everything, then."

"Yes."

"But he was a policeman, Illi."

"Trust me."

She shook her head. She would have preferred a student.

"Only because you like *young* men," Ilic said.

She grinned.

"A student wouldn't bring you a weapon, Louise."

They stared at each other in silence. A weapon. In Günterstal she'd agonised over this problem. She needed a weapon in case she found Lončar.

Liebermann would solve the problem.

"I'm worried," Ilic said.

"And yet you're helping me?"

He nodded.

For a while they didn't speak. They were thinking, probably about the same question. What would she do if she found herself face to face with Lončar?

She didn't know. Was she intending to get her own back because he'd used her to find the Niemanns and because he'd killed Carola?

She didn't know.

Calambert came to mind, who usually only entered her thoughts in winter. Who had died in the snow in January 2001, on a road outside Munzingen, two bullets in his body, both from her service pistol. Shortly before, she'd found the girl in the boot of his car. Annetta, folded in two like a piece of paper. Raped, beaten, strangled. She had survived for four more days.

The sticker on the rear window: *It's a man's world.*

She had thought long and hard about this. Maybe she'd done it because of the sticker.

At least one of the bullets had been unnecessary, maybe the one from which Calambert had died in the snow.

But her memory of the episode was no longer complete. Even at the time, in those last few minutes, she hadn't been able to think clearly. A case which had taken every member of the task force to the very limit, both physically and mentally. Barely any sleep, barely any hope. For days they had searched for Calambert and the girl, half-dead from exhaustion.

She had found the two of them in a strangely surreal moment, out in the silent whiteness. A nightmare of cold, despair, fear and exhaustion, in which thoughts were no longer present, only emotions and reactions.

One of the bullets had been unnecessary. She couldn't remember what had been going through her mind when she fired the second shot. She would never know. It was lost in the obscure, white memory.

Bermann had suspected something. He'd never enquired. Had been satisfied with the bare minimum of detail and made sure that nobody else enquired either.

She looked at Ilic, his eyes now lowered. René Calambert four years ago, now Antun Lončar?

He looked up. "Don't go getting lost in Slavonia."

She nodded. In his eyes she read the same question that was going through her head.

What road are you on, Louise?

Later Ilic asked how she was. After Au and all that. Whether everything was O.K. now.

Not really.

She was a fairly tough officer. But Au . . . Perhaps Au had been too much. The straw that broke the camel's back.

They looked at each other. Like Peter Mladić's murder for you, she thought, and knew that again Ilic was thinking the same thing she was.

*

Ilic had bought a prepaid mobile for her in Zagreb. The simplest model, the cheapest one, he said, smiling – there was no budget this time. Liebermann had the number, as did he, of course. The mobile already had both numbers saved. He showed her how to check how many kunas she had left and how to put in numbers that allowed you to make a certain number of calls at half price, whether you were in Croatia or abroad. In the first month seven, after that only two per month. But hopefully you won't be here that long. He smiled uneasily. To put more credit on the mobile you need a S.I.M.P.A. card like this one. He placed a shrink-wrapped plastic card on the table. It gives you fifty or a hundred kuna. It says here what you've got to do.

She took the card out of its wrapper and followed the instructions, tapping in characters and numbers, after which she now had one hundred and fifty kunas of credit.

"Excellent," Ilic said. "Now you're all set for Slavonia."

"Now," she said, "I'm really hungry."

Čevapčići with Thomas and Iva Ilic in a traditional restaurant in the street that seemed to consist of nothing but cafés, not far from the metal woman with the bun. Iva talked a lot; Ilic and she confined themselves to a few comments. Ilic looked nervous, he was sweating profusely and his hands were shaking. She wondered whether it was because he was worried about her, or perhaps he just wasn't used to eating in public anymore. He was only slowly surfacing from his illness and isolation. She was pleased to see him again, but she wished it were under different circumstances. Again he was being sucked into her abyss. Again he was supporting her in one of her not especially responsible solo efforts.

Again she was taking him with her up the Rappeneck.

Except this time, she thought, he knew his boundaries. This was progress, for sure.

*

Her bed was the sofa in the sitting room, but only intermittently could she think about sleep. This room also gave onto the street, and the cars seemed to drive straight through it, every few seconds there was a duet of juddering tyres and engine noise. Voices and music droned from a television in Iva's room half the night, and then, of course, there was Lončar, who came into her dreams and would not leave her alone.

Ilic, whose slow, heavy footsteps she kept hearing in the hallway.

At around 3 a.m. she woke for the umpteenth time. The television was off and for a few seconds no car came shooting down the street. When she heard Ilic in the hall she slipped on her jeans.

They went into the kitchen.

"I really am worried," he said.

"I know."

He seemed to be wondering whether it was right to be helping her. Perhaps he was contemplating ringing Liebermann and calling the whole thing off.

"What are you going to do if you find him? You can't arrest him, you can't take him back to Germany. Surely you can't . . ."

A pause.

"Would you?"

She shook her head. "No."

"Can I take your word for it?"

"Yes."

"Good. I think I have to be able to take your word for it."

"Illi, I'm not a killer."

For a moment she saw Calambert lying in the snow. The second bullet had been unnecessary. *Was* she a killer?

But the memory wasn't complete.

"Of course not."

"So don't worry."

Ilic nodded.

"A beer, Illi?"

"Yes."

She bent down to the fridge and took out a one-litre plastic bottle. Karlovačko, one of many Croatian beers. Ilic smiled as she handed him the bottle. Hostess and guest.

"I could do with one now too," she said.

The smile froze.

"It's a joke, Illi."

"I'm not used to your jokes anymore."

"There's a lot you're not used to after an eighteen-month break."

"Yes. No."

"It's time you went back to work."

"Yes."

"Stop worrying, Illi."

"I need to be able to take your word for it."

"You can," Louise said, hoping that he couldn't hear the doubt in her voice.

She set off around 9 a.m. Iva had already left and Ilic walked her to her car.

They embraced.

"Maybe this is a mistake," Ilic said.

"Yes, maybe."

She promised to pass on his greetings to Liebermann. To call regularly. To watch out. And definitely pop by on her way back.

To do the right thing if she found Lončar.

But what was the right thing?

There it was again, the question of right and wrong.

"What is the right thing, Illi?"

Ilic shrugged weakly.

She kissed him on the cheek and got into the car. There was still time to decide what the right thing was, she thought as she drove away, heading for Slavonia, without knowing where this road was taking her.

24

Two hundred kilometres of motorway, half of it along the Bosnian border, parallel to the other Slavonian river, the Sava. Hardly any traffic, plenty of sunshine, an unknown country and her old rock cassettes cranking out of the car stereo – no wonder, she thought, that this morning almost felt like work. At a service station she tried to order cappuccino *iz aparata* and got the instant version again. The turn-off to Požega, where forty-four years earlier Andreas Eisenstein had boarded the train for Germany, immediately brought back the images and feelings that had afforded her so much discomfort during the first couple of weeks in Günterstal. Three men in Poreč near Požega, trying to shed their own identity and language, so at the end of a long road of suffering they could adopt a foreign identity and language. Three men, and once again she was unable to comprehend that Antun Lončar, Carola's and Henriette's killer, had been one of them.

She passed Slavonski Brod, from where the Schwarzers and the Eisensteins had made their way to Osijek in November 1942 after the resettlement, while the other Schutzbergers had travelled on to Poland. Slavonski Brod, she had checked, meant "Slavonian Boat", another Croatian puzzle, a town with the name "boat". Here lay the border crossing to Bosnia–Herzegovina, and on the other side of the Sava began the road to Štrpci, which she would take with Ben Liebermann at some point in the coming days.

A few kilometres after Slavonski Brod she left the motorway and followed the road to Osijek, where the Schwarzers and Eisensteins had lived for two years. She knew nothing about this place because she'd forgotten to ask Eisenstein. Maybe Osijek/Essegg wasn't a place of pain for Lončar, as Valpovo would be later, but rather a brief moment of peace in spite of the war and an uncertain future, a moment of childhood. A town of nice memories, and perhaps after so many years of suffering that was all that mattered.

Her first impression of Osijek was ambivalent. Large stores, advertising hoardings and unsightly apartment blocks on the edge of town, the roads increasingly worse, burst tarmac, cracks like wounds in the surface. But all of a sudden the view of the city opened up for a few seconds and in the sunlight she could see the slim red tower of the neo-Gothic church in the centre, where her hotel was located. Then the gaps between the buildings closed again and she was swept into thick traffic at a roundabout.

Ilic guided her: blue words, arrows and lines on the photocopy of the map.

Bonì checked into her hotel at around 1 p.m. It was right on the main square, a large, old, simple hotel in a row of buildings with late-nineteenth-century façades, or at least that was how she imagined the style from this period to be. The receptionist, who spoke a little German, had trouble with her French name, enthused for a while about the unusually warm day, then sent Louise up a wide, curved staircase. High ceilings, red carpets, and her room – bright, functional, acceptable – was at the end of a long corridor. On a small table stood a large, superfluous black object, which she stared at in anticipation. How long was it since she'd last watched television? She wouldn't be switching this one on either.

The room gave onto the pretty bell tower and forecourt of the church, and cafés with huge awnings. It didn't look so bad after all.

She sat on the bed.

Osijek.

She had arrived in Antun Lončar's world.

She sat on a chair with a green cushion outside one of the cafés, ordered a cappuccino *iz aparata* and waited anxiously. *Mala Kavana*, she had checked her dictionary, "small café", a place where in other circumstances she might have spent entire days, with the view of the red church to her left, the beautiful main square adjoining the church forecourt opposite, and an impressively pretty orange building to the right, which looked almost Romanesque, Louise thought, even though it wasn't genuinely Romanesque, but imitation Romanesque, and in any case she didn't know exactly what Romanesque looked like.

When the cappuccino arrived it was a cappuccino.

She walked across the square towards the Drava. A triangular space, closed to traffic, but with trams running parallel to the houses. The corners of the square, or triangle, were cut off – this was where the roads began and ended. More cafés with large awnings, many of the tables occupied, but only by locals, it seemed to her; she couldn't see any tourists. Only now did she notice the almost fist-sized holes in the façades of many buildings, and it took her a moment to realise. These were bullet holes from the Yugoslav War. Osijek, Hoffmann had said, was besieged for several months, which meant it must have been shelled too.

Minutes later she was beside the Drava, passing one of the few tall buildings in the centre, a hotel tower, fifteen storeys at least. An arm of the river with no outlet, a mooring for a few boats and two floating restaurants, and behind this the Drava itself, not that much water and not particularly wide, she thought, for a river that had travelled hundreds of kilometres from Italy to here. On the other side of the river it was magnificently green; she saw woods, fields and only the occasional house. On this side of the Drava there were endless cafés with music drifting from them, sometimes loud music, and again many tables occupied in the shade of vast awnings, as if the sun were a natural enemy of the Croats.

And one hundred and fifty metres further on, at the end of the café promenade, an elegantly curved concrete footbridge suspended by wire rope.

Ben Liebermann was already there, a slim, unshaven man in the diffuse light of the low December sun. He was a few centimetres taller than her, with longish, slightly curly dark-blond hair, jeans, sweatshirt, not a handsome man at first glance, she thought, but definitely at second glance, over a glass of something in the evening at one of the promenade cafés, when all those lines around his eyes moved and he talked of Sarajevo and why he should want to live in a place that had been at war.

Perhaps at some point when everything else had been sorted out.

"First time in Osijek?"

"Yes."

Liebermann nodded. "It's a very liveable city."

"So it seems." She turned to look upstream, facing the sun, a hand shielding her eyes. "Call me Louise, will you?"

"Sure. As ex-colleagues. Ben." His voice was not too loud, deep and agreeably firm.

She heard him light a cigarette and smelled the smoke. "And now accomplices."

"Yes," Liebermann said.

The hand holding the cigarette appeared before her eyes, pointing left, pointing right. "Slavonia, Baranya. One of the main areas settled by the Danube Swabians. If you drive through the villages of Baranya you still see a whole host of German houses. Many are derelict now, but some have been renovated. In 1991 the Serbs invaded Baranya, the front line was over there by the edge of the woods. As they retreated they mined the area, and many mines still haven't been cleared. From there they shelled Osijek for ten months. Don't ask me why they didn't take the city. There was barely anyone left here, only around twenty-five thousand of one hundred and twenty thousand. But they didn't make a serious attempt. They'd taken Vukovar, they were to the north, east and south of Osijek, but they just bombarded the city instead. Maybe because too many troops were tied up in Vukovar ... They say that Tudjman sacrificed Vukovar to save Osijek."

She nodded. War stories – these seemed to be standard fare when you were dealing with Croatia.

And Vukovar, Vukovar over and over again.

But was it maybe just the passion of a man obsessed by wars?

"You need to know this if you want to understand Osijek," Liebermann continued. "If you want to understand the people here. A friend of mine says that many people in their mid-thirties are traumatised. They guzzle sedatives and whatever else. I don't know whether that's true." He leaned on the railing beside her. "Lončar was stationed here during the Yugoslav War."

Long shadows lay across the fields and woods of Baranya on the other side of the Drava, and the tips of the two bridge columns were still bathed in sunlight. It had suddenly turned chilly. They were sitting in one of the cafés on the promenade, which for the sake of simplicity Liebermann had called "Picasso" because a few metres further on stood a statue of the artist. Antun Lončar was in Osijek in 1992, enduring the siege for several months, then was injured in a grenade attack and taken to hospital. He was granted leave in Poreč, and then he and his family vanished.

"To Štrpci," Louise said.

"Yes."

"He'd lived in Osijek before, from 1942 to 1945."

"At Europska Avenija 16, not far from here."

"You're well informed."

"Thorough preparation. One of my hobbies."

She smiled and wondered whether he'd done thorough preparation on her too.

Anything I need to know, Illi? Any skeletons in her cupboard?

Liebermann shrugged with a smirk.

Good, that was that resolved, then.

What was still a mystery was how, after only an hour, they could be communicating without speaking. A smile, a smirk, all resolved.

Liebermann had gone to see the house at Europska Avenija 16. A clinic, no apartments anymore. If Lončar was staying there he would have to be sleeping in the front garden or one of the hospital beds.

The waiter came with a cappuccino and a bottle of beer. Osječko, she read laboriously.

They drank and said nothing.

One more thing needed to be resolved.

"Why are you helping me?"

Liebermann lit a cigarette. "Your plan is interesting. Crazy, and interesting. I wanted to know what you were like. What kind of woman hatches plans like this."

"And?"

He inhaled smoke. "Interesting. Strange, a bit sad, very interesting."

"I don't like strange."

"Unlike other people. Unusual."

"And sad?"

"Well, just a little bit. After everything that's happened."

She smiled. "And I'm fixated."

"I understand."

"Tomorrow Valpovo and Poreč, the day after, Štrpci. Have you got the time to do this?"

"I've taken time off."

"But I can't pay you."

Surprised, Liebermann gave a dismissive wave of the hand.

"Only the gun. I'll pay for that, of course."

"A present from the city of Osijek to an interesting visitor."

"A leftover from the war?"

He nodded. A Yugoslav pistol, model 57, licensed version of the Russian 7.62-millimetre Tokarev. It had probably belonged to a Serbian soldier and via a circuitous route had ended up in the hands of a friend, in whose hands everything ended up that could only be transported via circuitous routes. Louise was no expert in pistols, she knew a few Walther models, a few H. & K. models, as well as the weapon Liebermann had just described, produced from 1957 in the Belgrade headquarters of Zavodi Crvena Zastava. In summer 2003 they had found at least a hundred specimens of this model in an illegal weapons cache near Kirchzarten.

A reunion in Osijek.

"Life is odd sometimes," Liebermann said. "Amazing, all the things that've come from the Breisgau to Osijek."

For a moment they looked at one another in silence.

"You ought to smile when you say things like that."

"Yes," Liebermann said, but he still wasn't smiling.

A few minutes later she got up, put twenty kunas on the table and said, fancy dinner somewhere? Are you free?

Plan their journey, a working dinner, so to speak.

The gun, Ben. I need the gun.

Liebermann said nothing, just pointed at one of the floating restaurants on the arm of the Drava: "El Paso".

"Half past eight?" she said. Liebermann nodded and smiled.

She liked the smile. A dark, melancholic, soft smile.

Yes, *very* attractive at second glance.

Osijek in the darkness seemed darker than any other city she knew. Maybe because it was so foreign, because every word she heard or saw was foreign, just like the faces of the people, the buildings. Because she felt foreign here. Unlike in Zagreb, where she had found her foreignness agreeable, here it was oppressive. Europska Avenija began not far from the café promenade, at a cinema with a tall, curved gable, the "Urania". Number 16 was a magnificent building, now run down, behind a wrought-iron fence. It may have dated from Austro-Hungarian times. For a long while she stood on the other side of the street without really knowing why. Lončar was hardly going to come past right now, an evening stroll on an unusually warm December day. Again she had a clear sense that something wasn't right, just like with Johannes Miller in Kanadaring in Lahr at the end of October. She hadn't known the old warrior's name then, but she simply couldn't picture him there. He didn't fit in Kanadaring, he didn't fit in Osijek. Lončar wasn't seeking peace or nice memories, he was seeking hatred and pain.

At the hotel she rang Ilic and reassured him that everything was O.K., he needn't worry. Then she called Landen and reassured him that everything was O.K., everything under control, a few more days, a week maybe, then she was coming home. She showered, had a bit of a doze and waited in her dream for Lončar. When he came, she woke up drenched in sweat.

Pizza in Osijek, of course, Liebermann said with a shrug. Half of Osijek ate pizza in the evenings. Pizza it is then, she thought, not yet ready to sample the no doubt exotic dishes of Slavonia.

They sat near the bar and open kitchen in "El Paso". Beige chairs, the radio playing, a gentle rocking whenever a motorboat drove past. The Drava was carrying little water; the floating restaurant was ten to fifteen metres below the level of the promenade. They didn't have a view of the town's lights, but of the concrete slope of the riverbank.

As they waited for their pizzas Liebermann talked about the group of buildings in Europska Avenija that included number 16. You could find them in every guide to Osijek, half a dozen buildings in a row, art nouveau, late historicism, secession style, yellow, blue, green, probably planned as an ensemble. Jewels in a largely unadorned city, all of them going to rack and ruin because there wasn't enough money.

"You should see them during the daytime," he said.

She raised her eyebrows, he smiled.

Ben Liebermann taking secret detours. Was he there when you thought you were alone?

"When everything else is sorted out."

"I'll show you the fortress by the Drava too: Tvrđa, a little town in itself. Eighteenth century, built by the Habsburgs because they thought the Turks were coming back. Today it's the city's party mile: cafés, pubs and hundreds of young people at the weekends.

"You love this city."

"It does me the world of good. It's pleasingly modest. Not beautiful, but everywhere you encounter beautiful, bizarre or surprising details." A small city that has seen a lot and gone through a lot. The Romans, the Hungarians, the Turks for a century and a half, the Austrians, plus the Slavs, the Danube Swabians, other peoples. Taken by the Nazis in 1941, liberated by the partisans in 1945. Besieged by the Serbs in the early 1990s. And the traces of this history are everywhere . . .

Louise nodded. "At some point, Ben, not now. Now I'd like to talk about Valpovo."

He nodded. Valpovo was a small, unspectacular town with a baroque palace. The camp didn't exist anymore, of course. Where it once stood there was now a supermarket, an Austrian chain. A few cafés, a large paper manufacturer, several hundred detached houses in quiet side streets – that was Valpovo.

Valpovo was also the shadowy figures who had migrated down from the Danube in her dreams, it was a strange longing, a strange word she wanted to enter as if it were a place. A strange sadness because this word would always elude her.

She talked about the cemetery. A photograph of wooden graves with German names, perhaps there were still German graves in Valpovo cemetery.

"Are you thinking of Lončar's mother's grave?"

"It's a possibility."

Liebermann nodded. "What time do you want to set off in the morning?"

"Around eight."

"Shall we take my car?"

"No, mine."

He didn't question her on this. Perhaps he suspected the reason. Lončar knew the colourful Mégane. If he saw it, he would come. At least that's what she hoped.

"Do you really think you're going to find him, Louise?"

She shrugged. A question to which she had no answer.

"He could be anywhere," Liebermann said. "In Croatia, Bosnia . . . anywhere."

"I know."

"But you're still looking for him?"

"Yes."

She got up to go to the lavatory. For minutes she stood by the sink, staring at herself in the mirror. A minor shock in the evening, something had got muddled.

He could be anywhere, Herr Niemann.

Of course, I know.

You won't find him. Not like that.

No, maybe not.

And even if you did. What then?

*

The pizzas arrived along with another beer for Liebermann. They ate in silence. Still in silence, he took from his briefcase an object wrapped in a plastic bag. She felt the weight of the gun in her hand for a moment, it seemed heavy compared to the Walter or Heckler & Koch – no surprise, seeing as it must be twenty years old. Liebermann was staring at her. She looked into his eyes but found no questions there, questions such as the one Ilic asked her and she asked herself: what road are you on, Louise?

Would you—?

"I'm not going to help you kill him," Liebermann said.

"I don't intend to kill him."

She put the bag with the pistol in her shoulder bag and went on eating. There it was again, the question of which road, and she realised that Ilic was right to be worried, as was Liebermann when he said that he wouldn't help her kill Lončar.

She knew exactly which road she was on.

Taking the weapon from her bag, she gave it back to Liebermann and left.

25

In Osijek too there were roads that went on for ever. One of them, J. J. Strossmayera, began at the main square and headed westwards out of town. Liebermann had made himself comfortable in the passenger seat. He'd brought two coffees, switched on Radio Otvoreni – supposedly the best music station in Croatia – and every so often gestured the way with his coffee in hand. She caught herself thinking about him; she wanted to look at him, talk to him, get him to show her around Osijek. She wanted Ben Liebermann to help her forget Antun Lončar for a few hours or days.

Forget Carola.

She knew she couldn't forget yet.

Josipovac, a village on the western margins of Osijek. So far as he knew, Liebermann said, it had been founded by ethnic Germans. He pointed with his cup at the houses on either side, Do you see? Typical Danube-Swabian architecture, the narrow end facing the street, arcades with columns, they used to have inner courtyards and utility rooms as well. Beyond Josipovac was countryside; she drove past pasture, woods, fields, pursued and overtaken by impatient locals. "What the hell is that?" Liebermann said, pointing at the bullet hole in the dashboard. Louise began to talk about Taro, the Japanese monk, but then realised that Taro, Niksch and Hollerer didn't belong here, somehow even Ben Liebermann didn't belong here. She had to deal with Valpovo herself.

"Later," she said. "When everything else is sorted out."

*

Petrijevci, a small, elongated municipality that meandered with the winding road. Liebermann pointed to both sides: German houses here too. Then they were on a country road again until he indicated right and she turned off. Valpovo.

Valpovo, around thirty kilometres north-west of Osijek, the last four or five kilometres on a narrow road leading into the town, to a single tower, not a church as she had suspected, but the baroque palace. Liebermann navigated her through this unremarkable jumble of a town, one hundred metres of a 30 k.p.h. zone as they passed the palace in the centre, a pretty, restored building in a park. To the right, the pedestrian zone, three or four cafés and a glimpse of the church as they drove past. After a few more junctions they would be at the end of Valpovo, which then passed seamlessly into the next town. Liebermann pointed at a supermarket on the left, which was still in Valpovo. Roughly there, the camp was, he said. She drove into the car park and switched off the engine. So that was it, that was Valpovo, the place she'd felt a bizarre longing for, the place she'd dreamed of, thousands of shadowy figures on their way to Valpovo, including her, a sort of promised land in spite of the unusual intonation, the tricky first syllable, Valpovo, a word which had accompanied her day and night, which she had looked for on maps and in books, driven by this inexplicable, absurd longing to go there one day, to the place and the word, to the Land of Valpovo between the Sava and Drava.

A faceless centre, a baroque palace, a supermarket, a car park. So that was Valpovo.

Liebermann said nothing, did nothing. He let her weep in peace.

Valpovo cemetery lay on the arterial road slightly out of town. In silence they wandered down the paths in search of gravestones with German names and 1945 or 1946 as the year of death. Liebermann seemed edgy; he kept looking up and glancing around. Louise was going to tell him that he needn't look out for Antun Lončar, that she would sense it if he were nearby, but that was an exaggeration, in fact it was rubbish, Bonì.

What's happening to you?

The longing for a foreign place in a foreign country, a completely insane journey, the intermezzo with the pistol, the tears in the car park because Valpovo was just Valpovo . . .

But of course it hadn't begun with this, she thought, it must have begun much earlier, deep inside her, where perhaps there was a real longing for a homeland, without her ever having realised it.

It was high time she found this out.

A few minutes later Liebermann pointed to some kind of memorial in a distant corner of the cemetery, a concrete slab set at an angle, into which a large cross had been carved. A bit brash and showy, Louise thought, as memorials generally were, but it clearly fulfilled its purpose: it had caught their attention. As they got closer she saw that behind it were dozens of simple graves in no discernible order, some with weathered gravestones, others with wooden crosses, a striking contrast to the other graves arranged in straight lines and spruced up. "This must be them," Liebermann said. "Your German graves."

Now they were standing by the memorial, reading the inscription: "*To our innocent victims of the genocide 1945–46 in the camp at Valpovo. Danube Swabians from around the world. Never forget!*"

"Unbelievable," Liebermann said.

"Not now, Ben."

"Just unbelievable."

"The innocent victims, Ben. Not the guilty ones. Perhaps that's how it's meant."

"Innocence and genocide, that's how they rewrite their history."

She touched his arm. "Let's look for the grave, O.K.?"

"There's the other side too, Louise. There are the guilty victims." He took a packet from his pocket and lit a cigarette.

"I know."

"Innocence and genocide." Liebermann laughed angrily, there was no stopping him right now, Innocence, of course, but an S.S. division too, made up entirely of Danube Swabians, Louise, the Prince Eugene division, renowned for its brutality. Hitler euphoria in many towns and villages in south-eastern Europe, demonstrations by *Volksdeutsche* brandishing swastika flags, anti-Semitism, here too people benefited when Jewish property was put up for sale, as they benefited in the Banat from the occupation, in Croatia from the fraternity with the Ustaša. And genocide. Of course there were murders, expropriations, expulsions, arrests, all manner of atrocities committed against Danube Swabians, mass murders that rivalled ethnic cleansing. But genocide? For Christ's sake, how could ...

He broke off and stubbed out his cigarette. "Schwarzer, wasn't it?"

"Yes."

"Do you know the first name?"

"Emilie."

"Let's look for her then."

Together they walked amongst the graves behind the memorial, reading the German names: Fenninger, Hauk, Flatscher, Heim, Seligmann, Steiner, Kräuter, Thalwieser, Schmidt and many others, almost all of whom had died in 1945 or 1946. Most of the graves were cared for to some extent, decorated with fresh flowers, eternal lights, others appeared as if perhaps nobody had looked after them for years or decades. The wind and weather had worn away inscriptions and many of the crosses were crooked. Some of the graves were no more than a horizontal slab that one day would disappear beneath the grass, others consisted of a cross rammed into the ground with a metal plate bearing no more than a name. The German section – if this was what you could call it – looked like the fraying end of the cemetery, growing beneath the trees, into the bushes, beneath the grass, as if trying to hide, trying to disappear. She thought of Jenny Böhm, who found peace and mercy in cemeteries. Not here, Jenny, no way. Here you would just see the pain and the suffering, the violence and the anger that seemed to be chiselled into these vanishing, nondescript graves.

And then they found it.

A rusty metal cross, blown crooked by the wind, in ankle-high grass, a narrow enamel plate, *Emilie Schwarzer, 1917–1946*. No gravestone, no slab, no flowers, no eternal light – one of those graves which had almost disappeared, which nobody was caring for.

Emilie Schwarzer, died of hunger and exhaustion at Valpovo camp in 1946, married, one son, not yet four, who sat by his mother's body, swatting away the flies and mosquitoes, and the ants crawling across her face.

Who probably hadn't visited his mother's grave in years.

"Wait here, Ben."

She left the cemetery and bought a bunch of flowers at one of the stalls, yellow flowers. She didn't know the name, but they were beautiful, gentle flowers. Louise didn't know what she was doing or why, perhaps she wanted to give Lončar a sign, in case he came by in the next few days, but perhaps simply to prevent Emilie Schwarzer from disappearing so rapidly.

Liebermann looked at her but said nothing.

She laid the flowers in front of the cross, yellow flowers in the ankle-high grass.

Emilie Schwarzer, 1917–1946.

Now the enamel plate was shining and the cross was straight.

A café in the pedestrian zone, a few more impressions of Valpovo, a few more minutes in this place which bore such peculiar significance for her just then. They sat on low, brown-leather armchairs, a flat-screen television on the wall behind Liebermann, behind her a second screen playing music videos, and the radio blaring from a set of speakers. She was grateful to Liebermann for remaining silent rather than talking about Antun Lončar or Emilie Schwarzer. She realised that she understood herself less and less, and that increasingly she was undertaking things she couldn't explain, such as this whole trip, the hunt for Antun Lončar. It had begun, of course, with the word and the idea of Valpovo. You've got to get out of there, she thought, get out. This wasn't only true of Paul Niemann, it was true of her too.

The question was: what had she got herself into?

Bonì stood up.

"Poreč?" Liebermann asked.

"Poreč," she replied.

26

Poreč near Požega, fifty kilometres from Valpovo in the heart of Slavonia, evidently a tiny village marked only on large-scale maps. They drove along narrow country roads, twenty kilometres of highway until Našice, where they stopped and ate börek with minced meat. Liebermann drank bottled beer and was noticeably quiet. He kept looking at her, and again she thought how she'd rather be preoccupied by him than by Lončar. But that wasn't possible, not yet. She felt him close to her, his warmth, his serenity, and she sensed that something had been happening between them ever since they first met.

For the moment this had to suffice.

And yet her head was full of questions. Why Osijek? What is it about you and war? Illi said something about an abyss, what kind of abyss? And why did you do that earlier in Valpovo, clean the nameplate and straighten the cross?

She shot him a glance. At some point, Ben Liebermann, when this is all sorted out, but he didn't understand the glance and said, "What?"

"Nothing."

He nodded. "Do you really think we're going to find him?"

"If we don't, then at least we'll find traces that show he's been there in the past few weeks."

"Would that be enough for you?"

She shrugged. Would it be enough? She didn't know.

But maybe this wasn't about finding Lončar, maybe it was just about trying to understand him by visiting those places he was associated with.

"Poreč or Štrpci . . . What do you think?"

"I think you're asking too many questions today."

Liebermann laughed softly. "Would you rather I asked questions or smoked?"

"Today I'd rather you smoked."

"Actually, I was trying to give up."

She smiled.

"Poreč or Štrpci, Louise?"

"I think Poreč. That's where he lived the longest. It's where his wife and daughter were from."

"The closest he has to a home town."

"Yes." But then she realised that something else was getting muddled. *She* would go to Poreč because it was the closest he had to a home town. But perhaps Lončar wasn't looking for a home, for nice memories. Perhaps he really was looking for hatred and pain.

Poreč might be a sort of home. What about Štrpci?

The resettlement, the return with his family. The flight to Germany, the forced repatriation. The murder of Biljana and Snježana.

Štrpci, a lifelong nightmare.

Eighties rock on Radio Otvoreni, sunshine, a winding road through hills between Našice and the Požega plain, and Ben Liebermann's shoulder so close to hers that she could feel his warmth again without them touching, as if the heat molecules were leaping between them. She couldn't remember the last time she'd felt something like this, certainly not with Landen, that had all been very one-sided in the first few months, and Landen wasn't someone for whom you felt emotion that went beneath the skin. Certainly not with Mick, either. Back in 1994 she had just been stupid and insecure, had persuaded herself that maybe in her desire to be an independent and unconventional woman she was on the wrong track, and in a moment of weakness had tried to save herself from her own abyss – a terrible mistake. And before that . . .

Now Liebermann was looking at her.

"Let's talk," he said.

She nodded. Talk to calm the molecules down.

"Lončar," Liebermann said. "What if he's somewhere else entirely?"

"Where, for example?"

"In Germany."

"Because it's not over yet?"

"Maybe he's going to kill Paul Niemann too."

"He would have done that long ago."

And in any case, she thought, Lončar wouldn't be able to get at him for months.

Niemann was back in Munich in a psychiatric clinic, suffering from shock and severe depression.

He'd gone back to his home town a sick man.

Half past one, the Požega plain, or *Požega kotlina*, the "kettle". Small villages, everything green, in the distance the chain of hills where the valley came to an end in the south. Up above, Kutjevo, Liebermann said, a monastery worth a visit, fantastic wines, beyond it Požega with its mediaeval churches, lots of baroque, arcades in the town centre, a really attractive town and over there . . .

Talk to calm the molecules down.

At around three o'clock they reached Poreč, which was even smaller than all the other little villages they had driven through that day, just a handful of houses on either side of the road, secluded behind bare trees and wide strips of grass separated by battered wooden fences. An old woman in front of a Danube-Swabian house watched them as they drove slowly past, an old man opposite, otherwise nobody to be seen. The first thing that struck Louise, even before they had got out of the car, was that this was a place of total tranquillity and inertia.

"What now?" Liebermann said as they passed the last house.

"Let's ask about him."

"Too dangerous, Louise. If he's here—"

"If it's too dangerous for you, Ben, stay in the car."

"Who will interpret for you?"

"Well, come on, then."

They got out and walked slowly back down the road, Liebermann looking to the left, Louise to the right.

She knew he was irritated because he thought her reckless and couldn't understand what she was doing. Nobody on the hunt for a killer would show themselves openly in the street.

Only someone who wanted to be found.

But maybe he had understood that.

The old man simply shook his head, the old woman remembered and began to talk, Yes, a family by the name of Lončar, father, mother and daughter, they'd vanished a few years ago and never come back, the house stood empty and was falling into disrepair, the house back there, the house belonging to Antun, Biljana and Snježana, who'd both grown up in Poreč. There had been an uncle too, Igor, a short, sad man, he'd died long ago and now lay in the cemetery on the road to Kula. And there had been another man too, a tall, gaunt man who'd arrived with the uncle and Antun shortly after the war, when many were either leaving or arriving in Poreč.

Davor Vejnović, Louise said, but the woman didn't recall this name.

"Ask her whether Lončar ever came back alone."

Liebermann translated and the woman answered.

"No."

"How could she possibly know?"

"Louise, everyone here knows everybody else, everyone knows everything."

"Ask her if she ever heard of him again. Whether she heard where he went."

"She's already said no."

"For God's sake."

Liebermann said nothing.

"Let's take a look at the house."

Liebermann and the old woman talked. "She says we can't go in. Nobody ever checked whether there were mines inside."

"Serbian mines?"

Liebermann shrugged. "Or Croatian ones. His wife was a Croatian Serb, wasn't she?"

Here he was again, the other Antun Lončar, who probably hadn't returned to the war for Biljana's sake, but had gone with his family to Štrpci to bring them to safety. The Antun Lončar she felt sympathy for, because he'd lost so much.

A half-derelict German house, the roof partially fallen in, the windows without panes, no doors, most of the render crumbled away from the walls. No fence, the courtyard and loggia overgrown with tall grass, and stones had fallen from the arches between the pillars. This was where Lončar had first lived with Andreas Eisenstein and his uncle Christian, later alone with Christian, and then with Biljana and Snježana until the family moved to Bosnia in 1992. Twelve years on, the house was uninhabitable, but they didn't know what it had looked like before, when it was built, whether it had ever been renovated. Whether bombs had fallen on the roof in the 1990s.

"Shall we go?" she said.

"Where? Osijek, or straight to Štrpci?"

She thought for a moment, then decided on Osijek, even though it wasn't much further to Štrpci. Valpovo and Poreč in one day, that had been a bit much. Now she needed a café by the Drava, a restaurant on a boat, a place without Antun Lončar and his past, as far as that were possible. A harmless evening with Ben Liebermann, to let the molecules start jumping again.

Talk, talk, talk, to pass the time until all this was over.

27

Although Liebermann had warned her in advance, it still came as a shock. A few kilometres after the Croatian–Bosnian border she saw the first bombed-out, burnt, collapsed buildings, black patches of grass, charred trees and only the occasional new house, some painted in garish colours as if this might somehow mitigate the spectacle of destruction. The Bosnian Republika Srpska, one of the main theatres of war. Not enough money to clear away the damage, Liebermann said, and maybe not enough desire, you wouldn't really know what goes on here. An hour's drive through a land still maimed, dismal little villages, a bigger town, then to the right a long lake, a turn-off to the left up a hill and a sign that read "Štrpci".

Louise stopped the car a few metres after the turn-off. Too many thoughts and emotions to be able to concentrate on driving.

Štrpci, Schutzberg, the beginning. Carola, Carola's hand, her silent death, the end. In-between a life determined by twentieth-century wars.

Up on the ridge stood a gleaming white church, surrounded by bare, winter hills, meadows, woods and harvested fields. Everything had begun up there on the Dornenberg; it was there that Antun Lončar had been born Heinrich Schwarzer.

And everything would come to an end there too.

Štrpci/Schutzberg, the last stop on her strange journey.

Halfway up the hill Liebermann became uneasy. "Drive to the church," he said. "We'll start with the pastor. Then the mayor, then we'll see, O.K.?"

"O.K."

How she would love to be alone now, she thought. Liebermann came with a rhythm and a road that weren't hers. As in Valpovo, she sensed that he didn't belong here.

As in Valpovo, she had to deal with Štrpci on her own.

Lončar.

But Liebermann was here. She had brought him along, she couldn't send him away.

She saw him bend to reach under the seat. When he sat up he was holding two pistols. He carefully removed white adhesive strips, wiped the guns clean with a tissue, and checked the magazines and triggers.

"I don't need it, Ben."

He shrugged and put the Yugoslav Tokarev into the glove compartment. "Just in case you change your mind."

She nodded. "What about you . . .?"

"Me?"

They glanced at each other.

"You're here as an interpreter, Ben. You don't need to do anything else."

"Yes," Liebermann said.

"You can't do anything else."

"Yes."

"What do you mean, 'Yes'?"

"It's too late."

"Too late for what?"

"I think you know what I mean."

She said nothing. The molecule thing. And all the other things that came from the Breisgau to Osijek. Too late for Ben Liebermann to *not* do anything else but interpret.

She smiled. A man who was willing to plunge into her abyss.

But maybe it was his abyss too.

*

356

Štrpci had a different appearance from the other villages they'd driven through. She saw only a few destroyed or derelict buildings, and lots of new-builds painted white or yellow, some with unrendered brick walls like those she'd seen in Slavonia. Not a prosperous place, but somehow it looked tidy and content.

They stopped at the top of the hill in front of the church. Only now could she see the extent of the village. For kilometres it stretched in the December greyness along narrow streets across the ridge.

While Liebermann went looking for the rectory, Louise headed over to the beautiful Orthodox church, which must be visible from a distance in all directions. She recalled Eisenstein saying that the centre of the Serbian village had been in the centre of the German village, a church and school for the scattered Serbian farms. This must be the church he'd spoken about, newly renovated, painted, perhaps partially rebuilt.

She heard Liebermann's voice and saw him talking to a man outside a house. The man was pointing, Liebermann was pointing – somewhere down the road.

Ben Liebermann. A strange story. They'd known each other for only a couple of days and yet her head was churning with thoughts, full of emotions, possibilities, longing.

They knew so little about each other, but perhaps what they did know was decisive.

A strange, sad policewoman with a crazy plan. A burnt-out ex-colleague who couldn't get away from the war.

Things like that.

Was it simply the right life, and the right time?

The church was surrounded on three sides by graves. No wall, no fence. The dead had been laid in the hilltop, in the village, in the lives of the inhabitants. A beautiful, peaceful, silent place. A place for Jenny Böhm, she thought, the peace of the dead and of nature. A bizarre peace, for presumably Biljana and Snježana had been buried here too after they had been murdered, and the land around Štrpci was still marked by war.

But perhaps this contradiction meant it was important to forget as well as remember.

To forget after remembering.

She didn't have to look for long. A simple black grave with no photographs, unlike almost all of the others, just two names and a date: Biljana – Snježana 06.04.1999.

"You're not on your guard," Liebermann said right behind her.

Startled, she spun around.

He was right. She ought to have been keeping an eye out for Lončar.

She was tired.

She was tired of being deep in something, without knowing how she was going to get out.

"Jesus Christ, you're not being careful."

"No, I'm not. Have you seen the grave?"

"Yes, but come on now," Liebermann growled.

They wandered back to the car and got in.

"What did the pastor say?"

"He's new here, he said we should ask the mayor." Liebermann paused. "We can drive back to Osijek if you want. Leave everything as it is, accept what's happened, drive back and forget all about it. Is that what you want?"

"No."

"Then for Christ's sake watch out!"

She switched on the engine and said, "I'd really rather be alone now."

"Too late for that."

"Indeed. But we're going to go down my road at my rhythm."

"And where's your road going to take us?"

She smiled. "To the mayor."

The mayor proved to be a mistrustful individual who wouldn't give an answer until Liebermann had shown him some sort of mysterious I.D. He was short and stout, with a very high voice and vacant eyes, and he talked without any facial expressions or gestures. Louise wondered who would vote for this unpleasant man, but perhaps he had hidden qualities.

Five minutes passed, in which Liebermann asked questions, growing increasingly restless, while the mayor answered him in monosyllables. Then he went back into the house and closed the door, and Liebermann said, "Let's go."

In the car he explained everything.

Lončar was here. Not in Štrpci, but in the area, in a hut somewhere in the woods. From time to time he came to the village and popped into the house where he'd once lived or visited the grave of his wife and daughter. Then he would vanish again, but nobody knew where he went. Sometimes he was away for weeks, then suddenly he was back, standing in the cemetery or outside the derelict house. Police officers had come in mid and late November, in response to the request for mutual assistance, but because of the mines they hadn't dared go into the woods. Only Lončar ventured into the woods; he knew which paths were safe and which not.

Not Osijek, then, not Poreč, Louise thought, but Štrpci, where everything had begun in November 1942, and everything came to an end in April 1999.

"You found him," Liebermann said.

"Yes."

"Isn't that enough, Louise?"

Time to turn around, drive back to Osijek, forget?

But she couldn't forget.

She pushed her sunglasses up into her hair and looked at Liebermann. "I have to follow my road to its end."

"No," Liebermann said. "You *want* to follow it to its end."

She nodded. "So, will you come with me?"

Liebermann turned away and pointed. "Up there on the left."

The house where Lončar and his family had lived under Biljana's maiden name wasn't rebuilt after the fire, the mayor had said, and he was correct. The last house in the village, near the former German cemetery, a ruin, only the walls still standing, blackened by the fire, one of the walls with a crack from top to bottom like a seam. Another destroyed house, Louise thought as they got out, just like in Poreč. Like in the villages of Slavonia, on the road through the Republika Srpska.

Like in Merzhausen.

In her mind she saw the other ruin, the smoking black skeleton of steel girders, ceilings, stairs and in her head Carola saying, "Has it completely gone? Is it all gone?"

Liebermann wandered around the house. When he came back his face was tense and his right hand was on his holster.

"Ben."

"What? Shall I wait for you in a café?"

She touched his arm. "He's not going to come."

"He *will* come. I know my Bosnians."

She looked at him and realised. "The mayor?"

Liebermann nodded. He'd told the mayor he had a message for Lončar.

The policewoman from Germany was here.

Liebermann shrugged. "So we don't have to wait for days."

Louise said nothing. Again she thought how she would have liked to be on her own. That she wanted to go down *her* road, not

Liebermann's. Only then could she be certain that ultimately she'd do the right thing.

That ultimately the right thing would happen.

There was nothing left to see of the former German cemetery, no walls, no graves. Near the house was just a small, bare, winter copse, a path covered with dried leaves leading into it. Liebermann went ahead, very slowly and circumspectly, there could be mines here too. After fifteen or twenty metres they saw a stone grave slab in the undergrowth and a second one a few paces away. There were no gravestones, and they came across no other graves.

A cemetery that had turned into a wood.

Even the dead Germans of Schutzberg had disappeared.

Louise went back to the car while Liebermann walked around Lončar's house again, then a little way up the road into the village and in the other direction. Leaning against the passenger door she looked at the hills, the woods, the road. It was approaching midday, the sky was overcast, but at least it wasn't raining. Yet again, Louise thought, she was doing what she'd spent too much of October having to do: waiting for Lončar without knowing whether he would come or what he would do. But this time *she* was the foreigner, the intruder.

His country, his village. His life.

His dead.

"What are you going to do if he comes?"

"I don't know."

"Talk? Are you going to talk to him, Louise?"

"Maybe."

Now beside her, Liebermann put his hand on her arm. "To a—"

"Don't, Ben."

He withdrew his hand. "Talk to a killer?"

"He's not just a killer, he's a victim too."

"Not according to the criminal code."

"But here with us in Štrpci he is, Ben. The criminal code doesn't count here. So something else has to instead."

"I wonder what that might be."

She just nodded.

"Take the Tokarev, Louise."

"No."

"He's killed two people. Don't forget that."

She looked at him. How could she ever forget?

But she knew that at some point she would have to.

Remember, then forget.

Liebermann's patrols got shorter the longer they waited; he came and went with greater frequency. "If he waits till it's dark . . ." he said.

"If he comes at all. He hid from the Bosnian police."

"Maybe he wants to talk too."

She didn't respond. This was no time for sarcasm.

"Am I right in thinking he hardly speaks any German?"

"Yes."

"Even though he lived in Germany for five years."

She shrugged. So many questions still unanswered.

There was one question she did want an answer to, though. The thing about the war, why Liebermann had left Germany to live in a city that had been at war.

He laughed. "I was drunk when I wrote that."

She said nothing.

"I can't explain it, Louise. When I worked in Bosnia . . . A country that's so beautiful and has suffered so much destruction. Sarajevo, so beautiful and so destroyed. I don't mean the buildings, you can rebuild those. Or the state structures – the police, the authorities – they can all be rebuilt too. But when you wander through Sarajevo you get the impression that something inside these people has been destroyed, something you can't rebuild."

"Like in Osijek?"

"Like in Osijek."

"And you need that?"

Liebermann shrugged. "Perhaps I just don't know where I belong. I want to lose myself amongst broken people."

"Other broken people."

Liebermann hesitated. "When everything else has been sorted out, Louise." He smiled and set off on another of his patrols.

She saw Antun Lončar long before Liebermann did. A lone man who suddenly appeared on the ridge of the hill and started heading across the fields towards her. For minutes she stared at him, trying to understand why she felt nothing, neither hatred nor pity, no fear, no relief and why, in spite of this, tears were welling in her eyes.

Lončar vanished behind trees and appeared again.

Now Liebermann, who was outside the nearest house on the road, had spotted him too. "What should I do, Louise?" he called out.

"Wait, Ben. Just wait."

"If he's got a gun I'm going to shoot."

She said nothing. She took her road, Liebermann his. Ultimately each of them had to decide which was the right one.

Lončar appeared to be looking only at her, ignoring Liebermann. She saw his hands: no gun. The hands blurred behind tears, now Lončar was just a hazy figure, a silent shadow walking across the dark fields, and she had the same impression as Niemann back in Merzhausen, that he was a part of this place, part of these fields, the hill, the woods, that he had always been here. She didn't know why she thought this, because in the meantime she had realised that Lončar lived in his own world where nobody could get through to him anymore. A world with its own logic which told him that hundreds of kilometres from here a house had to be burned to the ground because a house had been burned down here, and that two women had to die because two had died here.

Lončar stopped by the road no more than twenty metres from her. She could feel him staring at her, although she could see barely anything through the tears. The tears kept coming until Lončar, the road and the hill disappeared altogether.

When she felt a hand in hers, she thought at first that Liebermann was standing beside her, but then she realised it was Carola's hand.

The hand began to twitch, Carola fell and Bonì fell with her.

An eternity passed, nothing happened. She realised she was lying on the grass beside the car, she felt tears still running down her cheeks. Images and thoughts raged inside her head, she saw a man walk across a field, then the man was a child and the child was running across the field, running away, running and running, a girl with red hair ... Then a voice whispered in her ear, He's gone, Louise, and she opened her eyes and saw Antun Lončar going back the way he'd come, returning to his world.

They sat close to one another in the grass, silently watching Lončar get ever smaller before he vanished over the ridge of the hill and didn't reappear. Liebermann didn't try to comfort her and she was grateful for this. Štrpci and Carola and Lončar, she needed to deal with these herself. He hadn't helped her up and she was grateful for this too. He just sat beside her quietly, letting her be what she was, letting her fall into her abyss and coming down too without disturbing her. They remained like that long after Lončar was gone. At some point Liebermann asked how much longer she wanted to stay and she said until the end. He didn't understand until minutes later, when an explosion tore through the tranquillity of Štrpci, a dark, distant bang from somewhere in the invisible woods on the other side of the ridge, a sound she had never heard before, the sound of war.

They said nothing during the drive to the border. Bosnia – for Louise that meant Štrpci, Lončar and Carola. Terrible days and weeks in Merzhausen, in Günterstal. She couldn't talk anymore in Bosnia.

Then, in Slavonski Brod, börek with cheese, coke, cappuccino and Ben Liebermann, who was nervous in an attractive way. "What now, Louise?" he said.

"Remember and forget."

He nodded. "Where, Louise?"

"Hmm. What's December like in Osijek?"

"Don't ask," Liebermann said with a dismissive gesture.

"Do you get snow?"

"Sometimes it snows, yes."

"Snow could be a problem. I hate snow."

Liebermann smiled thoughtfully.

"I am strange and a little sad, after all, Ben."

"Sounds interesting."

"Well, you have to like that sort of thing."

"I do." He laughed. "What do you think of me, Louise? A forty-two-year-old, falling in love on the first day like a teenager."

"On the first day?"

"It might have been the second."

She managed a smile. Liebermann and her, what a peculiar tale, three days and now she wanted nothing more than to surrender to the thoughts and emotions, the possibilities, the longing, now that everything else had been sorted out.

Remembering and forgetting in Osijek with Ben Liebermann.

They would talk about Carola, of course.

Talk about who he was, who she was. What existed between them.

Sit in a café by the Drava, talk, talk, and perhaps finally understand what had happened to her in these past weeks and months.

What might happen in the future.

"I need an answer, Louise. What do you think of me?"

"I've already given you my answer."

"Have you?"

She nodded.

December in Osijek.

Author's Note

The characters in this novel are fictitious. Any resemblance to persons, living or dead, is coincidental and unintended. The information on Schutzberg/Štrpci was mostly drawn from the book by Ferdinand Sommer: *Geschichte der deutschen evangelischen Gemeinde Schutzberg in Bosnia 1895–1942* (*A History of the German Protestant Community of Schutzberg in Bosnia, 1895–1942*).

I would like to thank everybody who helped me with this novel, first and foremost Detective Chief Superintendent Karl-Heinz Schmid from Freiburg police, but also Chief Superintendent Armin Bohnert from Lahr police, Detective Chief Superintendent Ralph Trefz from Baden-Württemberg police academy in Wertheim, as well as their respective agencies, for the openness and friendliness with which my requests were met.

Thanks to Hilda Beck from Lahr social counselling service for resettlers and Waldemar Held from the Landsmannschaft der Deutschen aus Russland e.V. (Association of Germans from Russia), the immigration office of Munich district council, Richard Benda (Vienna), Stefan Moser (Klagenfurt), Colonel Viktor Musil from Völkermarkt police, as well as to Othmar Mory, Roland Gerdey and A. in Bleiburg.

Thanks also to the many individuals who answered my questions about the Danube Swabians, including staff at the Johannes-Künzig-Institut für ostdeutsche Volkskunde (Johannes-Künzig-Institut for the Cultural Anthropology of Germans of Eastern Europe) in Freiburg and those at the Museum of Danube Swabians (Ulm), as well as Nikola Mak and Renate Trischler (Osijek) and Tomislav Wittenberg (Požega).

Heartfelt thanks to those in Osijek and the surrounding area: Alex and Sascha for two sensational months; Iva for finding me an apartment; Igor for his "chauffeuring" services in Slavonia and Bosnia and for many amusing moments; Daria for her valuable conversations and e-mails; Antun for moments of true enlightenment; and the wonderful Olga for equally wonderful Sunday lunches. I'd also like to thank Paula Thomaš for interpreting in Valpovo, Požega, Poreč and Štrpci.

Thanks are also due to the Robert-Bosch-Stiftung (Stuttgart), which subsidised my research visit to Croatia and Bosnia with a "cross-border" grant, to Sandra Lüpkes and Thomas Koch from the jury of the "Tatort Töwerland" Juist residency, as well as the Bockelmann family on Juist for accommodating me in "Haus Brunke", to the Extra family for breakfasts in Pension Charlotte, and to the Rose family for dinners in Kompass restaurant.